UNDERSEA MISSION

Seaton said, "I must go. The attack will begin at dawn." As he turned to step into the sub a figure moved toward him out of the darkness on the pier. Without looking he knew it was the girl.

"Goodbye, David." She leaned forward and kissed him. Her kiss was soft but ice-cold. As if they were both already dead.

Drake called from below: "All set, Skipper?"

Seaton lowered himself into the tiny sub. "Piece of cake," he said. His eyes met Drake's and they both grinned.

It was the only way.

DOUGLAS REEMAN

SURFACE WITH DARING

A JOVE BOOK
PUBLISHED BY G.P. PUTNAM'S SONS
DISTRIBUTED BY JOVE PUBLICATIONS, INC.

This Jove book contains the complete
text of the original hardcover edition.
It has been completely reset in a typeface
designed for easy reading, and was printed
from new film.

SURFACE WITH DARING

A Jove Book / published by arrangement with
G. P. Putnam's Sons

PRINTING HISTORY
G. P. Putnam's edition published 1976
G. P. Putnam / Berkley edition / October 1978
Jove edition / August 1982
Second printing / February 1984

ISBN: 0-515-07620-1

Jove books are published by The Berkley Publishing Group,
200 Madison Avenue, New York, N.Y. 10016.
The words "A JOVE BOOK" and the "J" with sunburst
are trademarks belonging to Jove Publications, Inc.

To Kathleen Nathan
In friendship

Contents

Author's Note

When I am doing the research for my books I am constantly being reminded of the courage of ordinary men and women in times of war.

At no time was I more aware of this fact than when I was re-visiting Norway for *Surface with Daring*. I saw the fjords and harbours which had been penetrated by British midget submarines, and had the privilege of speaking with some of the Norwegian Resistance who once helped to make each operation a reality.

Even in the face of constant danger and brutal reprisal, results were achieved which, looking back, seem totally impossible.

D.R.

1

The Men

THE CAMOUFLAGED three-ton Bedford slewed round on the narrow track, its wheels churning in a mixture of dirty snow and loose stones, and came to a shuddering halt.

The Royal Marine driver glanced first at his solitary passenger and then at the grey stone building which lay astride the track like a wall, and said cheerfully, 'This is it, sir. 'Ome sweet 'ome.'

Lieutenant David Seaton lowered himself stiffly from the cab and felt his back and muscles protesting at the discomfort of the ride and the many varied miles before it. He took his case from the driver and nodded. 'Thanks for the lift.'

The truck hardly needed camouflage, he thought. It was covered with mud and filth from end to end, a product of hard and continuous use.

He stood in the bitter wind until the Bedford had manoeuvred back towards the main road. If you could call it that. Then he looked at the grey building, examining his feelings, hoping for some sort of comfort. There was an entrance porch in deadcentre of the wall, and a small, sand-bagged hut, within which he could see a muffled figure watching him curiously.

Seaton picked up his case and walked quickly towards the entrance. Perhaps it was because he was tired from the journey, but the strong north-westerly which blew from the Atlantic felt extra cold, his body less able to withstand it.

He paused once again and slitted his eyes against the wind to peer down at the pewter-coloured stretch of water below the hillside. Loch Striven, a strange, compelling place, which gave an impression of secrecy and danger. It was surrounded by barren rock slopes, and these, with just two days of the year left on the calendar, were streaked and patterned with snow.

There were several blurred vessels anchored in the loch, as if they had never moved. One, a straight-funnelled ship, her outmoded hull surrounded by a clutter of pontoons and tenders, was half-covered by snow, as if she were freezing solid.

He smiled, despite his unusual apprehension. H.M.S. *Cephalus*, submarine depot and repair ship. Even at a distance she seemed more welcoming than this isolated building.

A petty officer emerged from the little hut and saluted.

'Oh, it's you, sir.' He grinned. 'Good leave?'

Seaton considered it. It should have been good. They had all been looking forward to it. Getting away. Hiding by losing identity in the crowd.

He thought of London. Battered, brave and tired. Christmas carols in a pub somewhere, while bombs had rattled the glasses behind the bar.

Seaton realised the P.O. was staring at him and said, 'Fair enough.'

Inside the building the wood-panelled walls were bloomed with damp, and the trailing Christmas decorations gave an added touch of something past.

He must be one of the first back, he decided. Those who had taken local leave would return last or late. It was always the same.

He thrust open the door marked 'Wardroom' and saw some logs burning in the big fireplace at the far end. It must have been a snug place in peacetime, he thought. Then it had been called The Lodge Hotel, and people in tweeds had come to shoot and fish, and to tramp the hillsides above the loch. Then they would come back here. To this big room with its fire, and a welcome which was carefully hidden by the stone exterior.

2

Above the long mantel was the new name and crest, H.M.S. *Syren*, with the proud motto beneath, 'Out of the deep we are here.'

A door opened and a white-coated steward peeped in at him.

Seaton sat in one of the many battered leather chairs and raised his feet to the fire.

'Tea, sir?' The steward regarded him bleakly. 'It's too early to open the bar as yet.'

Seaton yawned. 'Tea then.'

Four hundred miles and a bit from London. Train, bus, train, launch, and finally the camouflaged Bedford. It had taken two days. *Well, sir, there is a war on.*

Seaton looked up at the dangling paper decorations, remembering the pre-Christmas excitement, the drunken laughter and flushed faces. like end of term. A festival. Perhaps, if just once somebody had admitted it, they were all surprised to be able to celebrate. To be alive.

He realised with a start that he was unnaturally hot, just as moments earlier he had been half-frozen. He stood up, realising he was still wearing his heavy greatcoat. No wonder the steward had looked at him so strangely. Maybe he was fixing him in his mind, another face to remember. To add to the list.

Seaton walked to a wall mirror and threw his cap and greatcoat onto a bench seat. For a few moments he studied his reflection, as if seeking something. To reassure himself.

He was twenty-six years old, but felt ten times that age. The face which stared back at him was pleasant, with dark brown eyes and unruly hair which he should have had cut during his leave but had forgotten to do so. He looked very pale, and the lines on either side of his mouth were deeply etched. Strain. Probing tension. It was all there.

He wrinkled his nose and turned away from the mirror. Going round the bend. No doubt about it.

The steward re-entered with a tray and some hot scones.

'Local,' he said proudly. 'Got them myself.'

Seaton watched him pour the tea, knowing the man was bored and lonely. But he did not want to talk. Not to anyone just yet.

The steward left the wardroom and slammed the door. *Bloody officers.*

Seaton sat down again and studied the empty chairs. Some would soon be filled. Others....

He sipped the tea and thought back over the months. In two days it would be New Year's Eve. How would 1944 be different from the other years?

It was more a sense of disappointment and anticlimax, he decided. They had gone through so much, and the cost had been high. His eyes strayed to the crest again.

Syren and the elderly depot-ship anchored in the loch were the headquarters and training base of one of the Navy's midget submarine flotillas.

He ate the first scone very slowly, to make himself think.

At first most people had thought it was just one more harebrained experiment to postpone the inevitable stalemate of war. The Italians and the Japanese had had varied successes with their human torpedoes, 'chariots', and the Royal Navy's own attempt to sink or cripple the giant German *Tirpitz* in her Norwegian fjord had not failed for want of determination.

Then had come the midget, the X-craft, a submarine in her own right. With a crew of four, two heavy explosive charges to be laid beneath a suitable target, it had been accepted by both Admiralty and War Cabinet with cautious optimism.

For David Seaton and many others it had all started here, in Loch Striven. They had come from all sections of the Service. They had been volunteers, from the regular Navy and from the Reserves, drawn together by an eagerness to do something vital, or out of curiosity, and because there are some who will volunteer for anything if it sounds dangerous enough.

Seaton did not know why he had sent in his name. Like the bulk of the Navy, he was a 'temporary-gentleman', an R.N.V.R. Maybe that was why he liked the enclosed world of midget subs. There was no formality. Just total self-reliance. Dependence on the little team around you.

He had served in a destroyer, and had then transferred to conventional submarines in the early days of the war. When there were nothing but retreats, or strategic withdrawals as the pundits called them. As junior watchkeeper in a submarine Seaton had seen the strain turn his commanding officer into an old man. He smiled tightly. He must have been about my age then. While German U-boats had made the Atlantic into their

4

own killing-ground, British submarines had had to grope closer inshore in search of targets. The North Sea, the Baltic, or trying to knock off Rommel's supply ships in the Mediterranean. That was when the memo had been sent round. Quietly, without fuss. *Volunteers required*.

From the moment he had first come to this grim-faced building Seaton's life seemed to have been speeded up, like a faulty but exciting film.

Training and exercising in a fifty-one-foot X-craft. Creeping about the bottom of the loch, playing hide-and-seek with the M.F.V. tenders and two First World War submarines which were permanently attached to the base.

There had been a lot of mistakes, and too many accidents. X-craft had dived to the bottom and stayed there. Several men had been killed even towards the end of their training. But there had been few complaints. It was like nothing else. It was thrilling, frightening, but held on to its exclusive members with a grip of steel.

You were no longer an onlooker, one more carried along as part of a job. You *were* it. Or so it had seemed then.

1943 had been a violent year, but for once had leaned over to help Britain and her allies. The hurt of Dunkirk and Singapore, of blasted cities and great ships sent to the bottom faded a little as the last of Rommel's once invincible desert army was driven out of North Africa. In the summer the Allies had made their first stab to regain a foothold in Hitler's Europe, and with Operation Husky, the greatest amphibious operation ever envisaged, they had landed in Sicily, and had stayed there.

Seaton and many of his companions had been there, and two months later when another invasion had been launched on Italy's mainland he had been promoted to his own command.

As he thought about it, one scone still untouched on the plate, Seaton's fingers moved up to his jacket. The Distinguished Service Cross and Bar. Not bad for twenty-six, they said.

They had been recalled to Scotland after the Italian job. Those who had survived.

Seaton had immediately been given a new command, a slightly larger boat, and only just off the experimental list.

For months they had thought about it. The biggest target of

all. Never mind the great floating docks and harbour installations which were vital to the enemy's survival, a battleship, and the greatest one ever created, the *Tirpitz* was something else entirely.

With the war progressing in Italy and the Americans making impressive strides in the Pacific, it was clear that every major warship would soon be needed for the final acts of each campaign. But many British units were kept constantly moored at Scapa Flow and other harbours just in case *Tirpitz* or her graceful consort *Scharnhorst* should venture from their Norwegian lairs and break into the Atlantic as *Bismarck* had once almost done. The valuable troop convoys and deep-laden supply ships from Canada and America would be easy prey for such massive armament, and even if both ships were eventually sunk the damage to morale, the setbacks in men and machines might be overwhelming.

Seaton could recall the excitement when the raid had been announced, the X-craft which had been chosen to attack *Tirpitz* had been given the final briefing. They had been at the other base, but everyone here had known about it.

Tirpitz was lying deep in her well-defended fjord with nets and booms and every modern anti-submarine device available to protect her. The attack might succeed. But if not, another had to be ready. Seaton's boat and the two others which made up the new flotilla were put at first-degree readiness. Towing-submarines, passage crews for the midgets, plans, charts and recognition signals. Seaton had felt that he could find his way blindfolded to The *Tirpitz* in a dinghy.

Then the news had arrived. Not much of it, as the X-craft crews had all apparently been either captured or killed during the operation. But according to reports from the Norwegian Resistance and local intelligence agents, *Tirpitz* had been hit, and badly so. If she was not out of the war for good, it would be for long enough, or until more conventional means were employed to finish what the midgets had started.

It should have been a great moment, and yet despite all else, and the uncertainty of what had become of the crews, of faces which were familiar to many of Seaton's companions, there was a sense of shock. Of loss.

Never mind, somebody said. There's still the *Scharnhorst*. We'll go for her instead.

The day after Christmas the news had broken. *Scharnhorst* had died as she had endured, fighting to the end. In an Arctic blizzard she had gone down under the guns of Admiral Fraser's *Duke of York,* with few to survive those bitter waters.

The last of Germany's major warships had gone. The battles would be for the supply routes, as they had always been, and for mastery of the narrow seas, to protect invasion ships, and to ferry back the wounded.

Seaton looked at the motto on the wall. 'Out of the deep we are here.'

There did not seem to be much left for midget submarines any more. His head lolled and he was asleep.

The bar of the Royal Hotel was packed wall to wall. Lieutenant Geoffrey Drake stood with his stomach pressed against the polished counter, holding on to a hard-won beach-head. Around him uniformed figures of every service and rank surged in a noisy throng, and the beer flowed like a tide-race. The little fishing village of Port Bannatyne had never really recovered from the shock of the friendly invasion.

Now, Service boats came and went from the piers, and the whole loch was reserved as a submarine exercise area. The Royal Hotel was the most popular of the drinking haunts, and even though it was a hard trudge uphill from the waterfront, the beer and genial host made the trip worthwhile.

Geoffrey Drake was almost six feet tall, with the wide shoulders and slim hips of an athlete. He was very fair, with level blue eyes and a firm mouth, and looked like an open-air man. And as the gold shoulder flash on his jacket proclaimed, he came from New Zealand.

He yelled, 'Two pints, Pete!' He twisted at the bar and gave a thumbs-up to a sub-lieutenant who was guarding his place at a table. 'Not long now, Dick!'

He turned back to the bar again, feeling the same twinge of uncertainty. Guilt. Just seeing him there, relaxed, calm-faced, brought it home to you. You never really knew with Dick. Sub Lieutenant Richard Niven, Royal Navy. He always appeared to be so cool. But seeing him there. Drake shivered. When had it started? Why the hell had he let it happen at all?

He knew he had merely been putting it under the carpet. Don't look at it and it will go away.

They had met in the old flotilla in the early part of the year.

7

Niven had been new to X-craft, a diver with no combat experience at all. Drake had lived near the sea all his life, and his present submarine existence was like an extension of what had gone before. Off duty ashore he had found himself discussing his pre-war days of underwater exploration, with nothing but a pair of good lungs and a spear gun to protect him from marauding sharks.

Niven knew no other life but the Navy, and had entered the R.N. College at the tender age of twelve. In the past months he had proved himself in one difficult action, but his outer reserve had changed little, Drake thought.

God, if he knew. He felt the sweat prickle under his shirt. And it had started, as so many things do, with an act of kindness.

When the flotilla had been re-planned to allow for casualties and transfers, they had been given a week's leave. It had been then that Drake had met Decia. He had not even realised Niven was married. He seemed too young. Unfinished, in some way.

Decia was living with her father in Harrogate. Drake was to learn that her family was very rich, and although her father had come up the hard way, Decia wanted for nothing. The business was wool, and with three armed services to clothe and keep warm, Britain needed the mills as never before.

Drake had thought of going south to London. Harrogate sounded quiet. A backwater. But it was obvious that Niven wanted to repay him for his encouragement, and as he had no people of his own in Britain, a shared leave seemed the obvious thing.

Just thinking about her made him uneasy. She was small and very dark, with a husky laugh and a way of looking at you. Direct. Testing you.

The glasses slithered across the wet bar. *'Next,* gentlemen!'

Drake handed him some money and pushed through the packed bar with his beer.

They had all made him welcome, and he had had a royal time. The next occasion when they had invited him for a short leave he had accepted without hesitation. Knowing why. Hating himself for it, but still imagining he could break off his interest when he chose. She and Niven must have been having a row about something. There had been tension. A stiffness between them.

She had invited Drake to go for a ride on one of her horses, and Niven had appeared almost relieved at the interruption.

Later, in the big Yorkshire house, she had been showing him the library, and had climbed up to get a book for him. One of her ancestors had taken his share of the wool trade to New Zealand.

She had stumbled, and he had caught her. He could feel her lithe body now. Even here. Her breast against him, the amusement in her dark eyes giving way to sudden uncertainty.

He had found himself touching her hand, casually, if he crossed a room. Gauging her reaction. She never appeared to notice. But she never removed her hand either.

He sat down at the table and said abruptly, 'Here we go, Dick. Better cadge a lift to the base after this.' He watched him over the glass. Before it had been bad enough. Niven had been in another boat. They met most days, but it was not the same as now. The base captain had told them before this last leave.

'Promotion has come through for Tom Latham, so you'll need a new diver. Dick Niven is the lucky man.'

It was never a good thing to break up a team, and Latham, the previous diver, had been in the flotilla from the beginning. But he deserved his chance like everyone else. It still did not help Drake's conscience. To *see* Niven sitting in the midget submarine, going over every detail together. Knowing all the while that he wanted to see his wife. No, he *needed* to.

He could ask for a transfer. He dismissed it instantly. It would be wrong. Drake would rather cut off his hand than let down the skipper, David Seaton. With a new diver to get used to, and then to lose his Number One as well, it was asking for a disaster.

And it was quite obvious something was in the wind. The leave had been shortened by two days. The Navy did not waste telegrams just for the hell of it.

God, what a bloody mess.

Richard Niven watched two R.A.F. officers having a beer-drinking competition, their faces rigid with concentration.

It would be strange to start in a new boat, he thought. He did not know much about his commanding officer, David Seaton, other than by reputation. How he had survived was a mystery after what he had done, and his deeds were common knowledge. But as a man he seemed vaguely distant, withdrawn. But once in his little command it would be different. He glanced at Drake.

9

He and the skipper were close friends. That should be good enough.

Niven pushed his immediate future to the back of his mind. He could do the work, and had been reared and trained as a naval officer. For a career, and not as another exciting section of life as it seemed to be to Drake and many of the others.

He caught sight of himself in a mirror on the wall and imagined he could hear Decia's voice. 'Don't you *ever* relax, Richard? Can't you forget what you are, just for a few hours?'

He sighed and knew Drake was watching him. Niven was one of the youngest officers at the base, but one of the very few who had married. In wartime, they said . . . He downed the beer angrily. When you thought like that you were halfway dead. He had to keep a sense of proportion. The war might last for years and years. He loved Decia. She was *right* for the family.

Niven thought of their last night together. The angry words, and then her hands coming to him in the darkness, exploring him, wanting him.

And he had been unable. He still did not understand why. Worry about the recall? Actual fear which he had so far failed to recognise?

He had felt her move away, her perfume hanging to the pillow like a final bitter taunt.

'I'm ready.'

Drake looked at his watch. 'The bar will be open at the base.' He looked across the room and added, 'Hell, there's old Alec. We'll take him along with us.' He waved and started to push through the crowd.

Petty Officer Alec Jenkyn watched the lieutenant's fair hair rising above the drinkers like that of a Norseman. He was small and wiry, with narrow shoulders and the sallow complexion born of many engine rooms. Jenkyn was twenty-nine, but looked much older, and had spent thirteen of those years in the Navy. As he followed Drake's thrusting progress towards the table he thought back to when he had transferred from an ordinary submarine to X-craft. His mates had pulled his leg. And on the strength of it, it had sounded odd. Three officers and one rating cooped up together in a steel cylinder.

It wouldn't work. Couldn't. But it had.

As engineroom artificer of Lieutenant Seaton's stubby command he was satisfied. Glad to be back.

Drake towered over him. 'Hi, Alec. We're off. Thought we might go together.'

Jenkyn nodded. 'Right, sir.' He looked warily at Niven.

Drake said casually. 'This is Sub Lieutenant Dick Niven. Our new diver.'

'Glad to meet you, sir.'

Jenkyn stood up, suddenly confused, and angry with himself because of it. He had seen the straight stripe on Niven's shoulder. A regular. Like himself. But oh how different. Tom Latham had been a car salesman in civvy street. This one had all the signs. *The day he calls me Alec I'll hang the bloody flags out.*

Drake asked, 'Good leave?'

The petty officer searched for his small bag under the table. *Good leave.* South London. Bombed streets. A cat crying at the door of a house for its food, and there was only the wall with the door left standing. And his mother. With her beautifully laid table which quivered each time a train thundered past on its way to Clapham Junction. Knives and forks arranged like soldiers. Jelly, bread and butter. The chairs facing the table. Waiting. How she managed such a spread on her rations and what he could fiddle from the P.O. chef at the base was a bloody miracle.

He fumbled with his bag, giving himself more time before he faced Drake and the impassive subbie.

Jenkyn had wanted to sit down at the table and get through his mother's carefully prepared 'tea'. But she had tapped the old clock on the mantelpiece and had said reprovingly, 'Just hang on, Alec. Wait for your Dad and Jimmy to get here from the works.'

It happened each time. It was a nightmare. A relentless, haunting nightmare which his mother seemed to move through unscathed.

He could picture the table, starkly, in his mind. The tea-cozy. The ticking clock. The room he had seen on countless leaves from a dozen ships and from every corner of the world.

His father and his young brother Jimmy had been killed in a hit-and-run raid over Wandsworth on their way home from the factory. Blown to bits in the wink of an eye. Nothing. That had been six months ago. And she was still waiting for them. Her broken mind unable to accept it. The police, the A.R.P. people, the Welfare, even relatives had failed to budge her.

Good leave? It had been bloody hell.

'I know where we can get transport, sir.' He faced the others.

Drake winked. 'Knew it. Old Alec can fix anything.'

Jenkyn followed them to the door. You don't know the half of it, mate.

Outside it was already as black as a boot, and they felt sleet on their faces like cold spittle.

At the bar an artillery officer held out his glass for a refill. He said to the landlord, 'They seem a cheerful bunch.'

The landlord glanced at the young officer's uniform. Brand new, like its owner. He remembered Drake, and all the others who had come and gone through that door, although he was not supposed to know what they were doing.

'I expect they've got their troubles too, sir.'

2

The Machines

DAVID SEATON crossed the depot ship's deck and stood by the guardrails to look at the pontoons alongside. He had come out from the austere surroundings of the shore base immediately after an early breakfast, but here, aboard the *Cephalus*, the daily routine was well under way. Thuds and clattering drills from the workshops deep in the hull, while some oilskinned seamen tried without much success to clear the overnight ice and slush from the decks.

Below the ship's side, barely moving between the massive pontoons, were three midget submarines. With their rounded hulls covered in ice and frozen snow, they looked for all the world like dead whales.

Seaton moved to the accommodation ladder, treading carefully to avoid a painful fall to the deck and thereby raising the first laugh of the day for the onlookers.

The officer of the day, his nose glowing red over a woollen scarf, saluted and grinned.

'Going aboard, sir?'

Seaton nodded. Even he did not really know why he had come out.

The O.O.D. added, 'The buzz says that there's an operation in the wind.'

'I know.' Seaton tested the top tread of the ladder. 'But I've not been told anything.'

He touched the peak of his cap lightly with his fingers as he began to descend the ladder, while the O.O.D. and gangway sentry sprang to attention and saluted. Although he was going from the tall-sided depot ship into a tiny submarine which was not much bigger than one of her power boats, Seaton was still a commanding officer, and tradition and custom decreed that he should be treated as such, no matter how strange it might appear to an outsider.

Below on the pontoons it was colder. Much colder. And the wind which pushed a procession of noisy cat's-paws along the ship's pitted waterline explored his body as if he were naked. He was wearing a stained dufflecoat over blue battledress, a thick sweater and his seagoing leather boots. The latter were so old and scuffed that they were more brown than their original colour, but like him had survived everything. He sometimes felt that if he were to change them, so too would his luck.

His own boat was the outboard one, her number, XE 16, almost covered with crusted snow. He glanced at the other two, XE17, Rupert Vanneck's command, and XE 19, whose urbane commanding officer, Gervaise Allenby, looked upon her much as the owner of a private yacht.

Seaton paused, his gloved hand on the safety chain around the pontoon. There had been another of the new midgets too, *XE 18*. She had been exercising at sea, under tow by a conventional submarine. The midgets needed to conserve their limited fuel, just as they had to save the energies of their crews until the last possible moment. They were towed underwater to a point as close as possible to their selected target, with a passage crew aboard for the same purpose. The transfer, surfaced and in hostile waters, had to be made by rubber dinghy, and as rapidly as possible to avoid detection. It was the X-craft's most vulnerable moment, and everyone tried to think of new ways of cutting the time without increasing the danger.

XE 18 had been doing just that, practising under real combat conditions and in a heavy rain squall. Out of nowhere, a homebound minesweeper had loomed above the little hull, and even as the towing submarine had signalled frantically for the other vessel to stand away, there had been one, terrible crash. A search had been carried out, but nothing had come to the surface. Not even a drop of oil. *XE18* had dived deep, taking her crew of four with her.

Seaton sometimes thought of them, wondering what he would have done. Would he have flooded the hull? Or would he have sat with his three doomed companions in the steel coffin, waiting to gasp out his life?

Hazard of the game. Just one of those things. The trite expressions came readily to hand, as they always did. But Seaton knew that carelessness, a momentary lack of vigilance, killed more good men than enemy action.

He walked round to his own boat and saw that the after hatch was open. Even as he watched an E.R.A. in a filthy boilersuit emerged, carrying a toolbag and a torch, like a burglar.

He saw Seaton and smiled. 'Sweet as a nut, sir. We've taken good care of her for you.'

Seaton stepped on to the narrow casing and steadied himself against the periscope guard. Now he really felt back. Maybe it was because of people like this E.R.A., the unknown team who looked after every unpredictable thing. There was a strong bond between them and the men who actually took their little charges to sea. Rather like the rapport between mechanics and pilots on the muddy airfields of the Great War.

He lowered himself through the circular hatch and switched on the inspection lamps which were connected to the old depot ship. Even that link seemed vaguely symbolic, he thought.

Old and dented she might be, but the *Cephalus,* or *Old Syphilis* as she was affectionately known, could make just about anything in her outmoded workshops.

Seaton hesitated and drew in his breath very slowly. It was probably cold in the small control room, but compared with the icy wind across the loch it felt almost humid.

He caught the familiar smells of diesel and grease, of some new paint and of wet metal.

XE16 was slightly larger than the other XE boats, and larger still than the original X-craft. Even so, she was only fifty-four feet from her snoutlike stem to her rudder, and six feet in the beam.

He let his glance move along the motionless dials and control levers. The gyro compass, the wheel, the periscopes. He sat down on the bunk which covered a chart table. Everything was in miniature. Right aft there was a watertight door which led into the engine space where diesel and the electric motor shared their world with purifiers and cooling plant, with pumps and fuel. Every inch of space had to be used, and used again. Forward from where he sat there was another oval watertight door which led into the W & D compartment, the 'Wet and Dry', into and from which the diver could leave and enter the boat by way of the fore hatch. Forward through yet another tiny door was a further space. Just long enough for a man to sleep, but crammed too with stores, batteries, fuel and ballast.

A small but completely independent vessel.

Seaton thought of his companions, seeing them in his mind's eye as he studied the control room.

Geoffrey Drake was the same age as himself and a real asset to the boat. If they all survived, he should get a command of his own soon. He was totally reliable, and rarely out of humour. Before the war he had been a marine biologist employed by the New Zealand government amongst the islands. Seeking out new kinds of fish, sources of nutrition, although he always told everyone he really did it for the boating and swimming. 'Which they actually paid me for!' Drake's only trouble was his height. There was no headroom in most of the hull, and even then only for the 'less than average'. In fact Jenkyn, the E.R.A., was the only one who could walk from one bulkhead to the other without stooping.

His eye moved to the helmsman's seat where Jenkyn sat for much of the time to steer the boat. A good mechanic, and very loyal in some indefinable way.

He thought of the new diver, Sub Lieutenant Niven. He sounded all right. It was strange to find a regular officer in so junior a role, he thought. The position of diver tended to tie a man to the job and perhaps miss the many swift promotions which only presented themselves in wartime. He was married, and at first Seaton had been troubled that he might be a death-or-glory boy, with an unhappy homelife, looking for the hard way out.

But Drake had been to Niven's temporary home several

16

times. He had said that Niven's wife was a 'real cracker'. He had not mentioned her lately. That meant one of two things. Either Drake had got out of his depth with her, or vice versa. Seaton bit his lip. It would soon blow over when they had work to do.

He glanced at the basket-wheels, one on either beam. When on actual operation, *XE 16* carried a massive explosive charge on either side, like a pack animal. Crescent-shaped, to lie snugly against the hull, each contained over two tons of amatol and a time fuse. Enough to blow the guts out of a floating dock, or a battleship, for that matter. You set the fuses, spun the wheels and allowed the charges to float to the sea-bed beneath the target, like two great, obscene leaves. Then out and away before the bang.

Seaton touched his forehead and looked at his fingers. Wet with sweat.

It had been in the last Italian harbour, dropping the charges under an enormous dock. Unbeknown to anyone on the mission, and almost everyone else, the Italian forces were to change sides against their German ally once the Sicilian invasion had begun.

The dock was important for any heavy surface unit which might need urgent repairs, and the Germans would soon seize it once they knew what was happening. It had to be sunk. Just to be on the safe side.

Seaton turned his head to listen, as if expecting to hear it again. It had been in another boat, but the memory was too stark to quibble with detail.

Within seconds of releasing their two charges, Seaton had heard the sudden rasp of metal, the hull around him quiver violently, as if in a great vice.

The men on the dock had in fact decided to flood their ballast tanks, to prepare to take on a damaged cruiser. With each terrible second it was getting lower and lower in the water, pushing the little submarine towards the bottom, trying to stamp her into the mud, to lie helpless beside the two fused charges.

Bumping and scraping, swaying from side to side, Seaton had conned the midget clear, although why nobody heard their progress, or saw them break surface to fix their bearings, he still could not understand.

As Tom Latham, Niven's predecessor, had said hoarsely, 'God must be saving us for something *really* nasty!'

Seaton reached up for the hatch, the memory becoming less sharp as he turned away from it.

He thought momentarily about his leave. Although Scottish by birth, he had lived for much of his life in England, and before the war had been understudy and assistant to the manager of a large Hampshire estate. It was strange when you thought about it. While Latham had sold cars, and Drake had explored the depths, and both Niven and Jenkyn had followed the ways of the Navy, he had helped to watch over land and animals, tree planting and caring for the houses of the estate tenants.

It had given him time to be on his own whenever he had wanted it. When he had enlisted with the nearest unit of the R.N.V.R., the officer in charge had snorted, 'I'd have thought you'd be more use in the damned cavalry!'

Then the war had come and everything had changed. Seaton had been appointed to a ship, and months later when he had gone to the old estate he had known that nothing could ever be the same again.

The man who had owned the estate, as generations of his family had done before him, had been getting on in years, and just as Seaton was being trained to take over from an elderly manager, so too the owner had been putting all his hopes in his son. The son had died at Dunkirk, and the old man had sold up and gone away.

The fields and little houses were still there, but tanks, not horses and tractors, churned up the earth, and instead of the local cricket match outside the pub, the only activity was the stamp of feet and the bark of commands. A new army in the making.

Seaton's parents had got divorced while he was still a boy at boarding-school. His mother had gone out of his life completely after re-marrying, and his father had gone through a succession of young girls, and had alleged he was 'just beginning to live'.

And he was still trying. But he drank too much, and had got a lot older. On this last leave Seaton had felt really sorry for him. He had been in a pub buying a drink when he had heard a man say to his friend, 'look at the stupid old sod. Thinks he's a real dog. Can't he see that bloody girl's laughing at him?' It had been Seaton's father. Red in the face, tweedy suit, and buying drinks for everyone in reach. The unknown man had been right. The girl who had been knocking back the gins had been laughing, not with him, but at him.

Perhaps it was why the marriage had broken up. In those few moments Seaton had felt that he had known his parents for the first time in his life.

He slammed the hatch and looked along the curved hull with something like affection.

It was risky work, but a man could die crossing the road in the blackout.

He thought of Drake, and looked at his watch. Almost time for the meeting. He had better catch a boat ashore. But the gently-pitching submarine held him a moment longer. At least you were your own master, he thought. Well, almost.

The people you worked with became real and open. Unlike some of the synthetic gentry you met in the wardrooms of bigger ships. There was no use for sham in one of these little chaps. He swung on his heel and headed towards the depot ship's ladder.

Captain Clifford Trenoweth, D.S.O., Royal Navy, sat back in his leather chair, his fingers interlaced comfortably across his stomach.

He was very broad and heavy, with ginger hair, although very little of it, and a pair of bright twinkling eyes. He was a happy man, and often found it hard to be magistrate, executioner and general presence to H.M.S. *Syren*, of which he was captain.

In the Great War he had been a submariner of some distinction, at a time when underwater craft were quite prone to dive and stay dived. Between the wars he had climbed slowly up the ladder of promotion, and then with the rank of commander only just announced he lost a leg while trying to rescue a merchant seaman who had been trapped in a blazing freighter.

Trenoweth had been a passenger in the ship which had gone speeding to answer the S.O.S. He had joined in the rescue without hesitation, and the master of the vessel in which he had been traveling had been more than grateful for his aid.

Then there had been an explosion in the burning ship's

engineroom and the injured man had been killed. Trenoweth had been trapped, his leg caught between two jagged plates like a bear trap.

There had been no time. It had been a race between the rising water and the flames.

The merchant ship's master had sent his doctor across, and Trenoweth's left leg had gone down with the wreck.

H.M.S. *Syren*, formerly The Lodge Hotel, had needed a man like Trenoweth. Someone who could train and inspire the stream of volunteers who came to learn about midget submarines, how to endure and, if necessary, how to die with a minimum of fuss.

If anything, the bluff captain's jerky walk added to the old sea-dog image and helped to break down the barriers of rank and profession, of class and status.

And to the captain himself, what had first sounded like 'better than nothing' after being invalided out of the Navy, now seemed an immeasurable reward.

The base, the depot ship and her tenders, the two training submarines from his own, earlier war, and the X-craft themselves gave him a pride he would have found hard to credit a few years back.

He looked around his dark panelled office with its glass cases of large fish, caught and mounted many summers ago. As if the previous occupiers of the building had left them just to prove their true ownership and to mark their rightful claim once the war was over.

Outside he heard a man's voice and then a woman's quiet laughter. The former was Edgecombe, his operations officer, and the girl with the laugh was Second Officer Helen Dennison, a delicious creature who acted as secretary, communications officer and Trenoweth's secret weapon against interfering spies from the Admiralty and Whitehall in general.

There was one here now. Captain Venables. He was the cause of all the flap, the signals and the eventual recall. As if it couldn't have waited. Any man on the base, even the old 'stripey' who kept the boilers going to heat this building, had more than earned a nice long leave.

He frowned. Venables was so different from himself. More like a bishop than a sailor, with the same booming and insincere tones you heard on traditional state occasions. But he was important. His retinue, and his communications priority, proved that.

The voices beyond the door fell silent, and seconds later it opened. Captain Walter Venables was tall and lean, with polished dark hair and deceptively mild eyes.

He nodded. 'Good morning.' He sat. 'May I?'

Trenoweth struggled to hold the smile on his face. 'Of course. Right on time, I see.' With a man like Venables the remark sounded superfluous.

'Quite.' Venables folded his arms carefully, as he did everything else, and studied him. 'There is to be an operation. Absolutely top secret.'

'Is it all right for me to know?' Trenoweth sighed. It was useless trying to joke with this one. It only made him feel foolish into the bargain. He added, 'It's a bit sudden, isn't it?'

'Well, of course, up here one would tend to get a little out of touch with the mainstream, so to speak. In London, however . . .' That last word spoke volumes.

Mercifully, there was a tap at the door and Second Officer Dennison peered in at them.

'The three commanding officers are here, sir.'

She was not pretty, but had a pleasant, lively face. Captain Trenoweth was very fond of her, and hated being so much older, and having only one sound leg.

Unknown to him, she did not care about the difference in their ages. She *thought* she might not mind about the leg either.

'Send them in, please.'

The door closed and Venables remarked, 'Seems a nice enough girl.'

'She is.' It came out more firmly than intended, but Venables was getting under his skin.

'I will only need the one boat, of course.' Venables was on another tack. 'But we must be ready for last minute setbacks.'

Trenoweth thought of the letters he had had to write to parents and widows. *Setbacks.*

The door opened again and three lieutenants entered and stood hesitantly across the carpet like actors waiting for a prompt.

Seaton was on the left. Next to him, Lieutenant Rupert

Vanneck, D.S.C., R.N.R., a merchant navy officer before the war, and now the successful survivor of several missions, both in X-craft and prior to that in the two-man crew of a 'chariot', a human torpedo. He was darkly aggressive, with a heavy jaw, and a way of standing with his head thrust forward as if seeking an argument.

Against him and Seaton, Lieutenant Gervaise Allenby was completely at odds. A very elegant, well-groomed regular officer of twenty-four, he possessed a face which was totally lacking in expression, like a smooth, slightly contemptuous mask.

Venables looked at them gravely. From Seaton's crumpled battledress and scuffed boots, across Vanneck's barely concealed irritation, and finally to Allenby's protective shell of well-being.

He said, 'I was sorry to have you recalled, gentlemen. We all were. But . . .'

He turned, frowning slightly, as Trenoweth said, 'Sit down, please, chaps.'

They sat. Seaton found a place by the bookcases where the captain kept all his official reading. From there he could watch the rest of them, and wondered how this Captain Venables would see them. He felt something touch his foot, and when he glanced down saw it was Trenoweth's old labrador. Originally brown, he was getting very grey and faded, and spent much of his time in front of a fire, stretched out as he was now. His name was Duffy, and he was something of a mascot around the base. Even as their eyes met, Duffy's closed again and he gave an ecstatic yawn.

Venables coughed. '*Now,* gentlemen.' But he kept his gaze on Seaton. 'I am sure you all thought that much of your role had been made redundant at this stage of the war by recent events and successes. But roles, like war itself, adapt to fit a changing pattern. You have been trained to use your undoubted skills in a certain way. Those skills will be vital in your future operations. Some of your people will have to adjust, of course.'

He looked swiftly at Trenoweth who was leaning forward as if to voice a protest, and continued coolly, 'My department has been in full consultation with the Chiefs of Staff *and* Flag Officer, Submarines.'

Seaton glanced from one captain to the other. Venables was a swift mover. He had displayed his power, and the support he could muster, if need be.

Venables was saying, 'In the past we have been feeling our way. In future your missions will be even more personal, individual. One boat, one job, with no risk of being accidentally betrayed. Obviously I cannot discuss this new mission, but I want you to keep it in mind while you are preparing yourselves. The target will be Norway.'

Seaton heard Vanneck gasp, and knew what he was thinking. With the attack on *Tirpitz* only three months old, Norway would be a hornets' nest.

Captain Trenoweth asked quietly, 'Asking for trouble, surely?'

Seaton tried to relax his muscles. Good old Trenoweth. Moving in to protect his charges like a roused bear.

'So much the better.' Venables smiled wryly. 'In this case. You are all seeing the operation like those gone before. It's plain on your faces.'

It sounded like a well planned speech. A sales talk.

'The problems of the long tow to the proposed attack area. Crew transfer. Getting through the defences undetected. All these hazards before you can even begin. No wonder the strain has been too much for some.' He looked at each lieutenant in turn. 'But *suppose*, gentlemen, just for a hypothetical exercise, suppose you were in position *before* the target?' He nodded very slowly. 'I can *see* it makes a difference in your minds.'

Vanneck said bluntly, 'There's still a question of fuel consumption, sir.'

'True,' Venables was enjoying himself. As much as he could. 'But again, imagine there was fuel available for you *inside* the target area?'

Vanneck shrugged. 'I'd say the Jerries had gone bloody mad, sir.'

Trenoweth said quickly, 'Less of that, if you please!'

Venables turned to Allenby. 'What do you think? From all your experience...'

He faltered as the elegent lieutenant drawled, '*Actually,* sir, I am the very least experienced of we three.' He gave a gentle smile. 'Lieutenant Seaton will be a better guide, I'd say.'

Trenoweth felt his heart pounding warmly. Venables had played the dirtiest stroke so far. Setting up Allenby against the others because he was a regular officer and they were not. He did not know anything about Gervaise Allenby if he thought that would work.

Seaton said, 'I can't see how it could be arranged, sir. But if it was, it would make the mission a one-way affair, and halve the risk.'

He glanced at Allenby and saw one eyelid blink. Allenby didn't give a damn for anybody. He came of an old naval family, but he really *didn't* care. It was no act with him. Spicer, his first lieutenant, said he was raving mad, but would go with nobody else.

'Exactly.' Venables took out a silver case and examined a cigarette very intently before lighting it. He did not offer one to anybody. 'As I said earlier, we must adapt. The Department of Special Operations at the Admiralty has of course been interested in your work from the beginning.'

Seaton relaxed slightly. He was getting Venables' measure. The way he used the words 'of course' whenever he needed to show that all possible arguments were quenched before they were put. Special Operations *had* always helped. He was right there. They, whoever *they* were, had often provided intelligence reports and advice which could only have come from agents and men of the Resistance in any of the occupied countries. Ship movements, local patrols and strongpoints, navigational aids or the lack of them. It took iron nerve to discover such things, more still to pass the information to London on one of those tiny radio sets.

If they were caught the Gestapo would ensure that they lived as long as possible under the most hideous torture, whether they divulged any secrets or not.

Seaton had often found himself wondering what might have happened if the Germans conquered Britain. If they succeeded in the future. There would be the same mixture of traitors and heroes as in Norway or France, he thought.

Trenoweth asked, 'I still don't see where the difference lies?'

The other captain looked at him calmly. 'Distance mostly.

Before, it has been a matter of laying charges or attaching mines to some valuable target and then getting away without giving the enemy a chance of detection and so taking avoiding action. *Now,'* the word hung in the unmoving air, 'our people will have guidance from here and from whatever territory they are using. Military and Naval Intelligence, as well as the more unconventional units, have built up an excellent chain of agents in every important area under German control. When the next mission is put into operation, and it will be weeks, not months, I am afraid, those involved may meet some of the people who have risked their lives to help our cause and their own.'

Seaton did not look at his companions. Another twist of the screw. He had imagined at first that Venables' visit was to boost morale and try to sweep away the anticlimax. At the other X-craft base and depot ship further along the loch, he had heard much the same feeling existed. Venables had changed all that. Seaton was not sure if he was excited or alarmed by the news.

Venables continued in his dry tones, 'There will be risks, of course. But it will be of great value, and with any sort of luck should tie down even larger units of enemy troops when they are needed elsewhere. Next year, for instance, I shouldn't wonder if our soldiers are treading French soil once again. We have made a good beginning. It is up to all of us,' he looked at each of them again, 'and especially to officers like yourselves, to pave the way.'

Trenoweth cleared his throat, and Duffy awoke by the fire, startled.

He said, 'That will be all, gentlemen. Tell your people the bones of the job, and be ready to meet Captain Venables' er, assistants after lunch.'

They filed out of the room, and Vanneck said fiercely, 'We don't *know* anything else to tell them, do we, for Christ's sake?'

Allenby picked up his cap and smiled at Second Officer Dennison. 'Oh, I wouldn't exactly say that, old son. In this sort of work there are two main categories, either it's rewarding or a challenge. The first means there's no extra money in it, the second implies likelihood of a premature death.'

Vanneck grinned. 'You cheerful bastard!'

Along the passageway and left into a wide, low room with a

good floor. Snooker and billiards had been the pastimes here, but now it was hung with charts and maps, and littered with cheap folding chairs. *Syren's* operations room.

The rest were already gathered. The crews of the three boats, two staff officers and three lieutenants who would act as passage crew stand-ins whenever required.

They separated into their own little groups, and Seaton explained to Drake and the others what might be expected of them. That now, as from the beginning, any man could drop out. But later would be *too* late.

Each member of the three crews was then given the usual medical examination by the base M.O. He was such a vague character that Seaton suspected he would have missed even a case of mumps.

Then across to the *Cephalus* by launch, and a quick rundown on the boats with the base engineer officer. Next, lunch.

At the back of the grey stone building was a broad paved yard. Originally for horses and vehicles, the outbuildings which surrounded it were now used mainly for garages and naval stores. Promptly at 1400 the three crews of nine officers and three petty officers assembled in the yard, getting as much cover from the biting wind as they could. Lieutenant Commander Edgecombe, the operations officer, consulted a list, and Captain Trenoweth tried not to look anxious or protective as he watched from the opposite side.

Venables was not to be seen, but right on cue a straight-backed marine major, still impeccable despite his loose leather jacket and rubber gumboots, marched into the yard and saluted Trenoweth.

He turned and looked at the twelve waiting figures and said tersely, 'I am Major Lees. I know that all of you are experts in your own field of operations. Please accept my word that I am the same in mine. I am here to tell you in the short time available how, if it becomes necessary, you can kill the enemy.' He held up a gloved hand. 'I *know*, I have read most of the details of your work. Hear me out. But I do not mean killing at long range. I mean face-to-face, where an enemy is flesh and bone like yourselves. When you can feel his breath, see him for what he is. If I and my people can instruct you in certain matters, your own lives will be saved, and thereby those of many others who daily risk their sanity and families to help *you*.' His tone sharpened. 'This sort of war is real and deadly. You do not put up your hands and surrender when you've tried everything you've been taught by the good book. Because if you do the enemy will be unkind to you.' His clipped moustache lifted slightly above a brief smile. *'Very.'*

Doors squeaked and feet shuffled, and then two of the outbuildings were opened to the wind. Inside Seaton saw tables of weapons, machine pistols, commando daggers and grenades, a veritable marketplace of death.

'Walk around, if you please.' Major Lees remained in the centre of the yard. 'In a moment I'll be introducing you to the little team who will explain things more fully.'

Drake said quietly, 'God, they've certainly laid on a show for us.'

'It's no' just a show, sir.'

They turned and saw a giant figure with the beret badge and shoulder flash of the Scots Guards.

'The weapons are for use, d'you see?' He grinned. 'Sergeant McPeake, at your service. I am to show you the benefits of close combat, and the uses of hands, feet and knife.' He looked down at Jenkyn and beamed. 'Och, it's a grand affair. It gives you a chance to knock your officers about, and me the opportunity of jumping on top of an Englishman without being charged for it!'

There were others, too. Quiet, dedicated men from all three services. They would explain about the different sorts of explosives, about codes, enemy uniforms and weapons. It was like starting all over again.

As Lees explained, 'It is not so that you may do any of these things, but so that you will understand what others are doing. Not so that you can be heroes, but in order that you will not become a hindrance.'

After three hours of it they took a break.

Drake asked, 'What do you think, David? Is it a bluff, or are we really hopping out of the pan into the fire?'

Seaton thought about it. 'I believe it's real. Lees and his men are too busy to waste their time here, and Venables doesn't have the imagination for it.' He nodded slowly. 'In some strange way it makes sense, too. There we are, right in the middle of some enemy harbour or base, and what do we do, apart from drop our charges and try to stay alive? Maybe we could add a few tricks to our bag, eh?'

The door banged open and Sergeant McPeake marched in rubbing his big hands.

'Now, gentlemen, outside if you please, it's dark enough.'

Vanneck eyed him coldly. 'Enough for what?'

The sergeant was unmoved. 'We'll be down the hill to the loch in a few minutes. The major says you're to steal a boat and get out to the depot ship.' He became very serious. 'Three separate parties. And I'll not be wanting to hear you've been spotted by the sentries.'

Vanneck exclaimed, 'For God's sake, Sergeant, we're not bloody pongoes!'

'True, sir.' McPeake regarded him bleakly. 'If you were, I'd not be troubling myself.'

Gordon Lennox, Vanneck's first lieutenant, said quickly, 'It might do us good, Rupert. Show Gervaise and his scruffs just how much better we are.'

McPeake said softly, 'Well spoken, sir.' He opened the door and glared at the black sky. 'Let's be about it.'

And that was how it was to continue. For most of the night and into the following day they were chased, instructed and harried by Major Lees and his 'professionals'. Even throughout the day after, which was the first of 1944, and a Saturday at that, the three submarine crews could be seen bustling about the foreshore or stripping and reassembling weapons as if their lives depended on it.

Captain Trenoweth tried to stay out of the way, although every fibre within him demanded he should keep his crews company. He was usually on a hillside, perched on a shooting stick, binoculars to his eyes, watching their efforts until rain or sleet drove him back to his H.Q.

There he would find his dog asleep by the fire, and Second Officer Dennison ready to scold him for being out in such bitter weather. It only reminded him of his age and his missing leg, but she was putting his health before his displeasure, and usually got her way.

Two weeks later, as quietly as they had arrived, Major Lees

and his men departed for the mainland. Another day passed, and then orders arrived on Trenoweth's desk.

XE 16 was to proceed with towing submarine and escorts to Scapa Flow. Upon arrival there would be a final check on the midget and her crew. An exercise or two would be carried out against anchored warships and boom defences. And then? But the target remained shrouded in secrecy.

Soon after dawn on the prescribed day, Seaton watched his three companions climb through the after hatch and into their own private world. They had been seen off on *Cephalus's* deck by Vanneck and the others. Just handshakes, and a few jokes which only they understood.

It was still very dark, and the waters of the loch seemed unusually restless. A paler shape idled beyond the moored depot ship, the towing submarine standing by, shrouded in a haze of diesel as she continued to charge her batteries while she had the opportunity.

It was too dark to see the shore but Seaton knew there would be others there, too. Waiting. Remembering.

Seaton watched the line-handling parties bustling around the pontoons and heard the lower, but no less confident mutter of his own diesel engine.

He touched his cap to the duty officer. 'Be seeing you.' Just like the song.

'Stand by to cast off.' The man's voice through a megaphone sounded unreal. A spirit of the loch. Seaton shook himself, and then with a final glance around, flashed his torch towards the depot ship's high bridge.

Muffled in greatcoat and scarf, Captain Trenoweth saw the brief flicker of light. It seemed to come from the water itself.

He thought of the motto. *Out of the deep we are here.*

It was freezing on the hillside, and his eyes were streaming with the cold. But he would not have missed it. Beside him, a thermos of coffee in her gloved hands, Second Officer Dennison watched him anxiously as he slowly straightened his back and balanced himself on his game leg against the wind. He could see nothing, but his ears had picked up the familiar beat of diesels. Slowly the captain raised his hand in salute.

She whispered, 'They'll be all right, sir. You see.'

He turned and looked at her fondly. 'I hope so. But it's not that.' He took her arm and they started back up the hill. 'I was just wishing it was me.'

3

A Very Long Way

'WAKEY, WAKEY, SIR.' The hand on Seaton's shoulder gave another shake. 'Time to start.'

Seaton rolled over on the bunk, squinting his eyes against the torchlight. Reluctantly, and then with gathering speed, his mind came out of the deep sleep, and he asked. 'What's it like?'

The seaman placed a steaming mug of tea beside the bunk and answered, 'Blowin' a bit, sir, and as cold as charity.'

'Switch on the lights.'

Seaton yawned, lowered his feet to the deck and glanced at his watch. Five-thirty in the morning. He looked around the unfamiliar cabin, his ears collecting sounds above and below him.

It never seemed to improve. You thought you could take it in your stride, get used to it. But the actual moment still seemed to come as a shock. It must be like that for a condemned prisoner, he thought, as he sipped the hot tea. At some agonising time of the last night on earth he might nevertheless fall asleep. And then the hand on the shoulder, sad but final. 'Come on, son. Put a brave face on it.'

Seaton listened to the creak of metal, the thuds of booted feet overhead. *Christ.* He was starting to sweat.

To steady his mind he thought back over the past ten days. Exercising *XE 16* in Scapa Flow, using the moored battleships and carriers as innocent targets. Nosing at anti-submarine nets and defensive booms, as much to test the Flow's protection as for their own benefit. It was only a rumour, but someone had suggested that the enemy might have captured one of the X-craft which had attacked the *Tripitz*. Communications and weather had been so bad in Norway that nobody really knew who had survived or who had been lost in the attack.

But if the Germans had captured an X-craft intact, it was more than likely that Captain Venables' opposite number in the *Kriegsflotten* would be quick to use her against the big ships in Scapa Flow. Nobody had forgotten the sinking of the battleship *Royal Oak* by a conventional U-boat at the very beginning of the war. The sounds made by a midget submarine, or lack of them, on the underwater detection gear might do something to prevent a similar disaster.

Within days of their arrival the final orders had been delivered. *XE 16,* with her towing submarine, escorts and salvage tub would quit the Flow and head still further north, to the last barren outpost in the Shetland Isles.

Seaton put down the cup and methodically began to shave and dress himself.

The waiting and suspense were over. They were here in the Shetlands, at Lunna Voe, and despite all his usual qualms and apprehensions, he could appreciate the great difficulties which Venables and his department had had to overcome. They had been well escorted for every inch of the way. The Navy had no intention of allowing another *XE 18* collision. Before leaving the protection of the Flow, however, the boat had been hoisted bodily from the water and swung inboard of a submarine depot ship for final inspection, and more important, to have her lethal side-cargoes of explosive clamped in position on either beam.

Seaton checked his pockets, wondering how any of them could have imagined this operation was going to be called off.

He had spent the last few days aboard the big salvage tub, and outside the cabin flat he could hear someone whistling *South of the Border Down Mexico Way*. He smiled. Geoffrey

Drake did not seem to care for any other tune.

And they still knew nothing of the actual mission, except that they were going to Norway. He shivered, despite his thick submarine jersey. Some two hundred miles to the east of where he was standing.

He listened to the rattle of equipment and tested the sluggish movement of the deck beneath him. *Blowing a bit,* the bosun's mate had said. But this tub was a great pile of steel and lifting gear, and was snugly moored within the land's protection. He hoped they would be able to get clear and find the most comfortable cruising depth without mishap.

They walked along to the chart room. It was already full of pipe and cigarette smoke.

Seaton saw Niven and Jenkyn standing side by side at the big chart table, yet somehow a mile apart. He would have to change that. With all the scurrying about under Major Lees' instructors, the arduous haul to Scapa, and then here to this last stepping-off point, they had remained a team, but separate.

He forgot them as he looked at the others. The bearded lieutenant commander with his first lieutenant. He was the captain of the towing submarine. His role was vital. The tug's skipper, a met. officer and the depot ship's gunnery and torpedo wizard were all standing around with a few faceless subordinates doing things in the background. The door opened and Seaton saw it was Captain Venables.

He nodded to everyone and strode straight to the chart table.

Seaton smiled. No nonsense about him. No sentiment or use for false platitudes. It was to be hoped there was something of value on the other side of the scale.

Venables said, 'Everything is prepared.' He seemed to see Seaton for the first time. 'Ready?'

'Yes, sir.' It sounded foolish. 'I don't think we've forgotten anything.'

He watched Venables peering at the chart and comparing some notes on his pad. He wants me to ask him. Plead with him.

Venables looked up sharply, and for an instant Seaton imagined he had spoken aloud.

Venables said, 'Now to the mission.' Everybody crowded closer as the captain laid one finger on the chart. 'Almost directly opposite to where we are, loosely speaking, is the small

port of Askvoll, about seventy-five miles north of Bergen.
There's a little island nearby.' He glanced at the bearded submarine commander. 'One of your people landed an agent there
recently to confer with the Resistance. They can watch the port
from there. Askvoll has seen a lot of German activity, until, that
is, the weather became impossible.'

The lieutenant commander nodded. 'I was near there a year
back, sir. It seemed quiet then. The enemy were relying on
Bergen as the big base, with floating docks, submarine pens and
all the rest of it.'

'Quite so.' Venables sounded disinterested. 'You will tow *XE
16* to within thirty-five miles of the coast.'

Seaton listened intently. It was like hearing about somebody
else. The towing part was normal enough. Thirty-five miles was
fairly safe from both offshore patrols and R.D.F. while they
slipped the tow.

Venables added sharply, 'An agent will make contact with
XE 16 as laid down in the intelligence folio.' He studied Seaton
impassively and gave a slight smile. 'Something to read on
passage.'

Seaton asked, 'And then, sir?'

The finger moved along the chart again. 'If, and I stress *if* the
signs are right, you will proceed into the deep fjord to the north
of Askvoll. There you will be given shelter by the Resistance,
fuel, additional stores, anything which is not too impracticable.'
Again the little smile.

He's actually enjoying all this, Seaton thought. Seeing his
'baby' take its first faltering steps.

Venables continued, 'It is as well not to know *too* much. You
can leave the nuts and bolts of the matter to the men on the spot.
But we have firm information that a ship, at present lying in
Askvoll, is going to be moved into that fjord. You will be there
when she arrives. When you leave, *she* will be on the bottom.'

The met. officer, speaking with all the ease of one not actually
involved, asked, 'But won't they have laid the defences already,
sir? Like they did in Altenfjord?'

Venables did not look at him. 'This is different. The Germans
have been clearing out the surrounding area for months, but had
to diminish operations because of bad weather. They intend to
boom off the fjord *after* the ship has gone inside, and apart from

34

one small entrance, the place will be a fortress, a nut impossible to crack.' He looked at Seaton again. 'By the old methods, that is.'

It was all suddenly crystal clear. Venables' hints at Loch Striven, Major Lees' quiet instruction. Get in before the target and you were halfway home and dry. If the reports and information were accurate . . . he twisted his mind away. They *had* to be accurate.

Drake asked quietly, 'This ship, sir? Why is she so special?'

Venables took out his familiar silver case. 'She is a floating laboratory. Fuel induction. That kind of thing.' He was being very vague. 'The less you know the better. Just lay your charges under her.' He examined each of them in turn. 'Remember what I said when we first met. This is vital work. Not merely an exercise to boost newspaper circulation. The Germans have put a lot of work into their project. Askvoll is well guarded, and there are regular air patrols from Trondheim, and of course plenty of sea activity too. If the enemy succeed in carrying out their intentions, indeed, if they have moved the ship already, an attack will still have to be launched. But any success would be costly, the chances of survival minimal.'

Seaton said, 'This agent you spoke of, sir. Suppose I'm not entirely satisfied with what he says?'

Venables shrugged. 'You will find separate rendezvous times for meeting with the towing submarine. Use the first if you think there has been a serious hitch. Choose one of the other dates as you see fit.' His eyes hardened. 'But the Germans must not capture the boat, your secret orders or, if possible, yourselves. They have become increasingly embarrassed by our commando attacks, and are hinting that they will not be obliged to treat any captured raiders under the terms of the Geneva Convention. In other words, they are getting worried.'

Drake grimaced. 'Me too.'

Venables ignored him. 'Half an hour then.' He glanced at the others. 'Carry on, if you please.'

The submarine commander hesitated, then held out his hand. 'Good luck.' He was probably thinking of previous operations with X-craft. But this time there would be no passage crew, no rest for Seaton and his companions for the two-and-a-half day crossing to Norway.

They all shook hands with him, and Drake said, 'Try not to let the tow snap, eh?'

Then the chart room was empty but for *XE 16's* crew and Venables.

He said, 'Do not forget, when you leave Lunna Voe you must be constantly alert and single-minded. The objective is all that can concern you.' He took out another cigarette and added, 'Off you go then.'

Outside the chart room and on the tug's high bridge deck Drake murmured between his teeth, 'That bloke makes Jeremiah seem like a bloody optimist!'

Niven said nothing but stared down at the activity alongside, where two launches were dipping and swaying against the moored *XE 16.*

The towing submarine had already cast off, and Seaton saw the pale sweaters of her crew on the after casing as they arranged the towing gear. They had had plenty of practice, which was something, he thought.

Heaving lines snaked out of the gloom, and more men appeared on the tug's deck below the bridge. Seaton took a deep breath. Time to move on again. He said, 'Let's get started.'

He walked to the ladder, knowing some of the tug's crew were staring as he passed. Envy, pity, it was hard to guess. He imagined Venables on the bridge watching their departure, but dismissed the thought at once. Not him. He was no Trenoweth. Venables would be getting ready to leave. Most likely back to the Admiralty, a million miles away.

Seaton had noticed that neither of the other midgets had been mentioned. If *XE 16* was destroyed, no doubt the next boat would already be standing by in the Shetlands, and the third after that. He chilled. It made sense if you could stomach it. If he and his command were captured, he would be unable to tell the enemy anything, no matter what they did. For he would know nothing. It was another war entirely.

Jenkyn went first, cat-footed and easy, his boots not even catching a droplet of spray which sloshed amongst the swaying hulls. As if he were eager to go.

Niven next, not looking down, his face deeply shadowed with determination.

Then Drake, his lips pursed in a silent rendering of *South of the Border,* and lastly, as tradition decreed, the captain of this tiny but deadly craft, David Seaton.

Diesels coughed and spluttered before settling into a steady beat, and the lithe shape of the towing submarine angled in towards the tug, the heaving lines swiftly bent on to the towing wires. The last of the tug's seamen secured the tow and then leapt back into their own launches, one calling, 'Give 'em a bloody nose, sir!' Someone always said that.

Seaton glanced along his own little deck, shining like black glass in the gloom. No conning tower or structure of any sort to break the low silhouette. He gripped the periscope guard and yelled, 'Cast off!'

He saw the big submarine moving slowly away, almost crabwise as she took the strain of the tow. He felt the first pressure, saw an arrowhead of choppy water widening between *XE 16* and the tug's bulbous hull.

His mind recorded all these details and yet remained firmly on the main points of his job. To get clear of the anchorage and wait for the signal to dive. After that it was a question of adjusting the right trim and depth, following in the other vessel's wake like a snared shark.

Two-and-a-half days. It would be the first time without a passage crew. An extra strain on all of them.

He swung himself down the after hatch and noted that his companions were all in their positions. Drake sitting aft and facing to starboard, working the pump controls, while Jenkyn sat loosely at the wheel, his eyes on the gyro as it ticked round obediently to the pull of the tow.

Niven, whose work of diver was shared with that of navigating officer, had already removed the bunk from the chart table and was busy with parallel rulers and pencil.

Seaton slammed down the hatch and secured it, feeling his ears react to the pressure. He pressed the button of the periscope hoist switch and crouched to meet and control it as it slid out of its well.

Not much to see. Lapping white crests, and then the narrow stern of the other submarine. Further away a frigate, one of their escorts, was sliding into darkness. In fact, she was anchored, and added to Seaton's sense of separation.

He sighed and swung the periscope in a slow circle. Time to

begin the checks, before they got into open water. He felt the boat sag and shudder against the tow. He looked at his hands on the periscope grips. They were quite steady, although he felt far from cool. Here we go. *'South of the Border'*.

The passage went more smoothly than Seaton would have believed possible. After the hazardous business of getting clear of the Shetlands, with an angry sea and short, steep rollers, they had dived in the wake of their towing submarine.

Again, luck stood by them, and unlike a previous mission when the slender telephone link between the two hulls had parted at the first dive, communications had remained excellent.

The first day had been a busy one. Checking every gauge and circuit again. Stores, some carelessly stowed by depot ship ratings, had to be rearranged, the trim of the boat adjusted to compensate.

Seaton found he had been able to delegate more things to the others, and it had been then, perhaps for the first time, that he had realised they had all become professionals in their trade without noticing it. This was no groping, anxious procedure, with startled eyes and embarrassed grins when something went wrong, when the nearness of danger had insinuated itself within the damp steel plates. Each man did his job with minimum comment. Every task for the passage was shared, helm, pumping controls, food, sleep.

Four men, moving back and forth, barely pausing to consider their slow-moving shell, its unreality when compared to the world above.

Seaton took great care to study his secret orders. To memorise some points, and to discuss other details with his companions.

Everything seemed to depend on the agent they would have to contact. He often recalled Lees' words about seeing and feeling an enemy for the first time. *Flesh and bone like yourselves.*

Drake, who had kept a close eye on the pumps and the boat's trim from the first moment of getting under tow, marvelled at the way Seaton appeared so matter of fact whenever he disclosed titbits from his intelligence folio.

He looked on Seaton as a friend in the fullest sense. Seaton would come and help him, if he needed him. No matter if it were here or they were to become separated by two oceans. Drake felt the same towards him. They never discussed it. It was just *there*.

But back in the tug's chart room he had accepted the one difference between them. When that pompous ass Venables had been going on about the agent, and Seaton had asked calmly, 'Suppose I'm not entirely satisfied with what he says?'

That was the guts of the whole thing. Not *we*, but *I*. Seaton was in command, and right or wrong it would have to be his decision alone.

Drake hoped he would be able to react in the same way if he were offered a command. But he doubted it.

He had thought a lot about Niven's wife, too. Decia. Just thinking of her name felt like betrayal. Once or twice he had tried to place her and Niven together in his mind. Knowing all the while he was testing his own will, or the lack of it. *Get this job over and in the bag and I'll forget the whole thing.* Even a straightforward lie like that did not seem to help any more.

Jenkyn kept himself busy all the time, and the only moments he was not crawling through his engine space, watchkeeping or doing some mechanical work or other he was trying to sleep. For the passage he shared his watch with the skipper, which suited him very well. Seaton trusted him completely, and it was mutual as far as Jenkyn was concerned.

Keeping active helped to put his last leave to the back of his thoughts. The spread table. The clock. His mother with her patient smile. What the hell would she do, or become, when she allowed her mind to accept the truth? It was enough to make a bloke go round the bend.

Apart from checking their snail's-pace on the chart and sharing watchkeeping duties with others, Niven had little to do. His diving gear was ready. So, he told himself, was he.

Whenever he looked at the small watertight door which led to the W & D compartment he could feel a kind of elation. Apart from being the 'heads' for the boat, it also led to the adjoining compartment in the bows. Used for those purposes it was hard to see it in its more important role.

Sitting there, feeling the water rising around you. Knowing Seaton would be watching through the toughened-glass scuttle in the door. It always made him feel a man apart. Worthwhile. And that was important to Niven, or it had become so since marrying Decia.

She always seemed to crave some kind of excitement. Riding, or driving fast cars, for which she always seemed able to get petrol when nobody else could. And the way she could goad or tease him whenever she felt like it. His defences always flew to the winds, and he had felt like hitting her more than once.

She was beautiful, passionate and demanding, and he wondered how she still managed to find energy for all her other interests.

By and large, the four-man crew of XE managed to conceal their personal worries. Seaton imagined that one of the reasons for discarding a passage crew was so that nobody would find time to brood on his immediate future. They were part of Venables' master plan. They were also expendable.

Then, on the morning of the second day, everything changed again. The waiting was over.

After tidying up the boat they went quietly to their stations, and after one final check started the main motor. It barely made a vibration as the hull continued to fight against the tow.

Seaton looked at the bulkhead clock and consulted his watch.

'Stand by to surface.'

He found he was sweating, despite the clammy, lifeless air around him.

Drake crouched over his controls, his face set in a frown as he manipulated the pumps which trimmed the water back or forth between the tanks. After a moment he was satisfied and moved the hydroplanes very gently, studying the immediate response on his inclinometer. If the craft was badly trimmed, or if the tow-line snapped at the moment of surfacing, *XE 16* might plunge headlong to the bottom before they could gather power on their own single screw.

It already seemed more spacious in their tiny control room as Niven was in the W & D waiting to leave via the fore hatch and slip the towing shackle. It was all vaguely casual.

The door to the compartment was open, and muffled against the cold and wrapped in a watertight suit Niven sat on the heads and regarded the others with his usual level gaze.

The hull, vibrated and hummed, and Seaton said quietly,

'Soon now.' Sighing against the sides he heard and felt the subdued roar of compressed air as the towing submarine blew her main ballast and began to surface.

Seaton was suddenly very calm. Detached even.

Drake said, 'Check complete.'

'Very good.' Seaton shot him a smile. No unnecessary jargon. They knew each other too well. 'Two-five-oh revolutions. Periscope depth.'

The electric motor purred more insistently through the after bulkhead and the hull gave another slow shiver. Drake was juggling with his levers, his eyes unblinking on the depth gauge. 'Nine feet.'

Jenkyn's shoulders flinched as the periscope hissed up from its well and Seaton bowed almost to his knees to peer through it.

The boat was sliding rather than rolling, and Seaton watched the little picture take shape through the lens. Jagged waves and black-sided troughs. He could feel them lifting the boat but could hear nothing. Like going deaf. Being drowned. Like nothing else on earth. The sky was very dark, for it was still early morning. But the other submarine was already up and waiting, men vaguely visible on her casing.

He pressed the periscope button.

'Surface!'

The deck tilted, and with the tow giving them added impetus *XE 16* lurched violently to the surface.

Seaton handed Niven the weighing bag with Venables' secrets inside and snapped, 'Open up, Richard. Slip the tow.' He clung to the periscope as the hull staggered violently and added, 'Make sure you've got your harness clipped on.' He thought that Niven hated being reminded of something so routine. But he could take no chances. A resentful diver was more use than a dead one.

He raised the periscope again, holding firmly to the grips as the little hull was pitched about. He saw a brief splash as the weighted bag went over the side. Too bad if he had forgotten anything now.

He saw Niven stooping and fumbling along the casing, like a mis-shapen giant in the crosswires.

Seaton made himself stop counting seconds. Niven was doing his best.

He sighed as the tow relinquished its grip and the midget

almost slewed beam-on to a large, white-crested roller.

The forehatch thudded shut and Niven reappeared in the W & D, bringing with him a small cascade of sea-water.

Seaton heard a muffled roar as the other submarine once again dived to her proper element, her job done.

He looked at Niven and smiled. 'Good show.'

He took a quick glance through the periscope and then pressed the button.

'Dive, dive, dive. Thirty feet. Eight-five-oh revolutions.' He turned to watch Jenkyn's shoulders. 'Course zero-nine-two.'

The corticine deck levelled and settled down into a slow, regular pitch, and Drake let out a long breath. 'Thirty feet.'

Seaton pictured *XE 16*, freed from her protective tow, heading away and towards the invisible coast. They would make contact at dusk. All being well.

To Niven he said, 'I will try to get a better fix when we're closer inshore.' He watched him, seeking some sort of reaction. After all, there was a bloody minefield to cross before they could do anything.

But Niven merely replied, 'I'll work on it, sir. We can alter course when it suits us best to make the rendezvous.'

Just like that.

Drake looked at them. 'If you'll take over, Skipper, I'll make us some breakfast, or lunch, or whatever it is.'

Niven said stiffly, *'I'll* do it, Geoff.'

The tall New Zealander grinned. 'Thought you might.'

Seaton leaned over the chart, studying his and Niven's pencilled calculations. The towing submarine would have fixed their position exactly. With luck the final approach should be equally efficient.

He lowered the chart light closer to the table. It was a very wild-looking coast, he thought grimly. Fjords, and scatterings of little islets, some no larger than reefs.

And there was the port of Askvoll and the diamond-shaped island almost touching it on the chart. He examined the carefully plotted rectangle which showed the minefield across their line of approach. He had never had any trouble with mines before, except once when he had grated against a cable.

Eternal vigilance. The enemy was always thinking up new devices to overwhelm attacks or to hoodwink their opponents' defences.

He heard Jenkyn humming to himself, the occasional tick of the gryo repeater. In the fore-ends Niven was groping around for some tins of food. It was strange how you could be hungry despite all the risk and uncertainty.

Seaton studied the chart, trying to memorise each small detail and lay it in his mind beside the information which Venables' people had collated. He thought about the agent who was somewhere out there waiting to make contact. His must be a very special kind of bravery.

Jenkyn said, without taking his eyes from the compass, 'Ah, char up!'

Niven lurched through the oval door with his mugs and some very stale-looking sandwiches.

Drake rubbed his hands. 'Smashing! Just like mother used to make!'

Niven exclaimed, 'For God's sake, there's no fresh food left!' He shrugged apologetically. 'Sorry, Geoff. I'm a bit on edge, that's all.'

Seaton took one of the sandwiches. Spam and pickle. Not too bad. While they had been sitting on the bottom of that Italian harbour waiting to attack the dock, he had devoured a stale bun and some marmalade which had tasted of diesel, and had really enjoyed it.

Perhaps because he had believed it to be his last meal ever.

He thought of Niven's brief spark of anger. The passage had taken more out of him than he realised. Out of each of them probably.

He stood up, ducking automatically. 'I'm going forrard to get my head down for a couple of hours, Geoff. Take over.'

Seaton crawled through into the most forward compartment, tightening his stomach muscles against the motion and the smells which seemed more condensed here. Then he laid down on the bunk boards above the ranks of batteries and closed his eyes.

At least you were on your own here. And he needed to gather his strength. Prepare himself for whatever he was required to do.

It all seemed a very long way indeed from The Lodge Hotel.

4

Trevor

SEATON PRESSED his elbows on the chart table until they hurt. It took physical effort to stay still, and to keep his restlessness from affecting the others.

Lying in the the fore-ends had not helped, and peering at the chart until his eyes blurred was no better. His head and imagination could only contain so much. After that, even a firm decision arrived at earlier became confused and uncertain.

He looked down at his wristwatch. What was worrying him? It was all going like an oiled machine. Even allowing for the drift and the powerful thrust of tide and current, they must be through the minefield. To strike one of those moored killers was unlikely in such a tiny craft, and even conventional boats had made their runs along the coast to see what they could get a shot at. Shallow-hulled motor torpedo boats had made hair-raising dashes at top speed across the same track as *XE 16* to drop agents, to try to recover them later.

But there was always the chance, of course. Some submarines and small craft had vanished with neither trace nor a claim by the enemy.

He half listened to Niven mopping down the hull with great

wads of towelling. The plates were running with moisture and condensation, and but for their thick, protective sweaters and waterproof suits they would be too chilled and damp even to think properly.

Drake called, 'Soon now, Skipper?'

'Yes. I must get a look at the weather. Visibility is *supposed* to be good, but you know how it goes.'

Drake fell silent again, knowing Seaton was trying to think.

If they failed to make contact with the agent, and there was no sign of suspicious activity by enemy patrols, they would have to find a billet to set down on the bottom and wait for the next try.

The orders loomed in his mind. *Use your discretion.* They had probably given the same instruction in Nelson's day, he thought.

Jenkyn said, 'It all sounds quiet enough.'

There was no point in prolonging it. He said, 'Come over here, Richard.' It was strange, but Niven was not the sort you could call Dick. Seaton could not explain that either.

He felt Niven beside him, his breathing heavy in the bad air.

'If visibility's good up top, I'll get a fix for you.' He tapped the chart with his dividers. 'There's a stone tower the north end of the port. Should be easy to see.'

He glanced at his watch again. It was a worry. The dusk could close down on the Norwegian coast like a blanket. Equally, it might stay bright for an extra hour if there was a clear sky and plenty of snow on the hills.

Niven said, 'There's the beacon, too.' He leaned over the chart. 'So long as we don't get the islands mixed up.'

Seaton looked at him briefly. So even and calm. It was unnerving.

'Right. Here we go.' He turned and moved to the periscope. The conductor arriving on his rostrum. The idea made him smile.

Drake saw his mouth lift and shook his head. How could he do it?

He forgot the smile and said, 'Trimmed for diving.'

'Very good. Periscope depth. Two-five-oh revolutions.'

The sharp thrust of compressed air, and Drake's deft response to control the boat's eagerness to break higher than

46

intended showed he was on his metal.

'Nine feet, Skipper.'

Around the greasy periscope their eyes met. *One more time*.

Seaton bent himself to his knees, every muscle protesting with cramp and because of the thick layers of clothing. He held his breath and pressed the button, just in time to see the darkness changing to turbulent patterns of grey and silver.

He flinched as the eye of the lens broke surface, as if expecting to feel the spray hitting his face. It was always like that.

He moved slowly in a circle, his mind excluding the control room and the three silent figures around him. His body was here, but his vision and his brain appeared to be floating on the water. The sea was a dull shark-blue, undulating towards him like a moving glass desert.

Seaton raised the periscope further and said quietly, 'The stick keeps getting smothered.'

Nobody answered. Each man knew Seaton was speaking to himself. To the boat.

Seaton examined the sky with the same care. In this silent world you got no warning at all. A carefree gull could change in a flash to a diving fighter-bomber. A cloud might conceal a whole squadron of patrolling aircraft.

Seaton blinked his eyes again. He was straining too hard. He waited for the hull to lift slightly and saw the coast sprawled across the edge of the sea. Topped in a layer of snow and blue ice, it looked dead. Menacing.

He moved the periscope to starboard. It was almost perfect. There was the nearest island, etched against the mainland beyond, round-shouldered, like a giant, half-submerged mushroom.

He said sharply, 'I can see the tower.' He cleared his throat. 'I *think*.'

More precious seconds lost while he swung the periscope again before training it back towards the pale shape of the old tower. It had been a lighthouse in the old days. Now it was said to be derelict. But it made a good aiming mark. Behind the island was the rest of the port, the entrance and whatever local defences the Germans had installed.

He gripped the handles and moved the little periscope further still. He said, 'I've got the beacon.' His mind was very clear, empty of everything but those two flaws set against the forbidding landfall.

'Take down the fix.' The periscope vibrated in his hands even though the boat was moving through the great swell at little more than a knot. '*Now!* Stone tower bears green two-five.' Round again. 'Beacon bears green eight-zero.'

Jenkyn called hoarsely. 'Ship's head zero-nine-two, sir.'

The periscope hissed down swiftly, as if grateful to be safe.

Seaton was on his knees, steadying himself against the porpoise-like motion. He felt out of breath. As if he had just run a race.

Niven was working at the chart. Then he said, 'It's fine, sir. But we should alter course in fifteen minutes. Bring her round to one-four-zero.'

Seaton nodded. 'Yes. It will take us in and will also give us sea-room if the natives get bloody-minded.'

He pictured the fragile, vertical pillar of the beacon. Perched on the seaward end of a line of rocks. Marking the safe channel. Revealing the lurking danger to anyone who was trained to recognise it.

Seaton pressed the button again and waited for the lens to clear. It had not been imagination, or a case of seeing what he had wanted to see. The scene was as before. There was massing cloud further inland, so that the paler sky between it and the snow looked like part of a crazily made layer-cake.

Nothing moved, but he thought he saw a haze of smoke by the stone tower. He lowered the periscope again. No sense in inviting danger. *XE 16* was invisible to interested eyes ashore or aboard a distant patrol vessel. But small and slow though she was, she would still be a ready prey to a low-flying aircraft.

When he had been serving in a conventional submarine Seaton had once been given a flight by a friend in the R.A.F.'s Coastal Command. They had flown over an incoming submarine to give her protection. The submarine, although moving at periscope depth of thirty feet, had stood out as plainly as a basking whale. It had been a very worthwile reminder of vulnerability.

'Dive, dive, dive. Ninety feet. Eight-five-oh revs.' He glanced at Drake. 'Be on the safe side.'

'Suits me.'

Drake grinned and took charge of his pump and hydroplane wheel, while Jenkyn opened the vent valves.

Seaton stood up, rubbing the ache in his knees, before joining Niven by the table.

'Once we've altered course, Richard, you can change into your diving suit.' He glanced at him curiously. 'Feel all right?'

'Yes, sir.'

'Fine.'

He looked at the chart. When they raised the stick for the next look round it would be pitch dark. But they had got through the mines, and the weather was better than expected for the time of year. One step at a time. Like getting Niven into his suit, for instance. There was no need for it. On paper. But wars were fought with cruder weapons than paper.

He turned slightly as Drake reported, 'Steady at ninety feet. Eight-five-oh revolutions.'

Seaton crossed the control room in two strides. 'I'll take over, Geoff. You make something hot for us, eh?'

Jenkyn said, 'A nice woman'd do me.'

Drake staggered past him to the watertight door. 'She *would*, too!'

Seaton watched Niven struggling out of his woollen clothing and into his tight-fitting diving suit. A rotten job, he thought. Outside their protective shell. Entirely alone if things went wrong. It had happened to others often enough.

A hot drink would help, provided it didn't make him sleepy. This was the most testing part. Making the proper rendezvous at the right time. He reminded himself of the recognition signal, *Zebra Able*. Even that would seem too long for the poor devil who had to send it.

He thought suddenly of his father. Probably sitting in his office in the City of London, still getting over his lunchtime drinks. If his favourite pub was still standing. He was an architect with a highly reputable firm. There was not a lot for them to do with the bombing going on. After the war there would be more than enough work for everyone who could draw a plan and estimate the cost, street by street.

He sighed. His father must have been a first-class architect once. Otherwise his parners would have got rid of him long ago.

In just over an hour the pubs would be opening their doors offering snug little havens behind their blackout shutters and sandbags. For lonely servicemen and women, and for men like his father.

Jenkyn said brightly, 'Char up!'

Here, a few miles off the coast of enemy-occupied Norway, at a depth of ninety feet, they were performing a routine as regular as his father's.

He slipped out of the seat and changed places with Drake.

The latter said thoughtfully, 'Pity we've not been able to go in at full bat on the surface.'

'Yes. That would have to have been during the night, which is no good for the agent, and useless for the tides.' He smiled gravely. 'There's always something.'

He ducked his head and walked to one of the steel lockers. It had been at the back of his mind.

He said, 'I'll hand out the pistols. We'll do this one by the book.' He hesitated, the blue-barrelled revolver glittering in his hand. As Lees had said. The war would become closer. Within reach.

Drake began to whistle very softly.

'This is it then.'

Seaton sank on to his knees and rubbed his eyes with his knuckles. No matter what lay in store on the surface, it would be heaven to get a lung-full of salt air. In the boat it was thick and foul enough to touch.

During their two-day passage they had been able to ascend to periscope depth at the prescribed times, to start their diesel engine and suck fresh, clean air down the induction trunk, the 'snort'. But in such a tiny hull it did not last for long, and he was surprised how they had managed to endure it without complaint. And, as far as he knew, none of them had taken any benzedrine. Later maybe, but right now was no time for the false energy to fade and the taker to go spark-out.

'Trimmed for diving.' Drake was watching his inclinometer like a hawk.

'Ship's head one-four-zero.' Jenkyn sounded dry and strained.

Seaton tried to make his own breathing regular again. Nerves before the job. Afterwards you tried to make a joke of it. But now . . . he glanced at the bulkhead clock.

Suppose, in spite of all Venables' care and security, somebody had let the cat out of the bag? He thought of the posters he had seen in shops and railway stations, the cartoon characters gossiping about a supposedly secret convoy. And Field Marshal Goering under the table, grinning his head off. *Careless talk costs lives.* Or, Be like Dad . . . keep Mum!

He rubbed his eyes once more. Must be going round the twist. Or the air was so bad it was destroying his mind.

He said, 'Eight minutes exactly.'

The thought returned like a barb. There were always more people involved than they said. Those you actually met at the hush-hush briefings, the ones like Venables. But what about the others, those who duplicated the triplicate orders and left them lying about while they drank their tea?

His father had always said much the same about the yearly Budget. It was supposed to be secret, but it all had to be typed and printed, handled by dozens of people before the Chancellor gave his dreary predictions in the Commons.

Jenkyn said, 'Six minutes.'

Seaton looked at his hands. *Steady.*

The pub door would be opening about now. 'Good evening, Mr. Seaton. Any news from that son of yours?' *Christ.*

He reached for the button. 'Two-five-oh revs. Periscope depth.'

Very slowly this time, as if Drake was holding the boat in both hands.

When he spoke even his voice was hushed. 'Nine feet.'

Seaton crouched down and then raised his eyes level with the periscope as he lifted it so gently towards the surface.

God, it was dark. He moved the periscope carefully in a full circle. The cloud had arrived, but it was broken here and there to allow a few pale patches to show themselves. He saw a few small whitecaps, but not enough to break the line between sea and land, land and sky. Not any fishing boats about. That was good. No sense in adding to the confusion.

The motion was still fairly regular and steep, but slightly better than before, he decided. They were much nearer to the land, although for all that he could see they could have been in mid-Atlantic.

He lowered the periscope and glanced at the others. The main lights had been switched off an hour ago to allow their eyes to get accustomed to it. The little control room was lit by a gentle red glow, so that the dials and gauges shone from either side like additional power units.

He nodded. 'Surface.'

After that he seemed to move like a machine. One moment he was crouching in the centre of their dripping, dimly-lit hull, and the next he was fighting his way through the hatch, the breath smashed from his body by the bitterly cold air.

Groping for hand and footholds he seized the periscope guard and felt for the intercom handset. An improvement on the first ones with their terrible voicepipes, but still something extra to go wrong when you least expected it.

'Time?'

He heard Drake's voice, tinny and far-away. 'One minute.'

Seaton felt the need to keep whispering into the ice-cold metal. To hold the link open.

'Black as hell, Geoff. I can just make out the island on the port bow. No craft about.' He clamped his jaws together to stop himself from gasping aloud. 'Any second now.'

'Take care, Dave!'

The deck was visible at last, a narrow, dark wedge surrounded by swirling spray and foam. It always seemed as if even a blind man would see them, although he knew *XE 16* was virtually invisible.

Seaton realised he had not connected his safety harness and clipped it in place, imagining himself falling overboard and freezing to death far astern while his three companions remained in their hull, unsuspecting, steering to oblivion.

He turned his head, his eyes streaming, as a beam flashed out of the darkness. Very low down, but dangerously bright. He moved his lips in time with the stabbing light. *Dash-dash-dot-dot.* A brief pause. *Dot-dash.* Zebra Able.

He switched on the handset. 'Recognition signal. Alter course two points to port.' He did not wait for an acknowledgement but felt the deck tilt sluggishly as Jenkyn followed his order.

Seaton moved his head carefully and ignored the crust of salt and frost on his lips and around his eyes. Now he heard the steady thump of an engine, and sensed something like panic.

Right on the button. But suppose it was not the craft it should be, but a bloody great patrol boat, her cannon and Spandau machine-guns already trained on *him?*

There it was again, the carefully flashed signal. The engine sounded much closer, and he felt the tension freezing him in a vice.

He raised his handlamp and pointed it towards the hidden land. Just one letter. *R.* He triggered it quickly. *Dot-dash-dot.*

The beat of the other vessel's engine responded instantly in power and density, and he wanted to drop to the deck, expecting the darkness to be ripped apart by tracer.

Then he saw it, rising above his line of sight like a great, ungainly shoe-box.

Seaton called, 'Hard aport.' He could see the small bow wave, apparently swinging in a tight arc as Jenkyn put the wheel over. 'Midships. Steady as you go.'

Voices merged with the sounds of sea and engine, and Seaton saw pale shapes bouncing down the other craft's flat side like puppets. They had thought of everything. Rope fenders to avoid damaging the little submarine, or worse, the nearest side-cargo of amatol.

The diesel-powered barge, for Seaton could now see it for what it was, looked about two hundred feet long, with a small, lumpy wheelhouse right aft, like a tank-landing craft. He could smell something other than oil, dank and vaguely familiar. It was strange but true that after being sealed in any kind of submarine you emerged with the keen senses of a fox.

He watched narrowly as the barge continued to pound nearer, to run parallel and stay between *XE 16* and the shore.

Seaton said, 'Port a bit. Enough. *Steady.*' He held his breath as one of the massive fenders bumped past him and nudged into the hull.

'They've arrived.' He kept his tone light, knowing that down below his boots the suspense was much harder to take.

A figure swung above the deck plates, and he heard a voice call out in Norwegian. Then the newcomer skidded on to the midget's casing, and would have gone all the way across and over the port side if Seaton had not seized his arm.

The man gasped, 'Bloody hell!' Then, gripping Seaton's belt, he turned to wave up at the barge. But it was already falling away, the engine beat mounting to throw a long roller across the midget's hull and leave her rocking violently in the wake.

Seaton peered at his visitor. Mis-shapen in rough clothing which stank of fish, he could have been anyone.

He said, 'Welcome aboard. You run a tight schedule.' He guided him towards the hatch where Niven's head was showing to lead the way below.

'So do you, Captain!' The man hesitated as Seaton touched his shoulder. 'What is it?'

Seaton moved his head. 'Aircraft.' He waited, swaying. 'Get below, please, quick as you can manage.'

Then he thudded through the hatch and almost knocked the man headlong.

'Dive, dive, dive. Eight-five-oh revolutions.' He loosened his collar. 'What's the depth?'

'Plenty, Skipper.' One hundred and eighty fathoms hereabouts.'

Seaton remained by the lowered periscope. 'Hold her at ninety feet.' He listened and waited. Nothing.

The deck seemed to lift again, and Drake said, 'Ninety feet.'

'Good.' Seaton turned and looked at the new arrival for the first time. 'I'm David Seaton.' He grinned. It sounded so ridiculous he wanted to burst into a fit of laughing.

The other man tugged a woolly hat from his head and replied, 'Trevor.'

It was the name which had been written in the folio. False, codename or his own, did not seem to matter.

He allowed himself to be led to a kapok cushion on one of the lockers.

'This is quite a ship!'

He did not look much like a secret agent, Seaton thought. In a word, he was medium. Height, colour, voice, everything. *Medium.* An ordinary, homely face which you would hardly notice on a train or in a restaurant. Apart from needing a shave, and looking rather tired, he could have dropped in from anywhere.

Trevor said, 'Sorry about the stink. Got picked up by a fisherman.' He did not explain further. 'Is that your chart?' He got up from his seat and moved to the table. From a pocket of his coarse reefer coat he took a small square of paper. He laid it on the chart and then said, 'I suggest you make your approach now. The target is supposed to be leaving port sometime tomorrow. If you go around the island you should cut quite a lot off the distance.'

Seaton looked at the chart. 'Does anyone know we're arriving?'

Trevor chuckled. 'That barge is going there, too. Laying on a reception committee!' It seemed to amuse him.

Seaton picked up his parallel rulers. It was not for Niven now. The decision had to be laid in the same place as the blame.

He could feel the other man watching him.

'You've done a lot of this sort of thing before, eh?' Trevor sighed. 'Good job. It's going to be no picnic.' He could not control a great yawn.

Seaton said, 'It'll be a tight squeeze.' The depths and bearings on the chart flitted through his mind in time with his pencil. 'Even for us.'

Trevor nodded and pointed at the port. 'They've got anti-submarine booms everywhere there, and there. Regular patrols begin at first light, and air cover through the day at *irregular* times, weather permitting. As we've been pretty well iced up for the past week, there'll probably be quite a few planes up tomorrow. The forecast is good. Clear and bright. No snow.'

He took the dividers and touched the fjord very lightly.

'There. That's the place. I've arranged to have a boat of sorts. Just to signal if the coast is clear.' His tone sharpened. 'How long?'

'Take twelve hours.' Seaton studied the chart gravely. 'More or less. It'll be early daylight when we get there.'

'Hmmm.' His fingers rasped across the stubble of his chin. 'Pity. Can't be helped. If we take another day the ship'll be there before us, and Jerry *can* move when he has a mind to.' He nodded firmly. 'I'll leave it to you.'

'All I want is to lay my head somewhere.' Trevor looked at the little door in the after bulkhead. 'There?'

Drake grinned. 'Engines, chum!'

Seaton said, 'Show him the space forrard. We'll rustle up some tea.'

Trevor shook his head. 'Forget it. I need *sleep*, and you want to get on with the job, right?' He waved to the others. 'See you around.'

Niven returned a few moments later and said, 'He fell down on the bunk boards and was asleep before his head touched the blanket.'

Jenkyn's eyes glowed in the compass light. 'Poor bugger.'

Seaton straightened up until his hair was touching the wet deckhead.

'Alter course, Alec. Steer zero-two-zero.' He looked at Drake. 'When we're on the next leg bring her up to thirty feet, at four hundred revolutions. There may be some crafty Asdic trawler up there, just lying doggo and listening.'

'Will do.'

'And—'

Drake showed his even teeth. 'I *know*, David! Watch the trim.' He gestured towards the W & D door. 'And I've allowed for the extra passenger!'

'Ship's head zero-two-zero.'

'Very good.'

Seaton pictured the mushroom-shaped island. A good golfer could hit it easily with a ball from this point. It would need all his care and skill to slip past undetected.

Compressed air hissed into the tanks, and eventually Drake said, 'Thirty feet. Four-oh-oh revolutions.'

Half an hour before the next alteration of course, and with luck a quick look through the stick. He glanced at the clock.

And his father would still be enjoying himself at the pub.

5

Time of Arrival

SEATON RAISED the periscope gingerly and blinked his eyes to clear his vision. Strain. Sheer, mind-breaking strain.

God, it was much lighter than the last time he had looked.

'Alter course. Steer due north.'

He lowered the periscope and looked at the deck. He could still see the slab-sided rocks, the crowded little houses of the port, two tall cranes perched like prehistoric monsters waiting to pounce.

'Due north, sir.' Jenkyn sounded very calm.

It had been going on for hours. And as the first hint of grey had touched the clouds above the land, Seaton had realised how much the passage had taken out of him, just when he needed to be at his best.

Constant alterations of course. Up and down for quick looks through the periscope, to check that they were not being carried by an inshore current or were heading for an anchored patrol boat. On and on, mile after aching mile. The mushroom-shaped island which had lain across their approach had moved slightly with each peep through the stick. On the bow, then falling back like a massive curtain to reveal the channel, the sleeping town

57

beyond. The moon had showed itself, mercifully very briefly, and several of the windows above the port had shone suddenly with its unearthly light, as if the whole place had been alerted of their presence.

He heard Niven speaking softly from the W & D and knew Trevor was emerging from his rest.

Seaton pressed the button, trying to recall how many times he had done so.

He saw the feeble light touching the water below the headland, gunmetal grey, swirling angrily towards him. Beyond that steep slope, which was still hidden in blackness, lay the fjord. There was still a long haul after that.

He lowered the periscope and asked, 'Those chaps in the barge? Are they to be trusted?'

Trevor smiled gently. 'Completely. And they are so much a part of the scene here the Germans have ceased to bother with them. They carry cement from the port to the fjord. Where the Germans are building their new installations.' He did not elaborate. Not yet.

Seaton looked at him. *The less you know*. But the smell was coming back to him, opening up all those impossible pictures of another life. Green fields, farm workers trudging down to the Lamb and Flag for a pint. All those sties and cowsheds he had seen built. No wonder he had recognised the dusty smell of cement. Especially at sea.

Trevor added in his level voice, 'The stuff is unloaded at a special pier in the fjord. It was originally for timber from inland. They used to collect it there and take it by barge to Askvoll. From there it was shipped just about everywhere. They are good people.'

Niven said, 'We've been told that the enemy are clearing out most of the local population.' It sounded like a question.

'Further up the fjord, yes. But the Jerries need the people from here. At present.' He sounded grim. 'What a war this is developing into.'

Niven persisted, 'It can't last much longer, surely? No matter what the Germans do.'

'They told you that too, did they?' Trevor turned towards Seaton. 'How are we getting on, Captain?'

'Nothing moving. You were right about the patrols.' He

smiled awkwardly. 'Sorry, I didn't mean it to sound like that.'
He had been thinking so hard and so long about *XE 16's* part he
had momentarily forgotten the terrible risks Trevor had been
taking for much longer, and with no protection.

Trevor grinned broadly. 'I'm not *always* right, y'know!'

Seaton raised the periscope very slowly. Trevor's presence in
the boat had helped in some odd way. He froze, his knuckles
white as he gripped the handles. He jabbed the button. 'Depth?'

'Ten fathoms.'

Seaton's mind was racing like the screw. 'Flood Q. Thirty
feet.'

He scrambled across to the chart, his mind grappling with the
details.

'Steer three-five-zero.'

He listened to the pounding inrush of water, the instant
downward thrust of the hydroplanes. It would be a near thing.
He had been following the inner curve of the island as close as he
could, but this would take them even nearer to those frothing,
rocky teeth. He looked at his companions. Nobody spoke until
Drake reported the boat at the required depth.

Then Seaton explained, 'Motor launch. Moving very slowly.
Left to right.'

Trevor remarked, 'It shouldn't be there.'

'Well, it *is*!' He saw Trevor's guard drop. The boat had been
little more than a shadow on the swirling water. Like a drifting
log.

Drake cocked his head. 'I can hear the bastard.'

They looked at the dripping deckhead, as if expecting to see it
cut through the metal. *Thrum-thrum-thrum.* Like a motor cycle
ticking over at the kerbside.

'Ship's head three-five-zero.'

Seaton ran his fingers through his unruly hair. It felt matted
and dirty.

'Reduce to three hundred revs. Dead quiet everybody.'

Five minutes dragged by, then ten.

Seaton could feel the sweat gathering in his jersey and
running down his thighs. He could not risk waiting any longer,
He dare not.

'Two-five-oh revs. Periscope depth again, please.'

Drake said through his teeth, 'My pleasure.'

Even before he had raised the lens to his eye Seaton felt the more unsteady motion, and when it broke surface he saw the nearest rocks almost alongside. Another minute, a few more yards, and . . .

'Starboard fifteen. Steady, Resume original course.'

He swung the periscope round, his knees banging painfully on unyielding objects. The motor launch had vanished.

He took a slower examination of the out-thrust headland which marked the fjord's entrance.

The boat had behaved better than ever before. No leaks or weeping glands. No gauge faults or engine failures.

Seaton heard Drake and Jenkyn murmuring their alterations, adjusting the trim.

He had almost cracked wide open over that bloody launch. He had seen the dismay on Niven's face, uncertainty on Trevor's. And no bloody wonder. They're depending on me. Not the other way round.

He pressed the button. 'We'll alter course again in fifteen minutes.'

There was a click and he saw Trevor examining a deadly-looking machine-pistol. German.

Trevor looked at him and said, 'Pity we don't make guns like this. It can cut a bloke in half. Never jams either.'

Seaton tried not to think of what had happened to the pistol's last owner.

At his estimated time Seaton raised the stick yet again and saw the fjord opening up as if to swallow him. The inner reaches were still in total shadow, so that the snow-capped slopes and crests held the entrance like a great inverted black pyramid.

But between the entrance and his slow-moving eye he could see the water moving vigorously, feel it trying to shake Jenkyn's grip, challenge the strength of helm and screw. It was on the ebb. Much longer here and they would be hard put to get to their next rendezvous at all. He made a decision.

'Increase to eight-five-oh revs. Steer zero-eight-zero.'

Trevor waited for the alien world which surrounded and jostled him in response to Seaton's unhurried voice to settle before saying, 'Another half an hour at this rate, Captain.' He thrust the pistol inside his reefer. 'God, I'm ravenous.'

Seaton glanced at him and smiled. *You too?*

Then, as Jenkyn announced they were on the new course, he forgot everything but that last picture. The fjord opening on either bow.

It would look one hell of a lot better going the other way.

Seaton said huskily, 'I can see the pier. Starboard bow. About a cable away.'

He took a slow look around, his heart thumping painfully. It was almost as if he had been expecting total failure from the start. Seeing the strange, sloping pier, exactly as Trevor had described it, was more unnerving than any sort of assurance.

He moved the handgrip and saw a pale triangle of sky above him. It was still shadowed down one side of the fjord, and he could sense more than judge the depth of water. On the opposite side he could just make out little clefts, filled with snow like bushy eyebrows, and a solitary hut perched on a twisting track, as if it had fallen there by accident.

Trevor asked, 'Any boat?'

Seaton trained the crosswires on the pier. It was like a gaunt longhouse, its full length enclosed by roof and corrugated iron sides, open to the weather in only two places. Nestling against it he saw the boxlike cement barge, but no sign of movement aboard.

'No.' He heard Trevor's intake of breath. 'Not yet.'

He swung the periscope violently as something moved. But it was a large piece of ice and rock which had somehow detached itself from the top of the nearest land to bounce and rebound into the fjord below.

Trevor muttered, 'It was all arranged. A signal.' He was repeating it for his own benefit. 'The time is right. *We've* not put a foot wrong.'

'Perhaps the boat's been held up.' Drake sounded doubtful.

Seaton lowered the periscope, picturing the pier drawing closer. At their minimum revolutions they still had time left to change their plan. But it must be soon. He looked at Trevor.

'I can't stay out here all day, and the bottom's no use for putting-down. It's too deep, and too damn risky,' He waited, measuring the other man's reaction. 'Well?'

Trevor said, 'The Jerries might have heard something. A tipoff.' He shook his head. 'Unlikely. Collaborators get short shrift from the Resistance.'

Jenkyn called, 'Havin' a bit of a job, Skipper.' He was moving the wheel more deliberately than usual. 'The current's a sod for holdin' on course.'

Seaton sighed. Dead slow. One screw. Drake and Jenkyn had done marvels already to meet Trevor's unbreakable schedules.

He replied, 'I'll take another look. After that, if there's no red carpet, I'm getting the hell out of it.'

He saw Trevor's guard drop, the strain and tension of his mission giving way to obvious diasppointment.

Seaton added, 'But I'll try again. I promise.'

He pressed the button and dropped to his knees, his thoughts pushing Trevor's problems into the background.

It was like feeling your way in the dark. As if you were not entirely trusted.. Was it really for their own good, or because they were not yet tested in this sort of work?

He steadied the crosswires on the cement barge. The light was much stronger, and he could even see the dents and scars along her ugly, flat hull.

But he fixed his eyes on a small lantern which had appeared on the wheelhouse. Since his last look. He licked his lips, they felt dry and tasted of oil.

'Here. Take a look.' He seized Trevor's elbow and pushed him against the periscope. 'Use these grips. Adjust it either way.' He watched the man's uncertainty fading, the way his jaw tightened as he peered through the lens.

Seaton tried not to count the seconds. He had to know, be as sure as he could that he was not heading for destruction and worse. Only Trevor could help. All the same, their tiny stick of periscope might be seen, their approach greeted with a hail of steel and mortar bombs.

Trevor moved aside. 'It's a signal. The barge skipper would never risk his friends and family unless it was important.' He eyed Seaton grimly. 'Beneath the pier there is a long underwater shelf. About a hundred feet by twenty. Carved out of the rock wall to hold the lower foundations. They've been getting it ready for you for weeks.' He smiled, in spite of their combined anxiety. 'Probably before you even knew about this caper.'

Seaton stared at him. A berth under the pier. It made perfect sense. Barges might come and go, but security was usually to be found in everyday situations, not in isolation.

Trevor was not smiling as he added, 'But it might be an ambush. I have to tell you.'

Seaton thought of the pier and the moored barge. They would be very near. Once in the prepared berth their haven might well turn into a trap. Boat, crew and Trevor. Just like that.

He said calmly, 'We'll go in on the surface. The tide's dropping and we will be able to motor under the piles. Equally, we'll have room to come about and run deep if things get nasty.'

He felt better for saying it.

Having committed them he added, 'Richard, man the W & D. Stand by to surface.'

He groped for the unfamiliar holster at his belt, trying to see the three X-craft crews behind the old hotel while Lees' fierce sergeant had explained things. It all seemed a lifetime away.

Trevor said, 'Better let me go first.'

Seaton crouched below the after hatch testing the locking wheel and clips.

'No. You're too valuable. If I get strafed, Geoff can take you out.' He looked at the tow-haired lieutenant. 'Okay?'

Drake nodded, his eyes strangely sad in the dimmed lights. 'Too right.'

Trevor had drawn his deadly-looking machine-pistol. 'Just as you say, Captain.'

Seaton was thinking of the pier. 'Hold her on the 'planes as much as you can, then make it fast.' He looked from Drake to Jenkyn's narrow shoulders. 'Fit?' They nodded.

'Surface!'

He knocked off the last clips and thrust up at the heavy hatch with all his might, feeling the water surging across the narrow deck, the icy sting of spray in his eyes as he hauled himself into the grey light.

'Starboard a point.' Now he was standing upright, clinging to the snort, which he had raised in time with opening the hatch, the handset touching his lips. *'Steady, now!'*

Faces appeared on the barge's low bridge, and another man was running like a maniac along the outside of the pier, hopping from pile to pile, apparently indifferent to the risk of drowning or being crushed by the barge if he fell.

Seaton felt something coursing through his body like emotion and relief all in one.

This was no carefully staged deception. If anything, these unknown Norwegians were risking disaster in their brief moment of success. What they must have suffered as they had worked and schemed on some hazy instructions from Whitehall, Seaton could only guess. Fear of betrayal, for the safety of their families and friends. Knowing that any sign of precaution, or change in their daily and regulated routine, would draw suspicion and instant investigation.

He knew Trevor's head had appeared through the hatch, and wondered how he was feeling at this moment. Maybe he was hardened to such things.

Seaton said, 'Tell Richard to open-up and come on deck.'

A bearded man was waving down from the barge's high side. It looked like a bottle in his hand.

He heard Trevor murmur, 'Look at them, for Christ's sake. Now you know what you're doing is worthwhile. To them at least.'

Niven was on the fore-casing now, his hands reaching out to secure a line which had been lowered through the centre of the pier. The little submarine headed between the slime-covered piles, squeaking in protest as she nudged away from a hidden cross-beam.

Shielded by the moored barge outside the piles, *XE 16* continued to edge along the full length of the pier, while above and on either beam waving figures perched on precarious footholds like acrobats.

There was no cheering from these muffled, unknown people, but the warmth of their welcome was as obvious as if they had yelled it up and down the fjord.

Seaton saw another line being lowered so that Niven could attach it like a spring.

'Stop main motor!' He felt the hull shiver and lurch against the massive piles. 'All right, Trevor, or whatever your name is, over to you.' He smiled, feeling the tension like claws. 'We *made* it!'

At the top of the sloping pier was a tiny room, no more than an extension to the machine shed which controlled the solitary derrick.

Seaton was guided without delay or ceremony through a small door, conscious of the unreality which seemed to increase every minute. He had left Drake and the others aboard *XE 16*. Everything looked safe enough but, dedicated or not, these excited Norwegians knew nothing about midget subs. It would be hard to explain to Venables if a line parted and *XE 16* rolled gently along the bottom of the fjord and filled with water.

The contrast between the submarine's unsheltered deck, then the numbing cold of the pier, changed in an instant as he allowed somebody to lead him into the little room. It was like a furnace. The solitary window was well covered with battens and sacking, and in the centre of the room stood a huge, pot-bellied stove, which glowed pink in the darkness as if about to explode.

Trevor solemnly shook hands with the figures which had entered the hut. There were five of them. Muffled to the eyes, and mis-shapen with fur-collared weatherproof coats and filthy boots.

Then Trevor said, 'This is Jens.' He stood aside as the man loomed towards Seaton like a bear. 'He is the leader.'

The man Jens placed one hand on each of Seaton's shoulders and said in a deep, throaty tone, 'You are very welcome.' He peered nearer, a thick beard almost brushing Seaton's face. 'You will never know how much.'

They moved closer to the glowing stove, steaming and wilting in the great heat.

A head peered round the door and whispered something, then withdrew.

Trevor explained, 'All clear for the moment.'

A lantern was lit and hung above a rickety table, and the little group sat around it, pressed together in silence as the leader produced a bottle and some glasses.

He said simply, 'First we drink. Two of us speak your language well enough, Captain. The others,' he showed a set of gleaming teeth through his beard, 'will be told later, yes?'

It was Norwegian aquavit, colourless in the lantern light, but with a grip of mellow fire.

Then Jens said, 'We could not use the boat, Trevor. The Germans sent a patrol in yesterday and landed it here.' He looked at his strong hands. 'I felt like putting them in a bed of concrete!'

Trevor tossed back his drink and allowed a man to refill his glass.

He asked, 'How many?'

Jens shrugged. 'Six. No officer.'

Seaton said, 'They must have been put ashore by that launch I sighted.'

They all turned towards him, hearing his voice for the first time. Five pairs of eyes. He removed his salt-stained cap and laid it on the table.

'I'd be glad if you'd call me David. Captain sounds a bit grand.'

Jens thumped his arm and translated to the others, and they all seemed to emerge from behind their various defences, drawn by his simple request. Fur and woolly caps were dragged off and hair shaken in the unrelenting heat. One figure reached out to touch the mildewed badge on Seaton's cap.

Seaton stared, seeing the slender wrist, the well-shaped hand. The girl returned his gaze gravely. She had a thick scarf partly over her head, and Seaton could see she had short, disordered curls, fairer even than Drake's.

He knew the others were watching him intently, with impatience or amusement, he did not know or care.

'Welcome to Norway, David.' She held out her hand. 'I am—'. She hesitated and shook her head, spilling more hair from under the scarf. 'No matter. Just say I am a friend, yes?'

Seaton smiled. 'I am sorry if I stared too long.'

He watched her eyes as she looked down at his cap on the table. He would never be able to forget them. They were blue-green, like the sea through a periscope when the sky above it was being kind.

Trevor cleared his throat. 'We'd better get on. The workers will be arriving soon.' He looked at Seaton. 'They're Russian prisoners of war. Slaves would be a truer description. Their job is to keep the track clear of snow and fallen rock, all the way from here to the road. They load the trucks, too.'

The war had intruded into the warmth, stripping away the brief deception.

Jens nodded. 'But you will be safe here, David. You can

charge your batteries whenever you wish, our generators make enough noise to cover an avalanche. We have diesel oil in good supply. The work is important for our German masters!' He spat out the last part. 'They will live to regret it, *some* of them, by God!'

He recovered just as swiftly. 'Now.' He looked at Trevor. 'It is as we thought. The ship will be arriving late today. And work will begin at first light. They have been surveying the anchorage since we first heard something was being planned. Now they are ready.' He dragged a gold watch from one of his capacious pockets. 'The patrol boats will be here very quick, I think.'

A man with weather-beaten cheeks turned away and spat on the stove.

Jens explained quietly, 'He is in charge of the unloading here and has to meet the Germans more than any of us. I hope he can control his hatred a little piece longer.'

Trevor touched Seaton's arm. 'Any problems from your end, David?'

Seaton tried to think clearly about it. The plan was a good one. They were here, secure and well hidden, with people other than themselves to watch and worry over them. Safe from underwater detection, and well placed to observe the enemy's preparations and defences. When the time was right all they had to do was leave the pier and drop their charges right underneath the moored ship. It sounded easy if you said it quickly.

'I think I should know about the target.' He saw their quick exchange of glances.

Then Jens replied, 'Yes. Of course. The waiting is done. You have all our hopes with you. Our lives, too.'

Trevor interrupted, 'The Germans are building a great concrete ramp just to the north of us. It has been going on for a long time under maximum security. And you know the Jerries. I mean *security*.' He waved towards the covered window. 'The target is nothing less than a floating laboratory and factory. As the weather improves, more and more equipment will be transferred to the installations ashore. The ramp is a good site for practice shots. To iron out any last problems.'

Seaton was conscious of the stillness, of the girl's hand on the rough table beside his own. It looked tanned, and had freckles on it.

Trevor added slowly, 'It's a rocket, David.'

Seaton chilled. All the music-hall and radio jokes about Hitler's secret weapons were suddenly no longer amusing.

'And it's your job to knock it out before they can get into business ashore. If, I mean, *when* you've destroyed it, it'll take them time to get going again, *priceless* time which we must have if we're to invade Europe, or anywhere else for that matter.'

Seaton looked at him. Just him and his companions, and a little over four tons of explosive. It would seem cheap at the price.

Trevor seemed to read his thoughts. 'There's no other way. Deep in this fjord the target is safe from bombing attack, even if our people could reach this far without being shot into the drink. Every mile of coast from here to Bergen, or north to Trondheim, is bristling with flak, fighters and everything but the kitchen sink.' He kept his tone as level as his gaze. 'It's a must, David, no matter what they told you at home.'

Seaton wanted to lick his dry lips, but was almost afraid to snap the tension. They were watching, weighing the chances, wondering probably if they had made a mistake. It was vital they should trust him.

He said, 'I'd like to get hold of the known details of the ship. Size, tonnage, name. What she was used for before this.'

Jens said, 'I will arrange it.' He looked at the others and nodded.

The girl said quietly, 'You have made them very proud, David.' Her hand touched his lightly. 'You are a brave man.'

Jens asked, 'Is there anything we can do for *you.*'

'Sleep, something to eat which has not been dropped straight out of a tin, but mostly a good hot bath.'

He forced a grin, seeing their satisfaction. It was as if he had already been labelled as dead once the mission was completed. Proud? Brave? What did those words mean?

'There is a concealed place in the roof above us here.' Jens was on his feet. Eager to begin. 'I suggest you stay there during the day. Your men can remain in the submarine. They can lie submerged on the ledge in complete safety.' He gripped Seaton's hand. 'But you, I think, should go up there and watch your enemy.'

Seaton looked at Trevor, who said, 'You'll never get a better chance.'

'True.' Seaton stood up and jammed the cap on his head, the drowsiness from the fire dragging at him like hawsers.'I'll go and put the others in the picture.'

As the door closed behind him, and he followed one of the Norwegians back along the pier, Jens asked, 'Picture? What *picture?*'

But the girl said abruptly, 'You didn't tell him all of it, did you?' The blue-green eyes watched Trevor with something like anger. 'Was it because he is not strong enough? Answer me!'

Trevor picked up the bottle and emptied it into a glass.'I've seen him at work, and I know a bit about him. He's been through a lot in this bloody war.' He downed the aquavit in a gulp. 'It's not his strength I'm worried about.' He looked at the others. 'It's his humanity.'

6

No Choice

'I'VE BROUGHT you a hot drink.' Trevor squatted on the floor beside Seaton's rough palliasse and watched him curiously. 'Your Number One gave some coffee to Jens. The first good stuff they've tasted for a long time.'

Seaton rolled over on to his back, every muscle hardening like an alarm system as he grappled with his whereabouts.

The hiding-place in the roof of the pier was, naturally enough, triangular, and separated from the rest of the building by a brick bulkhead. It was possible to stand upright in the centre, but the roof sides sloped to floor level, towards the land, and out across the fjord. It was lined and very warm, the heating provided by the metal stovepipe from the little room below.

Trevor asked. 'Sleep well?'

Seaton struggled up in the blanket, feeling crumpled and dirty in his battledress. He had been dreaming about the girl. Thinking of her. Wondering how she would look without her padded clothes and scarf. When Trevor had shaken his arm he had almost believed she had come from dream to reality.

'I feel like hell.'

'Splendid. I'll let you rest. There's nothing for you to do just yet.'

Sounds, muffled and indistinct, probed into the hiding-place. The grate of metal, a far-off shout followed by the noise of engines.

Trevor said casually. 'They're loading cement on to some trucks. They've been at it since morning.' He smiled at Seaton's dismay. 'Yes, you've been in the Land of Nod until now.' He peered at his watch. 'Nearly dusk.'

Seaton lay back and said wearily, 'For God's sake. I'm not a child, you know.'

Trevor was unmoved. 'You need all your beauty sleep.' He stood up and grappled with part of the roof. 'Take a look. The beast has arrived.'

Seaton was on his feet in seconds. Trevor had unclipped a portion of the roof, about the size of a brick. Through the narrow slot he could feel the icy air like something solid.

For several long moments he said nothing, nor did he move. It was all so incredible and unreal, this could be another wild dream.

He had arrived here in semi-darkness, and now with the fjord already falling in shadow once again everything had changed. Instead of empty, swirling space there was a ship. Against the bleak shoreline she looked huge. Invincible.

Seaton moved his head from side to side, trying to see more. A few power boats surged this way and that, and there were plenty of arc lights on the ship's maindeck. There was no need for blackout this early.

He asked, 'What is she?'

Trevor replied, 'Jens has made enquiries. She's the *Hansa*, sixteen thousand tons. Used to be on the Deutsche Ost Afrika Linie running out of Hamburg, before the balloon went up.'

Seaton examined the ship as calmly as he could. It was not hard to picture her in sunnier days. Two fat funnels and a spacious boat deck, and three lines of scuttles down to her waterline. Now, her tall hull was garish with pale dazzle-paint, and she had the look of a vessel which had been hard-used since those far-off times.

He studied the two masts, the twin derricks which were weaving and dipping above her decks as if independent of human hands.

72

Trevor said, 'She was the usual mixture. Passengers, mail and cargo. Paid her way.'

A long launch moved slowly against the stream, pushing back a broad moustache of white froth. Seaton watched it, surprised that he was so calm, unable to accept it. There were German uniforms in the boat, and a bright scarlet flag with a black cross and swastika curling from her staff.

The enemy. He should feel something, surely?

He said, 'Have they begun work on the nets yet?'

'Tomorrow. There's a tug and supporting craft farther down the fjord. It's just as you were told. The enemy are starting from the wrong end.'

Seaton wiped his eyes. The bitter air was making them weep. It still eluded him. That down below the pier, and under this tiny room, was *XE 16*. A little midget of fifty-four feet, in which were three people, probably sleeping to save air. The launch which was edging past the cement barge was at least seventy-five feet long, and there were doubtless plenty more where that one came from.

He looked again at the big ship. All those men and weapons, and he was going to wipe them out. It was then that he shivered. It was better not to see them so near. So real.

'Satisfied?'

Seaton asked, 'What are those extra deckhouses for?'

They were like metal tanks, without scuttles, but he could just make out a door in each of them. They spoiled the vessel's otherwise stately outline.

Trevor answered vaguely, 'Equipment, most likely. The whole ship is crammed with the stuff, and enough eggheads and boffins to start another war.'

Seaton rubbed his chin thoughtfully. 'This one is enough, thanks.'

He stood aside to allow Trevor to seal the slot again.

Then he said, 'It will make a bang, believe me.' In his mind he could visualise their cautious approach, the agonising moments of setting the charges. But after they had left the explosion would roar along the fjord like a tidal wave. 'The rock walls will make it worse.'

'Yes. Jens has arranged to evacuate the pier in time. His

village will be safe enough and shielded from the blast.'

Seaton sat down on the box, thinking about it. How many would die? What must it feel like? He shook himself angrily.

'When?' His voice was sharper than intended, and he added, 'I'm getting old.'

Trevor lit a cigarette and puffed at it. 'Day after tomorrow. Sooner, and they might shift the moorings. Later, and the bastards may lay more nets around the hull with detection gear on.'

Seaton pulled in his stomach muscles, testing himself. Day after tomorrow.

Trevor said, 'It'll be a Saturday.' That seemed to explain everything.

'Yes.' It was funny, but you never thought of the Germans as people who had 'Saturdays off', like the British. All their efficiency and clockwork precision seemed to exclude such weaknesses. 'Saturday then.'

'Look, if you're bothered about something?' Trevor changed tack. 'I mean, if I can help in some way?'

Seaton smiled at him. 'Forget it. It's like a first-night. All will be well when the curtain rises. Where will you be?'

'That depends.' Trevor looked away.

'I mustn't ask.' He yawned. 'Sorry.'

Trevor moved to the concealed hatch. 'I'd better check with Jens. The Russians will be on their way back to camp by now, poor devils. But Jerry may throw in a patrol, just to impress the new arrivals.' He hesitated. 'You'll want to discuss it with your people.'

'Yes. Geoff Drake can surface the boat as soon as you give me the word.'

'It's snowing just south of here. That will keep the patrols tucked out of sight.' He snapped his fingers. 'Almost forgot. I've fixed it so that you can all have hot baths. One at a time, of course.' He chuckled. 'Just like Claridges!'

Trevor knelt down and raised the hatch half an inch. 'All clear. I'm off then.'

Seaton said, 'The girl.' It had come out. Just like that.

The hatch dropped softly into place again. 'Girl?'

'You know.'

Trevor turned slightly, his eyes in shadow. 'There's no point,

74

David. I tell you, then somebody else knows. You tell another, and so it goes on.'

'I see.'

'Do you?' Trevor moved closer. 'There's a man not far from here, a farm worker, an ordinary, simple man. The Germans made a swoop, looking for suspects, for members of the Resistance, for anything. They took this simple, ignorant farm-worker to their camp dentist, and they drilled *every tooth in his head*. Can you imagine it? Each tooth, through it and the nerve until there was nothing left. On and on. Until the man was almost crazy with agony and terror. Then they let him go. Because he knew nothing.' He stubbed out his cigarette and added quietly, 'Could *you* remain silent? Knowing just a name might help to ease the torture, eh?'

Seaton said, 'I've a lot to learn.'

Trevor raised the hatch again. 'We all have.' He nodded. 'See you later.'

Alone again, Seaton lay back and tried to think clearly. About Trevor, this extraordinary man who could joke about hot baths, worry over secrecy, and chill with his descriptions of brutal torture.

And the girl who must remain in the distance, unformed, like someone you see in a train as it pulls from the station leaving you behind, in ignorance of her and her world.

He scrambled up, and after a few attempts opened the peep-hole again. It was darker, and the cargo lights on the *Hansa's* deck were extinguished.

Seaton measured the angle of attack with his eye, calmly and professionally.

Then he closed the peephole and sat down, thinking of the man with the drilled teeth.

Why had Trevor really told him? Because of security? Or was it that he thought he was getting soft, unable to go through with the attack?

And Venables. Seaton had a sudden picture of him in some Admiralty corridor or a deep secret bunker.

'Not taking this Saturday off, Venables, old chap?'

Venables would not have that or any day off while his project was under way.

The day after tomorrow.

Captain Walter Venables would be peering through the wall, across the bleak North Sea, up to Norway. Seaton shuddered. To here. *Heads you lose. Tails I win.*

Down below he heard somebody stoking up the fire, the clink of cups. The working day on the pier was ending. Tomorrow would seem very long indeed.

Sub Lieutenant Richard Niven stood motionless on the pier and allowed his eyes to become used to the darkness. Somewhere below his sea-boots *XE 16* lay snugly against the piles while Drake and Jenkyn carried on with their battery-charging. He could not hear them because of the louder rumble of the cement barge's generator. It still took a lot to grasp, let alone get used to. All the din in the world, when his original training had laid stress on stealth and quiet.

He knew that some Norwegians were posted at each end of the pier, just to be on the safe side, as Trevor had explained. But no trouble was expected from the Germans.

Niven kept telling himself to stop thinking about it. After all, why *should* the Germans be worried? There had been no incidents here before, they were well protected, and their precious ship was deep inside a steep, dangerous fjord. The nearest Allied soldier was more than two hundred miles away. To someone who lived in Dover, just across the English Channel from the most invincible military machine ever created, the distance would seem like the Pacific.

He heard someone singing from the small bridge on the cement barge. Again it did not bear thinking about. Seaton was aboard right now, having a bath.

Niven plucked the sweater from his skin. He had already had one. Caution, anxiety had gone momentarily with the first blast of a piping-hot shower. He had ducked and panted, letting the water sluice across every inch of his body, until Drake had peered in at him and drawled, 'Come on, you gorgeous thing, don't make a bloody meal of it! Remember the poor Colonials!'

He was so different. Nothing seemed to worry him.

A torch flashed up through the rough planking by Niven's feet. The battery-charge was over for the present. He relaxed slightly and walked hesitantly along the pier.

It must be a hard life, he thought, even in peacetime. He could smell oil and dust, salt and fish. It was all completely alien.

Decia would ask him about it when he got back. He could see her. Her eyes direct and changing from amusement to impatience.

'What do you mean, you don't know, Richard? Why won't you *ask* people? Find out what life is about?'

He had watched her curled up in the big house while she and her father had listened to Drake talking about New Zealand, the islands, about sharks and exotic-sounding foods. Decia had been fascinated.

Niven reached the end of the pier and braced himself for the wind which he knew was waiting beyond the corrugated iron barrier.

What could he say to her about his work which would impress, or satisfy? The strength had to come from within, not like some stupid film, a cavalry charge with Errol Flynn to the rescue. He was walking more quickly in time with his resentment. Decia's father was partly to blame, and heaven alone knew what he said to her when they were parted.

He stumbled over an iron ring-bolt, and would have fallen headlong into the darkness if someone had not caught his arm.

'*Hell,* I'm sorry!' He straightened up, getting his balance again. 'I don't know what—' He froze, unable to move or breathe.

The man who had stopped him from falling was a German soldier.

David Seaton dragged a comb through his hair and regarded himself in a steamy bulkhead mirror. Even though he had dressed in the same clothing as before, he felt tingling and alert from the hot shower. He touched his chin and smiled at himself. Shower and shave, what simple things to prepare a man.

He looked slowly around the tiny bath space, making sure he had left nothing which might throw suspicion on the Norwegian crewmen.

Lastly, he buckled on his pistol. That too brought it home. With little trouble he could hit Saturday's target with this revolver from the nearest scuttle.

Seaton opened the door as he heard Jenkyn's voice in the passageway.

'What is it, Alec?'

Jenkyn stopped dead and stared at him, his eyes glazed under the deckhead light.

'You'd better get up to the pier, Skipper. Chop, chop. There's been some trouble.' He swung round to follow as Seaton strode past. 'Mr. Niven's been in a spot of bother.'

Seaton barely heard him. This was how it came. With the speed of light, the deadly accuracy of a bullet.

Two or three Norwegians stood aside as they hurried past, and Jenkyn added, 'Number One's standin' fast on board.'

It was Trevor's voice which Seaton heard first when he was still some twenty feet from the little room with the stove.

'What do you mean, *you didn't think?* You bloody half-wit, don't you realise what you've done?'

Seaton threw open the door and stood just inside. Everyone had frozen at his entrance, like figures in an unfinished picture. Jens sitting at the table, his big fingers interlaced in front of him. Niven, pale, fists clenched at his sides, his mouth quivering with both anger and humiliation. Two other men stood by the far wall, while Trevor was facing Niven, hands out-thrust as if to seize and strangle him.

'That's enough!' Seaton stood very still, conscious of his own heartbeat. 'If you have anything to say to one of my company, then tell me first!'

Trevor looked at him and groaned. 'I give up. I really do!'

Jens said, 'We have a problem, David.'

He gestured to a patch of shadow, and Seaton realised for the first time that a man lay on the floor.

Trevor added bitterly, 'A bloody Kraut, that's *all* I needed!'

Seaton crossed to the side and looked down at the soldier. He was dressed in field-grey, long coat and muddy jackboots. He wore a gasmask container, a short bayonet, and his helmet stood upside down near his head like a chamber-pot.

He was tied up with codline, and had a gag which was so tight he was nearly choking. Above it, his eyes stood out white and bulging, and his forehead was dappled with sweat.

About my own age, Seaton thought.

Jens stood up and joined him, his towering shadow rising

across the wall like a black spectre.

Sadly he explained, 'He is one of the guards from the prison camp. The Russians were gone, but this man found he had left his torch behind. Rather than get into trouble for losing it, he came back.'

Seaton asked, 'Past your men?'

'They were taken by surprise. By then it was too late. In any case, they know this man, just as he knows most of us.'

Trevor exclaimed, 'But for Sub Lieutenant bloody Niven here, it would all have gone off all right. Might even have helped to lull suspicion later on. As it is . . .' He did not finish.

Seaton watched the German's eyes. They had fixed on him, and he guessed that the sight of a uniform, no matter how crumpled and alien, would do much to steady his nerves. He probably imagined up to now that he had stumbled on a Resistance meeting, or a black-market sale. Either would mean his death.

Seaton asked, 'What happens now?'

'Good question.' Trevor was in control of himself again, but only just. 'Give me time to think.'

One of the others murmured something and Trevor snapped back, 'I *know* that he's got to be killed, for God's sake. *How* is worrying me.'

Seaton looked away. *Killed.* It sounded quite different from killed in action, missing, failed to return, and all those other things they put in the reports. This was like slaughtering a pig.

He saw Niven watching him, his face creased with worry.

'Tell me about it.'

Niven spread his hands. 'I was walking. After the battery-charge. I must have forgotten.' He sounded dazed. 'Then I tripped and would have fallen off the pier.'

Trevor said, 'Pity you didn't!'

Seaton asked calmly. 'What came next?'

'The German was coming round the corner, and caught me, stopped me from going over. I thought—' He shook his head. 'I—I don't know *what* I thought!'

Jens murmured, 'Knut, one of my men, arrived at that moment.' He made a slicing motion with his hand. 'He took care of the German.'

Trevor left the table and said quietly, 'Look, David, it's not what you're thinking. We're not all killers, enjoying ourselves like kids every time a Jerry gets the chop.'

'Go on, I'm listening.' Seaton turned away from the two bulging eyes in the corner.

'This German, *our* German, is going to be missed sooner or later.' Trevor was ticking off the points on his fingers. 'If we kill him here and drop him in the fjord, the Germans are going to keep searching and will probably wreck this mission. If they find his corpse they'll take hostages, call in the Gestapo from Bergen, and begin making reprisals everywhere. And if we don't dump him in the water, they'll find him and do the same anyway.'

Jenkyn cleared his throat and asked thickly, 'Beg pardon, but can I say somethin'?' They all looked at him. 'Why don't we put 'im in the barge and *they* can take 'im somewhere.'

Jens answered, 'If the barge-master even *knows* we have a German soldier here he will lose his nerve. He has already risked enough.'

Trevor sighed. 'Nice try, Alec, but we'd still be left with the search parties after the barge had left.'

Seaton said slowly, 'I suppose we could take him with us when we leave?'

Trevor smiled at him. 'After your charges explode the Jerries will come down on this area like the fiends of hell. Any suspicion will put other lives in serious danger. Would *you* hesitate, David, if you saw a hundred Germans in your crosswires, let alone this one?'

'No. All the same . . .'

'There's too much at stake.' Trevor sounded impatient. 'I'll not risk any more because of *him*.'

The door opened a few inches and Jens strode over to speak with somebody.

He came back and said quietly. 'They have found this man's motor cycle. On the top road. It is why he was not heard in time.'

Seaton felt sick. There was no emotion. It was a discussion, but a man would die.

He said, 'Suppose the attack was brought forward to tomorrow? We are ready. The Germans would probably think this soldier had been lost in the explosion.'

Trevor grimaced. 'Good try, David.' He rubbed his eyes. 'But the cement barge is not permitted to leave here until Saturday, and the Germans never budge from their orders. Especially this time. After the barge passes through the defences the entrance will be sealed.' He waved one hand around the room. 'The pier will be abandoned. They have all the concrete they need now.' He tried to smile. 'And when the barge goes through the gate, your submarine will be with her. Now you know why it has to be Saturday!'

Jenkyn said anxiously, 'I'd better get back aboard, Skipper. Number One'll be wonderin' wot the 'ell is 'appenin'.' His South London accent was more pronounced than usual.

'Yes.' Their eyes met. 'Richard, go with him.'

At the door, Niven swung round and faced Trevor. 'What will you do with him?'

'What he would have done to you, but for Jens' man.' Trevor seemed to relent, and he added, 'Thank God he had a motor bike. We take it up the road and skid it into the side of the fjord. There are rocks about ninety feet down. They'll think he went over the top by accident.' He shrugged. 'I *hope*.'

The door closed and Jens asked, 'Drink, David?'

'Not just now.' He felt the others moving restlessly. Wanting to get it over.

Trevor said, 'We're not like the enemy. But it's them or us. It's not a bloody game.'

He nodded his head and they dragged the German to his feet and untied his legs. He was making gurgling sounds, and Seaton knew he was vomiting into his gag.

Seaton could see it as if it had already happened. As if he were there. First the motor cycle. Then a quick removal of codline and gag and the German soldier would follow. Out and down into the wind and darkness. If he found breath to give a last scream it would only add authenticity, should anyone hear.

The door was open and he watched the man being bustled outside. His eyes never left Seaton's face. Pleading.

Then Trevor said, 'Sorry about that. You've got enough to think about.'

Seaton eyed him calmly. 'So has young Niven. We'll be relying on him too on Saturday, just in case you'd forgotten it!' He went out, slamming the door behind him.

Down the ladder and along the black casing, and then through *XE 16's* after hatch. He sank down on a locker and looked at the others.

Drake asked, 'Okay, Dave?'

Seaton took several deep breaths. He had imagined that after the crisp air ashore, the relative freedom of movement, it would be hard to come back. Instead it was like a homecoming.

He answered quietly, 'I'm getting over it.' He looked at his friend's eyes. 'But I'll never get used to it.'

Jenkyn remarked, 'I wonder who the Jerry was?'

Niven turned on him wildly. 'For Christ's sake drop it, will you! I slipped up, but don't *you* ever make a bloody mistake?'

Jenkyn met his stare coldly. 'Just the *one*, sir.' He turned towards the forward watertight door. An' that was when I agreed to serve alongside you.'

Seaton said, 'Enough. Both of you. It takes time to adjust. We've not been used to having others around, or so many depending on us, for that matter.' He watched the tension draining out of them. 'The methods alter but the objective is the same, and is sitting on the other side of the fjord. Waiting for us to finish what we came to do.'

Drake said, 'Don't worry, Dave. It'll go like clockwork. The Old Firm.' He patted Niven's shoulder. 'Forget it. This isn't the Royal Yacht, y'know.'

Jenkyn showed his teeth. 'Wish it was.' He stood up. 'I'll wet the tea.'

Seaton leaned back and allowed his limbs to relax. The flareup had been quelled. This time.

For most of the following day *XE 16* lay submerged under the pier, while her company went through their routine. Once again the sturdy little boat presented no problems. The checks had to be doubly thorough, there was no second go. Occasionally they heard the vague rumbling of machinery from the big cement barge, as she too prepared to set out on her return passage. It was a reminder of finality. Of purpose.

Soon after dusk, and Jens' signal that all was clear, they surfaced between the piles in a manner born. The 'signal' consisted of a large spanner being lowered on a line to clank three times on the casing. It was in no instruction book, but it worked every time.

Seaton left his companions to complete the topping-off of the fuel, the loading of some fresh food and bread which Jens' wife had sent for them.

Even the little room seemed and felt different. For one thing, it was cold and the stove stood black and empty. Seaton guessed that the hiding-place in the roof had also been stripped, to leave no sign of his brief stay, and of others who had gone before.

The many thousands of unknown people. Who did what they could, even if it was only in kindness. Or like the cement barge skipper and his men. They would never believe just how important their part was to the whole. Men like Jens, and the women who waited for their return, or the dreaded kicks on the door.

Jens and Trevor were waiting for him.

Trevor spoke first. 'It's all quiet. A patrol came here this morning. They found the body and the motor bike. The soldier had told someone he was coming back for his torch.' He shrugged. 'So it all worked out very well.'

Jens said, 'The *feldwebel* with that patrol seemed more worried about getting the torch back than losing one of his men!' But he did not smile.

'Let's get it over with.' Trevor sounded unusually tense. 'Sit down, David. I wasn't going to tell you, but I've been outvoted, persuaded that it's not right you should be in the dark.'

Jens said, 'You'd find out anyway when you reached England. I would not wish you to think badly of us, or that we did not trust you.'

Trevor continued, 'Those steel deckhouses aboard the *Hansa*. I *do* know what they're for, as it happens.

Seaton watched him, conscious of the tension, the sudden feeling of dread which he could not explain.

'The Germans started it in Denmark. The R.A.F. were getting so successful with pin-point bombing of important objectives that they decided to take tougher precautions. They filled the top floors of all the priority targets with Danish prisoners, political, Resistance, suspects, anybody. After that, any success achieved by the R.A.F. would be tainted and devalued by the loss of so many loyal Danes. London agreed to step-up aid to the Resistance and leave the work to them instead.'

Seaton looked at him. 'The *Hansa* has prisoners aboard, too?'

Jens said, 'Yes. Many good men. I know some of them myself. This is why your attack must succeed, if only to prove we are not beaten, and will never give way to such barbarity!'

Seaton saw with surprise that there were tears in the man's eyes.

He asked, 'Couldn't we find a way of releasing them before the attack?'

Jens shook his head. 'It is not possible, my friend. The Germans would unleash such reprisals that the horror of the whole nation would prevent any further resistance against the Germans. We would lose our country forever. Also our pride.'

'Even if we succeeded,' Trevor was looking at the floor, 'where would the escaping prisoners go? Two hundred miles to the Swedish frontier? Bringing more terror to those very people who might try to help them.' He raised his eyes to Seaton's. 'They'd not wish that, not a man of them.'

'That is true, David.' Jens watched him sadly. 'We thought it right to let you know. Not just what you were doing, but why you were doing it. Prisoners are soon forgotten, no matter what they have suffered.' His eyes blazed suddenly. 'But martyrs are never out of our memory!'

It was so quiet inside the room that the silence seemed to press into the eardrums like a vice.

Seaton said, 'I must leave. The attack will begin at first light.' He barely recognised his own voice. Flat and impersonal. A stranger's.

Jens nodded. 'It is better. We all have a great deal to prepare tonight.'

He thrust out his hand. 'God protect you, my boy.' He put his arm around Seaton and hugged him. 'We will meet again some day.'

Trevor said simply, 'Good luck. I'm sorry it had to be like this.'

They shook hands and Seaton replied, 'Take care of *yourself,* while you're at it.'

They walked out into the gloom and Seaton stared at the double line of waiting, anonymous figures. Nobody spoke, but as they passed, here and there a hand would reach out and touch him. Seaton was glad when he had reached the ladder, but he was deeply moved.

As he was about to step down on to the slippery rungs the last figure in the line moved toward him. Without looking he knew it was the girl.

She said quietly, 'Goodbye, David.'

She did not flinch as he pulled the scarf down over her shoulders.

He thought of Trevor's words, that he had been 'persuaded' to reveal the presence of the prisoners in the ship. She and Jens must have done it. It was as clear as her eyes, which were all he could see as he murmured, 'I shall turn up again. You don't get rid of me that easily.'

She leaned forward and kissed him quickly. Her mouth was soft but ice-cold. As if they were both dead.

He watched her step away to join the others. Then he raised his hand to his cap. It was not how he felt, but how they would want to see him go.

Drake called, 'All set, Skipper?'

Seaton turned and lowered himself down the ladder.

'Piece of cake.'

Their eyes met and they grinned. There was no other way.

7

Start the Attack

SEATON LOOKED at his watch and tried to ignore the rumble of the barge's diesels alongside the pier. The disturbance would help to conceal *XE 16* if she broke surface when she began to move. It was virtually impossible for Drake to trim the boat properly while she was idling on the shelf which had been their haven for three days. It seemed much longer, and the realisation made the hull's vibrating motion all the more unnatural.

The main motor was humming smoothly, and he could tell from the way that Drake and Jenkyn were sitting that they were well aware of the importance of the next minutes.

The red second-hand of the control room clock passed the hour. Seven in the morning exactly.

There was a loud clang overhead and they all flinched, even though they had been expecting the signal from the pier.

'Two-five-oh revolutions. Periscope depth.' He glanced at Jenkyn's back. 'Wheel amidships.'

How loud the air sounded as it forced water from the tanks, and the vibration changed to a gentle pitch and roll as *XE 16's* keel detached itself from the man-made shelf.

Seaton watched the depth needle creeping round until it

touched nine feet. He pressed the button and stooped to peer through the sticklike periscope.

He had to be very careful or he might buckle it on a crossbeam, or fracture it enough to endanger the boat.

A huge, slime-covered pile edged across his sight and he breathed out slowly.

'Starboard a little, Alec.'

'Aye, Skipper.'

'*Steady.*'

Bump, bump, bump. The hull tested a line of smaller supports with her port flank and continued at less than a knot against swirling undertow.

It was almost pitch-dark in the lens, and Seaton had to concentrate on the picture in his mind and take immediate obstacles for granted.

The shelf which supported the heavier piles was one hundred feet long, and the cement barge which lay alongside the full length of the pier was two hundred feet. But she was lying well back, and below her ugly stem was a fifteen foot gap before the rest of the pier's supports merged into criss-cross of beams and frames which would snare the midget's hull like a web.

He saw the water reflected in the barge's side and knew exactly where he was. Below the derrick and the little room. Cold now, its stove black and empty.

He heard Drake say, 'Seems a good trim.' He was speaking to himself.

Seaton swung the periscope towards the bow. Paler still, not long to go. The deck lifted and swayed under him, and he heard something metallic rasping along the side. He wondered if Jens and some of the others were peering down at the surging water, trying to see him.

'Stand by!'

He bit his lip, almost ducking as a long, rusty chain swung across his vision like a bridge.

He pictured the fjord. Once outside the pier and the barge the bottom plunged downwards to a depth of eighty fathoms. A great axe-cleft in the coast. He imagined the boat lying in the pitch-black ravine. Soundless, motionless. Dead.

Sweat trickled down his neck and he blinked to clear his vision. There it was. More rust, some lines of rivets and then the edge of the barge's stem. It looked as if it and not the submarine was moving. A massive iron gate swinging back.

He said, 'Port fifteen. Increase to four hundred revs.'

He pressed the button and crouched down, remembering the way he had planned it. How it had looked from his little rooftop spyhole.

Seaton watched the gyro ticking remorselessly round.

'Steady.'

The hull rocked heavily, and for a few moments the depth gauge seemed to defy Drake's efforts to hold the boat down.

'Steady. Steer zero-two-zero.'

They were out, without even clipping the barge or pier. Seaton wiped his face with his glove.

When he glanced forward he saw Niven sitting on the heads, his hands gripped together. He looked like a diver on display in an open tank.

'Ready, Dave.' Drake looked at him.

'Dive . . . dive . . . dive. Thirty feet. Eight-five-oh revs.'

No matter what each man was thinking, the checks must be made. So they were ready to attack.

Seaton pictured the little hull creeping along through the dark water. Up diagonally from the pier, then a slow turn round towards the target.

'Trimmed for diving.' Drake sounded almost cheerful.

'Good.'

He scrambled to the chart and his pad of printed bearings and distances which he had plotted so carefully. Depth, current, time. His mind tackled each item and linked them into a pattern. He glanced at the clock. There should be some daylight by now on the side of the fjord which mattered.

'Alter course. Steer three-zero-zero degrees.'

He let Jenkyn get on with it. He made it look easy. Like driving an Austin Seven.

The deck tilted and levelled off in response to hydroplanes and rudder.

'Ship's 'ead three-zero-zero.'

It was so quiet that even the motor seemed subdued.

Seaton glanced at the basket-wheels and wondered why he never thought of the two massive charges as dangerous to his command. But if a depth-charge burst against the hull, or one of the side-cargoes exploded prematurely as it left the boat, it would be a quick and terrible death.

He said, 'Reduce to four hundred revs. Less and we'll lose steerage-way.' He waited for the hum to fade even more. 'Periscope depth, Geoff. Let's take a peep.'

If he thought anything in the next seconds it was about himself. How was he able to play this role? To pretend that everything was just like the other times. What would his three silent companions think if they knew about the hostages? *The sacrifice.*

He pressed the hoist button and tried to steady his nerves. As the lens broke surface he forgot the others and Trevor, even the German's eyes as they had pleaded with him for mercy.

It was exact. The big cargo liner lay diagonally across his cross wires, the bows slightly towards him. Despite the dull light and the undulating water he could see it all, even a big mooring buoy below the bows, a twin of the other which the Germans had painstakingly laid astern of her.

She looked close enough to touch. Seaton held the periscope for a few more seconds, checking what he already knew was a fact or conclusion.

The *Hansa* was five hundred and fifty feet long, and beneath her great keel the bottom of the fjord flattened off more comfortably than the opposite side. Which was why the place had been chosen by the survey team before they laid their mooring buoys. Both of *XE 16's* charges would lie there with equal comfort.

Seaton pressed the button. 'Set the fuses.' He looked at Drake. 'Start the attack.'

He brushed his lips with the back of his glove. It had become a habit when he was under stress, but he had not noticed it until today. It reminded him of the brief contact. Her lips against his, barely touching, and yet...

'Engines, Skipper!'

'Damn.'

Seaton pressed the button and dropped right down to control the periscope as it broke surface.

'It's the German tug. Bearing red four-five. Hauling some lighters.'

He watched the blurred outline thoughtfully. She was moving

slowly. Coming up from the boom gate just as Trevor had predicted. He was probably sitting on the hillside somewhere, watching through his binoculars. If he stayed there he would get his head blown from his shoulders.

Hansa carried enough explosives, rocket fuel and God knows what else to reduce the ship and anything nearby to small pieces.

The periscope hissed down again. 'Steady as you go. The tug will probably go alongside the *Hansa* while those lighters are unloaded.'

Drake nodded, his lips pursed in a silent whistle.

Seaton rubbed his chin. It was all too easy. The silent approach was making him jumpy. No anti-submarine devices or thrashing patrol boats, nothing.

He kept thinking about the girl. How her hair had felt when he had uncovered it. Fine and soft. Who was she? Where did she fit?

Niven was climbing back into the W & D and said, 'Both charges set and live, sir. Two hours from now.'

He sounded so clipped and formal, Seaton wondered if he was still worried about the German or Jenkyn's sudden outburst.

What on earth would make a man at the very start of a naval career get married and immediately volunteer for this sort of madness? His father was a very senior officer, and there had been a Niven at Trafalgar.

Seaton raised the periscope again and looked at the target. He swung it round still further and exclaimed, 'The tug's at *work,* for God's sake!'

Gouts of smoke puffed from abaft her superstructure, and a buoy seemed to pop up almost alongside one of the lighters. He saw men moving purposefully, then another buoy glinting astern of the slow-moving group.

He lowered the periscope and said quietly, 'They're laying a net.' He squinted to get a better picture in his mind. 'Not a kind I've seen before. Take her down to forty feet. We'll just have to chance it.'

Seaton listened to the air being forced out of the tanks, and thought of the scene he had just witnessed. A new sort of net, perhaps temporary, but no less dangerous. Very light, with a small mesh. *XE 16* would have to get out before the net held her between it and target. To explode in one great detonation.

When Seaton raised the stick again he dropped it just as swiftly and held his breath. Two figures had appeared on the forward mooring buoy, and seemed to be working on a ship-to-shore telephone wire. Like men walking on the water. One had been looking directly at him.

He dabbed his lips with his glove. The man would have seen nothing. It was crazy to start getting the jumps.

'We'll cross beneath her from the starboard bow to the port quarter.' He glanced at the clock. 'Steer two-nine-zero.'

It was lucky they were in the fjord. The water was murky from its winding travels down hills and rocks on its way to the sea. In the Med they would have been seen. Like fish in a barrel.

Seaton couldn't wait any more. The periscope crept out of its well. This time the ship was right above him, like a steel cliff. He could see the flaking dazzle-paint, a man in a chef's hat looking from one of the scuttles. High above that, the boat deck and two mounted machine-guns. And he had seen one of the steel deckhouses, too.

He snapped, 'Eighty feet. Stand by to release the starboard cargo.'

Drake juggled with his controls as the boat tilted towards the bows. He was ready to compensate for the sudden loss of weight, and for anything else.

Seaton watched him. He could *feel* the great ship rising above his head.

'Let go!'

The wheel squeaked once.

'Cargo away.'

They waited, trying not to think about it as it floated, leaflike, towards the bottom.

'Stand by, port.'

Seaton looked at the curved deckhead as an engine sound murmured faintly against the hull. One of the *Hansa's* power boats most likely.

Another glance at the second-hand, then, 'Let go!'

This time the deck did roll more steeply. As if glad to be free of its lethal cargo.

'Alter course to port, Alec. Steer two-six-zero. Five minutes and we'll come up to periscope depth again.' They exchanged quick glances and he added, 'Time to think about getting out of it.'

'Ship's 'ead two-six-zero.'

When *XE 16's* periscope probed above the surface again, Seaton thought for a moment the gyro compass had gone berserk. A quick look round told him otherwise. The *Hansa* lay as before, except that now she leaned away across the submarine's starboard quarter. And on the opposite quarter, pale against the landmass beyond, he could see the cement barge, her foredeck almost hidden in a great haze of diesel fumes.

He trained the periscope ahead once more. 'Two-five-oh revs.' It would make the boat difficult to handle in the strong undertow, but he dare not risk throwing up even a small feather of spray.

The crosswires found and settled on the tug. But it was her stern, and she was forging along and well to port of *XE 16's* track, the sailors on the lighters working as feverishly as before.

From bow to bow he saw one glittering buoy after another. It was no use brooding about it, or wondering how the Germans had found such a quick method. All that mattered now was that an unbroken net barrier lay right across their retreat.

He lowered the stick and said, 'They've cut us off with their bloody net.'

Drake stared at him. 'Can't we haul round ahead of the tug?'

Seaton shook his head. 'Too wide a detour. The cement barge is getting under way. By the time we doubled back, and that's if we *could* outpace the tug, the boom will be shut, with the cement barge on the other side of it.'

Drake murmured softly, 'Here's a fine thing.'

Seaton said. 'Thirty feet. Four hundred revs. Dead silent routine.'

If only it were dark, or pelting down with snow. Then he could surface, slip over the net between a pair of buoys and run deep again on the other side. But even in this murky light they would be sure to be sighted, and the patrol boats would be down on them like a ton of bricks. And the Germans would still have time to move the *Hansa*. The tug could tow her clear of her moorings whether the *Hansa* had steam up or not. It might damage the ex-liner, but she would be safe from the two charges.

He said quietly, 'We'll have to cut the net.'

Niven answered, 'Right, sir.'

'It'll be damned cold, Richard.' Drake turned from him to Seaton. *I'll* go, if you like. No problem.'

'No.' Niven was already adjusting his tight diving suit. 'It's what I'm here for.'

Seaton looked at the clock. 'Watch your step. We don't know if they've got any detection gear above the net.' He held Niven's gaze and added, 'It's vital we get clear. But take your time. No heroics.' He forced a smile. 'I'll not go without you.'

Drake said, 'Nearly there.' His eyes moved swiftly from the clock to his gauges. 'Here we go.'

The hull gave a slow shudder, and Seaton felt the periscope press his arm as the little submarine's snout probed against the net.

'Dead slow.'

He strained his ears, waiting for the warning grenade or something worse. He pressed the button. It was too dark to see much more than a grey blur. He tensed, seeing the net rising above him and stretching away on either hand, vague and indistinct, like a huge, eerie web.

Drake and Jenkyn would have their work cut out to hold the boat bows-on while the diver got on with his work.

He held a faint rustle of metal as the net dragged slightly on the stem.

Niven was already squatting on the heads, fixing his noseclip and testing the oxygen supply.

Seaton reached through the door and helped him to fasten the face-piece and clip it tight. It was a bad moment for any diver, let alone one like Niven. But there was no more time. He patted his shoulder and ducked into the control room and carefully secured the watertight door, sealing Niven inside. It was up to him now.

Shut off from his companions, Niven was surprised at his own sense of self-control. He went through the motions like a robot, his breathing regular and unhurried.

He saw Seaton watching him through the thick glass scuttle and nodded. Then he reached out and opened the valve which enabled him to flood the compartment and leave the boat. The response came instantly, and the water pounded across his feet in a miniature tide-race. It was coming in fast, and the pressure against his limbs and then his waist and chest mounted noticeably. He kicked his flippered feet up and down and plunged his hands into the frothing water. For the first time he realised just how cold it was, and felt something like anxiety. Suppose he could not hold on because of the cold, or he was unable to work the cutter?

Grinding his teeth together he allowed the water to surge over his head. All at once it was very quiet. The pump had stopped, and he could barely feel the faint tremor of the motor as it held the boat against the net. It was like the training establishment. One movement at a time. He methodically unclipped the hatch, and using great care, raised it slowly above his head.

He felt slightly dizzy, his body temperature changing as the current swirled around his head and shoulders. Gripping the rim of the hatch, he allowed his body to arch up and out of the boat.

The pressure of water around his thighs and arms, the first sense of sickness which usually came to a diver under such conditions, faded as he took stock of his position.

How small the boat was now that he was crouching on her casing. It seemed impossible that she contained living men. People he actually knew.

He adjusted his oxygen, his jaw tight with concentration. *Don't fumble. Keep your head.*

He groped forward, his fingers aching as he released the heavy cutter from its bed inside the casing. He stared at the net, at the misty, ash-coloured surface above. It looked as if he was working in a strange, unreal world, encased under a muslin sky.

Niven swore to himself as his knuckles scraped on steel and a thread of blood wound ahead of him through the net. He stood up, the cutter resting on the mesh, his free hand paddling back and down to maintain his position.

Seaton would be watching him through the stick, he thought. He liked Seaton, although they seemed to have nothing but the boat in common. He was the sort of person he would like to speak with, to open his heart and tell about Decia.

One of his fingers slipped from the mesh, and he lost valuable seconds regaining his position. It both angered and frightened him.

Keep your mind on the job. Nothing else matters.

95

The cutter jumped in his grip as he started on the first part of the mesh above the submarine's stem. The net was of very fine wire, but stronger for its size than any he had seen. He felt his heart banging against his ribs, and the cold dragging his legs down, probing into his groin like some obscene hand.

But he kept working, forming a large inverted V, which when completed would allow *XE 16* to push through.

It was agony, and he had to squeeze his mind almost physically to keep it from straying into panic. If the cold finished him before he had done his work, the boat might never get free. In any case, he would not have the strength to re-enter the hatch.

What would he do? He worked blindly, another pair of strands curling away like hooks. Would he have the courage to let himself drift into a frozen death, or might he be unable to resist the temptation to try for survival?

He had a terrible picture of himself being dragged from the water, beaten and kicked, as they took him to see the recovered body of the German who had saved him from falling. And then the torture...

Niven was being pushed harder against the net as his strength ebbed with the persistent cold.

Just a few more strands. His mind was reeling as he set the cutter against the wire. *Snap*. Pause. *Snap*. Through his pain he thought it reminded him of the sound of a cricket ball. Lazy summer days. All the pink-faced cadets at Dartmouth. Seeking praise for their efforts. Admiration from the other chaps' sisters. Congratulations from fathers.

He could see his own father. Grave and smiling. But the smile never really got beyond his mouth.

Niven looked up, screwing his face in agony. Christ Almighty. Just a bit more.

He stared at the dark shadow which had appeared by one of the buoys. Must be going mad. Yet he was sure it had not been there before.

It was changing shape even as he watched, and he felt despair adding its talons to the numbing water.

The shadow must be a small boat, and the sudden extension, which even now was moving smoothly along the wires, was a frogman.

The man faded in shadow, and sobbing silently Niven

attacked the last part of the V with the fervour of madness.

The net gave a quick jerk, and he watched with disbelief as *XE 16* began to slide forward, the door he had cut in the mesh bowing away from her stem in submission.

Almost choking, Niven slammed the cutter into its pocket in the hull and began to drag himself to the open hatch. Seaton could not move yet for fear of catching his diver's body in the jagged wires, but the current alone was pushing the hull steadily with a power of its own.

Niven had lost all sense of pain, and only his hands seemed to retain any sort of strength and purpose. He found the smooth rim of the hatch, and prepared himself for the last pirouette to take him round and into safety.

Something pale flashed past his face, and with sick horror he saw a man's hand reach down and fasten to his wrist like a steel band.

Sobbing and retching, Niven clung to the hatch, while the other man, vague but immensely powerful, tried to wrench him free.

It was a screaming nightmare, and Niven wanted to cry out, to drown, anything to get away from the frogman. The man's knee drove up between his legs, and then another blow from something metal brought blood across his eye-piece.

God, oh God! He was screaming inside himself. *Help me!*

Then his torn fingers reached down, remembering without his aid, and fastened around the diver's knife.

Terror, hatred, humiliation; all these and other emotions flooded through him. Only when he felt the blade jar against solid bone, and watched the frogman's blood foaming around him like dull smoke, did he realise what he had done. How many times he had stabbed him he did not know, and as the hatch started to close over his head he saw the man drifting away and down into darkness, one arm moving weakly in his trail of scarlet.

He heard the pump beginning to drag at the water, then a sharp pain in his forehead as he slipped and fell forward against the steel door.

Somebody was holding him, pulling at his suit and mask, and then just as quickly, there was darkness. Oblivion.

Seaton lowered his body across the tiny deck-space,

loosening the collar and clasp and pushing Niven's hair from his tightly shut eyes.

Drake said harshly, 'Christ, look at the blood!'

Seaton felt the hull moving forward to the increased revs. It had been close. *Bloody close.*

He said tightly, 'Not all his, thank God.'

He remembered hearing the net sagging against the stem, knowing Niven had done it, probably in exchange for his own life. Then the urgent scratching and kicking on the casing as Niven had met and fought with an enemy frogman. Hearing had been worse than watching.

Seaton ripped open the suit and ran his hands over Niven's body. It was like ice, and almost blue from the water. But the heartbeats were strong enough, and the cuts and bruises were not adding much blood to the deck.

Seaton pulled some blankets across his limp body and returned to the periscope. It was not easy to leave him there, frozen and bleeding. But he had heard the thump of the cement barge's engines. There was more than one life at stake.

'Periscope depth.'

Seaton waited, listening, preparing himself. The air around him was thick with the smell of the sea, as if Niven had come from the depths and nowhere else.

He trained the crosswires on the barge. God, she was making a pall of smoke. For their benefit. He gripped the handles tightly to steady himself as shock and emotion gnawed at his reserves.

God, it had been a near one that time.

He said, 'Let her fall off to port, Alec. Steer two-five-zero.'

He was already swinging the periscope hard round, his foot dragging across Niven's outflung arm, as he brought the lens to bear astern. He saw the line of buoys bobbing slowly into the distance, the tug and her net-laying lighters already lost in the murk of the fjord. It was hard to accept there was a net there. That they had come through it. He peered briefly towards the *Hansa*. As before, motionless, remote.

Seaton pressed the button. 'Increase to eight-five-oh revs. That barge is faster than I thought.'

The deck vibrated to the barge's engines, and then Seaton raised the periscope once again.

He had to fix the picture, form his conclusions, translate them in mere seconds.

And it was all there. The stab of a signal light from the boom-vessel, renewed frothing from the cement barge's twin screws, the newly laid buoys rising above the choppy water like a line of beach balls.

Down periscope. Check the course against the barge's last bearing.

His voice said, 'Alter course, Alec. Two five-five. Take her down to forty feet.'

He looked at the clock, feeling the hull sway and level off to the new depth. One minute. Five minutes. Ten minutes.

Niven groaned once and felt down vaguely to his groin. Then his hand fell palm upwards on the corticine deck, like a dead fish.

Seaton stared at it, his mind focused into a narrow shaft. Fifteen minutes. Even allowing for the set of the current they were making less than seven knots.

Just thinking it was like a criticism shouted out loud. He touched the periscope as if in apology.

The barge's engines were fading now into a dull, sullen murmur.

Seaton glanced at the clock. Then he had to swallow twice to clear his throat as he said. *We're through.'* He scrambled over Niven and opened the first aid locker as he added, 'We'll go down to ninety feet as soon as we clear the fjord. Thank God we're not going back the way we came in.'

Drake said, 'Bloody good show, Dave. You did it again.'

Seaton looked at him. Wanting to tell him about the hostages. To share it.

Niven opened his eyes and muttered in a small voice, 'Are we? Am I?'

'Thanks to you.' Seaton wound a bandage round his head. It was a bad cut, and another where the frogman had hit him with something sharp. 'We're on the homeward run. Now all we have to do is find the right rendezvous.'

Niven's head fell back and he whispered, 'I didn't want to kill him. I thought it would be different.' He drifted into unconsciousness again.

Jenkyn said, "E's met more Jerries in the last two days than

I've *ever* bloody seen!' He added with something close to admiration, 'Not bad though. For somebody like 'im!'

Drake grinned. 'From you, Alec, that's better than a V.C.!'

The hands of the control room clock dragged round. A full hour had passed since the charges had been laid beneath the *Hansa's* keel.

Seaton thought about it, remembering how she had looked, what Jens and the others had said.

Even if the Germans found their dead frogman, and that was unlikely in the fjord's deep ravine, it would be too late for them to discover what had happened. Nothing had followed the *Hansa* into the anchorage, and by the time they discovered the hole in the net and realised it had been made by an outward bound X-craft, the charges would have exploded.

'Penny for them, Dave?' Drake was watching him from the control panel, his fresh growth of stubble making his chin shine like gold.

'I was thinking about those people back there. The sheer guts of what they're doing every day of their lives.'

Drake watched him as if fascinated. 'Thinking of one in particular, no doubt.'

Her voice seemed to penetrate the dripping hull. *Goodbye, David.* He wedged a kapok cushion under Niven's head. 'Yes, I suppose I was.'

Two more slight alterations of course, and *XE 16* dived deeper to retain her secrets. With luck they would rendezvous with their towing submarine around midnight. Due to Venables' preplanning and the Resistance in Norway, they had enough extra fuel to carry them to the next cross on the chart, even if they missed her.

Later on, while Drake was adjusting the trim to the new depth, and Seaton was making sandwiches with the freshly baked bread which Jens had sent aboard, they heard a sound.

Drake grappled with his controls and asked hoarsely, 'What's *that?*'

The sound rolled lazily around the hull, caressing it, raising and lowering it slightly before receding into the outer depths just as easily.

Their eyes met. All those miles astern, and yet they had felt it. From inside the fjord and around the headland, out and further still through the depths, until at ninety feet it had found *XE 16*.

Seaton looked at the clock. 'Both charges.'

Jenkyn whispered, 'Jesus.'

It was done.

Seaton dropped on to the locker and massaged his eyes. Somewhere, far away in his bunker, Venables would soon be on the telephone.

Mission completed. Target destroyed.

Must pull himself together. There was a long way to go yet.

He moved over to Niven and started to strip him, to pummel him with the last dry towel before dressing him in his sweaters and waterproof suit.

Next, Seaton took the helm, and Jenkyn made some hot cocoa.

Then, munching their sandwiches and sipping their custard-thick cocoa, they settled down for the passage home.

8

The Unexpected

Captain Clifford Trenoweth stood with his hands clasped behind his back and stared fixedly through a window. Not that he could see much, for what with the room's steamy heat and the slashing rain against the glass he could barely make out the track which led towards the loch.

A telephone jangled in the outer office, and seconds later Second Officer Dennison burst into the room without knocking. Trenoweth noticed she was wearing her large, round glasses, something she always tried to hide from him. So it must be urgent.

She exclaimed, 'Oh, sir!' Her eyes shone with excitement. 'That was a signal from Flag Officer Submarines.' Tears ran unheeded from under her glasses. 'They're *back* sir!' She seemed to realise what she was doing and pulled off her glasses, adding, 'I—I'm sorry, sir, I thought—'

Trenoweth limped round the desk and took her arm. 'Sit down.' He silenced her protest. '*Sit.*'

She watched him as he opened a cupboard and took down some glasses and a bottle of whisky.

He said, 'I've been saving this.'

'I don't usually drink, sir.'

'You do now.' He placed the glass firmly in her hand. 'Tell me about it.'

She said, 'They reached the Shetlands two days ago. The passage crew have taken charge of *XE 16* and she will arrive here next week.'

Trenoweth breathed out hard. 'I *wish* I'd known. I would have gone there to meet 'em.' He grinned. 'Though God knows how I'd have managed that!' He raised his glass. 'To them.' He clinked it against hers. 'And to you, Helen, for putting up with me. It can't have been easy.'

She blushed and swallowed some whisky. Between coughs she said, 'Once or twice you were a *little* difficult, sir.'

He beamed. 'Never!' And poured another glass for himself, remembering the morning when *XE 16* had left the loch for Scapa and the Shetlands. After that, apart from the routine signals, silence. If Venables knew anything, he had kept it to himself in London.

She said, 'Sub Lieutenant Niven was injured, although they didn't say how. He's being sent straight to Rosyth for treatment. Full report is following. The others are arriving here today.' She looked at her wrist-watch. 'At any minute. They must have laid on top-level transport for them. It usually takes longer to get from the Shetlands than it does to reach Cairo!' She dabbed her eyes. 'I'm so glad for them.' She looked up, her lipstick smudged. 'And for you too, sir!'

Trenoweth allowed the whisky to run through him like fire. Seaton and the others had done it. There had been times when he had found himself doubting, hating himself for not voting against Venables' plan. It was all such a different sort of conflict. He recalled his other war very clearly. The narrow-hulled submarines coming back from patrol, flags flying, and probably a band to play them in. Even in this war there was much the same attitude with conventional submarines. But all this cloak-and-dagger stuff. Secret agents and underhand methods were not right for his young crews.

He said, 'I shall go down to the pier. They'll be coming over from the mainland in the tender.' He looked at the dog, snoozing by the fire. 'I'll bet they're ready for some leave.'

'I'll phone for your driver, sir.' She was in charge again.

Trenoweth watched her admiringly as she brushed wisps of hair from her face. He had seen her lose her usual self-control, and *he* had been so confused he had called her Helen.

He prodded the dog with his stick. 'Get up, Duffy, you lazy old sod! We've work to do.'

Second Officer Dennison watched the mud-spattered Humber rocking past the window, Captain Trenoweth very straightbacked in the rear seat, and wearing his best oak-leaved cap. The old dog would be sprawled beside the marine driver as usual.

She raised her hand to the car and then sat down weakly. Things would never be quite the same after today.

'I thought I'd invite myself into *your* wardroom.' Trenoweth chuckled at the age-worn joke as he limped heavily from the car. It had been worth the bumpy ride. Just to see them getting off the tender, watching their first reactions. 'Splendid to have you back, and that's no flannel!'

Seaton walked into H.M.S. *Syren's* long panelled wardroom and searched his feelings. In truth he had not expected to see it again. Not when he had watched the net-layer through his periscope, knowing he must still go on with the attack, trapped or not.

It was strangely quiet in the granite building. He had already heard that Vanneck and Gervaise Allenby had gone with their own boats to Scapa to await news of the attack. Seaton had not seen them on his swift return from the Shetlands. In fact, he felt as if his feet had barely touched the ground.

They had met with their towing submarine exactly as planned, and from then he had only blurred recollections. A passage crew had been ferried over to complete *XE 16's* homeward run, while he and the others had manhandled Niven into the rubber dinghy to be pulled aboard the towing submarine.

Then, after handshakes and hot drinks from the submarine's company, most of whom looked in worse shape than they did, it had been a matter of collapsing into bunks.

One thing stood out in Seaton's mind, however. Apart from Niven, who had still been suffering from his underwater ordeal, there had been a real reluctance to leave *XE 16* in the hands of a passage crew. In the past it had been quite different, or so he thought. Not this time. He had looked astern at the glinting shape rolling to the tow-line and had wanted to say something. To mark the moment, and what they had done together.

He took a glass from the steward and tried to relax. It had been good of Trenoweth to come down and greet them. Typical, too.

Drake said, 'Cheers!'

Jenkyn, surprisingly ill-at-ease in his officers' quarters, gulped down his drink and said, 'Not 'alf!'

Trenoweth was saying, 'It's all laid on. Two weeks leave, although I'd have expected more.' He looked worried. 'Unless of course the Admiralty is brewing something else.'

Seaton glanced at himself in the wall mirror. Apart from fresh underwear, he was dressed in the same clothing as before, and looked more like a survivor than a victor. He thought of the other two midgets waiting in Scapa Flow. If he had failed, they would have been sent in. Without a chance in hell.

Two weeks leave. He must be dog-tired. The words had only just penetrated. What would he do?

Drake said, 'Poor old Richard. I hope they don't keep him in dock for long.' He looked at Trenoweth. 'Got quite a knocking-about. Did well, I thought.'

Jenkyn nodded. 'Yeh.'

The captain eyed Drake thoughtfully. 'I understand you were going to spend your next leave with him and his wife?'

Seaton watched them both. For a moment he had imagined Trenoweth was going to add, 'if you got back.'

Drake looked uncomfortable. 'Well, yes, sir. But under the circumstances . . .'

'I think it's a good idea.' Trenoweth rubbed his hands. 'I'm only sorry you can't talk about what you've done. Can't even give you a decoration while all this security stuff is going on.'

Seaton yawned. 'Sorry, sir. I'm feeling it now. The floor just came up and hit me.'

'Yes. Yes, of course.' Trenoweth nodded. 'I won't keep you any longer.' He shook hands with Jenkyn. 'Well done.'

The E.R.S. grinned. 'Thank you, sir.' He looked at the others. 'I'm going over to me mess. Then kip. For about a year.'

Trenoweth beamed. 'Mustn't forget your leave!'

Jenkyn turned away. 'I 'adn't, sir, believe me, I 'adn't!'

Trenoweth said, 'I just want a quiet word with you, David.' He glanced meaningly at Drake.

The New Zealander seemed pleased to go. 'Sure thing, sir.' He shook hands. 'See you when I surface. Better put down for a shake or I'll probably wake up when the war's over.' He winked. 'So long, Dave.'

He went out, and Seaton heard him whistling *South of the Border*.

'Sir?'

Trenoweth eased his remaining leg and perched on the edge of his chair.

'I think they've got a bit of a bloody nerve. That's my personal feeling anyway.'

They were obviously somebody high up.

Trenoweth continued, 'They want you to report to the Admiralty when you get to London.' He waited, watching Seaton's pale face.

'I was de-briefed at Scapa, sir. I can't add much to the report.'

He got a mental picture of the silent steel deckhouses. How many had died there? Had they known what was happening?

'Yes, yes, I know, my boy. I'd have thought it could have waited for two weeks. Until you were bright-eyed and bushy-tailed again, eh?'

Seaton said wearily, 'It's all right, sir. Better get it over with.'

He thought of his father. He would have to see him. It was only fair. He thought too of Drake. His face as he had spoken about his leave. If he was after Niven's wife, something would have to be done. One more raid like this last one and they'd be at each other's throats if that happened.

'I suppose so.' Trenoweth poured some more whisky. 'Venables wants to see you. And some of the Intelligence brains.' He added angrily, 'God, I wish I was going with you. I'd tell them a thing or two. Damned desk-warriors.' He grinned. 'I suppose I'm one of those as well!'

'Hardly, sir.' Seaton tried again. 'I'd like to talk about the attack with you, when I've had time to think.'

'Of course.' Trenoweth's voice was getting slurred. 'Be happy to. You know that.' He stood up carefully and leaned on his stick. 'But memories fade, given time. In war, they must.' He walked to the door. 'Ask the doc to give you something if you can't sleep. Tell him from me, I'll kick his arse for him if he starts moaning about it!'

The door closed and Seaton leaned back in the chair. It was the same one he had used when he had come back that other time. Eating the steward's scones.

Two weeks leave. He would break his journey to London. Go to Rosyth first and see Richard. His mind was getting confused. Or instead he could...a glass rolled across the floor, and he realised he had let it drop. He stood up, suddenly desperate, angry too at having to see Venables. Anybody.

'Damn and bloody hell!' His voice came back at him from the dark panels.

He walked unsteadily through the door, knowing a steward was watching him anxiously, and made for his room.

They were back. He must think of nothing else. Nothing more must concern him.

Working late in her office, Second Officer Dennison looked up as Trenoweth returned from the wardroom.

'All right, sir?'

'Not sure.' He leaned on her desk and added, 'He doesn't say much, but he's taking it badly.'

'I don't know how they put up with it.' She tapped her teeth with a pencil. 'Cooped up in that little hull. Wet, cold, and probable scared half to death.'

He nodded. 'They do it for nice young women like you, and for silly old buggers like me.' A smile spread across his face. 'But at the moment I'm feeling not-so-old. Come out with me and celebrate, eh?' He hesitated, unsure of himself. 'Please?'

She was already putting on her tricorn hat. 'I thought you'd never ask.' She was laughing. 'Sir!'

'Sorry to have kept you waiting.' Captain Walter Venables strode around the desk and held out his hand. 'Busy days.' He gestured to a chair. 'I'll try not to keep you too long.'

Seaton sat down and glanced around the big room. It was much as he had imagined. Spartan, severe, with any sign of luxury removed for the duration. He looked at Venables. Like the man. All the superfluous trimmings honed away.

The room was part of a complex, deep under a London

street. He had gone through several security checks to reach it, seeing busy typists from open doors, hearing the rattle of tele-printers, the vague stammer of morse.

'I've studied most of the reports.' Venables took out his silver case and withdrew it immediately. 'I forgot. You don't.' He lit a cigarette for himself and continued, 'Your attack was a complete success, of course.'

Seaton waited. *Of course.*

'The *Hansa* was blown to pieces, and much of the surrounding area damaged.' He flicked open a loose-leaf folder. 'Several patrol launches were also sunk. Everyone is impressed.'

'What about the enemy, sir?'

'Usual follow-up. Arrests and searches for arms and suspects but the local Resistance took good care to prepare for most eventualities. And we made certain the Germans knew it was an underwater attack, *after* you were well clear, naturally.' He closed the folder. 'The Germans have no excuse for mass recrim-inations against the Norwegians. That was how it was planned. No loose ends.'

Seaton watched him. Venables was genuinely satisfied. With himself. Because of the raid, or maybe because he had been proved right.

The captain added, 'By getting you into position before the target arrived, we cut the risk of discovery. By building up your chances of success, the risk of severe reprisals by the Germans was also halved.' He gave a small shrug. 'Some, naturally, will die. But as patriots they will be remembered. Not as the Germans would have wished, as mindless terrorists who brought death and destruction amongst their own people for a lost cause.'

'I *think* I understand, sir.'

Surprisingly, Venables smiled. It made him appear ten years younger.

'I'm glad to know that.' The mood changed just as swiftly. 'Two years ago, our Intelligence people, working with the Czech Free Forces here in London, planned a daring assassination inside Czechoslovakia. They were parachuted down to work with the local Resistance. The rest is history. They succeeded in killing Reinhard Heydrich, Hitler's right-hand man, and 'protector' of Czechoslovakia. But there was no thinking-through, no plans for the aftermath. The result? The Germans wiped out a complete village, Lidice, every man, woman and child. Then they ploughed up each street, razed the place to the ground so that not one brick was left standing.'

Seaton had heard about it before, but it was suddenly much more stark and horrifying. He thought of the steel deckhouses. The German soldier's eyes as he had been dragged out to die.

Venables said, 'It was appalling. Maybe Heydrich, the Butcher as he was rightly called, was a possible rival for eventual leadership in Germany. But dead, he became a lever for the occupying power to smash home its lesson of terror, once and for all.'

Seaton thought of the town above his head. Streets black with rain, shabby people, half-empty shops, and burned ruins where buildings had once stood. A city fighting for its life and, thank God, still free.

Venables looked at his watch. 'We must get on. I just wanted to speak with you first. I know how you felt. What it probably cost when you realised what had to be done. But war does not change in some things. It makes us soil our hands occasionally.'

Seaton stood up, feeling strangely uncomfortable in a clean shirt and his best uniform. It usually hung in a cupboard in the chilly room above Loch Striven.

'I have no intention of involving our people in reckless and profitless schemes.' Venables picked up his cap. 'We need friends in Europe and Scandinavia, not a vast army of terrified souls who are too frightened of brutal reprisals to help us.'

He led the way to the door. 'This will not take long. They are both busy men.'

Seaton almost smiled. For a moment he had imagined Venables had been considering his feelings.

He thought of his father's booming voice on the telephone. 'Home *again*, David? You have a fine time, you Navy lads!'

The room he was shown into was smaller than Venables', and slightly less grim. A desk, some map tables and steel cabinets were softened by a carpet and comfortable leather chairs. It was very quiet, its security made more apparent by a massive steel girder across the ceiling.

The two 'busy men' were standing, facing the door, as if

answering a cue. One wore the uniform of an air marshal, the other was dressed in a dove-grey suit. Apart from their ages, they had nothing in common.

Venables said, 'Air Marshal Noel Ruthven, newly appointed as head of Combined Special Operations.'

It was a firm, wiry handshake. Like the man, neat and confident.

Seaton got the impression Venables did not much care for him. The way he had laid a slight stress on the word 'Combined.' No service ever seemed to get used to another's involvement.

He looked at the other man. Thick build, with a broad, outdoor face which had once been handsome. But he had the mark of a heavy drinker. A man who enjoyed life in the fullest sense.

There was something vaguely familiar about him, and yet Seaton was certain they had not met.

'This is Rear Admiral Philip Niven. Naval Intelligence, of course.'

Seaton shook his hand. Niven, he should have known. He pictured the face he had seen at Rosyth. Tense and pale, but still one of youth. It was hard to find a young face in that of his father.

'*Proud* of you, my boy.' The admiral's voice was deep and rich. 'Damn good show all round, I thought. I'm sorry I've been too tied up to see my son, but—' He sighed and left the reasons unsaid.

Ruthven said crisply. 'But we have not brought you from a well-earned leave to bandy praise about, Seaton. Fact is, we're in a cleft stick. There may be an operation where you can be of use. Your success, your general behaviour and ability to make and change decisions, single you out as an obvious choice. Point is, could you do it again, so soon?'

Rear Admiral Niven sat down at the desk and said bluntly, ''Course he can. He's young. A lion, like we all were at his age.' He grinned. 'In the Navy at any rate.'

Ruthven did not rise to it. 'It is not a question of stamina.' He placed a paper-weight in the form of a First World War fighter plane on the edge of a table. 'We have no target this time. No set objective where we can say, go there and do *a, b* or *c*. Your submarine may become a means to something else.' He smiled, and it was genuine. 'I *am* sorry. You must be getting fed up with all this mystery.'

'Lieutenant Seaton accepts the necessity.' Venables spoke severely. Like a house-master protecting a promising pupil.

'Good.' Ruthven eyed him calmly. 'Really, Walter, you must not take everything I say as a criticism.'

Seaton said, 'My command is as good as the boat, sir. Apart from my diver, we have worked together for some time.'

The admiral said heavily, 'We know your record, and as for young Richard, he'll buck up his ideas all right.'

Ruthven said sharply, 'Your son had to *kill* a man, Philip. Not through a bomb-sight or range-finder, but with his bare hands and a knife. You make him sound as if he's malingering after the measles!'

'What I *meant,* sir,'—Seaton was suddenly tired. Drained— 'was that if I am told what to do, I will answer you then. But I was going to recommend my Number One for a command of his own. He's earned it ten times over.'

'Out of the question, just yet anyway.' Venables sounded relieved. As if he had been expecting an outburst of some kind. 'We need teamwork. Of the highest order.'

Ruthven rubbed his hands together. 'I'm satisfied. Your destruction of the *Hansa* will have made a tremendous blow to the enemy's production of a new weapon. I do not imagine for an instant that one success will seal the enemy's fate, and I hope nobody here would feel anything but caution. As our prospects for invasion in Europe grow more apparent, so Germany's determination to smash those chances will become more pressing, with less regard for safety. Weapons will be built, rockets and guided-bombs far better than those they used against our landings in Italy just five months ago. Bigger and more powerful, with no thought for those who might get killed in their manufacture and operation.'

The little speech seemed to embarrass him, and he said, 'Be off now, Seaton. Just wanted to *see* you, not build your image from two dozen reports and certificates.'

It was over, and they all stood up again.

Seaton asked suddenly, 'Did the Germans kill any of the Resistance who helped me, sir?' He could not stop himself, nor did he want to. 'I realise I'm not supposed to know. But I've had time to think about them. Of what they risked for me.' He looked at the massive concrete walls. 'For all of us.'

Ruthven regarded him curiously. 'Actually, it is difficult to collate all the reports. Many sources are lying low. Others are changing their locations, for obvious reasons.' His voice softened. 'One we do know, however, was the leader of the local group.'

Seaton stared at him but saw nothing. 'Jens.'

He nodded. 'Jens. The Gestapo were taking his wife away for questioning. Jens shot two of them before he and his wife were killed.'

Seaton murmured, 'I see. Thank you, sir. He was a good man.' He felt his eyes smarting again. 'His wife sent us food the day we—'

Venables said, 'You're tired. Better cut along now.'

Ruthven walked over to Seaton and shook his hand. 'Try and *enjoy* your leave. Don't be ashamed of showing your feelings. It's *men* I need, not machines.'

In the corridor outside it was cool and vaguely damp.

Venables looked at his watch. 'Leave your address with the duty officer. Just in case.' Then he was off, vanishing through yet another door of his complicated world.

Seaton slung his gas-mask over one shoulder and tugged his cap level across his eyes. He was glad to be getting out of the place.

A petty officer at a little desk looked up as he passed. 'Air-raid warning just sounded, sir.' He grinned. 'All go, isn't it?'

Seaton found he was smiling back at the man.

Perhaps they were all going completely mad, without knowing it?

Geoffrey Drake stood with his hands outstretched towards a roaring log fire and listened to the rain pummelling the windows. He looked at the massive stone fireplace with its ornate, carved scrollwork. It could have been Tudor, but Niven had told him it had actually been built for another wool tycoon just before the Great War.

Drake did not really want to think about Niven. Not just yet anyway. He needed all his wits to cope with the situation.

He had only been in Harrogate for a few hours, and yet he felt completely at home, all anxieties over what he had endured in *XE 16* banished from his mind.

A door opened, and he turned to see Decia watching him. She was wearing pale jodphurs and a green jersey, and her face was flushed with the cold.

'That's better.' She smiled at him. 'You look almost human.'

She had suggested he should change into slacks and sweater as soon as he had arrived. It had sounded like a command.

'Now.' She sat down on a long sofa and crossed her legs. 'Tell me about Dick.'

Drake moved away from the fire, off balance at her tone. There was no concern, and not much interest. Just something which had to be said. Got over with.

He shrugged. 'He was under water for a long time.'

She smiled, her eyes very direct. 'But he *is* a diver, surely?'

Drake felt cornered. 'It was pretty dicey. I thought he'd had it.'

'Bad as that?' Her eyes widened. 'Daddy said it was just shock and a few scratches.'

Drake replied bluntly, 'Your father doesn't go much on Richard, does he?'

'You are observant.' She wriggled her body, curling up like a cat. 'I like that.' She pouted. 'But you're probably right. I think that's why I got married so soon. I like to have my own way.'

He grinned. 'You do surprise me.'

Decia tossed her head. 'Well, I'm fed up with this war. I'm so bored. Everyone else seems to be having such a splendid time. Even Daddy is getting involved with the Ministry of something-or-other over wool production.' She laughed. 'He's after a knighthood, if you ask me!'

Drake stood looking down at her. 'You're not that hard, surely?'

She lay back, her lips slightly parted. 'Don't you be beastly, too. I couldn't stand it. What with one thing and another, and then Moonshine pushing me against a rail in the stables, I'm really not at my best.'

She looked like a wanton child. Drake felt clumsy, lost for words.

'Horses don't like this sort of weather,' he said.

'I'm not joking, you know!' She tugged urgently at her sweater and pulled it above the waistband of her jodphurs. 'See for yourself, you horrible New Zealander!'

Drake sat beside her and looked. There was a dull red mark on her skin with a tiny red scratch in the middle.

He said, 'You've got a splinter.'

He was trying to sound unruffled. Matter of fact. But the sight of her smooth skin, the way she was watching him, teasing him, made his blood pound like a pressure pump.

He bent over and touched the bruise, feeling her stomach muscles tighten, her knees coming together as if expecting a blow.

'God, you're lovely, Decia.' The words came out calmly, in spite of his reeling senses. 'Don't you know what you do to a bloke?'

She said, 'Take the splinter away, will you?' She winced as he pinched the skin together. 'Lucky you're not a vet. Any horse would kick you where it hurts, you sadist!'

He plucked the splinter out and threw it towards the fire.

'You deserve a reward.' She thrust her arms around his neck. 'Just this once.'

Drake felt the power in her, pulling him down. He expected her to push him off at the last moment, torture him with a laugh or a mocking reprimand.

If she wanted to play, so then would he.

But it was no game. As their mouths touched she pressed her face against his, her mouth opening wide, comsuming his breath, and rousing his desperate want of her. He felt her lips, then her tongue darting into his teeth, while her body moved beneath him, inflaming still further, if that were possible.

Drake felt his hand groping under her sweater, as if it belonged to someone else. Up and across the smooth skin until he was cupping her breast, pressing it under his fingers until she moaned with pain.

He pulled back, breathing hard. 'God, I'm sorry. I don't know what the hell came over me.'

She watched him, her eyes wide, her mouth glistening in the firelight.

'You're not, and you do!' Her arms dragged at him again. 'I *want* you. Here, by the fire!'

Drake said huskily, 'What about Richard?'

She slipped her hands down around his waist and touched him.

'You want *me* too!'

It was then Drake knew he was lost.

The police sergeant rested both hands on the polished counter and regarded the petty officer gravely. There was so much to do, what with shortages and partly-trained War Reserve constables and Specials to chase and watch over. But he was a kindly man, and had never got hardened by the demands of war.

Jenkyn looked at him dazedly. 'Night before last, then?'

The sergeant nodded. 'Jerry dropped a stick of bombs right across the main railway line. All the way from Nine Elms yard.' He lowered his eyes. 'To your street.'

Jenkyn thought of the shock, the stunning disbelief, when he had passed the shabby but so familiar corner shop. In the centre of the terraced street was one great gap. As if it had been gnawed out.

The sergeant added, 'Old Mrs Templer was looking in to see your ma. Bloody miracle she wasn't killed, too. Direct hit.' He shook his head. 'I dunno. Can't grasp any of it nowadays.'

Jenkyn put down his little case and stared around the police station. Notices about air-raid precautions. About ration books and hostels. A different existence from his own. A message would have gone up north to Loch Striven. *We regret to inform you . . .*

'Mrs Templer, did you say?'

He caught another picture. A grey, owl-like old girl, whose husband had worked on the buses.

'Yes. She used to drop in. Make tea. Try and cheer your ma up. She never got over losing your dad and brother, did she?'

Jenkyn shook his head. Seeing the table laid for tea. Glad she was not alone when hell had burst into her empty life.

'I was away. At sea.' Why had he said that?

The sergeant smiled. 'It's not only the armed forces who have to take it, y'know.' He added suddenly. 'Old Mrs Templer mentioned something strange when I visited her in hospital.'

'*Strange?*' Jenkyn tensed. Ice-cold. Knowing somehow what was coming.

'Yes. She said your ma was re-setting the table, like she always did. Not saying much. Then, all at once she looked up and said something like, 'They're back! They're coming home at last!' Then she ran to the front door. Just as the bomb hit the house. She wouldn't have felt a thing.'

Jenkyn picked up his bag. *She must have known.* Sensed the exact moment.

He said, 'I'd better go and find somewhere to kip.'

The sergeant said, 'I can fix you up, if you like.'

'No.' He forced a smile. 'I'll book into the Union Jack Club until I've settled things.'

The sergeant saw one of his men fidgeting with his notebook. A motoring offence, a death to be notified, someone caught out on the black market. It never stopped.

He said, 'Sorry it had to come from me. Another day and your commanding officer would have had the job of telling you.'

Jenkyn shook his head. 'Better from you, mate. I've known you a long time.'

The constable watched the petty officer, small but smart in best blue, and gold-wire badges, leave the office.

'Ma Jenkyn's son?'

'Yes.' The sergeant did not want to talk about it.

'How did he take it, Sarge?'

He thought about it. That was odd. Jenkyn had been shocked, but in some way relieved, too. Especially when he had told him about old Mrs Templer.

He snapped, 'How the bloody hell d'you expect? Now give me the notebook and shut up!'

Outside it was already dark, and the rain was getting heavier. Jenkyn followed his feet around the corner and into the street again. He stopped opposite the gap where the house had been. Where he had been born.

It was roped off, the shattered brickwork swept back to the edge of the crater.

The realisation struck Alec Jenkyn like a clenched fist. *There was nowhere to come home to any more.*

Brokenly he exclaimed aloud, 'God, I'll miss you, Ma.' Then

with the rain hitting his shoulders he turned and headed for the railway station.

'The fact *is,* David, things are a bit awkward, if you get my meaning?'

Seaton leaned against the dark-wood bar of the Snug and watched his father wearily. The pub was not very busy. The customers were probably waiting to see if it would be a raid-free night before they decided to come or stay home in their shelters or under the stairs.

His father seemed to have grown older. It was ridiculous in so short a time.

He explained, 'I didn't know I was getting leave again either.' *No, I thought I was going to be killed.* He asked, 'What is awkward?'

'I'm supposed to be meeting somebody.' He shook his head. 'I *know* what you're thinking, my boy, but this time you're wrong, entirely wrong.'

Seaton looked away. His father's hand was shaking badly, he must have been at it all day. Why should it matter? Any more than any other time? Yet he felt cheated in some way.

He said bitterly, 'I'm glad for you.'

His father moved round him, filling his vision again. 'You don't know. Wait till you get a wife. Then you will.' He coughed violently and spilled some gin down his tweed suit. 'They live off you until you're too worn out to protest. They drag you down, and keep telling you what *they* could have been, but for looking after you all those years, cooking and working for you!' He waved his glass to the barman. 'You see if I'm not right!'

What about you? What did you give *her?* Seaton said,'I'm tired.'

His father seemed to see him properly for the first time. 'You do look a bit done in. Been on manoeuvres or something like that?'

Seaton smiled. 'Something like that.'

He thought of Jens, and the strange man, Trevor. Of Venables, and his secrets about rockets and devastating new weapons.

Here, in the Snug, it didn't seem to count for anything.

He said, 'I'll buy you a drink. Sorry I couldn't let you know about the leave.'

Then he saw his father's eyes and turned as he greeted his friend.

Seaton felt sick. The woman was old enough to be his mother, but had dyed red hair and a great red slash for a mouth. Funnily enough, her bright clothes and make-up only made her look older.

His father was saying thickly, 'Er, this is, er, my son, David.'

She fixed her eyes on his. 'I can't believe it!' You with a grownup son!' But her eyes gave Seaton another message entirely.

It would almost be worth it, he thought savagely. Take her off him, just so he could see what he was doing to himself.

No wonder his sudden arrival had made things a bit awkward.

'I'll stay at a hotel, Dad.' He picked up his case. 'You have a good time. I'll phone you.'

'If you're *sure*, David?'

Seaton grinned at him. Poor, pathetic old boozer. But he was all he had.

'Quite sure.'

He pushed out through the bar and took several deep breaths. A good sleep and tomorrow it might all seem different.

As sirens wailed their nightly air-raid warning over southern England, Seaton sat on the side of an hotel bed and poured himself a large gin. He had had several, but they did not seem to make any difference.

Near Waterloo Station, Jenkyn passed the time with two other petty officers, tracing patterns in spilled beer on the table, swapping yarns which each of them had heard many times before.

In the naval hospital at Rosyth, Niven lay with his fists clenched at his sides, staring at the ceiling. The ward was dark but for the night sister's little lamp, and if he moved his head he could see her white cap as she drowsed over a book.

Near his bed, hidden by screens, he heard a man's gentle moaning. It had been going on since his arrival. Regular, unhurried. When it stopped, Niven knew it would seem louder. The man was dying.

Further south, and somewhere in between the scattered members of *XE 16's* company, Drake lay on his back, listening to the rain and the girl's deep breathing beside him.

He felt completely spent, but knew that if she needed him again he would be unable to resist. He could feel the press of her breast against his skin, the heat of her leg thrown carelessly across his own.

She stirred and reached out to touch him. To hold him until he was fired almost to madness.

She whispered, 'Darling?'

He looked at her pale outline in the darkened room.

'Yes?'

'Now.'

9

One Down

At the end of a week's leave Seaton was almost thankful to receive a summons to the Admiralty. He had spent the days walking around London, going to cinemas and theatres, anything to keep his mind off the war. But, if anything, it made matters worse. It was all escapism, a delusion which he was unable to share.

The streets were always full of uniforms. Americans, Poles, Free-French, Canadians, it was like a foreign country. Against their restless searching for enjoyment, the real Londoners made a drab but defiant backcloth.

Seaton often wondered how they put up with it. And the war showed itself in various guises. Like the morning after a bad raid, when he saw a double-decker bus standing on its nose against a shopfront, as if placed there with infinite care by a giant.

Or the time he had been sitting in the companionable warmth of a West End cinema watching Gary Cooper in *For Whom The Bell Tolls*. Without warning a young soldier had jumped to his feet in the next row and had screamed, 'You don't know what the bloody war is about!' He had been sobbing like a child when somebody had fetched a couple of military policemen to remove him.

At the Admiralty, Seaton waited for a sentry to check his identity card against a list of names. It was the same man as before, and he had the mad idea that Venables and Niven's father, and the newly appointed Air Marshal Ruthven, had not left the bunkers since his other visit.

'Right, sir. You can go on through.' The man watched him incuriously. Lieutenants, even those with decorations, were two a penny.

'Hello, Dave!'

Seaton turned with surprise and saw Drake rising from an uncomfortable bench inside the waiting room.

They shook hands warmly, and Seaton asked, 'Did they send for you, too?'

'That's right. So I came a-running. Something's in the air maybe?'

They fell in step and penetrated deeper into the building.

'How's Richard?'

Drake glanced sideways at him. 'I waited until he came down from Rosyth. Then I went to see a friend in Leeds. Chap I met in Malta.' He shrugged. 'Richard was fine. A bit wound up. But he's like that on the surface.' He changed the subject. 'What's it like here? Full of brass and brains?'

'Some of each.' Seaton showed his pass to another man at a desk. 'The Intelligence chief is Richard's father, by the way. Rear Admiral Niven.' He looked at him meaningly. 'Didn't want you to put your hoof into anything!'

'Thanks.' Drake grinned. 'It has been known.'

A lift carried them swiftly down to the concrete bunker, then into Venables' outer office where three shirt-sleeved Wrens were hammering typewriters as if their lives depended on it.

A bored-looking lieutenant said, 'Wait here, please. The captain is engaged.'

Drake raised his eyebrows. 'Who's the lucky girl?'

But the lieutenant merely gave him a frosty stare.

They sat down and waited. Then Seaton asked. 'Did Richard's father-in-law make you welcome?' He saw the guard drop.

Drake answered, 'Well, he was away, as it happens. On some government commission.'

'Just you and Richard's wife?'

'Right.' He turned and dropped his voice. 'Look, take it easy, Dave. It just happened.' He sounded bewildered. 'I still can't believe it.'

'Does Richard know?'

'For God's sake!' Drake lowered his voice again as all three typewriters fell silent. 'I'd not want to hurt him. I don't think she would either.' He was very serious. 'If you'd like me to request a transfer, I will. I don't see why you should get involved because of me.'

Seaton smiled gravely. 'Captain Venables says no transfers. Teamwork comes first.'

Drake shifted uncomfortably. 'Sod *him.'*

'What's she like?'

Drake spread his hands. 'Lovely. Full of life. Fantastic.' He looked away. 'I'm not proud of myself. I'd kill the bastard who did it to me. I should never have gone there.' He ran his fingers through his fair hair. 'Christ, what a bloody mess!'

'You sound like my father.' Seaton stood up. 'Come on. We are being called.'

Venables greeted them formally and shut the door.

'I would not have recalled you unless I considered it necessary.'

Good beginning, Seaton thought. No arguments for that.

'The operation I hinted at last week has become suddenly urgent. I have made a signal for your E.R.S., er. what's his name, Jenkyn? He will be on way to the base, I should think.'

Drake said, 'Niven's only just come out of hospital, sir. Not much of a leave for *him.*

'Quite.' Venables tapped his desk with a ruler, as if trying to make up his mind. 'I am well aware of that. But we need a boat like yours. Pity about Niven, but it can't be avoided. I don't want any changes at this stage.'

Drake was unimpressed. 'But what about the others, sir? They've had the same experience and training.'

Venables eyed him bleakly. *'XE 19* has been playing-up with mechanical failure. Lieutenant Allenby requires another week at least.'

He walked to a wall map and touched it vaguely. 'In fact, orders *were* sent to *XE 17.* Lieutenant Vanneck seemed most suitable.'

Seaton felt his mouth go dry. *'Seemed?'*

'*XE 17* was reported missing. No survivors.' He sighed. 'That's all I can tell you at present.'

Seaton looked at Drake, remembering Vanneck, tough, uncompromising, intensely professional. His courage went without saying. Lying somewhere with his crew of three, or scattered across the sea-bed for the scavengers.

He asked quietly, 'So that mission was aborted?'

'Correct.' Venables was himself again. '*XE 17* was not captured or, as far as we know, sighted. The plan remains the same, but has more urgency now.'

Drake tried to smile. 'What is it this time, sir? Dock, battleship, or the Gosport ferry?' But the smile would not come, and he added bitterly, 'It's all the same to us!'

'Return to *Syren* immediately. My people will give you the necessary clearance when you get there.' He looked at each of them in turn, his eyes cold. 'I wanted both of you here. Yours is a shared enterprise, but if one of you is unable to continue with the operation, the other must be ready. And this one is important, directly linked with your last success.'

A telephone buzzed and he lifted it instantly. 'Venables.' He nodded, his eyes on a wall map. 'At once, sir.'

He picked up his cap. 'Come. The admiral is ready.'

They followed him into the other office where Seaton had first met Niven's father. He was sitting at his desk, in uniform this time, a cigar in one corner of his mouth. Two lieutenant commanders waited just behind him, one with a large folder under his arm. Like a confidential clerk, Seaton thought.

The admiral half rose and sat down again heavily. 'Good of you to come.' He glanced at Drake. 'You're Number One, eh? Fine'.

'I told them about Vanneck's boat, sir.'

The admiral looked at Venables. 'Did right, Walter. Good thinking.'

The 'confidential clerk' took a cautious half-pace nearer the desk and said, 'Ready when you are, sir.'

'Don't fuss, Bannion!' He waved vaguely across the desk. 'These chaps are what it's all about.' His fingers strayed to the bright rectangle of medal ribbons on his chest. 'Oh yes, I know what it's like, believe me.'

Seaton saw the staff officer wince, and pitied him.

'All the same, sir.' Venables sounded impatient.These officers have to go north today.'

'I'd not forgotten.' The admiral eyed him grimly. 'Ruthven has his uses, it seems. He's been able to lay on a priority flight with the R.A.F.'

Seaton looked at Drake. It was that important.

Rear Admiral Niven stubbed out his cigar. 'You are going back to Norway.' He gestured to his aide, who laid out the folder between his powerful hands on the desk. 'Bergen, to be exact.' He studied Seaton for several seconds, and in that time it was just possible to see something of his son in him.

Seaton nodded. Bergen was just about the most important German base in Norway. U-boats were berthed and maintained there. Patrols which covered the south-western approaches and the entrance to the Skagerrak regularly fuelled and took on stores in the excellent harbour.

'And the target, sir?' Again Seaton was amazed at his own voice. Flat. Too bloody calm.

'No target. Not this time. Although your boat will carry side-cargoes in the normal way. In case . . .' He hurried on, 'The agents working in Bergen have something for you to collect and bring back here.'

In case. He had nearly let it slip out. Venables would not have hesitated. At least he seemed genuine. If *XE 16* was going on a special mission she had to *look* right, if she was captured or salvaged after a mishap.

The staff officer said, 'Here are some of the details.'

Seaton listened to the man's dry voice. But he kept thinking about Drake and Niven's wife. And of Bergen. It was not just any harbour. It would be like Piccadilly in the rush-hour.

His mind came back with a jerk as the officer continued, 'The trouble is, we have to keep our part of a bargain. In exchange for the handing-over of this highly secret piece of equipment, you must bring a passenger, too.'

Venables interrupted curtly. 'There is no other way. Fishing boats, disguises and false papers are out. This man is known to us. He has played a key role in German rocket research.' His eyes flickered to Seaton. 'We got some hint of the *Hansa* through him. To turn traitor needs more than courage. It requires certain promises from us. The Gestapo will have no mercy if they discover what he is doing.'

Drake asked quietly, 'And if we can't get him out?'

'We'll not discuss failure.' The admiral clipped the end of another cigar. 'Let me just say that we want him brought out alive. Equally, we would not want him to be *left* in Bergen in the same condition.'

'You mean kill him, sir?' Drake sounded very calm.

Venables said, 'The wheres and whys can be thrashed out later on. This is a team effort. You will be given all the aid and information which we have been able to muster. Intelligence, and the Norwegian forces in England, are ready to help. As I said before,' he was looking directly at Seaton, 'the enemy has instilled fear to his advantage. We must rely on mutual trust.'

The admiral stood up. 'That's it then.' He sounded impatient. 'No point in discussing it further at this stage.' He offered his hand to Seaton. 'I'll see you soon. Give my regards to my son. He's full of surprises, that one.'

It was suddenly over, and Seaton found himself standing with Drake at another desk while a Wren petty officer hastily scribbled out new travel passes for their privileged flight with the R.A.F.

Drake said at length, 'It's not quite what I had in mind when I volunteered.'

'You know what they say.' They fell in step again. ' A volunteer is a man who has misunderstood the question!'

Drake grinned. 'I expect so.'

They stood waiting for a lift to carry them up to reality again, and Seaton said quietly, 'look, if you're really set against this, I can have a word with Captain Trenoweth. You're due for a command if you're staying in X-craft, a transfer to something more comfortable if you're not. Venables is right about one thing. This has got to be a team effort.'

Drake watched him thoughtfully. 'The old firm. I told you. We'll see it through together. Captain Venables really got to you, didn't he?'

'I don't know. He's necessary. He sees the war for what it is. It's no use being a good, clean loser. But I'd not have his job for the world.'

A cold February drizzle greeted their appearance in

Whitehall, and Drake said suddenly, 'About Richard's wife.'
'Decia?'

Seaton saw the shot go home. Poor Geoff was even trying to
ease the guilt by not using her name.

'You'll not tell him, will you?' He sounded worried. 'I'll try
and sort it out.'

'You'd better.' Seaton waved at a cruising taxi. 'Otherwise
nobody'll have to tell him a thing. He'll bloody well guess!'

Drake sighed. 'For once, I'm not sorry to be going back to
work.'

Seaton looked at him. *If you only knew.* Aloud he said, 'It's
as good a reason as some.'

They crowded around the centre table of H.M.S. *Syren's*
operations room listening to the unhurried tones of an
intelligence officer, while outside the building the wind moaned
and hissed against the granite walls.

Seaton felt cold, in spite of the room's steamy heat. The
uncomfortable flight to Scotland, the changes from one transport to another, his nagging doubts about the proposed raid
were all having effect.

Maps and photographs were laid carefully across the table in
line with a giant chart and two coloured maps of Bergen. A
model of the port and the adjoining fjord, dates, distances,
recognition marks. A parade of efficiency.

All the lights in the room were out but for the large one above
the table. That too seemed to imply a compressing of
information and method, pinning it in the glare.

XE 19's company were also present. Time was obviously
running out. Gervaise Allenby's boat would be on immediate
stand-by, engine defects or not.

One of the two Norwegian officers was speaking now. His
low voice reminded Seaton of Jens. And the girl. Was she still at
the same place? Hiding in fear of her life. Or already...He made
himself listen, to control his anxiety.

'Some months ago there was an explosion aboard a freighter,
here.' The Norwegian moved a pointer along a plan of the
harbour. 'Accident or sabotage, we do not know. The vessel
took fire, and was a real risk to others close by.' The pointer
moved on. 'The Germans decided to warp her away. Let her sink

rather than allow the fires to spread. There was an ammunition ship quite close.' The man's sad face softened into a smile. 'No matter. One of your submarines sank the ammunition ship on her next trip.'

The other Norwegian, a bluff, heavy commander, said, 'So the wreck is lying apart from the main channels, well marked by buoys.' He looked hard at Seaton. 'The sea-bed is good there. You can set down on the bottom and await final instructions.'

The British Intelligence officer nodded. 'We suspect that the article you are to obtain for us is also in that wreck. We will know more when you have made contact.'

Captain Trenoweth had entered the room without anyone hearing. He asked quietly, 'Do you have any questions?'

Seaton turned, seeing Allenby watching him curiously, Drake's eyes shining in the overhead lamp above his shoulder.

'What exactly is this "article", sir?'

The intelligence officer cleared his throat. 'It is part of a guidance system for a rocket. We know something of the enemy's work in this field, naturally. But this would really tell us how far they have got, and what we can expect. Range and trajectory, some idea of the scope of the whole weapon, should it be brought to bear before we can knock it out.'

Trenoweth said coldy, 'Thank you.' To Seaton he added, 'Does that help?'

'Yes, sir.'

Seaton tried to make a mental picture of the man who held the secret. One who could bargain his country's secrets for some sort of sanctuary.

Trenoweth said, 'The man is not German, by the way.' He looked at the two Norwegians and added gently, 'We all have traitors somewhere along the line.'

The Norwegian commander shrugged. 'It may be difficult to make the local Resistance accept our 'bargain'. A Quisling deserves only death.' He looked at Seaton gravely. 'Be patient with them. They are fighting their war with no less courage than the rest of us, yes?'

The operations officer stepped up to the table. 'Now to work. *XE 16* has been overhauled and is at present on passage to the Shetlands. This time there will be the usual arrangements for

passage crew up to the moment of slipping the tow.' He smiled.
'We want you all bright and eager. There may be quite a bit extra
to do on this one. I suggest you all turn in and get some sleep.
You'll be picked up tomorrow and flown to the nearest airstrip.'

Seaton was glad it was over. Before the actual moment of
departure there would be more instructions, new ideas. Now, he
needed to be alone.

Outside in the draughty passageway Allenby said, 'I'm going
to have a noggin, old son.' He did not ask Seaton to join him. He
understood well enough.

Seaton asked quietly, 'Does anyone know what happened to
Rupert Vanneck's boat?'

'They won't say *where* it happened.' Allenby added bitterly.
'We're too young to be told! But apparently *XE 17* was on
passage when the tow snapped in bad weather. Worst part was
that the towing submarine never realised what had happened
until the moment to surface and do a battery charge. So nobody
knows exactly.'

Seaton tried not to think about it. The midget would probably have had her bows well trimmed down to compensate for the
tow and the bad weather. When the line parted she would start
to dive immediately, headlong and out of control, unless the
men on watch had been able to act at once. They obviously had
not. *XE 17's* fate might remain a mystery, which only the depth
of water could determine. Lying crippled on the sea-bed, her
crew dying in slow despair, or plunging into deeper darkness
until the small hull was finally crushed flat by the mounting
pressure. It was no choice at all.

He touched Allenby's arm. 'Bed.'

'Good idea, old son. Sorry I had to drag you into this because
of my mechanical problems. Still, your diver is better than my
chap. He can't find a hearse in a bloody thimble!'

Seaton went to his room and switched on an electric fire.
Then he sat on his bed and thought about Vanneck and about
his own crew. Drake with his guilt. Niven, strangely withdrawn
but outwardly unscarred by his experiences. And poor Alec
Jenkyn. Back from his leave, and another funeral. Seaton did
not proceed further to examine his own reserves.

Instead he thought of his father, recalling with sudden clarity

the stories about his service in the Army on the Western Front.
Of gaunt, ashen-faced infantry tramping up the line at night to
find death in the morning.

Perhaps that was what had changed him and turned his wife
against him?

He thought too of his last telephone call and the woman who
had answered it. It had not been the same one he had met at the
pub.

Somewhere outside the building he heard Captain
Trenoweth's old dog give three hoarse barks. That was his ritual
offering. Like the sunset gun.

How those two Norwegians must envy men like Trenoweth,
he thought. In his own country, with his friends around him.
And his silly old dog.

Seaton rolled sideways on to the bed and was instantly
asleep.

Forty-eight hours after leaving Loch Striven for the
Shetland, Seaton and his companions were on the move again.

As he lay on a spare bunk in the towing submarine's
wardroom, Seaton stared up at the curved deckhead and
listened to the throaty beat of diesels.

It was strange how you got used to things. When he had first
gone to sea in a submarine he had imagined it so suffocating, so
terribly enclosed, that he would be found unsuitable after one
trip. But now, after serving in the tiny X-craft, an ordinary
submarine seemed unimaginably spacious.

He felt the gentle pressure of the bunk against his body, and
pictured the boat thrusting steadily out to sea, keeping on the
surface for as long as possible to make good speed and to charge
batteries. Somewhere, lost in spray and darkness astern, the
little midget would be following obediently to her tow-line. The
passage crew would get little rest, he thought grimly. With the
tragic loss of Vanneck's boat on their minds there would be no
need to warn them about vigilance.

He heard low voices beyond the bunk curtains as two of the
submarine's officers prepared to go on watch. It felt safe and
snug behind the curtain. A private world.

Seaton thought suddenly of Drake's face just an hour or so
before they had sailed. An intelligence officer had been giving
some last minute details about coastal shipping around Bergen,

and had said, almost as an afterthought, 'By the way, Captain Venables wanted you to see these pictures. The R.A.F. managed to fly a photographic recce over your fjord. Some of the shots are quite good, under the circumstance .'

Even the term 'your fjord' had sounded obscene. Despite the stiffness of the aerial photographs it had all been there. The great, echoing explosion which had followed *XE 16* far out to sea. The devastation no less terrible because of distance.

Of the *Hansa* there had been nothing left to see, nor had Seaton expected it. But all along the side of the fjord the great juggernaut force of the combined explosions had scarred the land, as if a giant had scraped away the terrain with a wire brush. Pier, houses, all had gone, and every small inlet appeared to be filled with flotsam, broken boats and uprooted trees.

He had asked quietly, 'How many hostages were there?'

The officer had replied, 'Upwards of fifty. God knows how many of the Germans went for a Burton.' The casualness of one not involved.

Afterwards Drake had tried to explain his own feelings. 'I had no idea, Dave. Not the *faintest inkling*. I watched your eye at the 'scope, as I always do, I did what was expected of me. And all that bloody time you were carrying it, holding it all in your gut. Knowing what was going to happen.'

It had been a mixture of shocked admiration and shame.

'And to think I've been bothering you about my petty problems.' He had reached out impetuously. 'Christ, Dave, if it happens again, share it with me. I'll not be able to offer much, but at least you won't have to shoulder the whole works!'

Seaton heard the muffled shouts of orders, the warning klaxon in the control room. Diving, to the more peaceful stability below.

They would have to shake themselves out of their gloom, he thought. Only Niven appeared unreached by the pressures, and when you thought about it, he had no right to be.

He rolled over and pulled the damp blanket up to his ears.

On the opposite side of the wardroom Drake was also wide awake, his fingers interlocked behind his head.

Decia returned to his thoughts whenever he left his defences down, and he imagined he could feel her supple body writhing in his arms, her mouth driving him insane with passion. Above and below him, she had been everywhere. A torment, a frenzied

131

need.

His ears popped as the submarine's diesels cut out and were instantly replaced by the low purr of electric motors. Air hissed from the saddle-tanks, and as metal creaked and protested above his bunk the bows tilted downwards.

Drake remembered Seaton's pale face at the periscope as he had started that last attack on the *Hansa*. How could he do it? With a net being unexpectedly laid across his line of retreat, and knowing all the while about the wretched hostages who were soon to die, he had still gone through every motion as if they had been out on an exercise.

Nobody could stand that sort of strain for long. Everyone said so. But what was the answer? Like that bloody ghoul and 'your fjord'. Pity he didn't get out and discover what it was like.

Jenkyn was sitting in a corner of the petty officer's mess, keeping out of the way as the business of diving was completed stage by stage.

Jenkyn did not think much about the mission, but then he never did. What was the use? It only added to anxiety and sweat.

He did think about the funeral, however. The big grave, the rain, and the usual embarrassment.

There had been ten dead in all, caught along the line where the stick of bombs had come down. He had seen a few uniforms amongst the mourners, but mostly older faces, people he had known all his life. Uncles and mates, aunts and friends from work.

The vicar had been new though. Nice young chap with a posh voice like Niven. He had said something about an 'oration for the dead'. Jenkyn had told his friend Bill Turbett, who was the E.R.A. in *XE19*, about it. Turbett was a cynical bastard. He had said that an oration for the dead was just a hypocritical defence of the living. Poor old Bill, his missus had gone off with a bloke in the Black Watch.

Still, it was no use moping about it. He would have to plan things. Maybe he would even meet a nice little party and get settled. Feet under the table somewhere.

Just as the funeral had ended a train had rattled down the main line towards the Junction. Ma would have liked that. A sort of familiar fanfare.

The submarine's torpedo gunner's mate thrust the curtain aside and looked down at him.

'All right, chum?'

Jenkyn sighed. 'Yeh. It's like what they say. If you can't take a joke—'

They both grinned like conspirators.

'After this little lot I'm going to grow roses for a livin'!'

A few yards away, wedged against the chart table, Niven stood beside the navigating officer and watched the youthful captain at work.

Niven knew he ought to be resting, if not actually sleeping. But he could still feel the same sense of thrill and elation, like a drug which would not release him even for a minute.

He could not get over it. How she had greeted his arrival from the hospital, the way she had given herself to him. As if she had wanted to offer him anything his whim might desire.

Drake must have told her something about him when he had called there. Never before had she shown such passion, such hunger for him.

The submarine commander said, 'Thirty feet. Check with the tow that all's well, Pilot.'

Gauges quivered, and the tense figures in their oil-stained jerseys moved over the controls like minions around their god.

'Up periscope.'

Niven watched him, fascinated. He was always interested in the technicalities of his profession. Recently, some of that confidence had been badly jolted, and he had discovered something like shame at being so proud of 'your silly old Navy', as Decia had called it. She had certainly changed since then. Niven had felt slightly mean at accepting all her regrets and apologies, and when she had said she would make it up to him from now on, he had realised just what his experiences had given him.

If only he could go on the same way and perhaps end up like the young lieutenant commander who was peering through the periscope. Then perhaps even his father would find room to offer a little encouragement and praise.

'Down periscope. Ninety feet.'

The submarine commander crossed to the chart table and then glanced at Niven.

'Raring to go, Sub?'

'You get used to it, sir.'

It had come out wrongly. Stiff and pompous. He made to try again but saw that the other man was already thinking about something else.

'I—I think I'll turn in, sir.'

The first lietuenant said softly, 'Little prig!'

His captain looked up from the chart. 'Take it off your back Number One! W e were all little prigs once.' He grinned. 'At least we don't have to get out and walk when we reach a target, so be thankful for *that.*'

On his way to the wardroom Niven heard their quick laughter and clenched his hands into tight fists. Well, he would show them. As he had Decia. And as he would his arrogant, bloody-minded father! He calmed himself very deliberately; piece at a time, like parts of an intricate weapon.

He thought again of Decia, the way she had knelt at his feet, looking up at him like some tantalising slave girl. If he had beaten her, he doubted if she would have lifted a finger to stop him.

Perhaps he held too much power? And that would explain her earlier attitudes. She had always had her own way, and was ever ready for an arguemnt. Just as if she was taking charge of a new mount. It might also put a name to his father's aloofness. *Jealousy.*

A curtain moved slightly and Drake peered at him through the gap.

'You say something, Richard?'

Niven flushed. 'Sorry. Got carried away. Was thinking about that last leave, what there was of it.'

'Okay, was it?' He watched, almost afraid to breathe.

'I think you must have been filling her with stuff about me, Geoff.' He looked at him and smiled. 'I'll get to the bottom of it.'

Drake lay back and tried to relax. It was getting worse every moment. Like being sealed up with some destructive force or spirit.

'And another thing—'

Mercifully, Niven was cut short by a sleepy voice from a curtained bunk.

'For Christ's sake shut up and remember the bloody watchkeepers!'

Oblivious or indifferent to all of them, *XE 16* followed in the other submarine's wake. Like the patient shark, she could afford to wait.

10

A Problem

SEATON SCRAMBLED round in a tight circle, his eyes throbbing with concentration as he peered through the periscope. It was close on midnight, and as black as a boot. Just as it had been when they had surfaced to slip the tow and transfer from the other submarine an hour and ten minutes earlier.

He saw vague, soaring shadows rising away to starboard, the only way of distinguishing land from water. The hull was moving well. pitching only slightly in an offshore swell. *XE 16* had moved immediately towards the islands along the coast, and was now comfortably amongst them, following the mainland, and staying in the centre of the channel.

Seaton glanced at Drake, seeing his hands moving deftly as the boat dipped heavily and almost submerged the periscope.

Seaton said quietly, 'You'll get a lot of that. Freshwater pockets from various fjords and inlets. Be ready to blow some ballast if need be.' He saw him nod, knowing he was thinking of Vanneck.

He made up his mind. 'I'm going up. Get a better chance of seeing where we're heading.' He slung the binoculars around his neck and buttoned his waterproof jacket. 'Continue battery charging. We'll need all we can get later on.' Another glance at the clock. 'We should be through the outer minefield by now.' He forced a smile. 'All things considered.'

Jenkyn said between his teeth, 'Watch out up top, sir. Don't want to lose you just yet.'

Drake kept his eyes on the inclinometer. 'Besides, you're the only one who knows the way.'

Seaton unclipped the after hatch and opened it carefully, feeling the raw air scything across his face.

Once outside it did not seem quite so cold, and for several minutes he lay prone on the wet deck, balancing on his elbows as he trained the glasses from bow to bow.

After the sealed control room everything was larger and louder. The hiss of spray along the casing, the back-echo of waves from a nearby spit of land and *XE 16's* diesel making enough din to wake the dead.

He moved the glasses carefully, seeing occasional darts of white foam, the glassy restlessness of the water beyond the stem.

They were moving very slowly, reducing from six-and-a-half knots to just above four as the battery charge continued without a break.

They were through the outer minefield, but it took great confidence to believe anything. They were following the coast, south-easterly, weaving through the islands as if they did it every week. But it was hard to accept that once through the next pincer-like gap of rocks and islets they would be entering the last great fjord, and then Bergen itself.

He rubbed the handset with his glove, feeling the ice-rime on it like powdered glass.

'Ship's head?'

'One-four-zero.' It was Niven. Crisp. On the ball.

'Alter course ten degrees to starboard.'

Seaton held his breath and tensed as the deck sagged violently in another freshwater pocket. Spray, and then the sea itself surged along the casing, pulling at his sodden clothing, knocking one foot over the side before he was raised clear again.

'Ship's head now one-five-zero.'

'Better.'

He wiped the glasses and steadied them on the nearest land. It was better to have sea-room for the final approach. Just in case some sneaky patrol boat might be working the fjord.

He blinked and looked again. A light had flared up and died

just as suddenly. Like car headlights. Except that the glare seemed to be pointing out to sea.

Seaton peered at his luminous watch, feeling the edge of his cuff cutting his wrist like wire. Cold and salt water were cruel to skin.

He tried to lay out his plans and alternatives in his mind. Like the marine major's display of weapons at Loch Striven.

He would stick it out on the surface for another hour at least. *Right up to the gates.* It was going well. Eighteen miles up the approach fjord without diving once. It would save time in the long run. Give them more scope for putting down on the bottom to await events.

It sounded easy when it was discussed ashore.

He froze as another tongue of light swung up, over and down across the water, making the fjord glitter like black silk. He counted, feeling his breath clinging to his woollen muffler. Ten seconds. But it seemed like an hour. He snapped on the handset. 'I think Jerry has got one, maybe two, searchlights playing across the entrance.'

Niven's voice came back within seconds. 'The gap is less than a half-mile across, sir. Between two little islands.'

It came pushing through all the other facts and figures even as Niven spoke. A narrow channel. The Germans would have something there. Strange nobody had thought about searchlights.

Drake had switched on his connection. 'Plenty of depth hereabouts, Skipper.' A pause. 'We can run deep.'

Perhaps it was the intercom, or the surrounding darkness, or his own imagination, but Drake sounded different. Worried.

Seaton answered, 'No. It may be what they want. I'll lay odds they've got detection gear right along the bottom.'

He lost more precious seconds as the boat wallowed down and smothered him with freezing water.

'Anyway.' He tried to rake up something trivial. Casual. 'We've not finished the battery charge yet.'

He thought he heard Jenkyn laugh. It was a start.

'Alter course. One-four-zero as before.' He eased his limbs painfully on the rough plating. 'We're about dead-centre.' He watched the beam lick out across the water and hover momentarily on the surface like a giant spotlight.

As the boat moved steadily towards the islands it was very

hard to stay level-headed and calm about it. Seaton had been told often enough that searchlights looked far more effective than they actually were. That the men who worked them only saw what they expected to see. He watched the opposite beam probing out from the darkness. All the same...

The bitter air must be turning his brain into ice, he thought vaguely. He felt no actual fear. Just a kind of light-headed bravado. He reached out and readjusted the induction trunk, lowering it almost to its diving position.

Damn them to hell. He would continue charging batteries as they pushed through the gap.

He must have made more noise than usual, and when Drake called him on the intercom he said, 'Getting stiff. I'll be bloody glad to come inside.'

The next searchlight swept down and over the deck with alarming suddenness. It revealed every rivet and scrape, and glinted on his wrist-watch like a bright diamond before swinging away across the undulating water. Then it hesitated, and Seaton could feel his heart thumping against the deck-plates like a hammer.

Here it comes. The beam passes slowly over the hull, from port to starboard, touching the frothing bubbles around the screw and then cutting-out completely, making the night blacker than ever.

'Gone.' He strained his ears, imagining he could hear back-echoes from the islands. 'Nearly through.' His teeth were chattering uncontrollably. 'Press on.'

He tried to think of his visit to London. Of Hampshire before the war. Of his father, greeting everyone in the pub like a brother.

A searchlight made its play from the opposite direction, but barely raised a shine on the deck and periscope guard.

Seaton thought of the girl with the blue-green eyes. She might be just a few miles away, sleeping, or dreading the dawn. He retched, feeling the cold exploring his insides, grinding his resistance.

He peered dazedly at his watch. They had done it. He unclipped his safety-line and groped his way to the hatch. Niven had to help him down into the control room, and he almost pitched headlong as the boat took another playful wallow.

Drake watched him anxiously. 'God, you're blue!'

Seaton took several shallow breaths and rubbed his hands violently together.

Still without trusting himself to speak, he scrambled to the chart table and pulled the overhead light above their pencilled course. Twenty-five miles all told on the surface. He felt the warmth creeping back to his blood like elation.

'We'll dive in ten minutes. But we shall stay at periscope depth.' He made a small cross at the last narrow gap. 'By the time we've slipped past the opening at Langholm we should be able to see what we're at. Watch the trim, Geoff, more than ever now. Revolutions for two knots only.' He turned to look at him. 'Nice and easy.'

He hoped he looked and sounded convincing. But the strain was not letting go with the cold. Like steel claws, and it would be another six hours at least before they could snatch a small respite on the bottom.

Jenkyn said over his shoulder, 'I put one of th' thermos flasks under the table, sir. Drop of kye to warm you up.'

Seaton groped beneath the chart table, and seconds later was swallowing the thick, glutinous cocoa, feeling his nerve-ends responding just as gratefully as his stomach. 'Thanks.'

He peered at the chart again. Up and into the swept channel of West Byfjord and through the inner minefield. By that time it would be getting light. And busy, if the intelligence reports were accurate.

It looked so much worse on the chart than the last one. Weaving and probing deeper and deeper amongst islands and fjords, with no short-cut to get out again. Their return course would be over exactly the same ground.

Seaton touched his mouth with the back of his hand. One thing at a time.

He said, 'Stand by to dive.' He nodded at Niven. 'Check our progress minute by minute. This is a precision job.'

He thought of Venables in his bunker. Trenoweth and his dog. And Niven's father. Something was badly wrong between those two.

Drake said, 'Ready.'

'Dive . . . dive . . . dive. Thirty feet.'

Three hours after diving, *XE 16* continued to make good progress through the swept channel of West Byfjord. But they were the longest three hours Seaton could remember in his life, and every minute made new demands on his nerve and concentration.

The water around the hull seemed to vibrate and throb to countless engines, as if the whole fjord was packed with haphazard shipping, all determined to cause a major collision. Once, when he took the submarine up to periscope depth, Seaton had to call for a crash dive as the tall stem of an outward-bound fishing boat loomed into his lens like an axe.

When he chanced another look he saw that the sky seemed paler, and he could almost feel the dawn's chill approach. He sighted vessels large and small moving busily in the swept channel, trawlers and smaller fishing boats, a ferry, two landing-craft and a low-lying flak-ship, her deck crammed with vicious-looking cannon.

Niven said, 'We'll be entering the inner minefield in ten minutes.'

Drake muttered hoarsely, 'Great.'

Seaton had too much on his mind even to contemplate hitting a stray mine. The shipping was far worse than he had imagined, or the reports had suggested.

Wakes and bow waves intercrossed and sluiced around the small periscope whenever he thought it safe to raise it. But they kept going, diving every five minutes to twenty-five feet and then popping up again for a look around.

'Entering minefield *now.*' Niven sounded calm.

Seaton peered at his watch. It would soon be broad daylight up top. He felt the strain tugging at him, the ache around his eyes. Seven hours since they had left the other submarine. Was it really as little as that?

He tensed as a sharp, metallic ping struck the stern of the boat, like a tuning fork.

'Start a twenty degree zigzag!'

He felt the sweat running between his shoulders as another ping echoed along the hull. A patrol boat was up there amongst the local shipping, and was using her Asdic, underwater detection gear.

Ping.

Seaton tried not to flinch, feeling Niven's eyes on him from the chart table.

'Bring her up to fifteen feet.' He raised his hand. *'Easy!'* The sound of compressed air seemed like a tidal wave.

'Fifteen feet.'

They waited, listening, expecting the echo to find them. The patrol boat's skipper probably imagined he had touched an old wreck or a shoal of fish. If he had noticed anything at all. Men were never at their best around dawn.

'Periscope depth.' His mouth felt dirty. As if covered with an extra skin.

He pictured Niven's father, one hand laid on his medal ribbons. It was hard to imagine him ever being soiled. He looked like a man who bathed too often.

Seaton pressed the button and prepared himself with cold deliberation.

It *was* much lighter.

Plenty of shipping, but further abeam, being guided through another channel. He saw the mass of land too, the faint slopes of blue-grey where the hard snow marked the hills. When he moved the periscope he felt the unnerving sensation of being trapped, of driving deeper and deeper into a rocky vice.

A black hull throbbed parallel with the periscope, foam spewing up from twin screws. Another patrol, but no Asdic this time. He pressed the button.

'Twenty-five feet.' Seaton mopped his eyes and mouth, feeling sick, shaky.

He thought of the people in Bergen, getting up, trying to believe that things were normal. Going to work in the docks, the schools, the canning factory and the brewery. It was probably easier to delude yourself if you could keep from seeing a German uniform.

Some would be staring unseeingly across the harbour as they went to work. Who in his wildest dreams would imagine there was a tiny steel pod working steadily towards them, with four men sealed inside and two massive charges of explosives.

Like something from Jules Verne or Walt Disney.

'New course?'

Niven replied, 'Steer one-two-zero in,' he craned over the chart, 'five minutes.'

Drake gave a gasp as something clicked against the side. This time it was not an echo.

'Very easy, Alec.' He sounded so even, so assured, yet every nerve was wanting to scream. 'Bring her round just a bit to port.'

He heard the metallic rattle begin again, slowly, rasping over the curved flank.

Seaton felt his eyes following the sound down the side of the control room. With the set of tide and depth as it was, the mine would probably be just a foot or so above the periscope guard. He could almost see the rough mooring wire as it edged along the hull, looking for a projection to snare it, to drag the hideous death amongst them.

As the wheel eased over the noise gave one sharp clatter and stopped.

Seaton squeezed the E.R.A.'s narrow shoulder. 'Well done.'

The petty officer bobbed his head but kept his eyes on the gyro. 'Ta.'

Seaton raised himself to the table and looked at the chart, to the points of Niven's dividers as he said tersely, '*Here*, sir.'

'Good.' He wanted to let out a great sigh, laugh or burst into tears. But he said, 'Alter course now, Alec. One-two- zero.' He waited while they adjusted the trim and settled the boat on her new heading.

Then like conspirators they crept up to periscope depth again, and Seaton saw the entrance to the harbour for the first time. The light was very poor, but enough to see buildings and moored ships of all sizes, overlapping as if they would never move. A church, a slablike dock, and rising above all else, a towering gantry which appeared to be suspended on four great legs. It was unmoving, but gave an impression of watchfulness and menace, like some terrible prehistoric creature waiting to plunge down its head and snatch a helpless victim. It must be huge, he thought, but it had not been mentioned in his notes. So it was probably a floating gantry, recently constructed, or brought round from another port to help the Germans.

He found himself wishing this was the objective, instead of a human being and some nameless piece of equipment.

Drake darted a quick glance at him as he lowered the periscope. 'Okay?'

'On the button.' It sounded hollow and he added, 'We'll head for the adjoining fjord, where the wreck is.'

Niven said, 'Puddefjord, sir. About a mile and a half.'

Seaton looked at the clock. It was amazing what you could put up with. Depth ... speed ... distance. He massaged his eyes before returning to the chart and his pad of notes and bearings.

The fact they had been so near to death at the moment of entering the harbour approach had already departed from his mind. The resilience of war. The necessary protection against terror.

They rose to periscope depth and increased the engine revolutions to compensate for a strong tide and undertow which swept through the fjord.

A fat tug pushed busily towards the swept channel, two barges towering emptily astern. Nodding buoys and a few more small craft, and a circling mass of gulls, very white against the clouds. Seaton could see their beaks opening wide, their shrill screams mute in the periscope.

Later he picked out a green marker buoy, and dimly beyond it what looked like part of a submerged hut.

He examined his reactions like a surgeon with an unpredictable patient.

The 'object' was the uppermost part of the wrecked ship's bridge. At high water even that would be invisible. From there he would be able to watch the main harbour and rest his boat. The Germans had done well. If he had picked the site himself he would have found none better.

At exactly eight o'clock in the morning *XE 16* settled on the bottom, her hull plates almost touching the buckled side of the wreck.

While one of their number maintained a listening-watch, the others tried to sleep, or to await the future in their own different ways.

As dusk moved across Bergen's seven hills, *XE 16* rose warily to periscope depth, brushing against the wreck with a grate of steel.

Seaton felt no relief from his restless sleep, nor, at a guess, did the others. The strain had left him tired, cold and irritable. The noise of the wreck against the hull almost made him turn on Drake with a reprimand, when in far worse situations they would have made a joke of it.

He raised the periscope and swung the lens carefully in a wide arc. Nothing appeared to be moving, but it took extra revolutions to hold the boat steady against the thrusting current. No place for a swim. He thought about the secret equipment he was to carry back to base. It was to be hoped it would be worth the journey.

Seaton licked his lips. They tasted of oil. A great steaming-hot bath in some fantastic hotel. Pity. There never were hotels like those. Not on a lieutenant's pay.

'Anything?' Drake shifted his powerful frame on his little seat.

'We've a few minutes yet.' Seaton thought of the passenger. He would make a change.

Drake added, 'Just our luck if the gadget is too big for the bloody boat!'

Seaton moved his gaze from the periscope and stared at him, surprised and unreasonably angry that he had not thought of that. The most important detail, and nobody had mentioned it.

Drake looked at him. 'Sorry, Skipper. Just a thought.'

'That's all I need!' He turned back to the lens. 'Bloody hell!'

Niven said, 'Oh, they'd have taken it into consideration.'

He sounded so confident, so assured, that Jenkyn snapped, '*They* do make foul-ups, y'know!'

Seaton said softly, 'Boat coming.'

The others fell silent, Jenkyn stiffly angry, Niven coldly disapproving.

Seaton heard the boat's engine muttering through the water. God, what would happen to the spy systems and intelligence men if the time clock ever went wrong? It was amazing, unnerving. Something planned and discussed at a Whitehall desk was being executed before his eyes. Even as he watched he saw something flare up in the gloom, like a man lighting a pipe downwind.

The boat was slowing down, barely making a ripple as it continued towards the inner wreck buoy. Then the engine stopped altogether, and Seaton saw the hull rocking on the swell and two or three figures converging in the bows like shrouded monks. They had hooked on to the marker buoy. Waiting.

He cleared his throat. 'Revs for two knots. *Surface*.'

They had exercised and practised the manoeuvre countless times, and the little submarine revealed herself within yards of the buoy with no more than a sigh.

Seaton unclipped the hatch, very conscious of the hard pressure against his ribs. His pistol. It would not save him, but might give Drake a chance to get clear with the boat.

'Watch it, Skipper.'

Seaton glanced at him and nodded. Then he was up through the hatch, half expecting to be met by a challenge or a fusilade of bullets.

He saw the boat more clearly, a number painted on her bow to show she was official, one of the harbour master's own craft.

A rope was thrown, and he made it fast to a bollard while the men in the boat took the strain, hauling both hulls together.

One figure scrambled to the gunwale and peered across at him, ignoring the midget's tough hull as it pounded against the boat's planking.

'Hell's teeth, it's you again, is it?'

Seaton stared. It was Trevor.

He replied, 'Everyone else is too busy!' He looked round. 'Is it safe?'

'Enough.' Trevor was watching him curiously. 'The Jerries only patrol this part occasionally.' He reached out and gripped Seaton's hand. 'Bloody nice to see you, and I mean it.'

Seaton peered at the others. Resistance men, people forced by threat or promises, or just ordinary Norwegians, who could say?

He asked, 'Where's my passenger? Better get a move on. I've been told to collect him and the "package". The bargain is accepted by London.'

Trevor said, 'I know.' He tried to grin. 'What do you imagine we use here, bloody semaphore?' He became serious again. 'Fact is, we've a problem.'

Seaton sighed, remembering Jenkyn's bitter words. *They do make foul-ups.*

'The enemy have picked him up? Is that it?'

'Worse in some ways. The local Resistance boys have got him.'

'For Christ's sake! We're all supposed to be on the same side!' He took a firmer grip on himself. *Easy.* Don't snap his head off. He asked, 'What do you want me to do?'

'We need another day.' Trevor sounded worried. 'At least. You'll have to come ashore with me.' He hesitated. 'Right now, as it happens.'

Again Seaton was reminded of another's words. *If one of you is unable to continue with the operation . . .* Venables.

'Bit dicey, surely?' The crazy logic of his remark helped to steady him. A surfaced submarine in an enemy-held harbour, a British agent in a motor boat, everyone chatting as if it was a Sunday cricket match. He added, 'Well, why not? In for a penny...'

Trevor did not hide his relief. 'For a moment there I thought—' He hurried on, 'Quick as you can. I've got some gear for you to put on, but it's no problem once you're ashore. We've a lot of friends.'

Seaton lowered his head through the hatch. 'Take over the con, Geoff. Same routine. Just like the plan. You'll keep watch, and ventilate the boat, everything as we discussed it.'

Drake waited for Niven to take over his controls and then stumbled to the hatch.

'Where the hell are you going? You can't just take off!'

He winced as the boat surged and clattered against the hull and then saw Trevor.

'Oh, it's you, is it?'

Trevor grinned. 'Always welcome. The story of my life.'

Seaton said firmly, 'Forty-eight hours. If I'm not back by then, get the hell out.' For Trevor's benefit he added, 'Sooner, if you feel things are wrong.' He reached down and patted Drake's shoulder. 'Take it off your back. It will be all right.'

'With *him*?' Drake nodded, his face tight with anxiety. 'But if you say so.'

It was done. Seaton clambered into the boat, and by the time it had been freed from the buoy, *XE 16* had vanished. Only the wreck buoy's winking green eye remained.

The engine spluttered into life and they turned away towards the shore.

Trevor said, 'The local leader is a man called Brynjulf. He's one of the wild ones, not another Jens.' He sounded sad. 'There never are enough of his sort. But Brynjulf is a fighter, and he knows how to hit the Germans.' A flurry of light snow swept over the boat, and he asked, 'How's England, by the way?'

'Raining.'

'Good. You need something familiar to hold on to.' He peered over the bows. 'Ten minutes. Get this coat on, and if you meet some Jerries, just show you don't understand what they're saying. That's how the locals behave. Drives the krauts wild, especially as they desperately want to be liked.'

146

Seaton struggled into a thick, fur-lined coat.

'After what they've done?'

Trevor lit a cigarette and threw the match overboard.

'You have to understand the Teutonic mind.'

The boat passed beneath a massive stone jetty, and Trevor said, 'Here we go. Ready?'

The helmsman steered as close as he dared, and as Trevor and Seaton stepped off on to some slippery stairs he swung the tiller and headed away down the harbour.

They both stood in silence, listening to the wind, the water lapping over the stone stairs. Apart from the sound of some vehicles a long way off, it was very still.

Trevor said abruptly, 'We'll walk for a while. You get more time to react.'

Seaton slipped his hand into his pocket and gripped the pistol tightly. He was walking into Bergen. A few figures passed along the other side of this narrow street, stooping and muffled against the cold. It could be anywhere.

Trevor seemed to know his way about very well. They went swiftly through a small arch and down another narrow street, their feet slipping on the slushy cobbles.

On a windswept corner by a shuttered bakery Trevor paused and whispered, 'Got your gun?' He did not wait for a reply. 'There are two krauts coming. If things get awkward, you take the one on the left.'

Seaton swallowed hard. And he had been thinking it could be anywhere.

Then he saw them, two bunched figures strolling along the opposite pavement, collars turned up, heads down. But there was no mistaking the helmets, the machine-pistols slung across their shoulders. Seaton thought of the man he had seen bundled out of the little room to be killed.

The soldiers saw them and hesitated, peering through the soft snowflakes like men-at-arms from an ancient tapestry.

Trevor raised his hand. '*Guten abend!*'

The soldiers bobbed and grinned, and one called something in Norwegian.

Trevor walked on without looking back. Then he said, 'If you speak to them in German they think you're God's gift.' He looked at Seaton. 'But they shouldn't have been here. Probably looking for a drink, or a woman.'

A small, elderly van, overloaded with empty fish boxes, clattered across the cobbles and halted, steam rising from the radiator.

Trevor walked unhesitatingly to the cab and said, *'Kjor meg til Brynjulf.'*

The driver was so swathed in clothing and scarves that he looked like a mummy. He gestured at Seaton, and Trevor shook his head. *'Nej.'*

Trevor explained to Seaton, 'He wanted to know if you've been here before.' He opened the door for him. 'So you'll have to kneel down and put this scarf round your eyes.'

Seaton crouched and felt the gears grind into action. Who were they protecting? Themselves, him or their prisoner?

It was an uncomfortable journey, and Seaton tried to picture the various places they passed. He caught the heavy smell of fish and heard the clank of winches. Then more traffic sounds and a girl laughing. Snatches of song and music, the scent of hot food.

Eventually the van lurched to a halt, and Trevor said, 'Here we are.'

He helped Seaton to the ground, and when he removed the scarf he saw they were both inside a small hallway, with the street door closing behind them. He heard the van grinding away again.

An inner door was flung open, and Seaton saw a man in a leather coat and patched engineer's trousers. He was slightly built, but had great, compelling eyes which seemed to dominate his face.

He nodded to Trevor and then strode across to take Seaton's hand in his.

'Welcome. I am Brynjulf. I command here.' He glanced calmly at Trevor. 'No matter what you may have heard.'

There were several other men in the adjoining room, and one stepped into the hallway and asked, 'Are you armed?'

Seaton nodded and put his hand in his pocket.

But Brynjulf shook his head. 'No. Keep it. We trust each other here. Life is short otherwise.'

Trevor said curtly, 'I think we must talk.'

'Yes.' The man nodded impassively. 'But first we drink.'

148

II

The Trap

SEATON SAT with his elbows on the table, thinking of that other time, the great, glowing stove. Here it was not very warm, and the house had a damp and neglected air about it.

There was tension too, and as he watched the Norwegian, Brynjulf, pouring another round of aquavit, he guessed it was not the first time that he and Trevor had disagreed.

Trevor leaned back on a rickety chair, squinting against the one naked light bulb which lit the room.

'A bargain is a bargain.'

Brynjulf raised his glass. '*Skal!*' He smiled, his huge eyes glowing. 'Bargains can be changed, my friend.'

Seaton left his glass untouched. He said suddenly, 'My orders are to take the passenger and the device. What has *changed?*'

The Norwegian regarded him thoughtfully. 'From my point of view, nothing.'

Trevor said wearily, 'The passenger is Professor Paul Gjerde.'

Brynjulf snapped, 'Traitor! A damned collaborator! He should be shot, and that is better than he deserves.'

Trevor explained, 'Gjerde worked at the university here. As

you have been told, he is something of an expert in propulsion fuels. When the Germans occupied Norway, he volunteered to go to Berlin, and later to a secret laboratory in Stettin. I don't suppose he saw himself as a traitor, but he was most certainly an opportunist, a professional scientist who put his work before country. At the time it seemed unlikely that Norway would ever be free again.'

Seaton looked at Brynjulf. 'What is your plan?'

He grimaced. 'Kill the swine, and then get on with the war.'

Seaton thought of London, the patient hopes for an invasion into Europe. A sight of the end, if not the end itself.

'This secret equipment could be vital to the Allies. British towns and villages have taken a lot of bombing in the past four years. Another new hazard, more deaths and destruction might be too much. And at a time when we may be turning the corner.'

'You sound like the B.B.C.' Brynjulf shrugged. 'But you must see it our way, too. Bombing and possible invasions are difficult to translate into daily reality. We are occupied, you are not. You think of winning, we hope first for survival.'

Trevor said desperately, 'Traitor or not, Professor Gjerde is now prepared to help the Allies. Killing him would serve no purpose, and might do untold harm.' He looked at Seaton. 'I was to take you to him. Only by showing you to be what you are could we convince him of our intentions, and that we would keep our part of the arrangement. Instead—' he glared at the Norwegian, '—we have this bloody-minded bandit to contend with!'

Brynjulf smiled gently. 'Now, Lieutenant, this is *my* bargain. You have seen that great floating gantry in the harbour? It is the largest in Norway, and very new. I was one of those forced to build it. In turn, it will be used at the yard where they are to assemble U-boats in sections. But it is more than a mere crane, it has become a symbol. You can see it from all over the town, standing there like an idol from Nazi Germany!'

Trevor groaned. 'For God's sake!'

The Norwegian ignored him. 'In addition, it supplies power to the dock and several smaller installations.' He nodded slowly, his eyes like black olives. 'I can see you understand, Lieutenant!'

'You want me to destroy it.'

'Yes. Then you can take the Quisling and his secrets away with you.'

'And if I refuse?'

'We kill him anyway, and find another method of destroying the gantry.'

Even the other men in the room had crowded closer to watch Seaton's reactions.

Trevor said, 'You don't have to decide just yet.'

'But I do.' He was suddenly angry. 'I have a submarine and a company which relies on me. I didn't come here to play games, or to discuss the ethics of war. I'm one of those who has to fight the bloody thing, in case you'd all forgotten. But, unlike you, I have to obey orders. I can't go off and do little jobs here and there as I choose.' He looked at Trevor and said bluntly, 'I'd like to see this professor. It's what I came for.' He turned to Brynjulf. 'Then, I'm leaving.' He watched his face and added quietly, '*And* I'll knock down the gantry for you. Satisfied?'

Brynjulf looked at Trevor and spread his hands. 'You see? A most reasonable young man.' His face split into a grin. 'I will see it is done!'

Trevor sighed. 'Very well. Tonight you can stay here, David. First thing tomorrow we'll get you to meet Gjerde at wherever they're holding him. After that it will be up to you.' He grinned ruefully. 'We always seem to be giving you a lot on your plate.'

Seaton looked away. 'I'd not forgotten that either.' He thought of the devastated fjord, the scattered flotsam. 'That girl who was with you. Is she all right?'

Trevor nodded, his face expressionless. 'Yes. She is my radio-operator. A very brave girl.'

'I see.' He did not see at all. In some strange way he felt cheated, excluded by Trevor's news.

Trevor said casually, 'You'll probably meet her before you shove off. She's here in Bergen.'

Brynjulf was busy passing instructions to his companions. Then he pulled on a heavy coat and said, 'Take care, Lieutenant. You will be on the streets tomorrow. Watch your tongue, and every move you make.'

'Don't worry, I will.'

'Jens said you were a good choice.'

Seaton looked at him. 'You knew him then? I thought he was a fine man.'

Brynjulf walked round the table and laid one hand on Seaton's shoulder. 'You see, my young lieutenant? You are not one of our sort. Maybe you are all the better because of it.' He left the room without further explanation.

Trevor lit a cigarette and said quietly, 'He means that you are not made for this work.' He held up his hand. 'No, listen, David. Just now, he tricked you. He spoke of Jens, and you reacted as he knew you would to something or somebody familiar. You admitted you knew Jens, that you had met him before he died. Can you imagine what the Gestapo would have dragged out of you?'

Seaton nodded. 'I'm sorry. It's a different war.'

'No. Only the weapons vary.'

'I'll try and be more watchful.'

Trevor smiled sadly. 'You stay as you are, Daivd. Leave the dirty work to us. Together, who knows what we might come up with?' The moment of truth was past and he said, 'Now, about tomorrow.'

Brynjulf leaned against the wall and watched as Seaton gulped down some black coffee and finished the remains of a crude sandwich.

It was very early in the morning and intensely cold.

Brynjulf looked at his watch. 'Better you not shave, Lieutenant. You will look more like a fisherman this way, yes?'

There was no sign of Trevor, and Seaton was getting tired of asking questions and never getting a straight answer.

'What now?'

'I have a young guide for you. The son of a friend. His name is Thor and he has dreams of becoming a hero. His English is "not so hot", as you would say, but his head is firmly on his shoulders. He will take you to a café by the fish market. It will be busy there. Better for you, and harder for the enemy to watch what is happening.'

Somebody clattered past the house ringing a bicycle bell.

'Time to go now.' Brynjulf led him into the damp-smelling hallway. 'Good luck. Once you have spoken with Gjerde, and he knows who you are, we will proceed with our plan.' He shrugged. 'I regret I had to bargain. But it was necessary.'

A round-faced boy of about fifteen was waiting in the street.

'This is Thor.'

Brynjulf glanced quickly up and down the street and then stepped back into the house.

Thor nodded. 'We go.'

Curiously, it seemed less dangerous in the early daylight. There were plenty of people about, bustling through the narrow streets towards the harbour and the shops. Seaton tried not to think about Drake and the others, out there somewhere, submerged and enduring the damp misery of waiting.

A small scout car rattled past with four German soldiers inside it, looking neither right nor left, heads hunched down in their field-grey coats.

Seaton watched them, surprised that he could without flinching. *The enemy.*

Thor grimaced. 'Pigs!'

Seaton glanced at him. A pleasant-faced boy who could easily be scarred for all time by this sort of work. If he survived the war he might end up as some sort of gangster, his need of danger too strong for daily routine.

Seaton caught the powerful aromas of fish, and remembered the van ride. The driver must have gone in a complete circle to make sure they were safe. They had reached this far in less time on foot.

Some people nodded or called out to Thor, but were careful to avoid looking at his companion. Seaton wondered if they knew what he was up to.

'There!' Thor pointed across a small square. Jammed between two shops, as if for mutual support, was a café, its windows already steamed over and several people coming and going.

'I keep watch. You go in.' Thor was very definite, even if his English was poor.

'Who will I meet?'

Thor grinned. 'All ready, Chief. You know when you get there.' He stuck his hands in his pockets and strolled towards the next corner.

In the next few moments everything was compressed into a fast-moving sequence, as in a dream or a nightmare.

Seaton reached the door and was just beginning to push it open when it happened. There was a violent squeal of brakes and several harsh shouts. At that exact moment he saw the girl sitting at a table facing the door, exactly as he had remembered her and re-created her in his mind so often.

No wonder he did not need to be told who he was meeting.

Trevor would understand. Had understood.

He saw her eyes widen, even found a split second to see a customer's hand stiffen in mid air, coffee spilling unheeded across the table.

'Halt!'

Boots thudded on the street, and Seaton swung round, knowing he must keep away from her. He watched uniformed figures charging amongst the fish stalls, and a camouflaged Mercedes stopping further along the square.

Then he saw Thor. He was walking towards him, hands in pockets, his face as white as death. Beyond him a helmeted soldier stumbled and almost fell headlong as he yelled again, *'Halt! Hände hoch!'*

Thor kept walking, and when he knew Seaton had seen him and was not in the café he yelled, *'Run! Trap!'*

The rattle of automatic fire was the last thing Thor heard. The bullets ripped him across the back and shoulders, hurling him face down on the wet snow, blood running amongst the cobbles in a bright scarlet mesh.

Doors slammed on the far side of the square, boots grated and clattered as more soldiers ran towards the café.

The man who had fired his automatic-pistol walked warily towards the spread-eagled body, as if he expected Thor to leap up and attack him. It was a German N.C.O. who looked like something left over from the Kaiser's war. Fat and bulging in his greatcoat, his neck hung in folds across his collar.

Then he bent over and pushed Thor's body with his boot. The boy rolled on to his side, his eyes still wide open, blood flooding from his mouth.

Seaton forgot everything but the look on Thor's frozen features. He bounded across the cobbles and hit the N.C.O. in the stomach with all of his strength. He saw the man's face change from anger to fear as his helmet rolled away and Seaton hit him again in the face, the pain lancing up his arm like a bullet.

Then something exploded against his head and he was falling, and there were boots closing in all around him like an angry black forest. More pain, all over, agonising, then, mercifully, nothing. Oblivion.

Seaton did not know how long he was unconscious, and

when his reeling mind slowly returned to him the pain almost finished him again.

He lay quite still, knowing he was in a small, bare room without windows and that he was lying on a rough bed. There was a table and two chairs in the room, and he somehow knew there was a man standing just behind his head. His eyes moved painfully from table to wall. He found it hard even to do that, and his whole being throbbed with pain. He wondered if they had broken his ribs or given him some terrible internal injury. Then he tried to remember. Piece the fragments together. The girl's startled eyes, and Thor walking with elaborate disregard for the bellowing sergeant. The clatter of gunfire, the figures standing around the little scene like waxworks, bonded together in that split second of death.

Seaton heard someone whistling and a tap running. Feet clicked on the floor above, and he thought he could hear a typewriter. Where was he? Police station, or already in the hands of the Gestapo?

With a start he realised that his overcoat was missing and so was his blue battledress jacket. He was wearing just sweater and trousers and his old scarred boots.

So they knew. A British officer. Right here in Bergen. He tried again to think clearly, to prepare himself.

Feet grated behind him and he saw his guard for the first time. A German soldier with a machine-pistol cradled on his forearm, pointing directly at the bed. He was young, on edge. Maybe he had been one of those soldiers at the café.

The German moved away and pressed a button by the door. As if from miles away Seaton heard a bell ringing.

More feet in the passageway, voices in low pitch. Then the door was flung open and an N.C.O. marched into the room, his eyes fixed on Seaton.

'*Stehen Sie auf! Schnell!*' He gestured with his pistol. 'Up!'

Seaton saw two more figures entering the room, but all but lost them again in a swirling mist of pain.

'Take your time.' One of the misty figures moved around him like a ghost. 'You have had quite an ordeal.'

The soldiers, confused by their superior's polite attitude, struggled to assist Seaton to one of the chairs. He sank into it, gritting his teeth, trying not to faint.

The picture swam vaguely in front of him, then settled and sharpened. The table was no longer empty. On it was his battle-dress, the tarnished stripes on the shoulders gleaming faintly in the overhead lights.

In the chair was a naval officer, and just behind him another.

The one at the table pressed his fingertips together and regarded Seaton for several long moments.

'I am Kapitän zur Zee Hans Vogel. This is my assistant, Kapitänleutnant Gunter Habeit.' He touched the crumpled uniform carelessly. 'We know who *you* are, of course.'

Of course. Like Venables. In fact, he was very much like him. Austere, coldly efficient. Intelligent. The lieutenant commander had a white-topped cap beneath his arm. So he was or had been a U-boat commander. Maybe from the Bergen base.

The captain said evenly, 'Now, before you try and tax your brain with some wild story, let me explain your situation.'

Seaton felt sick, but made himself sit very erect and still.

The voice continued in accentless English, 'But for our arrival at the scene of your, er, arrest, you might have been kicked to death. As it is, you are a very fortunate man.'

'That Norwegian boy was less so, Captain!' He barely recognised his own voice. It was just a croak.

'One of the bitter facts of war. The military police wanted him for questioning. He failed to respond to the challenge and was shot trying to escape.'

Seaton felt a tiny warning in his mind. The captain was trying to draw him out. He recalled Trevor's words about being tricked. Would he have heard of his capture? It seemed more important that the girl should know he had been trying to warn her. Save her.

Captain Vogel said, 'Both my assistant and I have served in *Unterseeboote*, which is why it was doubly fortunate that we were able to save you. Now I wish to give you some advice. Please take it, for all our sakes.' He glanced at his assistant. 'Gunter?'

The other officer said harshly, 'We wish to know what you are doing in Bergen. Where you came from, and the name of your ship.' His accent was thick, his manner hostile.

His superior said, 'If you refuse, we cannot help. There are certain forces in Bergen who must be obeyed, even by us. You will be seen as a spy, a terrorist, and interrogated accordingly.' There was something like pain in his voice as he said, 'Believe me, I detest that such things should be. So give me some grounds to save you, and your safety will be guaranteed in a prisoner-of-war camp.'

It was all suddenly crystal clear. There was no point in lying. Nor was there any need. If he broke under torture everybody's life was in real danger.

He said calmly, 'I am the only survivor from a submarine.' He saw the quick glances and added, 'You will know about it, I imagine. The sinking of the *Hansa* in a fjord seventy miles north of here.'

Vogel nodded very slowly. 'Is that so? Tell me about it. I will judge the truth of the matter. But be warned, *Herr Leutnant*, time is short.'

Seaton tried to shrug, but the pain numbed his shoulders like a vice.

'It was an X-craft. We cut the nets after following some coastal craft through an outer boom. Then we laid our charges beneath the *Hansa*.' It was amazing how easily it was coming to him. By reversing the sequence of events and omitting the first part altogether, he could almost believe it had happened. 'Then we hit an underwater obstruction, maybe a spur of rock. The boat started to flood, so I ordered the main ballast to be blown.'

They were both staring at him, and even the two guards were listening fixedly, whether they could understand or not.

'Then?'

'We lost control, the boat began to founder. I got clear. The others went down with the hull. I expect she was destroyed in the explosions.'

Vogel nodded. 'That would explain why there was only one hole cut in the net where the dead diver was found.' He sounded satisfied. 'After that?'

'I must have been found by some Norwegians and hidden. One had a beard, I remember.'

He heard the lieutenant commander say quietly to Vogel, 'Jens.'

Seaton said, 'I was told to come here and try to contact a neutral ship.'

'You would have been captured anyway.' The lieutenant

157

commander smiled complacently. 'So you were in command of the X-craft?'

'Yes.'

Vogel tossed the battledress across the table. 'Your name is being damned by many, but it was a courageous deed on your part, one that any *Unterseeboot* officer would be proud of.' He rubbed his chin. 'Others will hold *very* different views, I fear.'

The door opened and a German sailor stamped to attention beside the table. He said something very quietly to the captain and withdrew.

Vogel sighed. 'I am informed that the officer in charge of this military police headquarters has returned. I will see him at once and explain that you are to be moved immediately into the naval base until an escort arrives.' He stood up, glad to be going. 'Believe me, there was no dishonour in telling you the truth. One day you will know it.'

His subordinate paused by the door. 'Later you will be expected to answer more questions about your operations.'

Seaton watched them leave. The ex-U-boat commander was probably from naval intelligence.

He leaned back in the chair, shutting his eyes against the agony and the pitiless anger which made them smart with emotion.

He heard voices, loud and violent, like dogs barking. Doors slamming, and boots clattering up and down the passageway.

The two guards were getting uneasy and shifting their feet, obviously worried at what was happening elsewhere in the building.

The door crashed open and a young, fair-haired officer in an olive-green uniform strode into the room. On his tunic he wore the death-head insignia of the Waffen S.S.

He stood directly in front of the chair and placed one hand gently under Seaton's chin, lifting it so that the light shone on his face.

'So.' He nodded. 'The British officer. The brave gentleman, *ja*!' His fingers were very smooth and smelt of fresh soap.

Seaton watched him, seeing the pent-up fury and hatred. The man looked half mad, incredibly dangerous.

He glared across Seaton's head at the two soldiers and pointed at the door.

Seaton heard the door close, felt the power of the other man closing round him like a trap.

'And now, I tell you something.' He walked slowly round the chair, his heels clicking on the bare floor. 'You think that because of the "code", the respect of one brother officer for another, that you will be safe.'

Seaton tensed, expecting a blow or worse. He clung to one thought. That he had to stay silent for two days, no matter what. Give the others time to get clear, pass a warning to Drake.

'Answer when I question you!' It was almost a scream.

'I am entitled—' He got no further.

'Here, I am in command. You are entitled to nothing beyond the limit of my orders! *Do you hear me?*'

'Yes.'

'Good,' His shadow moved round the lamp again until he was directly in front of the chair. He leaned back against the table, his features composed, even calm. 'I am glad to know it. If I had returned earlier things would have been different. I do not know if what you told the two officers,' he spat out the words with obvious contempt, 'is true or false. I care even less. But I promise you that when I have done my work you will be eager to tell me everything and anything. Your sort will always hide behind your out-moded conventions and *standards*. Play the game, eh? Or something is not cricket?'

The room was starting to spin again, and Seaton had to fix his gaze on the wall to stop himself from collapsing.

'The intervention by those officers of the naval staff merely delays matters slightly. It will give you time to build your strength for what is to come.'

There was a nervous tap at the door and the commandant swung round angrily. *'Herein!'*

It was a soldier with a sealed envelope. Seaton saw his hand shaking as he held it out to his officer.

He ripped it open and read the short note inside. To Seaton he said, 'A car and escort is waiting. You will go to the naval hospital.' He reached out and touched Seaton's face very gently. 'Enjoy your respite.'

He beckoned to some soldiers outside the door, and once again Seaton was hauled to his feet, his teeth grinding to hold the pain at bay.

Seaton watched the officer's squared shoulders as he strode ahead along a poorly lit passageway. It was an old building, the walls lined with glazed bricks. But at the far end was a narrow rectangle of light. Outside was reality. If only for a brief while.

A door to the left opened slightly and a man in a white coat, wearing small, gold-rimmed spectacles, waited for the commandant to see him.

Seaton felt his heart pounding. Perhaps they had their own doctor after all and had been playing with him, like a cat with a mouse.

The commandant said something sharply and pointed at the floor. There was water everywhere, and the air was heavy with a foul, acrid smell.

'Well, *Leutnant* Seaton.' The commandant faced him coldly. 'You may wish to see something.' He kicked the door inwards with a polished boot, while the soldiers gripped Seaton's arms and pushed him into the entrance.

After the passageway the overhead lights were searingly bright. There were several figures in the room, some in white coats, others in shirt-sleeves, as they paused to watch his reactions.

Lying spread-eagled on the floor, wrists and ankles cruelly tied to ring-bolts, was a naked, bloated 'thing'. You could not accept it as human. Every inch of the bloated flesh was discoloured by bruises and burns, but worst of all was the way the body itself was swollen to incredible and obscene proportions.

The sound which Seaton had heard through his pain in the passageway began again, and he realised with stunned horror that a rubber pipe which ran out between the pinioned man's buttocks was connected to a stirrup-pump which in turn was being worked into a new bucket of water.

He would have fallen but for the rigid hold on his arms. The body was starting to heave with the mounting pressure of water, and a series of inhuman grunts accompanied each powerful thrust of an S.S. man's arms on the pump.

The tortured creature seemed to realise that someone else was present. The head tried to turn, the eyes bulging from a contorted face.

'Enough.' The commandant stepped into the passageway, holding a handkerchief to his face. 'It will take more time yet.'

Seaton allowed himself to be half-dragged, half-carried towards the pale daylight. His mind was screaming, trying to shut out the regular squeak of the stirrup-pump.

Had Trevor recognised him? Did he in the last moments of unspeakable torture realise that Seaton was trying to spare his agonising degradation?

Outside a walled yard a camouflaged car was throbbing quietly, a German seaman sitting at the wheel, and several S.S. men waiting beside it with their Schmeissers.

As he was pushed into the car he turned and looked at the commandant. He was standing in the entrance, smoking a cigarette and smiling.

The car rocked and jolted over the cobbles and then turned towards a main road.

Everything was the same as before, and yet totally different.

Seaton stared out at the muffled townspeople, almost grateful for each stabbing pain as the car gained speed, if only to blot that scene from his mind.

He thought of Jens, of the brave and pathetic boy Thor, and of the girl. He was almost fearful of even remembering her in case she had been in an adjoining cell to Trevor. Waiting or suffering even worse torture.

Ideas wild and desperate played havoc with his thoughts. He would kill himself. Anything but give in to the smiling madman with the death-head on his uniform.

Seaton heard the driver swear under his breath and saw another German car parked across the road. A fish cart was upended, and while its owner waved his hands in the air the occupants of the car gathered round to watch. They were soldiers, and seemed to be enjoying their driver's argument with the Norwegian.

One of the soldiers saw the naval car and grinned hugely. He started to walk towards it, pretending to hold his fingers in his ears to shut out the argument behind him.

Seaton closed his eyes, stunned that his captors could take an interest in a minor collision after what they had just witnessed. After what they probably saw on every working day at the police H.Q.

The rear door was suddenly wrenched open and a voice filled the car. *'Hände hoch!'*

Seaton stared with disbelief. Now he knew he was going mad.

He had to be. The soldier from the other car had whipped a machine-pistol out of his greatcoat and had it trained on the S.S. guards, and as if to a shouted command the other soldiers were also running to surround the vehicle in a tight circle of guns.

The man with the little cart came last, unbuttoning his leather coat, keeping his huge eyes fixed on the motionless occupants. It was Brynjulf.

He saw Seaton and nodded slowly. 'Can you climb down, David?'

Seaton pulled himself towards a door. He heard the nearest guard move too, the sudden click of a safety catch. The response was instant, the murderous hail of bullets cutting the S.S. man down and spattering blood across the terrified driver and shattering the windscreen.

Seaton coughed in the smoke and allowed eager hands to aid him to the street. Their faces were starting to swim and fade.

He gasped, 'Trevor!'

Pistols clattered in the street and were immediately gathered up by Brynjulf's fake Germans.

The Resistance leader said quietly, 'Yes. I know.' His tone sharpened. 'Now. We get you away from here. Quickly.'

They all started towards the other car. All except Brynjulf. As the Norwegian driver swung his car round in a violent turn towards a side street, Brynjulf wrenched open a door and flung a grenade into the back.

Seaton was propped between two of the Norwegians for comfort and security. Nevertheless, the blast almost threw him to the floor, and when he peered through the rear of the careering car he saw a black crater and a swirling funnel of smoke.

Then and only then did his last reserve of strength give out.

12

Gesture for the Dead

LIEUTENANT GEOFFREY DRAKE wriggled his shoulders deeper into his various layers of clothing and made himself check the control panel. If nothing else, it kept him from falling into a dazed sleep, or from counting the minutes since he had last looked at the clock.

Jenkyn was asleep in the battery compartment, and Niven was stretched out on the bunk on the port side of the control room. His back was turned inboard, so Drake did not know whether he was awake or not.

It was cold and damp, with heavy drops of condensation falling from the curved deckhead like rain. On the corticine deck covering, over machinery and dials, and on Drake's head and shoulders.

The boat felt very still as it lay nestled against the burned-out wreck. Drake was uneasy about the one time he had surfaced the boat, just before the dawn which had followed Seaton's departure. A stiff cross-current had swung the hull wildly, and they had slammed against the wreck like a battering-ram. Quite apart from the grinding noise, he had been worried about possible damage. He still was.

Drake had always relied on Jenkyn as a gauge of the security, or lack of it. The little E.R.A. had spent hours going over his printed diagrams of electrical circuits and one of the tail-clutch. He always did things like that when he was bothered. Just to keep his mind busy and ready.

Drake reached up half-heartedly and wiped the steel plating directly above him. But the old towel was already sodden. Stinking with the boat's own sweat of water and oil.

He tried to think, but it was getting more difficult in the foul air. Despite all his watchful care, the air supply was running low. But they dared not surface to charge batteries and ventilate the boat. Even during the night he had heard the pounding vibration of fast engines. It was too damn risky.

It was late afternoon. He yawned hugely, the stubble on his chin rasping painfully on his collar. The skipper would come back tonight. He had to. They couldn't keep on like this. He almost envied Seaton's trip ashore.

He rubbed his gloved hands together. *God damn the cold.*

Niven rolled over and stared at him wearily.

Drake said, 'Go to sleep. Save the bloody air.'

Niven sighed and peered at the clock. 'Is that all it is?'

When Drake remained silent he said, 'Do you think he'll make it back?'

'What a stupid remark.' Drake looked away. 'Course he will. Dave's a real goer.'

Niven lay back and covered his face with his cap. 'This is enemy territory.' He spoke thickly, like a man who has had too much to drink.

Drake watched him. 'I *had* noticed.' He glanced at the door of the W & D compartment and added, 'I'm more worried about the state of the boat. The batteries are getting punch-drunk, and unless we can get weaving soon we'll not have the power to make the rendezvous with the sub.'

'I hadn't thought of that.'

Drake stared at him. 'You wouldn't.' It came out almost savagely. 'Christ, it's getting me down.'

Niven groaned. 'It'll be the same in a thousand years.' The thought seemed to rouse him. 'What d'you reckon will happen to the midget subs which have gone down? I mean, after the war?'

Drake waited, trying to curb his unreasoning anger. 'Depends who wins.'

'But does it?' Niven propped himself on one elbow, his eyes very bright. 'Take Lieutenant Vanneck's boat, for instance. We've written it off, accepted it as a steel coffin. But years from now, we or the Jerries, or even Ivan, will salvage her and stick her up on a plinth with a sort of pride.' He chuckled, 'Think of it, we'll all become valuable relics!'

Drake said sharply. 'You're round the bend, mate!'

Niven regarded him thoughtfully. 'How did you get on with Decia, by the way?'

Drake swallowed hard. 'Decia?'

'Yes. My wife, you know.'

Jenkyn almost fell through the door. 'We'll need more air from the after cylinders, Number One. What about it? I can brew some char then.'

Drake looked at him gratefully.

'Great idea. See to it, Alec.'

'She would hate it if anything happened to me.' Niven did not seem aware of Jenkyn. 'She *hates* wearing black.'

Jenkyn said quietly, 'I seen it 'appen before. We was stuck on the bottom for two bloody days while Jerry flung depth charges about like they was goin' out of fashion. Our navigator completely flipped. One minute he was studyin' 'is precious charts, an' the next 'e was strippin' off stark naked an' makin' for the connin' tower.'

Drake watched Niven's blank features. 'What happened?'

'The Old Man says, "'Ere, Pilot, where the bleedin' 'ell d'you reckon you're goin'?"' Jenkyn's narrow face split into a grin, remembering and savouring the moment. 'Mr. Thomas, that was 'is name, turns and replies, "I'm goin' up to speak sharply to them bastards!"' He rocked with silent laughter. 'An' us lyin' in a 'undred foot o' water!'

Niven flopped on his back and said in a small voice, 'I feel like hell.'

Drake crossed the control room and looked down at him. If anything, he seemed younger than ever.

What would happen, he wondered, if he really told him? That he and Decia had made love in every position he had ever imagined, and a few more she had introduced him to. That they had been too shagged out to move, let alone speak.

He heard air hissing into the pressure hull and breathed deeply.

That was close. Too damn close. But he had acted wrongly, as deep down he had thought he would. He had always wanted to share, be part of something special. David Seaton had left him in command, making him responsible for the boat and his companions.

At the first sign of over-submerged jitters he had cracked. He had *asked* this poor, ashen-faced subbie what he should do. He swore aloud, 'Oh, sod it!'

Then he tried to whistle, but for once *South of the Border* would not come.

Jenkyn watched him gloomily as he waited for water to boil for the tea.

'Just like mother makes!' He looked away, stabbed by his own attempt at humour. Poor old Ma. She was well out of it.

High above their heads, as the shattered bridge of the wreck showed itself through a dropping tide, its clinging weed reflecting the flashing buoys, other shipping went about its affairs.

A few launches pushed through the swirling water, eager to get home before darkness closed in, and two small fishing boats headed towards the quays.

Hardly anyone had heard the brief rattle of gunfire either that morning or later in the day where it was rumoured a German car had been ambushed. By terrorists or patriots, according to your point of view or how you had to earn a living. Either way it would mean trouble, and most people had enough of that already.

In his office near the docks, Kapitän zur Zee Hans Vogel sat behind his big desk, pretending to study the daily report of progress in the new U-boat pens. But his mind was with his son, who was also in the navy. The signal lay hidden under his blotter where his efficient assistant, Habeit, could not see it. *Missing.* His son's ship had been sunk by British motor torpedo boats near the Dogger Bank. *Missing.*

He rubbed his eyes and thought about the young British lieutenant he had seen at the police station. All at once he was glad he had tried to help him, and despite his background and inbuilt loyalty, he was even more pleased he had escaped from the S.S. butcher.

Perhaps, and it was only a small hope so far, his son would be rescued, and somewhere, even now, a British officer would be helping *him*.

From the other desk, Kapitänleutnant Habeit said, 'I have ordered the harbour patrol to be doubled.' He saw his words had not reached his superior.

Habeit knew about the signal. But it was war. The Leader needed firm, dedicated officers. Orders would be obeyed at all times without question. That British officer, for instance. He had known more than he had said. He had admitted being the one who had destroyed the *Hansa*. It might have set back Germany's victory by a year. And all his superior could do was praise him for his courage.

Darkness returned to Bergen's seven hills, and in the police station the thing which had once been a man at last mercifully died.

Seaton opened his eyes, the pain returning instantly. Part of it was caused by tensing his body, as if to protect himself or to withstand a blow.

He was in another room, and he realised it was lit by a small table lamp which was shaded by some cloth to protect his eyes. The lamp made a small arc of light against the opposite wall, and played on a framed picture of some hills, with the sea between them like water in a vast dam.

He tried to move, and realised two things. that he was naked between clean sheets, and that his whole body felt as if it were clamped in sections of armour plate.

A shadow detached itself from the wall and moved silently to the bedside. It was Brynjulf, his great liquid eyes hidden against the soft light.

'How do you feel?'

Seaton winced as the memories flooded back. Thor's blood running out between the cobbles. The German's helmet rolling away. The boots and the agony.

He licked his lips. 'What about the bargain *now*?' He felt the bitterness welling up inside him. 'God, I hope you're satisfied.'

Brynjulf shrugged. 'It was unfortunate. Nobody knew that Thor was wanted for questioning. About some small matter. I am sorry.'

Seaton raised his wrist and looked at his watch, which was

surprisingly unbroken. About the only thing which was intact.

He gasped, 'It's late! I must get up immediately.'

Pictures revolved in his aching mind. The wreck buoys, the launch, Drake listening for his return.

There was someone else by the bed now, a small, round man with scrubbed hands and a grave expression. Without asking, Seaton knew he was a doctor.

The doctor eyed him severely. 'You have suffered, young man.' He snapped on the overhead light, almost blinding Seaton. 'I think you should meet someone before you begin to assert yourself, yes?'

Seaton felt his heart pounding and made himself lie still as he looked around the bedroom. Small, and rather old and quaint. Pictures of fjords and square-rigged ships on the walls, a china Polar bear on the dressing table.

The doctor swung the long mirror of the dressing table towards the bed. 'I should like you to meet *you*.'

Seaton felt Brynjulf levering his shoulders from the bed, and then stared at himself with horror.

Most of his nakedness was covered in bandages and plasters, and the skin which still showed was blotchy with savage bruises.

The doctor pulled the sheets off him completely, reciting the injuries in the same severe tone. 'Four ribs cracked, and a finger on your left hand fractured. Severe bruising, and I did think that a lung might be injured.'

Seaton looked at his face. There was a great bruise above one eye, and he could tell from the soreness on his scalp that some stitching had replaced the Germans' field-dressings.

Even his groin felt on fire, as if his body was falling into separate halves.

Brynjulf said, 'I have had your passenger brought here. When I explained to him what had happened, he agreed to disclose where he had hidden his secret device.' He laid a hand on Seaton's shoulder, easing him back on the bed. 'So you see, my brave friend, you can rest now. I regret that your uniform was needed. It will be left many miles from here, somewhere the Germans cannot fail to find it. They will think you are heading for Sweden, as others have done.'

Seaton shook his head from side to side. 'You don't understand. My boat cannot survive just because I *want* it to. It is small, vulnerable, and can only exist on her very limited resources.' He watched the liquid eyes translating his words into reality. 'But how could *you* understand that?'

The doctor snapped his bag shut. 'I am going now. I have never seen you in my life.' He waved his hat with a flourish. 'Good luck.'

Brynjulf waited for the doctor to leave. 'I had not thought about that.' He rubbed his chin. 'What do you suggest?'

Seaton lay back, staring at a crack in the ceiling. 'We have missed the contact time. It will have to be tomorrow.' He thought of Drake again. *Please God let him be able to cope.* 'You will have to get us out to the wreck. I'll bet the Jerries are combing the whole town for me.'

'That is why your uniform must be found, and quickly.'

The door opened again and he saw her standing in the entrance watching him, her hair very pale against the landing beyond.

He tried to cover his nakedness, but Brynjulf said softly. '*She* took care of you until the doctor came.'

She stood beside the bed and touched his shoulder, her fingers cool, gentle.

'I am so very sorry, David. For what happened, for what they did to you.'

It all came back. The voice, her accent. The long, sloping pier in the fjord.

He reached out and gripped her hand. She did not resist, nor did she return the pressure. He saw that her eyes were wet from crying.

She said, 'Trevor died just now.'

Seaton squeezed her hand. 'Thank God.'

She smiled sadly. 'I saw you warning me in the café. Another minute and the patrols would have been questioning everyone.' She bent over and kissed him lightly, her hair touching the bruise on the opposite side of his forehead.

Brynjulf said, 'You must go now.'

Seaton held on to her hand, suddenly desperate. 'Where?'

'The uniform. I will take it to a train and place it well away from here.'

'No. Leave it. Don't risk your life again, *please*!'

She watched him gravely. 'You must be allowed to escape.

You will have a valuable passenger. We have come this far. It is too late for second thoughts.'

Seaton tried not to see the glaring cell, the water, the moaning, bloated body on the floor. Next time it could be she.

'You'd risk all this for a traitor's safety?'

She nodded. 'Yes.' She released her fingers very gently. 'God be with you, David.' Then she was gone.

Seaton wiped his mouth with his hand. 'You should have stopped her!'

Brynjulf smiled. 'She is doing it for us all. It is her way of showing things.' He looked away. 'The traitor is her brother.'

'Look, Geoff, what *exactly* are we going to do?' Niven was standing, his head slightly bowed below the dripping plates.

Drake swilled some cold tea round his mouth and then swallowed it. It made no difference. The taste remained. Stale and dank.

He had not really expected Seaton to return when he had surfaced the boat. But as the contact time had passed, and *XE16* had sidled awkwardly around the wreck buoys, he had felt disappointed and strangely unnerved. He had opened the hatch and they had sucked at the brittle, icy air as if it was pure wine.

He had postponed the moment of diving, and had hung on, still hoping.

Then Jenkyn had called, 'No go. Take 'er down, Number One.'

He had done that badly, too. They had glanced off a projection on the wreck's bilge, and it had taken long minutes to bring the submarine under control.

Another long day. Endless. Broken only by mechanical checks and taking turns at watchkeeping. Hot tea, benzedrine, a tot of brandy. It was all anyone could keep down.

The air fouled steadily through the day, and Jenkyn said nothing after checking the batteries. He did not have to.

Now it was evening again. Almost time to surface.

Niven said impatiently, 'We can't damn well stay here forever!'

Jenkyn looked at his filthy hands. 'It's a decision, ain't it? I mean, it's *your* decision, Number One.' Jenkyn tried again. 'Look at it this way. If the skipper's bought it, or bin nicked, us stayin' 'ere ain't goin' to solve a thing, right?'

Drake nodded. 'I suppose so.'

'Right then.' Jenkyn watched him. 'An' if either one of them things 'as 'appened, we've lost the bleedin' passenger, too!'

'He means–' Niven recoiled as Drake swung on him.

'I *know* what he means! That I've got to get the boat out of here and double bloody quick! Otherwise there'll be no towing submarine at the rendezvous, or else we'll not be able to reach the position for want of power! You don't have to spell it out.'

'*Sorry.*' Niven turned away, hurt and angry.

Jenkyn persisted, 'You'd leave the skipper, would you?'

Drake rested his head in his hands. 'There's no other way, unless . . .' He looked up. I could get into a suit and swim ashore.'

Niven stared at him. 'Oh, that would be *fine*! You'd go wandering round Bergen, while we'd be left here on our own. We'd never get free, just the two of us, but you'd be out there telling everyone you'd *done your best*!'

Jenkyn squared his shoulders. 'Steady, gents! Life's a bit dicky for all of us at the moment. Let's not start doin' a knees-up, eh?' He watched them, as a man studies the movements of dangerous dogs. 'We've all known this might 'appen one day. So let's get on with it. Surface and take a gander for the skipper. After that, we've no choice but to obey 'is last order.' Even the words seemed to choke him, and he turned towards the lowered periscope as if expecting to see Seaton there. 'But I'll *never* forget 'im, never as long as I live, an' that's a fact!'

His sudden show of emotion had its effect on Drake. He said, 'We will do just that.' He smiled, the effort making him look worse. 'And thanks, Alec.'

But as the time to move drew nearer, Drake felt the same gnawing tension more strongly than ever. They went over their checks, keeping their voices low, even formal, and when the electric motor purred into life it seemed to scrape at his mind like an additional claw.

The motor would not stop again until they surfaced clear of the fjord and switched to the diesel for battery charging. It set the moment of decision better than any recording in the log.

Jenkyn said quietly, 'Pressure's mountin' a good bit, Number One. Better watch it when you open the 'atch or you'll get blown out like a cork.'

Drake nodded, knowing Niven was watching him and waiting for the inevitable.

In fact, Niven did not wait. 'I'll go, shall I? You've all the experience with pumps and hydroplanes.'

Drake replied, 'Yes. Stand by to raise the stick as we lift to nine feet. I hope to God it wasn't damaged when we hit the wreck.'

Niven crouched by the periscope and rested his gloved hands on the grips.

Drake looked at him. *He's loving it. Every bloody minute of it.*

'All quiet.' Jenkyn slammed down his switches. 'Not even a rubber duck waitin' for us.' He glanced across his shoulder. 'Better get goin', Number One.'

Drake swallowed. 'Good idea. Maybe we can hook on to a buoy and listen for a bit longer.'

Cautiously, like one hurt too often, *XE 16* swam towards the surface. Using every ounce of skill and what they had learned on the two previous occasions, Drake and Jenkyn conned the boat into the current, watching the trim, the ticking gyro compass, everything which told them better than words how she was responding.

At nine feet Niven reached for the hoist switch, and after the slightest hesitation pressed it. The hiss as the thin periscope rose from its well was like one combined sigh of relief.

Niven moved round in a circle and then returned to the original bearing, a pinpoint of green on his eye as he picked out a marker buoy.

'All clear. Surface.'

It took another twenty minutes, nudging against a swift current and trying to stay clear of the wreck, before Niven could guide them close enough to the buoy for him to throw a grapnel and make the boat secure on a temporary head-rope.

There was quite a wind blowing offshore, and the surface was choppy with cruising whitecaps. It gave them good cover, but made the waiting uncomfortable. Especially for Niven as he lay prone on the casing as Seaton had done when they had approached the fjord. His teeth chattered violently and his feet felt numb with cold. And yet he was strangely alive and exhilarated. Like someone else.

172

The hands of the clock moved round, and twice a power boat surged noisily abeam, only to disappear into the darkness.

Drake listened to Niven's boots on the casing and then said, 'He'll not come, Alec. I just *know* it.'

He moved to the periscope and raised it quickly, swinging it towards the town, to the black mass of piers and quays where he had watched the boat carrying Seaton ashore.

How would he explain it when they got back to base? What would the others think of him? He shook himself like a dog emerging from a stream. What the hell was the matter with him? Worrying about other people's opinions when David was out there on his own.

The speaker above the control panel squeaked, and then he heard Niven's even voice. 'Boat approaching the next buoy. Could be it.'

Drake also heard the metallic scrape as Niven cocked his machine-pistol.

Jenkyn licked his lips. 'I never done it before, but I'm doin' it now.'

'What?'

'Prayin'.'

The journey from the 'safe house' to the harbour took longer than Brynjulf had expected, and for several reasons. The streets were full of military vehicles and small squads of soldiers, helmeted and heavily armed. Even if the Germans did not know exactly what had happened, they were taking no chances and putting on a show of force.

Another reason was Seaton himself. Once out in the open he felt worse, and had a powerful Norwegian holding his arm to help him from one street corner to the next. Other shadowy figures flitted ahead of them, or padded along to cover their slow progress from behind. Brynjulf's whole Resistance group seemed to be present, and as ready as their enemy to fight.

Brynjulf had sent some men to collect the secret device from its hiding place, although Seaton did not know where that was. What he did know was that the frightened professor, Paul Gjerde, was just a few paces behind him, protected and guarded by two villainous looking fishermen who kept their hands in their pockets.

No one in Whitehall need worry, Seaton thought bitterly. If the Germans came for them now, the girl's brother would die instantly at the hands of his captors.

He remembered his mixed feelings when he had come face to face with Gjerde. The thought of her speeding into the night to lay a false trail for the Gestapo and military police, with the real chance of capture and torture, made him sick with anger and disgust. At the same time he felt uneasy in the man's presence. He was younger than he had expected, with wide eyes and a sort of pathetic innocence about him. He could see the girl in his face, would have known them as brother and sister anywhere.

Seaton leaned against a wall, grateful for a pause, as someone darted up the street to consult with another lookout.

Brynjulf said, 'Not long now. The boat is waiting. We are a little late, but . . .' He shrugged.

A car roared across the end of an adjoining street, and Seaton said, 'You did not tell *her* about the gantry, did you?'

'No. As it happens, I neglected to involve her further.'

'That *was* good of you.'

Brynjulf ignored the sarcasm. 'And now she will be away when the explosion comes. One less in danger.'

'Will there be reprisals?'

'There are always reprisals, my friend.' He waved to the lookout and they started to move again.

Seaton's mind grappled with the complexity of what had begun as a well-planned mission.

As usual, the people at the top had failed to recognise the personalities on the ground.

Trevor and Brynjulf had bargained for the device and the hostage. The girl had been used to bring her brother firmly to the side he had deserted. But Gjerde had been too frightened, or had been long enough under German supervision, not to take even her presence for granted. He had understood Brynjulf and Trevor better than they had him, and had wanted to see an outsider, a British officer.

Seaton turned and glanced at the trio behind him. What was Gjerde thinking, he wondered? Because of his actions he had brought death to many. To the *Hansa's* ship's company, to the Norwegian hostages, to Thor and Trevor, and God alone knew how many others would follow. And probably it was too late to prevent the Germans exploiting his work anyway, so still more people would die when the secret rocket was brought to bear on England.

He caught the tang of fish and salt water and found he was quickening his pace, despite the pain in his battered body. He thought of her bathing his injuries, stripping away his crumpled uniform, touching him.

'We are here.' Brynjulf drew a pistol from his coat.

A few figures hurried from the stone stairs which led to the water and muttered with their leader.

Brynjulf nodded. 'It is in the boat.' He watched his men hustling the professor down the stairs. 'My men will take care of you. The harbour-master's men were unwilling to risk it this time.'

Seaton said, 'The device. Is it all there?'

Brynjulf gripped his arm. 'Yes. And so is the gantry. So we must trust one another, yes?'

Seaton peered at his watch. 'You had better stay here. The submarine may have gone.'

'I will wait for my men to return, with or without you.' He put his arms around Seaton's shoulders, as Jens had once done. 'Maybe we will meet again one day.'

Seaton turned to go but still hesitated. 'If you see her...'

'I will tell her you asked about her.' He pushed him to the stairs. 'Now *go*.'

The boat surged away from the stairs, bucking as it rolled amongst the choppy water of the harbour. An aircraft roared suddenly overhead, ripping the air apart with its throaty growl. Seaton noticed that four tiny warning lights had been switched on, as if on the clouds. Of course, the German air control would switch on lights above the gantry when a friendly aircraft was returning to base. Even as the thought touched his mind the red lights went out again. He recalled his intelligence folio and the section on local anti-submarine patrols. The aircraft was probably returning to Stavanger in the south.

A man seized his arm with excitement, apparently unaware of Seaton's injuries. He pointed across the port bow as something low and dark moved very slowly between the buoys.

Another man stood up in the swaying hull and tried to light his pipe. It took four attempts, with the matches flaring out like small Very lights. A crude but effective signal.

The launch swung round to run parallel with the little submarine, and Seaton heard the fenders being dropped over the side to withstand the shock.

He watched as someone, probably Niven, threw a line across, and heard him call, 'Is that you, sir?'

Seaton waved to him, realising he probably looked a total stranger in his borrowed clothing. *'Yes!'*

Far away across the harbour a narrow searchlight licked out and touched an anchored storeship. Seaton felt a new sense of urgency, but knew it was pointless to say anything. These Norwegians were unfamiliar with submarines of any size, and if he started to hurry them they would probably capsize the boat altogether.

The two hulls pounded together and a man fell headlong. Niven took in the slack of his line and then reached out to receive a heavy oilskinned bag which he then passed hastily through the hatch.

Seaton gestured to Gjerde. 'You next. Watch your step.'

He saw the man nod and scramble awkwardly across the leaping spray. Then he too was hidden within the hull. One of the Norwegians thrust his pistol back into his pocket. To the last he had expected treachery, and had been ready to kill.

The others watched Seaton pull himself painfully over the grinding gunwale, and, with Niven's help, make his way to the hatch.

With a coughing roar the launch swung away and headed back towards the shore.

Niven was shouting, 'You're hurt! Here, let me take an arm!'

But Seaton waited, knowing something was wrong. The launch's engine was too loud.

He gasped, 'Another boat! Patrol!'

As he spoke he saw a searchlight stab from the darkness and fix the harbour-master's launch with a great, glacier-like beam. He thought he heard someone yelling through a loud-hailer, and then saw the patrol boat moving across the water at top speed, the stem throwing back a great bow wave as high as her forecastle.

Red tracer ripped from her deck, swept across the escaping launch, surrounding her with leaping feathers of spray. Then the gunners found the range and poured a long volley into the launch, splitting it apart in a torment of broken woodwork and corpses.

The patrol slowed down, cruising through the broken water, thrusting the fragments aside with her raked stem. The searchlight remained switched on. As something dark floundered by a piece of wreckage a man on deck fired just one shot, and all movement ceased. The light went out.

'Get me below, Richard.'

With his face ice-cold from spray and pain, Seaton lowered himself into the dimly-lit control room. He saw their faces, the mixed expressions of anxiety and relief. The passenger was squatting beside the W & D door, like a trapped animal trying to avoid discovery.

'I–I thought that gunfire was for us.' Niven dropped to the deck with a thud.

'A bit longer and it would have been.' Seaton watched Drake's eyes. 'They killed all of them.'

Drake let out a great sigh. 'Thank *God* you're okay! You look as if you've been through a kind of hell.' He nodded to Jenkyn. 'Let's get the blazes out.'

Seaton was getting light-headed again. Perhaps the doctor had given him something.

He touched the curved deckhead and made himself move to the chart table. *XE 16* felt good. Was she pleased to see him, too? He felt vaguely disturbed, disappointed.

He said flatly, 'Belay that. We're not going. Not just yet.'

Drake stared at him. 'But, Dave, everything's going rotten on us. If we put down again, we might never make it to the rendezvous.'

Seaton lowered himself on to his elbows and peered at the chart, shutting them all out, sharing his thoughts only with the submarine.

Drake had been on his way. Running without waiting. He was obeying orders, but how often had he done that before?'

'I'm going to blow the gantry.' He heard someone gasp. 'I promised.'

He thought of the S.S. officer, watching him from the doorway, smiling. The one he had taken for a doctor, in a white coat with tiny flecks of blood on it. The silent people around the café, seeing a boy shot down and unable to do anything about it.

'And we don't have to wait too long. There have been several planes about. As soon as they switch on the aircraft warning lights I will start the attack.' He tapped the chart with a pencil. 'Richard, you plot the bearings as I give them. We know the approximate size of the floating platform, so we'll make the run-in accordingly.'

A symbol, Brynjulf had described it. Well, *XE 16* would leave a different one. The German staff and the Waffen S.S. too, they would all know that for once they had been caught out. He remembered the excited cruelty on the S.S. officer's features. *Something is not cricket.*

He waited for Niven to take over the chart and then staggered painfully to his place at the periscope. Each action was agony, and when he lowered himself to his knees he felt like an old man.

'Dive...dive...dive. Twenty feet. Steer–' He glanced at Niven. *'Well?'*

Niven replied, 'Course to steer is one-six-zero.'

'Right. Now stay with it.' Seaton realised that his mind was probably sharper than theirs. They had been penned in this terrible atmosphere for two days. While he...He snapped, 'Steer one-six-zero. Revs for three knots.'

He clung to the periscope, listening to the familiar sounds of inrushing water and murmuring pumps as Drake kept the boat trimmed.

Jenkyn said, 'Ship's head one-six-zero, sir.'

Seaton nodded. 'Very good.' There was an edge to his voice he could not understand, a sharpness which should have been doused by his pain.

'Twenty feet, Skipper.' Drake was different, too, Subdued.

Seaton watched the red second-hand on the clock ticking round, and pictured the harbour hidden in darkness overhead. The tension was almost physical, and he glanced around him, seeing the crouching Norwegian professor, still dazed by what was happening. He, like the others, probably imagined he was in the hands of a madman. One second he was being rescued from the Resistance, and the next he was safe aboard a British submarine. But escaping, no. He was suddenly involved in something over which he had no control at all.

A fast pair of screws rushed overhead, drumming against the

hull like a train tearing through a station. But no Asdic. It was probably a police patrol, or the one which had poured the murderous tracer into the launch.

He saw Niven, gripping his stop-watch as if life depended on it, a pencil held point-down on the chart. Jenkyn's narrow shoulders, his head thrown back characteristically to watch his controls.

Seaton looked at the oilskin bag, left where Niven had put it. It might contain a vital secret for the Allies, or a dead codfish, for all he knew.

Niven said, 'Now, sir.'

'Periscope depth.'

He dabbed his mouth with the back of his hand. His fractured finger stuck out away from the rest, and he had a desire to laugh. It reminded him of one of his father's old girl friends. Little finger sticking out as she sipped tea with borrowed refinement.

'Nine feet, Skipper.'

The periscope showed him very little, except that the sea was choppy, and often obscured the lens for several seconds at a time. Low cloud. No sign of a searchlight. He swung the handles carefully, every move on the deck a stabbing agony. How many ribs did the doctor say? Only four? They felt like a broken wicker basket.

He steadied the periscope and saw the far-off wink of green lights. They had come a long way from the wreck.

He said, 'Wreck bears three-four-zero.' He swung the periscope round once more.

Niven responded in the same strained voice. 'I suggest you bring her round to starboard in that case, sir. Steer one-six-five.' To the control room at large he added, 'The current seems stronger than I allowed for.'

Nobody answered.

Seaton gripped the handles until his hands were welded to them. There must be another plane coming in. He saw the four warning lights shining down from the sky, glinting red stars.

He said softly, 'Dead on course. The target is right across our bows. About half a cable.' He looked at Drake's stubbled features. 'Take her down. Sixty feet. Can't afford a second go. If we push our luck we'll hit the harbour wall on the far side.' His mind clicked into position. 'Revs for one knot.'

The deck tilted very slightly, but he kept his eyes on the ticking red hand.

'Should be under it now, sir.'

He nodded, afraid even to speak. He could see it in his mind, feel it towering over them, the colossus which Brynjulf and others had been forced to build.

The hull gave a violent shudder.

Seaton said, 'Stop engine.' He saw Gjerde wrapping his arms round his knees like a passenger in a crashing aircraft. He explained, 'It's all right. We've grounded.' He looked at Niven. 'Nice work. Depth, tide, all perfect.' They would have hit the wall, or ground into thick, suffocating mud if they had made an error of just a few feet.

For a moment longer they stood or sat quite motionless, listening, and imagining.

Only the soft purr of the disengaged electric motor remained to break into the stillness.

'Release starboard cargo. Four hour setting.'

Niven swung the basket-wheel and they felt a slight tremor as he reported, 'Gone, sir.'

Seaton pictured the massive platform above them. Almost square, it made little difference where they placed the charges. The height and tremendous weight of the gantry would do most of the work.

'Release the port cargo.'

Niven took the other wheel with both hands and put some weight on it. He said, 'Stiff, sir. I'll have another go.'

Seaton watched Niven's shoulders crouching over the wheel, could feel his frustration. There was a grating sound which ended abruptly in a loud click.

Niven turned and looked at him, his mouth moist. 'Cargo refuses to release, sir.' He gestured behind him. 'But the contact is unbroken.'

Seaton said, 'Try again.' He was amazed at the calm tone of his voice.

There had been tales of side-cargoes which had refused to budge, or had exploded prematurely when they dropped off. This was only different in one way. The charge was still fixed to the hull, but the fuse set to fire in four hours had engaged and would not return to a safe setting. *XE 16* had been transformed in seconds from a submarine to a live bomb.

Drake said softly, 'That's torn it.'

Niven shook his head. 'Still won't budge, sir.' He glanced up at the deckhead. 'If I went outside . . .'

'You'd probably detonate the charge.' Seaton kept his voice low, knowing how Niven felt. 'We've four hours. Time to get clear. If we have to ditch, we'll take our chances outside the harbour limits.'

He saw Gjerde staring at him and then at the control panel, as if to discover his fate.

Seaton added, 'Bad luck.'

They all turned as Niven said, 'We hit the wreck a couple of times.'

'You didn't say anything.' Seaton looked at Drake. 'Was it serious?'

Drake moved his hands in the air, his eyes red-rimmed with strain. 'How the hell do I know? I was worried about you, and when you came aboard back there all I could think of was getting out. Job done, medals all round, something like that.' He fell silent.

'I see.' There was nothing more to say. Perhaps it was true, but Drake had gone through enough hazards to know that only the ever-vigilant stayed alive. Anyway, once they started to move again the faulty side-cargo might explode instantly. End of problem.

'Stand by.' He steadied himself against the lowered periscope, wishing that his heart would leave his throbbing ribs in peace. 'We'll go out stern-first.'

Jenkyn adjusted his position on his little seat and said, 'They do *say* that if you keeps yer mouth open when the thing blows up it lessens the chance of a 'eadache.'

Seaton nodded. 'No doubt about it.' It was fantastic about Jenkyn. He had a sort of blind faith in him. Unshakable. Perhaps he knew there was no point in worrying about anything if the charge did explode.

'Slow astern.'

The screw vibrated steadily, and as compass and inclinometer moved together, *XE 16* slid off her muddy perch and backed slowly into the harbour.

Seaton could feel his teeth grinding together, the cold sweat running down his neck and chest. But there was no split-second realisation, no awful finality of an explosion.

He made himself study the clock's impassive face. It would be a final twist of fate if they had to swim ashore and be captured. He found himself wondering if he would have continued with the attack if Drake had told him about possible damage. He thought of Trevor and the others, and got his answer.

'Stop engine. Slow ahead. Steer three-zero-zero. Eight-five-oh revolutions.' He waited, listening to his orders being made into deeds. 'When you're happy, Geoff, raise her to forty feet.' To Niven he said, 'Give me a course to reach the next position.'

He thought he heard a small sound against the hull, and pictured the two-ton charge hanging from its pivot. The other one was lying astern, the timing fuse gnawing away the seconds and the minutes. One would be quite enough with all that top-hamper overhead. It would be like a giant iceberg capsizing.

'Course will be two-eight-five, sir.'

'Good.'

The depth gauges blurred suddenly, and he imagined that something was overheating. But when he looked round he saw that everything was out of focus, as if seen through a steamy window.

That was all they needed now. For him to pass out. He sat down very gingerly, taking his time.

Gjerde was staring at him fixedly. If only he could ask him what her name was. But he knew he would not ask anyone. Anyone but her.

13

–And Escape for the Living

IT WAS an unreal and nerve-stretching journey from the harbour to the big West Byfjord for each man aboard *XE 16*. Not only were the bearings and courses directly opposite to their original approach, but so too were their reactions. Or so it seemed to Seaton. As he fought against pain and waves of nausea, and tried to keep his command running at her maximum speed, he was aware of the tension around him.

Perhaps it was because they had begun to imagine they would be unable to get free of Bergen. And then when the side- cargo had failed to free itself from the hull the acceptance of death had already been reached. Only the frightened Professor Gjerde suffered in ignorance, knowing nothing of the real danger and fearing only for his own escape.

To achieve what they had, and then to realise that after getting through two minefields and out into broader reaches of fast moving water they were none the less faced with disaster, was enough to make anyone despair.

It was strange too how Niven had come to the fore. Seaton had known from the outset that he himself could not get back on deck without losing consciousness. His injuries gave him no peace, and it was all he could do to hold on. Drake's past skills were all needed as *XE 16* wallowed and porpoised through fresh-water pockets along the fjord, and Jenkyn removed from the helm would be like throwing the wheel and compass overboard.

Seaton had explained to Niven what he wanted, what to look out for. He had seemed almost eager to go on deck, and when he had reported to the control room that they were fast approaching the pair of small islands, still with their watchful searchlights swinging back and forth across the channel, his voice had been steady, matter of fact.

It was a chance they had had to take. To risk a dive and the possible detection by A/S gear laid out on the sea-bed was not worth thinking about, It was hard enough to keep the boat steady as it was. With one massive charge hanging to her port flank, her progress was often haphazard and crablike, with plenty of sweat and curses from both Drake and Jenkyn to keep her under command.

And so with her induction trunk all but lowered, and Niven lying half frozen on her casing, *XE 16* swept between the islands at an impressive speed of nearly seven knots, running her diesel engine and charging the batteries throughout.

As Jenkyn had remarked between curses, 'If only the bloody prof 'ere 'ad the savvy to make a pot o' char, things would be near bloody perfect!'

Seaton knew that Drake was trying to hide his resentment at Niven's role. Even though he was the obvious choice, and no slur against him as first lieutenant, it seemed hard to take, in spite of the nearness of violent death.

Seaton's head struck the periscope hoist and made him gasp with pain. Tired almost to exhaustion, and sick from a dozen different pains, he had nearly gone under, his forehead lolling forward like that of a corpse. If it had been the other side of his head, and he had banged the great, blackened bruise, he knew he would have screamed aloud.

None of the others had seen it, thank God. None except Gjerde.

Seaton's dismay seemed to bring him to life in some way. He wriggled past the chart table, scrabbling on his hands as the boat staggered violently in a deep trough.

He exclaimed, 'I forgot, Lieutenant. I have a flask. Some brandy, I think.' He started to search through his stained and creased overcoat.

Seaton was about to refuse his offer when Gjerde added vaguely, 'I must still have it. Nina said to keep it away from the others.' He pulled a small flask from his inner pocket and said, 'There!'

Seaton stared past him, his lips forming the name. *Nina*.

He took it and let the brandy trickle over his tongue. It was tremendous.

'Give some to the others.' He watched the man's face. It was pathetic to see his expression. As if he had been expecting Seaton to smash him in the face.

Jenkyn did not take his eyes from the gyro repeater but took the flask gratefully. 'Ta, mate.'

Drake had a quick swallow and nodded. Embarrassed? Confused? In these past hours it was difficult to accept that you knew anyone that well, Seaton thought.

He dragged himself to the table and rested against it, feeling the heartbeats of his small command throbbing through the frames, the chart table and into his own body.

He studied the chart with extra care, checking each of Niven's little crosses which marked their original passage towards Bergen. Time was fast running out. He would have to decide. *Now*. He peered at the nearest island. Beyond it, and the rest of the chain, lay the sea. Between the scattered islets, some no larger than humps of jagged rock, there were many marks to show where ships had gone down over the years. It was a dangerous place, and certainly with nowhere to beach the boat while they got ashore with their passenger.

At worst, the side-cargo would explode when the fuse ran out. At best, when it was freed from the hull. It was not the sort of hand you would play poker on, Drake would have said.

He turned. 'Blow all your ballast. Trim her as high as you can. Reduce to revs for two knots.'

Air hissed insistently into the ballast tanks, and the deck rolled more steeply as the top half of the side-cargo rose out of the water.

Seaton picked up the handset and said, 'Richard? Get your life-jacket blown up. We may have to ditch.'

To Drake he said, 'Take Professor Gjerde on deck. I'll sit in for you as soon as you've got the trim right.'

Drake was breathing heavily. 'All set.' He looked round desperately. 'I'll stay. You go, Skipper.'

Seaton smiled grimly. 'Like this? I couldn't get ten feet.' He added in a sharper tone 'Move over, and do as I say, for once.'

He caught sight of Gjerde's face as Drake hustled him to the hatch. Even in subdued control room lights he looked like the walking dead. It must be twenty times worse for him, he thought.

To Jenkyn he said, 'I need a volunteer, Alec.'

'Oo would that be d'you reckon?' Jenkyn chuckled. 'Ready, sir, Ship's 'ead is three-two-zero. Dead slow.'

Seaton heard the others moving uneasily on deck. It must be bloody icy up there. Not that it matters now.

He reached for the handset again. 'Geoff? I'm going to try and slip our baby in a second or two. If it blows, there's nothing to say except it's been nice knowing you. If it brews up after it starts to sink, you'll get a beating, but you should reach the nearest land, with any luck.'

He heard something like a sob and knew it was Gjerde. He snapped off the handset and said, 'All right, Alec. Leave the wheel.'

Jenkyn moved to the release gear and spat on his gloved hands.

'Fer what we're about to receive...' He looked Seaton straight in the eyes. 'You're a good bloke, *sir*.'

'You're not so dusty yourself.'

Jenkyn turned away and gripped the basket-wheel. There were fifteen minutes left to run on the fuse. And the one under the floating gantry.

The submarine was starting to yaw and roll through a larger and larger arc. Seaton could hear the frantic movements on the casing as the three men fought to hold on. *XE 16* was broaching-to and pitching from one trough to the next like a steel bottle in a tideway.

Jenkyn gasped, 'Gawd, it shows 'ow important a good cox'n is, dunnit?' He heaved again. 'Come on, you bloody cow! Move your bleedin' self before the 'ole boat comes to bits in me 'ands!'

The passage from Bergen, mostly surfaced and through lively

water and swift currents, must have had some effect. That, plus the boat's uncontrollable rolling.

The red light above the wheel was suddenly extinguished, and Jenkyn fell back with a gasp. 'Gone! Bloody well gone!' He scrambled across to the steering position and spun the spokes, his features screwed up to withstand the explosion.

The hatch was dragged open and Drake yelled wildly, 'Nothing happened! Dear Jesus, it's gone deep!'

Seaton said nothing but stared at the clock, seeing instead the great curved charge falling and pirouetting deeper and deeper into darkness. And it *was* deep hereabouts, with some great underwater canyons not even properly surveyed.

Then he said, 'Take your positions. Passenger to the control room!' As Drake struggled through the hatch, tugging off his life-jacket and showering cold spray over everything, he added, 'Regain original trim and increase to maximum revs. We're heading into open water in ten minutes.'

Gjerde groped past him, touching his arm like a blind man, unable to speak or help himself.

Seaton watched him. *Nina.* If only she and not her brother were here.

Exactly at the set time the faulty side-cargo exploded, the force of the detonation muffled deeply in the unknown place where it had come to rest.

XE 16 had dived by then, feeling her way through the islands and into the waiting sea. They all felt it. A sensation, shielded by the islands, but somehow triumphant just the same.

Their twisting and difficult passage through the various fjords to the open sea completely prevented their hearing the one in Bergen.

It was a very grey dawn, with an obvious build-up of more snow and sleet to come.

A few minutes after Seaton had made his last calculation and marked it on the stained chart, Niven reported. 'Submarine surfacing, starboard bow.'

After that it was a matter of picking up the tow from the other boat and waiting for a passage crew to be sent across in a rubber dinghy.

While some of the ratings from the towing submarine were fixing and testing a telephone wire between the two ill-matched craft, Seaton watched Gjerde being taken with his precious oil-skin bag up and through the hatch to the dinghy.

The control room was full of figures, or so it seemed as the passage crew hurried to their stations and the temporary skipper knelt down to say, 'God, David, you look rough. You'll be all right when you get to the other boat.'

Drake called down, 'Ready, Skipper?'

Seaton shook his head. 'Not going.' He reached out and touched the dripping metal. 'Not this time.'

The relief skipper stood up and nodded. He thought he understood. 'Clear the casing. Cast off dinghy. Call up the sub's C.O. and tell him what's happening.' He looked around at the wet hull and disorder, the litter of voluntary imprisonment. It must have been quite a show, he thought grimly.

Somehow Seaton got himself through both watertight doors and then sprawled out on the bunk-boards above the ranks of batteries.

Once more, they had made it. As weariness and pain closed over him again he thought of the girl he had left behind in Norway. Loss, and not survival, had become paramount.

David Seaton recalled very little of his return across the North Sea. The lieutenant commanding the passage crew had given him a new type of pain-killer with the instant effect of a club across the head. When some of his senses resumed working, nothing seemed to focus in his mind, so that time and distance became blurred and meaningless.

He was dimly aware of being transferred to a depot ship, where his injuries were examined and re-dressed. Then he was wafted out to a destroyer's sickbay, where after a painful injection his mind slipped away again.

It was like dying, he thought, with everyone around you imagining you already dead. Ship, ambulance, gentle hands, quiet voices.

And then one morning he awoke in a room with pale sunlight shining across a medicine cabinet and a small rectangle of carpet. Even without the smells he would have known he was in a hospital of sorts. But it was very quiet. So quiet it seemed to press on his eardrums.

He moved his hands, feeling the splint on his finger, the

constricting pressure of plaster bandages. The worst pain had gone, however, leaving him with a feeling of being badly bruised. And weak.

The door opened and a male nurse stood looking at him.

Seaton asked thickly, 'Where am I?'

'Hospital, sir.'

Seaton groaned. 'For Christ's sake.'

When he looked again the man had gone. Hospital. It was better than a mortuary. He felt terribly hungry. All of a sudden, and without any sort of warning. Ravenous.

The door opened again and a doctor bustled into the room. A surgeon commander, well, that was something. At least it was Navy.

'Glad to have you with us again.' The doctor took his pulse, his face frowning with concentration. 'You even look a bit better.'

'How long, sir?'

The doctor held up a bedside calendar and watched Seaton's head fall back on the pillow.

Seaton said with disbelief, 'Two weeks since the attack.' It sounded impossible.

The commander replaced the calendar. 'At least your eye-sight is not impaired.' He placed Seaton's hand on the bed. 'Fact is, you've had a rough time. Much worse than your Norwegian doctor really knew. One lung was scarred, and the fractures, due to the way you treated yourself after escaping, looked nasty.'

Seaton smiled ruefully. He could feel it now. Perhaps he had always known.

But the doctor had heard all about the attack and what had happened. So he was obviously in the know.

As if reading his mind the doctor explained, 'You are in a small hospital just on the fringe of Edinburgh. It is at the disposal of Special Operations. People come here to recover *quietly*.' His eyes were sad.

Or *die*, Seaton thought.

He said, 'Have you heard anything, sir? I–I mean, about the others?'

'A little. Your people were debriefed pretty thoroughly, and Captain Venables has been up here in the hopes of speaking with you. Now your companions are having a bit of leave.'

Seaton closed his eyes. His father would ask cheerfully, 'Home again? What do you chaps *do* in the Navy?'

'What about my passenger, sir?'

'Not my department.' The doctor grinned. 'Even if I knew I wouldn't be able to say, but I don't.'

'I want to get up.' Seaton moved his legs gingerly. They felt like lead.

'Possibly.' The doctor sighed. 'Frankly, you're a mess. You're lucky to be in one piece.'

'Luckier than some.' He did not hide the bitterness.

The doctor walked to the window. 'Yes. So I heard.' He shrugged. 'But you are my concern. I can't pop you off home, can I? No wife, and I gather your father is not used to looking after bomb-happy lieutenants?'

'No, sir.' God, they were thorough. Venables probably had a file on his father's latest girl friend. 'But I can't stay here.'

'I'll have a word. Something might be arranged. But Captain Venables won't stand for you being placed in one of these convalescent homes, y'know.' He tapped the side of his nose. 'German spies under every bed.'

He turned by the door. 'I gather you did rather well. Pity you can't get away on leave right now. But you know how it is in this regiment.'

The door closed.

Telephones must have got busy, for within a couple of hours Venables arrived. He got straight to the point.

'Sorry you had such a difficult time. It was not as I intended.' He gave a wintry smile. 'But neither was blowing that gantry, by the way.'

Seaton looked at him. 'Was it destroyed, sir?'

'According to aerial reconnaissance, the place is a shambles. Gantry, with two supporting barges, blown to bits, and the top of the crane itself fell across a minesweeper and put her down, too.' His voice hardened. 'I am not sure if I should congratulate you. You had the device and the passenger by then. You might have lost both by your display of bloody-mindedness.'

'It was more than that, sir.' He stared at the ceiling. 'A whole lot more.'

'I'm sure. Anyway, it came off. That time. The enemy knows we were a jump ahead of him. He'll also know before long about our Norwegian professor. I've had several reports of course, and he sounds quite a good catch. I have to trust the *experts* in that field, I'm afraid.'

'You didn't tell me that the Norwegian girl was his sister, sir.'

'I didn't see it would have done any good. We shall have to get her out when things quieten down a bit. She may blow her cover otherwise. And the wretched business of Trevor.' He looked away. 'Bloody awful.'

Seaton tried not to see the gasping creature on the cell floor.

Venables glanced at his watch. 'She and Trevor were quite close, I believe.'

'I see.'

Seaton bit his lip to steady himself and curb the disappointment. He had been a fool, a blind idiot. He should have known or guessed. But the realisation did not help at all.

Venables was watching him shrewdly, 'It often happens, I believe. Mutual trust as a first necessity, and then . . .' He did not elaborate.

Instead he became his usual formal self. 'XE 16 is undergoing a complete refit. She'll be ready for trials and tests in a few weeks. Then, we shall have to see.'

Seaton asked, 'Was it all worth-while?'

'What a curious chap you are.' Venables sat down on the room's only chair. 'Of course it was. Our agents in Europe have known since last year that the Germans were building ramps and launching bases for their new weapons. It was vital for us to get a foot in the door. Gjerde has given us that, and perhaps a lot more. The enemy has concrete sites from Calais to the Cherbourg peninsular, and this is not hearsay, it is confirmed by the R.A.F. Can you imagine what a serious new form of rocket could do to our invasion hopes?' He rubbed his palms together. It sounded like dry parchment. 'We cannot stop them all, of course, but the really big ones, like those being tested in Norway, are something else. They have to be smashed. Otherwise it's another stalemate. You cannot win a defensive war.' He smiled. 'Worth-while indeed!'

'That rules us out then.' Seaton searched his feelings. 'I can't see midget submarines in the streets of France.'

'Hmm.' Venables picked up his cap. 'Anyway, I'll be off now. But I shall be in touch.'

Seaton nodded. *Of course.*

'You've seen what happens in an occupied country. Weigh that against what you have had to do. If we make a mess of the invasion, we'll never get another chance, believe me.'

'Are you sure, sir?'

'As much as I am about anything. If we fail, the Russians will stand fast at some carefully selected line. In time they'll make a non-aggression pact with Hitler, just as they did before the war. The Americans will withdraw and content themselves with clearing out the Pacific and the Far East. It would all become suddenly very *lonely.*'

Seaton smiled for the first time he could remember. 'Just as well you told me, sir. I might have changed my mind the *next* time.'

Venables opened the door. 'You *are* getting better.'

Drake took another slice of toast from the rack and spread some jam on it with heavy, anxious strokes.

Around and above him the big Harrogate house was very still, although he knew Decia was in her bedroom and Niven was somewhere else speaking on the telephone.

Why the hell had he come? Drake munched through the toast without even tasting it. He had started immediately after the debriefing. Telling Niven he didn't want him tagging along, cluttering up the house. Niven had been insistent. Nothing had changed. Or perhaps he had felt the tension which had come between them in Bergen and on the return passage.

Anyway, he was here, but he intended to be damn careful. Maybe he had come because he was inwardly afraid she might blurt out something about their time alone together. Fly into a temper, as he had once seen her do, and let everything out in the open. The thought made him wince.

In fact, in the days since their arrival at the house he had watched Decia with growing astonishment. She actually seemed to be enjoying the situation. Teasing her husband, goading him with a casual comment or look. God Almighty.

The door opened and Niven came into the room. He was wearing flannel trousers and a pullover. The typical Englishman, Drake thought.

Niven sat down and picked up the morning newspaper.

'That was Dad on the phone.'

Drake had to think hard for a moment before he got back his memory of Niven's father. Big, impressive, with a chest of gongs.' 'Is that good, Richard?'

Niven smiled. 'I don't really know. You never do with him. Bloody man.'

Drake asked carefully, 'What's he want?'

He heard Decia's step on the stairway and waited, his fists clenched in his lap. She brushed past him, touching his shoulder lightly.

''Morning, both. What's new?'

Niven said, 'Dad phoned.'

'God.' She shook her head as Drake made to fetch one of the dishes from the sideboard. 'No. I'm watching my figure.'

She was wearing a black jumper which fitted her perfectly, and black slacks, the only patch of colour made by a small red scarf around her throat.

Niven grinned. 'I shouldn't bother. Everyone else here is doing that!'

Drake said, 'Tell us about the phone call, will you?' The blood was roaring in his skull, and he wondered why nobody else could hear it.

'It was about the skipper, actually.'

'Dave?' Drake sat up. 'What's happened?'

'They've got him in some special hospital in Scotland. They can't release him because he's nowhere to go.'

Decia touched her lower lip with her tongue. 'We'll have him here!'

Drake watched her. She would too. One against the other.

She added, 'What's he really like? I met him once. Looked a bit lonely.'

Niven tried again. 'Dad wants him down in our place in Sussex. He's got plenty of staff, naval and otherwise. It's not a bad idea, I suppose.'

'Poor Dave.' Drake felt uneasy. 'I should have tried to see him before this.'

'Get past Venables?' Niven smiled. 'You'll be lucky, I don't think!'

'He's a damn good bloke.' He looked at her. 'Brave, too.'

Niven said, 'He wants me to collect him myself.'

'I see.' Drake looked at his hands. 'Sort of official?'

'Yes. I feel rotten about going off like this and leaving you.'

Drake watched the girl's nail file flashing across her left hand. She had wanted to go with him. It was obvious. If only to get out of this place. She was bored.

She said, 'I wouldn't have gone anyway. Your father's a bit fruity for my taste.' She pouted. 'All heavy breathing and seven pairs of hands.'

Niven took it well. 'You don't exactly hide *your* light under a bushel, do you, *angel?*'

She chuckled, 'If you've got it, flaunt it!'

Drake examined each word as it left his mouth. 'Shall I come? I'd sure like to see Dave, talk over things.' He gestured vaguely to the newspaper's front page, filled with glaring headlines of the Allied progress through Italy. 'Won't be much left for us at this rate. We'll be off to the Pacific to join the Yanks.'

Niven looked at him thoughtfully. 'You think so?'

She exclaimed, 'Oh, for God's sake, you two! War, war, bloody war, is that all you ever think about?'

She walked towards the door, her eyes flashing. But by Drake's chair she paused and ran her hand over his shoulder.

'I'll have to try and take your mind off it while Mastermind here is with his daddy!'

Niven followed her into the big entrance hall, and Drake stiffened as he heard him say angrily, 'Must you behave like that in front of my friends? One of these days...'

'Well, *what?*'

Drake could see her in his mind's eye. Hands on hips, chin up, defying and yet tantalising at the same moment.

A door slammed and Drake heard nothing more.

Go as soon as he's left the house. But if I do that he will guess what has gone on between us and imagine far worse.

Sweat pricked his scalp. Perhaps he did know? And was deliberately forcing the pace to a point of disaster.

He stood up and walked to a window. Everything was getting greener, and there was a swaying patch of daffodils at the end of the garden, like yellow birds.

The war seemed a long way off. But it was still out there somewhere. He thought of Seaton's battered face as he had been lowered through the hatch, his eyes when he had showed his determination to blow up the gantry.

Another few minutes and *XE 16* would have gone without him. Leaving him to perish aboard the launch with the others.

But how can you *know*? How can you be sure?

He knew she had entered the room and was standing just behind him.

Drake said huskily, 'You had me worried a moment ago.' He turned and saw the excitement on her face.

'Nothing to what I'll have you in a few hours time, my handsome colonial!' She reached out and thrust a finger through the front of his shirt, scraping his skin with her nail.

He said, 'Watch it, for heaven's sake!' But he wanted her more than ever.

Niven came down later in uniform, carrying a suitcase.

'A taxi's coming.'

She crossed the room and kissed him. 'There's a good boy then.'

Drake watched them, unable to think clearly. How old was she? Nineteen, did someone say? She had the ways and wiles of a sorceress.

Alec Jenkyn leaned on the parapet of Waterloo bridge and studied the Thames beneath. It was slack water, and surprisingly peaceful. He could feel spring in the air, and no amount of soot or smoke could keep it out. There were even a couple of swans down by the pier, which was unusual these days.

But the air was still pretty sharp, and he could feel the cold stone parapet through his naval raincoat. *Perhaps I'm getting past it. Too long in submarines.*

He would have to move on soon, but the pubs were not open for two more hours. He could not face the hostel again for a bit. Blokes going on about the war, their officers, grub, women; he had had a gutful.

Behind him the pavements rang with countless feet, mostly the heavy boots of soldiers on leave, hundreds of them, from all over the world.

Where did all the civvies go, he wondered? He would like to find a nice village pub, like the ones he had visited with his dad on their rare holidays together in Devon. Full of brass and snug corners, red-faced farm workers with all their quiet jokes at the holidaymakers' expense.

He turned to watch a small girl coming along the pavement.

She was tossing a penny up and down in one hand, her face stiff with concentration. About three, he thought, no more. But all the kids were supposed to be evacuated? Things must be getting brighter. He saw who he supposed was the child's mother almost on her hands and knees trying to retrieve some potatoes which had burst from a carrier bag.

The penny hit the pavement and rolled rapidly over the kerb into the bridge road. The child gave a cry of despair and ran after it, seeing the penny and nothing else.

'Jesus Chirst!' Jenkyn darted from the parapet and charged after her, oblivious to the towering front of a double-decker bus, the shriek of brakes and shouts from every side.

He snatched the child and pulled her aside, then gasped with pain as the front wing of the bus pushed him over and on to the pavement.

People crowded round. 'What happened? Did you see the kid?'

And the shaking bus driver climbing down to add his piece 'Weren't my fault, chum! God, I'd 'ave killed 'er but for you!'

Then the patch of dark blue. 'Now then, what's all this then, who's been hurt?'

The crowd melted slightly in the presence of the London bobby.

'S'nothin'.' Jenkyn stood up and brushed down his raincoat. There was a slight tear in it. And it was brand-new from the pusser's store at Loch Striven. 'I'm okay.' He looked at the policeman and grinned. 'No, *really*.'

The policeman glared at the bus driver. 'Off you go then. Some of us have to work, y'know!'

Still shaking, but glad to be out of it, the bus driver moved away with a violent grinding of gears.

Jenkyn looked down at the child, who was sobbing breathlessly against her mother's shoulder. She was on her knees on the pavement, her carrier bag forgotten.

She looked up blindly and said, 'That was *brave*. I'd just looked away for a second. She's a good girl for most of the time.'

'Well then, if you're all all right?' The policeman waited.

But Jenkyn had not heard him. He was staring at the child's mother. Mid-twenties, and although she was poorly dressed and her brown hair was in disarray under a green headscarf, she had the face of a young beauty. Oval-like. With cornflower eyes and a fresh, smooth skin.

He reached down and took her elbow. ''Ere, let me 'elp.' He pulled out a sixpence and handed it to the child, who had fallen silent to watch him. ''Ave a tanner. I think your penny went down a drain.'

'I can't thank you enough.' She patted the child's coat collar into position. 'To think you nearly died, too.'

The policeman walked away. Unnoticed.

Jenkyn shrugged and winced. He'd have a massive bruise there tomorrow.

He asked awkwardly, 'You live round 'ere then?'

She did not reply directly. 'I've been to the War Office. We were just going over to the station. To catch a train home.' She shook her head. 'No. I live down the line. Wimbledon.' She sounded wistful.

Jenkyn was lost. War Office. Wimbledon.

She asked, 'And you? On leave?'

'Yeh.' He set his cap at a proper angle. 'I'm stayin' at the Union Jack Club. I–I lost my 'ome a while back. Blitzed.' He was angry with himself at once. She obviously had troubles of her own. He didn't have to tell her about it.

She said suddenly, 'Your coat! You tore it on the bus!'

She sounded so upset that Jenkyn said, 'Not to worry. Jack can mend most things.'

'Jack?'

He grinned. 'Yeh. The Navy.'

He felt the child's hand inside his and was strangely moved. *God, I must be getting bomb-happy.*

'I'll be off then.' Jenkyn did not want to go anywhere. Just to stay. Keep her talking.

'I don't want you to think...' She looked away, biting her lower lip. 'I'm not that sort.' She nodded suddenly. Making a decision. Something she had to do a lot. Jenkyn suspected. 'You could have our spare room.' She looked at the child to cover her embarrassment. 'Couldn't he, Gwen?'

The grip on Jenkyn's hand tightened.

He said, 'I'd like that a lot. An' don't worry. I'm not that sort either. People get funny ideas about the Andrew.' He grinned, feeling an uncontrollable happiness. 'Most of 'em true, unfortunately.' He spoke quickly. 'I'll 'op over to the club an' get me gear. Then we'll catch a train, eh?'

The girl smiled, watching him dazedly, as if unable to realise what she had started.

Jenkyn waved his hand to a passing taxi. 'We'll do it in style!'

Later, on the busy Waterloo concourse, he said, 'I'm Alec Jenkyn, by the way.'

She smiled. 'And I'm Sarah. Mrs. Sarah Woods.'

He nodded and said gently, 'War Office. Yer 'usband?'

'Yes. Missing. That's all they keep telling me.' Her lip trembled and she added firmly, 'But we'll not talk about that. We'll go home, and I'll fix that coat for you. I just hope you don't find us a bit boring.'

Jenkyn guided them towards the platform. Boring? His heart was almost breaking with the pleasure of it.

14

The Secret

THERE WAS nothing fake or pseudo about the Niven family home. It stood in a perfect wooded setting, surrounded by rich Sussex countryside, a rambling yet elegant place of mellow stone and brick. A neatly kept drive curved up from a tall gateway, and as the car moved slowly between an avenue of firs Seaton was conscious of permanence, of security.

Niven sat beside him in the naval staff car, watching his reactions.

'Used to be a fortified manor house, sir. Back in Queen Elizabeth's time. Great barn of a place really.'

Seaton nodded. The long journey had sapped his energy and made him realise there was a lot more to recovery than being wangled out here by an admiral. He wished Niven would stop calling him sir. It made things worse in some strange way.

He saw a maid and an elderly manservant in black jacket and pin-striped trousers coming down some stone steps to greet him. He noticed the steps were curved deeply in the centre, worn away by a million feet.

Niven held open the door while the marine driver went round to unload the cases from the boot.

Seaton exclaimed, 'My God, the *air*!' The words came out without conscious thought. The evening scent of shrubs and freshly cut grass brought it all back. The old estate in Hampshire. That special moment of peace at the end of a day.

Niven was pleased. 'Bit different from the boats!'

The car was already moving towards a long garage, which had apparently been converted from a stable block. In it were several cars, two of which were Rolls-Royces. Now carefully resting for the duration. In hibernation until things got back to normal again.

Seaton wondered if there ever would be such a time once this war was finished.

Niven saw his glance and said awkwardly, 'Some of my early ancestors were pirates, though we choose to call them privateers.' He grinned. 'I sometimes wish I'd lived in those days.'

The admiral was waiting inside a circular entrance hall, a great, glittering chandelier poised above his head, completing the picture.

He watched Seaton with a mixture of pleasure and uncertainty.

He said, 'Glad you came.' He gripped his hand. 'You look a bit bushed. Spot of leave will fix you up.' He glanced at his son. ''Evenin', Richard. All well?' Before he could answer he said to Seaton, 'Have to check everything myself. Richard here couldn't organise a bottle party in a brewery!'

A thin, vague-looking woman in a filmy grey dress emerged from an adjoining room and greeted Seaton with something like dismay.

'So you are the poor boy I've been hearing about. Let us hope you will soon be your old self again.' She took his hand. Like her, it was fragile.

The admiral muttered, 'God damn it, Harriet, he's not a *poor boy*, he's a chap who's done a good job! How many times must I tell you not to fuss!'

She did not even flinch. 'How many times have I told *you* not to blaspheme, Philip?'

She hurried up some stairs with the maid, followed discreetly by the old manservant.

The admiral winked. 'Bed, David? Or a large drink first?'

Seaton smiled. 'The latter, sir. All this takes a bit of getting used to.'

They went into a big panelled room, where decanters and glasses stood waiting. It was like stepping into history. On every wall pictures of sea officers stared out at their ships or at forgotten battles. It was all there, like a tapestry. A museum. The Saintes, The Glorious First of June, Trafalgar. Through another door Seaton could see a library, with even more pictures to mark the Niven family's record.

Dogger Bank, Jutland, and many more. One day there would be others, Seaton thought. Crete, Narvik, Matapan. He wondered if Richard Niven would follow the same tradition when his father died.

Rear Admiral Niven sat down heavily in a chair and poured some whisky.

'No point in waiting for Griffin. He's getting so doddery that the time between drinks gets longer each week.' He lifted his glass. 'Cheers.'

His son sipped the whisky and said, 'I suppose I'd better make a move.'

'Nonsense.' The admiral was already pouring another drink. 'Anyway, you'll not get transport to the north at this time. I'll get you driven up tomorrow. I've got some stuff to be sent by road.' He chuckled. 'So the journey really *is* necessary in this case!'

Seaton looked at his glass, at the scars on his hands where he had fallen or been kicked. *Go home now, Richard.*

He said, 'You did a good job in looking after me, Richard. I really can manage now, you know.'

Niven looked at him strangely. Did he sense the warning behind the casual remark?

The admiral said, 'I'll have none of it. You're my son, God help me, and your place is here until–' He did not finish.

Niven stood up. 'I'll give Decia a call then. Let her know we've arrived.'

As soon as the door closed the admiral leaned forward and asked quietly, 'What d'you make of him, eh?'

'I like him, sir.'

'Well, I *like* him. I like dogs too, for that matter!'

Seaton watched him, seeing the sudden fire in the man, the compulsion. Like some of the still faces in the portraits around the room. Strong, and with little time for indecision, he thought.

'He's done his job well, far better than I'd have thought for a fairly recent recruit to X-craft.' He was thinking aloud, but aware that the admiral was giving him his full attention. 'He has a detached attitude to his duties, as if they and not he are in control. I'm surprised he came into this kind of work at all.'

'You're shrewd. Walter Venables was right about you. Have another glass.' He ignored Seaton's protest. 'Fact is, I'm worried about the boy. He's a rebel, against the family, against all I stand for. He's always got to challenge everything I say or do. You probably think it makes me sound like a tyrant, well that's as may be. Marrying that girl, for instance.' He stared past Seaton directly at the images of his irritation. 'He picked a right one in Decia. Spoiled, arrogant little bitch. Richard could see I didn't approve of her and her bloody "ee-bah-goom" father. So he married her. To spite me.' A smile broke through his stern expression. 'Out of the frying pan and into the fire, as it often happens. She was marrying him to provoke *her* father! God, what a pair, it'll never last. May ruin the boy.' He looked at the window, at the purple shadows reaching down from the great trees. 'A man has to keep his mind alert when he's involved in danger. I could get him out of X-craft, I could *order* him out.' He shrugged. 'That would put me in the wrong again. But if I leave him well alone I might lose him altogether.'

'I think he's growing up fast, sir.'

It seemed to please him. 'Young devil! Had too much too soon. My old father used to keep me short of cash until he thought I was old enough to marry and settle down. But it was different for him. Richard grew up in the Depression. I suppose I spoiled him to keep him free of all the despair and gloom.'

Seaton could feel the drowsiness closing in on him. He hoped the hospital had not forgotten to pack his tablets. Without them, each night was a thing of terror and unbelievable dreams.

The admiral said abruptly, 'Bed for you, I think. It should all be ready now. When you're feeling a bit more get-up-and-go. I'd like you to drive over to one of our establishments. Quite near here. Old Noel Ruthven would be delighted to see you.'

A picture formed reluctantly in Seaton's blurred mind. The bunker. The trim air marshal, the new 'chief'.

Griffin, the old manservant, entered the room and announced, 'All ready, sir.'

'Good.' The admiral walked to the door with Seaton. 'Your Number One. Did he come through all right? You can't get the real truth from intelligence reports.'

Seaton looked at him. The admiral had said nothing so far that he had not intended to say.

'He's reliable, sir. We've been through a lot together.'

'Oh yes, quite. I agree. But not much there, I'd have thought? Bit of a hanger-on if the going gets rough, hmm?'

Seaton did not know how to answer. He said, 'I think he should have his own command. He's earned it.'

The admiral eyed him impassively. 'That's loyalty speaking. Friendship. But deep down you know, just as I've known for some while, he'll never rate a command. Not a submarine anyway. Never in a million years. He's a *nice* chap, good-looking, do-anything-for-you sort of fellow, but beyond that, nothing.' He grinned unexpectedly. 'Now go to bed, for God's sake, before you fall down! Forget Drake, the boat, the whole bloody war!'

Niven came from another room. 'She was out. I'll ring again later.'

The admiral drew a cigar from his case. 'Who answered?'

'Geoffrey. Geoffrey Drake.' He walked into the library.

The admiral turned and looked straight into Seaton's eyes. 'You see? Nothing beyond the moment. I'll bet she was there all right. If it wasn't for the work in hand I'd go and see that New Zealander myself, I'd tell him a few home truths, believe me!'

He watched as Seaton started up the stairs. 'But you put it out of your mind. Leave this one to me.'

Seaton felt his heart quickening, and knew it was not just his condition or the steepness of the stairs. *If it wasn't for the work in hand*, he had said. That implied only one thing, that *XE 16* was already earmarked, a little tin flag on someone's operations map.

Otherwise Rear Admiral Niven would never tolerate a situation which might involve his son and the family name. It was not in the man's make-up. His sort always used everything they had, from influence to ruthlessness, to protect their own.

He followed Griffin into a large bedroom and was desperately tired, barely able to remove his jacket.

Griffin might be old, but he knew his work like a true professional. Seaton found that his clothes had been removed from his body with barely a jar to his injuries. As he sat on the bed feeling rather like a small boy, Griffin slipped pyjama trousers round his ankles. He said, 'I'm sorry to be such a bother.'

The man paused and looked up at him. 'It's no *bother* , sir. I've been with the family all my life. And you're very like Master Jonathan, and about his age, I'd reckon, sir.'

'Jonathan?'

'Master Richard's older brother, sir. A fine young man. This was his room when he was home.'

'He's dead?'

The man sighed and buttoned Seaton's pyjama jacket. 'Yes. Went down off Malaya in the old *Repulse*. We still miss him, y'know.'

Seaton allowed himself to be helped into bed. Long after the door had closed he lay staring at the darkness, listening to the soft tap of a creeper against the window.

Jonathan had once laid here. Dreaming and pretending. Planning. Now he was just another name on the list. *Killed in action.*

Griffin had not said so, but Seaton guessed that the dead Jonathan had been the apple of the admiral's eye. The favourite. Just one more standard for Richard to compete against.

No wonder the admiral was worried. Perhaps too late. For good or bad, it seemed as if Richard held all the cards.

When Seaton eventually fell asleep he'd forgotten to take some of the pills. But for once, he did not need them.

To David Seaton the following days and weeks were strangely unreal. The admiral had returned to his duties in Whitehall, 'running the war', as he had described it, and had left Seaton with the run of the house and estate.

Gingerly at first, he had started to take short walks around the grounds, putting names to shrubs and flowers he had almost forgotten. Then with a stick and a good stout pair of shoes he had set off on longer journeys, to a nearby village, to a couple of farms, and even spent a whole morning reading inscriptions on the graves at a little Norman church. It reminded him of a short story he had once read in a naval magazine. About a sailor coming home on leave, visiting familiar places, seeing old faces.

Upon arrival at his own house he was astounded to find his mother in tears, a telegram lying on the table. The telegram told of her son's death at sea. *His* death. No wonder nobody had heeded his greeting or watched him pass. It was much like that here. He walked anywhere he chose, was looked after by the admiral's servants with barely a word spoken. Even old Griffin had hardly said anything since his first show of confidences.

In a way it suited Seaton. It gave him time to adjust, to think of the future, if there was one.

Reality touched him on his visits to the army Medical Officer at a nearby anti-aircraft battery. And when he passed a barrage balloon site on one of the farms. But, like the war itself, it was out of reach.

Daily he was getting stronger and consequently more restless. He scanned the newspapers and tried to work out what was happening. The army was doing well in Burma, and the Japs were falling back on the Imphal front. There were day and night raids by the R.A.F. and the Americans on targets in Germany and Occupied France.

One report he did find interesting. That of an R.A.F. raid across north-west France. One of the Mitchell bombers had carried a newspaper reporter. He had written about the air of desertion and stillness in that sector of France. No road convoys, few trains and, more to the point, no cattle in the fields. *So the Germans knew*. They really knew this time that an invasion attempt would be made, and soon.

They were getting ready. Moving supplies and livestock out of the area. The killing-ground. Digging in.

Seaton fretted about it. Feeling left out, forgotten. It was no use telling himself he was being stupid. It was the way he felt.

On one day he had visitors, Drake and Niven. They were on their way, not to Loch Striven, but to the West Country of all places, to the naval base at Portland.

It seemed that during their leave *XE 16* and her consorts had been moved south, where new training was to be undertaken without delay.

'Don't know what to do with us any. more,' Niven had suggested.

Drake had merely said it might be for final transporting to the Far East. Neither had made much sense. There had been a strained atmosphere, a curious feeling of apprehension.

When they left Drake had said, 'Don't be too long, Skipper. It's no bloody team without you.'

Niven had said, 'I wish I could have stayed here with you, sir. I can talk to *you*.' It had sounded rather old-fashioned, and had shown a side of Niven which his father had probably never seen.

Then, when Seaton was contemplating a visit to the Admiralty out of sheer desperation, the admiral had driven down to Sussex from London. With his usual methodical attention to detail he had stopped off en route to visit the army M.O. who had been treating Seaton's injuries.

He said cheerfully. 'Right as rain, the brown job tells me, Capital. You'll be ready to climb mountains now!' He sounded genuinely pleased.

At dinner Seaton broached the matter of Portland.

Rear Admiral Niven regarded him calmly. 'Big build-up there, and right along the coast from Falmouth to Pompey. Ships, landing craft, the whole potmess of invasion. The greatest armada *ever*. Not long now.'

'Do we have a part in all this, sir?'

'Of course.' He smiled. 'Some X-craft have already been over the other side. Surveying beaches, measuring anti-tank obstructions, picking up agents. In their element.'

'I'd like to go back, sir.' Seaton tried to hide his desperation. 'I'm all right now, the M.O. didn't lie.'

'So you shall.' He wagged a silver fork. 'But you were a mess, you know. Scars can go deeper than tissue. We have to be sure.'

It sounded like one of the doctor's own quotes, Seaton thought.

He said, 'That's fair enough.'

'Tomorrow I'll take you over to see Air Marshal Ruthven. I have to go back to London later, partly to see Venables, but mostly to collect Harriet. She's been shopping, or something.' He grinned. 'I took her with me to give you some peace. She'd have you believe you were at death's door, if you'd allow her.'

He became serious. 'I hear that Richard and your Number One called in to see you. How are things, in your estimation?'

'A bit brittle. I think they're probably glad to be back at work, for various reasons.'

'Good. That girl Decia.' He shook his head. 'If I was a bit

younger, I'd have a go at her myself. She's hot stuff, if I'm any judge.'

Seaton suspected that the admiral had had plenty of experience. It would certainly explain his wife's remoteness.

The admiral added, 'Pity you've not got a girl. Good for you. You could have brought her here.'

I can imagine. He said, 'I've enjoyed being here.'

'Yes. I've seen you meandering round the place. Used to be your line of country, I believe? Well, after this lot's over, you never know. I might be able to help. This place needs a proper hand at the wheel.'

'Richard...' He fell silent.

'It's all right. I expect you heard about my other boy. But Richard is not the sort to rusticate here and leave the work to others. He's a dreamer. The sort who might make First Sea Lord one day, or end on the gallows.'

He did not continue the subject, and Seaton was glad. He preferred the autocrat. Family confidences seemed as out of place as rocking chairs in a battleship.

The next day, bright and early, they set off to meet Ruthven. It was a pleasant drive, hampered only when they had to wait in a side lane to allow an army convoy to pass. It was impressive, truck after truck, packed with helmeted troops and equipment. Then tanks on long, flat transports, more vehicles and finally Tail-End Charlie, an M.P. on a motor cycle.

In months, maybe weeks, they would be across the Channel. Or underneath it.

At first sight Ruthven's hideaway was something of an anticlimax. Although surrounded by a massive perimeter fence of barbed wire, with sentries and checkpoints at every entrance, the place itself looked like a small and neglected farm.

But after they had been carefully scrutinized by the sentries, and a military policeman had phoned the house about their arrival, Seaton had seen past the general air of shabbiness. Barns were filled with jeeps and staff cars, and carefully shielded by camouflaged nets he saw several batteries of multi-barrelled A.A. guns.

The main farm building was now only a shell. Camp-beds, a field-kitchen and a guardroom filled the complete lower floors. Ruthven's H.Q. was deep underneath all that. Another complex of soulless concrete and glaring lights, passageways and steel doors.

Combined Special Operations were certainly well blended, Seaton thought. Wrens in a communications section, Waafs and A.T.S. girls manning screens and wall charts in other planning departments. An air of quiet purpose seemed to pervade the place, and he felt that once the war was done it would all be covered over and 'filled in' to make way for the return of that unknown farmer above.

'In here.'

The admiral nodded to a couple of tough-looking M.P.s. Each carried a Sten gun across his arm, and Seaton thought of the S.S. men in Bergen.

Ruthven was dressed in R.A.F. battledress. He even managed to make that look immaculate and tidy.

'Welcome to the club.' He waved to some chairs. 'You look splendid, Lieutenant. I'm glad for you.'

'He's going to Portland as soon as I pass the word, Noel.' The admiral sounded cautious. Not so relaxed.

'Fine. Better than I'd hoped.' He studied Seaton. 'I don't want you to take on anything until you're fit for it.'

A naval officer entered the room and said, 'Ready, sir.'

Ruthven swivelled his chair so that he had his back to the others. As if to a magic sign the lights in the room dimmed and the high map boards which covered the rear wall started to slide apart like doors. Beyond them was one huge window, and further still was another world of people and constant movement.

'Our ops room.' Ruthven had his fingers pressed together.

He must think of his responsibility each time those panels open, Seaton thought. The great wall charts showed the Channel, the coasts of France and the Low Countries, and further to the north-east, Denmark and the Third Reich itself. It did *not* show the countless men and women who daily risked their lives in Hitler's Europe, gnawing away at the German war machine from within.

On ladders and moving platforms a dozen girls or more were busy with cards and pointers, flags and coloured strips of paper. Wrens in white shirts and black stockings, Waafs in pale blue, the army girls in khaki.

Below, in a sort of square well, other people were working on glass-topped tables. Phones were in use, and a tape machine was spewing out paper intelligence. And it was all in total silence. It was like going deaf without any warning.

Ruthven selected one of his telephones, and down in the well a lieutenant commander picked up his receiver and turned to look at the window.

Ruthven said, 'Switch on the Victor lights, Tommy.'

In response to more magic, little red lights appeared along the French coast.

Ruthven said quietly, 'Rocket sites. We've known about them for a long time, and our bombers have flattened a lot of them. But some will still be in use, no matter what we do.' He paused as some more lights appeared on the wall chart. 'These are something new. Mostly in the Normandy area.'

Seaton stared at the chart. It must be one of the greatest secrets on earth. Why were they sharing it with him? Ruthven spoke curtly into his telephone and the scene was again hidden by his sliding wall maps. As the lights returned to full brightness he said, 'In war we accept casualties, no matter how hard it is to admit it. As Captain Venables has told you, morale is everything. Without it you have lost the stuff of battle, the tenacity which has carried us this far. At any time in the next few months, and maybe much less, the enemy is going to release some of these new weapons on England. My people have told me about two of them, the V.1 and the V.2, which we call Victor on the chart. The V stands for *Vergeltungswaffe* in Germany's handbook, their reprisal weapon. Your passenger, Gjerde, was working on a project for something even worse, which but for you might already have been falling on London.'

Seaton felt his face and wrists getting clammy. He recalled the anchored *Hansa*, Trevor's information about a launching ramp for testing the new rocket.

Ruthven was saying, 'The British people have had to endure much. But belief in survival, of not actual victory, kept them going. Now, with even victory a possibility, they cannot be expected to stand another serious, if not fatal, setback. With the Allies through France, no matter how rough it gets, we will win. But if the enemy can destroy our ports and towns, smash any hope of building up supply convoys on land and sea, we might just as well surrender.'

The admiral, who had been watching Seaton all the time,

said, 'You know of the build-up. Can you imagine what a new, powerful rocket, against which *there is no known defence*,' he let the words hang in the air and then added, 'would do to our invasion?'

Seaton asked, 'Where do I come in, sir?'

'No doubts, Lieutenant? No demands?' Ruthven smiled gravely.

Seaton found he could speak quite easily. Perhaps he had always known deep inside his soul it would be like this. Violent. Terrible.

'Well, sir, I know we have a good Air Force, and for the most part better than anything the Germans have, It's a long time since "The Few" bashed the many.' He saw the admiral hide a grin. 'So the target must be something that the R.A.F. and the United States Air Command can't cope with.'

Ruthven watched him. 'Right, so far.'

'It must be on the coast, as my *XE 16* has not yet been fitted with legs.'

What was he doing? Going crazy in this concrete tomb? He was making jokes about it. Like they always did in war films before they took a one-way ticket to Armageddon.

He said quickly, 'And it *won't* be a rocket-firing vessel of any kind, an X-craft would be the last thing to send!'

Ruthven pressed down a button and spoke into an intercom. 'Send in Bill, will you please?' To Seaton he said, 'Naturally I can't tell you the exact size and location of the target. You might not feel able to continue with the mission, you could just as easily step under a bus. And I think you, more than either of us, know the real value of secrecy.'

The door opened and an R.A.F. group captain came into the room.

'Ah, Bill.' Ruthven smiled. 'This is Lieutenant David Seaton.'

They shook hands, and Seaton could feel the questions and the impressions in the other man's glances.

The group captain said, 'I've been following your exploits.'

Ruthven explained, 'Bill's my chief intelligence officer.' He dropped his voice. 'He organised the Bergen job with Captain Venables.'

The silence moved in again as each man saw the memory from his own separate viewpoint.

Then the group captain said, 'This one is a lot tougher, I'm afraid. Earlier, we might have pulled it off without too much difficulty. But *earlier* we didn't know enough. Now we do. The Germans have constructed a new site, unseen by our recce boys because in a sense it was already there. Our agents on the other side, even the Resistance, have been in the dark, because the Jerries have cleared the whole area of civilians.'

Seaton nodded, thinking of the newspaper article, the fact that the Germans' attention to detail had not even overlooked the cows in the fields.

He asked, 'How do you mean, sir? It was there already?'

'A U-boat pen. You know they built them all the way from Norway to the Bay of Biscay. So deep and thick, not even a block-buster will penetrate.'

Seaton heard himself say, 'I saw some in Bergen.' Again the memory. Like a blow in the heart.

'Yes.' The group captain shot Ruthven a quick glance. 'This one is converted to take the launcher. Everything else goes in by water, underneath.'

Seaton had seen the exchange of glances, but he no longer cared. *They think I'm over the hill.* He must be anyway to agree to such a scheme.

Ruthven said, 'We think you could get in and drop your charges right under the bunker.'

Seaton held his breath, seeing all of it as if it had already happened. The rocket, which had become somehow human and fiendish. The bunker, and all the explosive and fuel pressured together by those masses of concrete, blasting apart in one great fireball.

The admiral cleared his throat. 'This time you will be supported, but I want *you* in overall command, see?'

Seaton touched his lips with the back of his hand. 'I see.'

Ruthven said calmly, 'Captain Venables originally wanted Lieutenant Vanneck, but you proved yourself twice over in Bergen that you are the man for me.'

Seaton looked at him thoughtfully. 'Anyway, sir, Rupert Vanneck is dead.'

There was an uncomfortable silence, then Ruthven said, 'Nevertheless, I'd not have expected you to risk your life again so soon. We have little choice. Only you have that.'

Seaton smiled. 'Do I, sir?'

The admiral touched his shoulder. 'When you put it like that, David, not much.' He stood up. 'I'll get my driver to take you to a nice pub. I'm off to London now. When I get back, you'll have your orders.' He grinned. 'Also a half-stripe, Lieutenant *Commander* Seaton!'

They shook hands solemnly and the group captain said, 'I'll walk you to the checkpoint. To see what daylight looks like.'

As they walked through the grim concrete passageways Seaton said, 'They don't know, do they? About all this?'

'Who?'

Seaton shrugged. 'People. Everyone thinks the war is made up of ships and planes, tanks and men. Then there are rations and blackouts, and *shortages*. Occasionally people die, but that only happens to others. Nobody ever thinks there are places like this, that someone actually *plans* their war for them!'

The group captain called Bill chuckled. 'Never thought of it like that.'

At the foot of the steps which led up to the farmhouse he said, 'I've enjoyed meeting you. I had been a bit worried. You know, *so soon after the last one*, and all that stuff.'

'You're not worried any more?'

Their eyes met. 'No. Only about having to send people to do things like this. *That* worries me.'

Somebody called his name and he said, 'Must dash. Never stops. I'll see you before the balloon goes up.' He beckoned to a W.A.A.F. officer who was crossing from one room to the next. 'Take him through the gate, will you, m'dear?' Then he was off.

Seaton turned to the pale blue uniform, a flight officer. Everything else seemed to merge into a haze as he said huskily, 'It's you! *Nina!*'

In this place they knew everything. That group captain certainly knew about his agents in Norway. Perhaps he had done this for both of them.

She said, 'Oh, David. Help. Take me out of here.'

Up in the sunlight he gripped her hands and turned her towards him. The sudden strangeness and the uniforms seemed to hold them apart. But it was the same girl. The same blue-green eyes, the pale hair which even now was rebelling around her service cap.

'I've never stopped thinking about you. Wondering.' He could not contain himself. 'Nobody would tell me...'

She watched his despair and replied quickly, 'It was my fault. I told them to keep my presence a secret from you. Because of me you nearly died, because of *me* you were used without thought or mercy.'

'It wasn't like that.' He looked at the ground. Beaten. 'Just to know you're safe makes all the difference, believe me!' When he looked at her again he saw her eyes were glistening. 'I'm sorry.'

She shook her head. 'Don't be. I was selfish. Thinking of myself, my own sadness.'

'Trevor?'

She looked away. 'Yes.'

'Don't talk about it.' Seaton glanced around at the sentries, the camouflaged guns. 'Not here.' He thought suddenly of the great house. 'The admiral's place.' He squeezed her hand, seeing the strain in her eyes, the uncertainty. *'Please.'*

She nodded without smiling. 'I will come. First I have to go back.' She watched his face. 'I *mean* it. I will come, but I cannot stay very long.'

He waited until she had disappeared into the farmhouse, knowing the sentries were staring at him, knowing it was all hopeless before he had begun. Had he met her *before* going into the bunker, would he have agreed to Ruthven's proposal so willingly?

He turned and walked towards the car. He must see she was not hurt any more. Not by him.

Seeing her again, knowing she was safe, was all that counted. It had to be that and no other way.

15

It Was to be Expected

THEY SAT opposite each other before a crackling log fire. For
despite the spring days the evenings still had a nip to them, and
old Griffin had seen fit to light a good fire.

Seaton felt almost afraid to move in case he spoiled it all. The
girl had taken off her shoes and had curled up her legs on the
chair, her eyes distant as she watched the flames.

An hour. It was all they had. This time.

When Seaton's hopes had begun to waver he had heard the
jeep growling up the drive, and once again felt jealous of the
voices which had followed her to the door. They had only been
R.A.F. officers giving her a lift, but to Seaton they had meant
one more barrier, a new threat to his momentary peace.

She said suddenly, 'Sometimes I think I can understand my
brother's actions. When the Nazis came to Norway he was there,
I was safe in England, a student. To Paul, science was
everything, and in those first terrible months there was absolutely no reason to suppose that Norway would ever be free
again. Country after country fell to the Germans. It must have
appeared much worse to Paul than it did to those who still had a
will to fight.'

Seaton recalled his own feelings when her brother had been brought aboard *XE 16*.

He said gently, 'You took a terrible risk by going to him. He might have been betrayed before your arrival.'

She turned to look at him. 'It was not the first time for me. Perhaps I wanted to prove something, to redeem the family honour.' She smiled, but it only made her look sad. 'When I was asked to help bring my brother to England, I saw no further than that. I did not consider all those others who would be at risk.' She shook her head. 'I think of them now!'

He wanted to go to her. to hold her, but knew that if he moved she might break away.

She continued in the same low voice, 'I had worked with Trevor several times. Officially as his radio operator, and sometimes as a contact with people I had known for most of my life. We were thrown together.' She looked at Seaton with a level stare. 'I never thought he loved me, but we were lovers. Sometimes life seemed very short, too precious to waste, even if it was substituting something for reality.'

Seaton said, 'If only I had known.'

'And then?' She shook her head again. 'It would have made you uncertain, when you needed all your strength. It might have made you fail, and so bring failure to the mission. I hated the way you were used, but it is the way of their war. No flags. Just courage and hatred.'

Seaton leaned forward and pushed another log on the fire. He saw her flinch, as if she had expected him to touch her.

She said abruptly, 'Paul, being Paul, thought he would take extra precautions, to seal his "bargain" and so save his life. He had his stolen piece of equipment lowered into that wreck in a watertight bag. If he had been killed, nobody would ever have found it.'

'He was playing a dangerous game. With both sides.'

She smiled at him. 'Both sides, David? In that war there are as many sides as you want.' She shrugged, even that movement bringing a pain to Seaton's heart. 'Now it is done. Paul has his safety, and no doubt will end his days elsewhere, possibly in America.'

'What about us?'

'Us?' She shivered and leaned towards the flames. 'We will

mend in time. If there is time. But I will not be going back to Norway until it is over. I was already being hunted by the Gestapo, and they missed me twice by minutes, I am told.' She stood up suddenly, her stockinged feet soundless as she walked to a window. It was almost dark outside, but he could see her framed against the sky, sense her barely controlled emotion as she asked, 'Did you see him, David?'

'Yes. He was alive, but beyond anyone's reach.' He had to speak very slowly to hold his voice steady. 'He was very brave, too.'

She turned easily and walked towards him. To his dismay he saw her fingers fastening the buttons of her tunic, just as he heard the sound of the returning jeep on the drive.

She placed one hand on each of his shoulders and said softly, '*You* saved me that day in Bergen. You, nobody else. When others used my innocence, or ignorance, call it what you will, you trusted me. And now that you know about Trevor you are still here with me.' She gripped his shoulders and he could feel the pain, hers and his own, as she added, 'That day on the pier, before you sank the *Hansa,* I wanted to shout to all the others, *here, take a look at this one*! So quietly confident, hiding your fear for the hostages aboard the ship.' She quivered as he put his hands on her waist. 'But instead, I just stood there with the rest and let you go.'

A bell jangled in the entrance hall, and Seaton heard Griffin's footsteps, slower than usual, even for him.

She said in a whisper, 'I must leave now. There is a lot going on–' It was then the truth seemed to hit her. 'Was *that* why you were there today? I thought the admiral had brought you merely to ...' She threw her arms round his neck, her voice lost in anguish and sobs as she said, *'No! Not again!* They wouldn't order you to go!'

When he stayed silent she stood back from him. 'You wouldn't have told me. Any more than my superiors.'

Griffin was in the doorway. 'The gentlemen with the transport are here, miss.'

'Thank you.' She turned slightly, so that half of her face shone in the firelight. Then she put her hand against Seaton's cheek, holding it there, very still, as she added, 'This time you will *not* be alone. I will be waiting when you return.' She bent down to put on her shoes. 'And before that, if–' She tried to brush past him but he caught her in his arms.

'If?' He could feel her heart trying to match his own.

'I should like to be with you.' Then she was gone.

Seaton was standing there long after the jeep's noise had faded.

Griffin entered the room and started to draw the heavy curtains.

'No air-raid warning, sir, and in any case we don't get much disturbance here. But the local warden sometimes makes a fuss, and as he's also our butcher, cook will not thank us for upsetting him.' He hesitated by the door. 'A most charming young lady, sir, I see she had a Norwegian flash on her uniform.' He ambled away. 'Most charming.'

Seaton sat down very carefully and looked at the fire.

It was not a dream.

Jenkyn paused in front of a mirror in his borrowed bedroom and looked at himself. He felt out of sorts, and unable to explain his sense of loss.

It was even strange to see himself in his new uniform. The promotion had come through and had awaited his return from Bergen. Chief Engineroom Artificer Jenkyn. Once it had seemed the impossible horizon. He grimaced. *Call me Chiefy*. Now it seemed much further down the list of things in his life.

Reflected in the mirror he saw the neat bedroom which he had enjoyed since that chance meeting on Waterloo bridge, when young Gwen had almost gone under a double-decker. His case and respirator lay on the bed, his new cap and mended raincoat hanging behind the door.

What a leave it had been. Like nothing he had known. Each day had been different. Trips to the cinema, to the river to feed the ducks. A picnic down the Thames by Hampton Court Palace, when it had started to rain.

At the end of each day, with Gwen tucked up in bed, he and Sarah had sat by the fire, listening to the wireless, swopping stories. Each had kept an unspoken promise, and when she had bolted the door of the little Victorian semi- detached house they had gone to their separate rooms.

They had been wonderful, simple days. Now it was done. The chit said Portland. So that was it.

He held up his sleeve and looked at the three brass buttons above the cuff, remembering that very first evening when he had peeled off the torn raincoat.

She had exclaimed, 'Are you an officer?'

He smiled sadly. 'Not exactly,' he had replied. 'We sort of carry the officers.'

The worst part was, he was off to Portland, and then sea duty again. But tomorrow all this would still be here, and he would have to forget it.

He picked up his case and gasmask and slung his coat over his arm.

Had he forgotten anything? He had given all his hoarded chocolate, his 'nutty', to the kid. She had thought it must be Christmas. And he had put some money in an envelope in the dresser. Sarah would find it when she looked for a clean tablecloth. She wouldn't like it, but it was no use to him.

There was a sudden crash of breaking china and something like a gasp of pain.

Jenkyn was through the door and down the stairs in a few bounds, his cap and case scattering in his wake.

It was all immediately clear, like some brutal photograph in a magazine.

The open door, with the single tree just outside on the pavement. The startled telegram boy, his bicycle propped against the gateway.

She turned and stared at him dazedly, her face streaming with tears. In her hand she held a telegram, in the other an empty saucer. The cup of tea she had been getting to send him on his way lay scattered and broken on the rug.

Jenkyn's experience took over. He nodded to the telegram boy and said, 'Thank you, son,' and shut the door. Then he put his arm round her shoulder and held her against his chest. 'Let it all go. You've carried it too long.' He didn't need to see the wording. It was all confirmed. Neat and tidy. *Killed in action.*

She whispered brokenly, 'What'll I tell Gwen?'

Jenkyn waited, letting her cry. Then he said, 'I want you to know, Sarah, that I've a great affection for you.' He felt her stiffen and added, 'I'll never be another Bob for you, but if you'll 'ave me, I'd like you think about it.' He squeezed her shoulder. 'I mean it, love.'

She looked at him, her eyes blurred. 'I *know* you do.'

'I'm only sorry I've got to go. I wish–'

She touched his mouth. 'I'm all right, really. I suppose I always knew Bob was dead. I didn't *feel* anything. It wasn't right somehow.' She seemed to realise what he had said. 'Write to me, Alec. Please. I'll think about you, and pray for you.'

Jenkyn picked up his cap. *Chief Petty Officer.* As a young boy from a working-class family it had seemed so high and mighty.

He said firmly, 'I've done me twelve years. When it's over, I'm leavin' the Andrew. For good. Nice little garage, that's it. Down in Devon or Cornwall. You could do teas an' that.' He forced a smile. ''Sides, it will be better for Gwen.'

'Oh, Alec. You're so good. So *decent*!'

Jenkyn was a small man, but as he left the house in Wimbledon he walked like a giant.

Seaton stood with Drake and Niven looking across the great horseshoe of Portland Harbour.

A navigator's nightmare. Every inch of jetty and pier, each buoy and pontoon seemed to have five-times too many vessels tied on to it. Escorts and supply ships, landing craft of every size and design, there was no end to the display of might. And it was like that everywhere, as far as he could judge.

In the clear sky thin vapour trails marked not dog-fights but constant and heavy fighter patrols. No enemy aircraft was to get even a sniff of the build-up of ships or of the fields and side roads which stretched inland like arteries of steel and armoured tracks.

It was strange, 'to be back'. It all seemed different. The crowded moorings, and the double sittings for meals in the wardroom of the naval establishment perched on the side of Portland Bill. People everywhere. After Loch Striven and Rear Admiral Niven's house it was like a menagerie.

He had seen Nina only once more after her visit to the house It had been a difficult affair, with the admiral's wife and two ladies from the W.V.S. who never stopped talking about raffle tickets.

He had watched her across the table, feeling the minutes falling away like blood. He had held her with his eyes, and had seen her mouth move in small, secret words. Torment. It had been almost worse than not seeing her at all.

Now he was here in Dorset. The Channel looked very grey for the time of year, the sunshine too fragile.

Drake said, 'The old *Syphilis* is tied up on the other side of the big depot ship.' He was pointing vaguely towards the harbour. 'Our boats are pretty well hemmed in there.'

Seaton nodded. H.M.S. *Cephalus* and her little brood had waddled all this way to play her part in things, whatever they were. At Loch Striven it must seem bare without her outmoded shape.

Drake added, 'It sure looks as if the balloon is about to rise to unprecedented heights.' He sounded cheerful, but he had lost some of his old carefree manner.

Niven, on the other hand, was much as usual. He said, 'We were all bucked to hear about your half-stripe, sir. It looks better for the whole flotilla, with all the other top brass hanging around.'

Seaton smiled, He did not *feel* any different. Not yet anyway.

He thought about the new addition to the flotilla, XE 26, and her C.O., Lieutenant Roger Winters, another veteran like himself. Seemed pleasant enough, and his small crew appeared to like him.

In the past Seaton would have wanted to know each one much more closely. Now he was almost afraid to reach beyond duty and routine. Perhaps that was what rank did?

Niven saw his smile and asked, 'Our new job will be fairly soon, I suppose, sir?'

Drake tapped his nose. 'Shh! Keep mum!'

Seaton turned and looked up at the rocky Bill. 'There'll be a lot to learn. New ideas, before we move.' He shivered. If only Niven's hope was true. Get it over with. And yet . . . He walked away from them, saying, 'I'll cadge a lift into Weymouth.'

Drake grinned. 'It's Sunday. The pubs won't be open for ages!'

When he reached the wardroom Seaton found several officers staring at the noticeboard. He pushed through them and read the neatly worded signal.

There would be no lifts into Weymouth. Not for a while. Leave was cancelled. All officers would report for orders forthwith.

Even as he re-read the brief notice he heard the tannoys

booming around the establishment.

'D'you hear there! D'you hear there! All ships' companies will go to first degree readiness at sixteen 'undred hours. All ratings attached to beach parties and L.S.T. disposal report to the dockyard immediately!'

Seaton walked to the window. The Channel looked even rougher now, and yet in his heart he knew it was not going to stop them. He saw Drake turning from the noticeboard.

'This it, Skipper?'

'For them. Not for us.'

'Maybe they won't want us yet after all, eh?' He rubbed his hands. 'Far East'll suit me. Bit nearer home.' He strolled away humming *South of the Border*.

Seaton left the wardroom and walked out into the crisp air again.

The tannoys kept up their stream of instructions, and presumably it was happening in a dozen other bases as well. Great surging mobs of seamen and marines changed into squares and platoons, into squads and to individual crews. Petty officers bellowed out names and ticked off their lists. Much as they had prior to Trafalgar, Seaton thought.

It would be something to be going with them. After all the hard knocks and disappointments. There'd never be another, or anything like it. He thought of the secret rocket, lurking somewhere in its concrete pit. It did not seem to belong with all this din of voices and stamping feet.

A seaman in belt and gaiters blocked his way, his eyes carefully averted.

''Tenant Commander Seaton, sir?' He sounded like Jenkyn.

'That's me.'

'Cap'n Venables' compliments, an' would you report on board *Cephalus* right away.' He studied Seaton's features and added hurriedly, '*Sir.*'

He found Venables aboard the ancient depot ship drinking sherry with her captain and a tight-mouthed lieutenant commander he had not seen before.

Venables introduced him as Alan Charteris, Mission Training Commander. They shook hands, each knowing they were not going to get on, equally understanding why Venables had made the arrangement. To hone away any last soft edges.

Seaton took a sherry. His long weeks of recovery made him wary of drinking too much. It made him light-headed.

'Fine lot of ships in harbour, sir.'

Venables nodded. 'Tomorrow you'll have the place almost to yourself.' He looked at the others. 'The day after that is Tuesday. That's when it all starts to happen. *Operation Overlord.*'

Seaton put down his glass. 'What about us, sir?'

The tight-mouthed officer said sharply, 'We get down to work.'

Venables looked at Seaton and raised one eyebrow. 'Fit?'

Seaton nodded. 'I'll send for my gear, if you'd excuse me sir.'

When he had gone Venables said quietly, 'I want you to *help* these crews. Don't start threatening them with hell. They've been there already.'

The process of re-training the three X-craft and working them into a team for one specific purpose was more demanding than Seaton would have believed. At any other time it might have been different, but after that particular June morning when the greatest seaborne invasion had punched its way into Normandy, any form of revision was pure torture.

Lieutenant Commander Alan Charteris, Royal Navy, was good at his job. Particularly if part of that job was to antagonise everyone to such a degree that he performed his work perfectly if only to spite the nagging, tight-mouthed instructor.

From first light each day they went through every possible evolution, cutting nets, some of which were exactly like those which had been laid to protect the *Hansa*, diving, surfacing, everything by the stop-watch. There had been several additional pieces of equipment added to the boats, one of which was a short-range radio telephone which could be used to link the boats while they were submerged and give support when it was most needed.

But at the end of each day it was back to the depot ship or ashore to the base wardroom, to listen to the news and try to determine what was happening.

One thing was certain, the moment of invasion had caught the Germans completely by surprise. Seaton could understand it. When he had seen the angry sea, low clouds made worse by a violent electric storm, he had expected the moment of attack to

223

be postponed. But D-Day had gone on. The troops had landed and in widening prongs of armour were spreading through the French countryside at an impressive speed.

The Tactical Air Force held the upper hand above the beaches and far inland, and each day that passed saw more and more equipment and men being ferried across the Channel.

Once again it sounded as if the top brass had over-reacted, been too cautious, as some had suggested earlier. Secret weapons, if there were any left, had not made a showing, and with the Russians advancing from the east and the Allied armies safely landed in France, what could go wrong?

Seaton watched the morale getting lower in his little flotilla. He had heard rumours that some of the crews, particularly the extra ones kept for passage or stand-by work, were thinking of volunteering for general service, if only to see some action.

The returning landing craft, with their lines and lines of wounded soldiers laid where the tanks had once stood, only added to the dissatisfaction.

Nina had written to him every week. Short but precious letters which he read when he was alone in his cabin. They did not tell him much, other than she was extremely busy. She mentioned that she had been allowed to see her brother, which suggested he might be on his way to another secret destination where she would not be able to visit him.

Seaton went into Weymouth and telephoned his father two or three times. His father never wrote, and even on the crackling telephone it was hard to find much to say. He had met another lady. 'You'd like her, David. You really would.'

Only Jenkyn seemed to be thriving. When not working XE 16 he was to be seen bustling about, writing letters, posting parcels and visiting the welfare office.

Seaton was sitting in his makeshift flotilla office in the depot ship when Jenkyn came to see him.

'Well, Chief?' It amused him to see the way Jenkyn's new rank seemed to have left him unmoved, as his own promotion had.

Jenkyn beamed. 'I'm gettin' spliced, sir. Really nice little party she is. 'Er bloke bought it in Burma. Got a kid, too. Really *nice.*'

Seaton walked round the desk. 'I'm glad for you, Alec.' He

shook his hand. 'That's the best news I've had for a long time.'

'Ta. But I'd rather you didn't let on to no one else. But I wanted to tell you. Special, like.'

Seaton was moved. He was sad too, that he out of them all was alone.

He said, 'We'll have a drink on it later.'

'There's one thing, sir.' Jenkyn looked uncomfortable. 'If anything goes wrong...'

'If it does, Alec, I'll go with you.'

'I know that, sir.' He shifted awkwardly. 'But if it's later on, when the crews split up, I–I'd like you to 'ave a word with 'er first. I saw 'er when th' bloody telegram come to 'er. It'd be better from you.'

Seaton looked down. 'Sure. Glad to.' He tried to smile. 'Thank you.'

The telephone rang on his desk and he said, 'Seaton?'

A bored voice replied, 'Outside call, sir. Hold on, please.'

Across the desk again Jenkyn watched him. Glad he had come.

'David?' Her voice was right beside him.

'Nina?' He gripped the handset and leaned forward as if to draw her closer. 'Where are you?'

Her voice faded as if she had turned away suddenly. 'I have been told that you have finished what you are doing?'

If anyone was eavesdropping he would not have a clue.

'Yes. All but the usual exercises.'

'There is a cottage. Twenty miles from where you are.' Her voice shook as if she was finding it difficult to translate clearly. 'The village is called Maiden's Nettle.' This time she did laugh. 'Sweet, isn't it?'

There was a silence and he said anxiously, 'Are you there?'

'Sorry, Daivd. I was being silly.' She cleared her throat. 'I am all right now.' In a stronger voice she added, 'I can have some leave.'

Seaton said, 'I'll meet you there. Oh, Nina, you don't know how much–'

She gave what sounded like a sob. 'Don't say any more. They'll cut us off. Bring all the food you can.' She started to laugh. 'I am told the cottage is falling down, full of what do you say, wet rot?'

'If I'm late getting there–'

She said quickly, 'I will be there, David. Just come.'

The bored voice said, 'I'm sorry, but this line is needed for a priority call.'

She said, 'Take the road to the north and turn left at Dorchester!'

Seaton could almost feel the switchboard operator dragging out the lead.

'What's the name of the cottage?'

She was laughing again. 'I don't know! It's the last one as you leave the village!' The line went dead.

Seaton put down the receiver and looked at it for several seconds. Then he realised Jenkyn was still there.

Jenkyn said, 'Seems I'm not the only one, sir.' He grinned. 'Smashin'.'

By the time Seaton had reached *Cephalus's* captain's office he had decided that nothing short of an immediate mission was going to stop him.

But, as is often the case, things went rather differently.

The captain met him with a broad smile. 'Funny you should anticipate a bit of leave, David. Captain Venables has just been on the line. Thinks you should shove off for a few days. It'll be good for you, and you deserve it more than the rest of them. Besides, it will give Gervaise Allenby the chance to act as your understudy for a bit.' He tamped down his pipe. 'But you will be on call. I'll see you get transport of some sort from the pool. I suggest you get going before Venables changes his mind.'

An hour later Seaton was speeding along the road in his transport, a jeep which had seen better days, but which had a very good engine.

Turn left at Dorchester. The roads and quiet lanes merged and divided as if in a dream. Once he stopped and bought a few items to supplement a bag of food he had begged from the wardroom chief steward.

The smaller roads were very quiet, and he could smell the hedgerows and the heavier aromas of hidden farms as he sped towards the tiny village of Maiden's Nettle. He need not have worried about navigation. The village seemed to consist of about a dozen cottages, a post office cum grocer's shop and a small pub called the Blue Boar.

He slowed down as he entered the village, conscious of a few curious glances, the twitch of a curtain or two. Sailors were probably rare here. Strange how naval men preferred to stay near the sea, even when off duty.

The cottage greeted him as he rounded the last bend past a tiny war memorial. Beyond was open road and the browns and greens of the Dorset countryside.

He jumped from the seat and hurried through the front door. A few more seconds of suspense, then he saw the W.A.A.F. cap on a chair, her tunic on another. There was a lot of wrapping paper scattered about, and two jugs filled with flowers on a table.

The far door opened and she stood looking at him, her hands hanging at her sides. She was wearing a white Norwegian blouse, with embroidery at neck and wrists, and a dark red skirt. His mind recorded all these things and more, but he only saw her.

She said, 'You were quick. I'm not ready.' She brushed some hair from her eyes. 'Oh, David.'

They came together in the centre of the low-ceilinged room and stood motionless for a long time, neither knowing what to say or wanting to break the spell.

Then he asked, 'Where were you when you called me?'

She looked at him, her eyes very bright. 'Dorchester. Air Marshal Ruthven offered me a lift, as he was on his way somewhere. He put the call through for me. Made it sound official. I–I could not wait back at the headquarters. I needed to be close, in case you tried to get out of seeing me!' She laughed and turned lightly out of his grasp. 'Mind where you tread!' She pointed at several very old telephone directories which were strategically placed around the room. 'There are rot holes in the floor underneath those books!' She could not stop laughing, and he sat at the table to watch her happiness.

She said, 'I feel terribly wicked. I think this cottage used to be a place where the owner took his girl friends for a black week-end!'

Seaton grinned. '*Dirty* week-end!'

'*So?*' She arranged the flowers around the room and then took his hands in hers. 'Now we are here. Do you mind?'

He stood up and held her tightly, feeling her body returning the pressure, the warmth of her skin against his cheek.

'I don't care if it's the moon.' He stroked her hair
'Anywhere.'

He walked with her into the small, overgrown garden. It wa
evening, and he could sense the peace of the place.

She said quietly, 'There is a telephone. I had to make sure.
knew you would be on recall.'

Seaton nodded, holding her shoulders more tightly. Ruthver
had probably engineered the whole thing. It was hard to imagin
him as the owner of the cottage, but he doubtless knew him wel
enough to borrow it.

'I like the sound of your boss,' he said. 'Full of surprises.'

While he telephoned the base at Portland to give the number
to the O.O.D., he heard her working in the kitchen.

He had brought some wine, which tasted remarkably good
considering the shake-up it had endured in the jeep, and long
into the evening they sat enjoying it, watching the trees' black
outlines, and then the moon touching them with metallic light

The cottage did not run to blackout curtains, but neither o
them had even considered the fact.

She placed her glass deliberately on the floor and turned
towards him on the old sofa, holding his face in her hands as she
had done before. He watched the oval of her face, the top of her
hair catching some of the filtered moonlight. Then they kissed
Slowly at first, and then with all the hunger of desperation and
want. When he slipped his hand down to her breast and further
still, she tensed and then pulled herself even closer. Just a
quickly she stood up, her voice husky as she said, 'There is a bed.
Then she took his hand, and they walked together into an
adjoining room.

She stood trembling as he undressed her with infinite care
pausing only to touch her body or to prolong the pain of their
need with another embrace.

Then with her knees drawn up to her chin she sat in the centre
of the bed watching as he threw his clothes in disorder on the
floor.

He knelt beside her, his hand exploring her perfect breasts
the gentle curve of her stomach. Neither of them said a word
But then, as he knelt over her, and she reached out to hold him
and to receive him, she said with a quiet fervour, 'I *want* you
David. I'll not live without you.'

It was like falling, and it was like nothing else. He felt her body responding to his desire, his love for her, and all that she had been before he had even seen her.

When they fell apart he leaned on his elbow, looking at her clean limbs bathed in moonlight, the depths and shadows of her body which he had found and aroused until both of them were completely spent.

She pulled his head down on her shoulder and ran her fingers through his hair. He kissed her body, tasting the heat, the returning desire.

Much later, when he had fallen asleep, she watched and held him tenderly, afraid to wake him, yet unable to leave him alone.

Captain Walter Venables looked at a half-empty cup of tea and rejected it. It was stone-cold, and his tongue felt raw from telephone calls and dictating signals.

Above his head, beyond the layers of steel and concrete, was a London dawn. Here, it could be anytime, anywhere.

A petty officer Wren, her lipstick unnaturally vivid against her tired face, looked in at him.

'Rear Admiral Niven has arrived, sir.' Her eyes, weary or not, flickered over the desk, the tables with their charts. Nothing to worry about. Neat and tidy.

Venables rubbed his eyelids and yawned. She would make a good secretary.

The door squeaked open and Rear Admiral Niven came in with big strides. Powerfully, angrily, a man of the moment.

He glanced at Venables. 'Been here all night, I suppose?' He sat down. 'So it's started.'

Venables nodded. 'Like the one yesterday, sir. Now we've had reports of two more flying bombs. Our people think they were launched from LeHavre.'

The Wren came back with fresh tea.

The admiral watched her. 'Casualties?'

'Civilians. But the point is–'

'The point is we've no more time, Walter. The Jerries must be going all out to stalemate the invasion and destroy any advances by an all out barrage of rockets. The other V- weapon will be over next, I suppose.'

They looked at each other. They were both thinking of the third rocket. The one nobody ever spoke about.

The Wren looked in and said, 'Your Mission Training Officer is here now, sir.'

As she withdrew the admiral remarked, 'Pretty girl.'

Venables fished out his silver case. *All you think about.* He could even smell the lingering aroma of whisky, or was it brandy? After a night of it down here, and the days before, he didn't recognise any of the ordinary things.

Lieutenant Commander Alan Charteris came in stiffly, his face lined, his chin blue and in need of a shave.

He saw the admiral and became very formal. 'Sir!'

'Sit down.' Venables hated to waste time. He took a folder from his private drawer. 'You've heard all about the flying bombs?'

'It was to be expected, sir.'

Venables dropped his eyes to hide his impatience. Men like Charteris were very necessary. They got things done. But they were as thick as two planks.

'Quite. I want the flotilla brought to readiness at once. Go yourself.'

'I've just driven all night from Portland to get here, sir!'

The admiral lowered his cup. 'So?'

Venables added, 'I'd come myself, but things are hotting up. I've just put a sabotage team of frogmen ashore in Normandy to help the Canadians. I'm still waiting to hear from them.'

Charteris had recovered his in-built caution. 'I'll leave now, sir.'

Venables thrust the folder across the desk, 'Sign for this. Don't let it out of your sight.' He watched the other officer scratching his signature on the flimsy. 'Operation Citadel. It was the P.M's idea. I suppose it does have the right ring to it.'

Charteris cleared his throat. 'Lieutenant Commander Seaton is still on leave, sir.' It sounded like an accusation.

'I know. I arranged it.' Venables smiled coldly. 'Leave all that to me.'

As the door closed Rear Admiral Niven breathed out noisily. 'Bloody man. A proper belt-and-gaiters type!' He yawned. 'But maybe he's like me, and doesn't go much on all this cloak-and-dagger stuff.'

Venables wanted him to go. So he could get on to the marines at Eastney and find out about their frogmen.

He said, 'It's the real war. A handful of determined men can change a nation. Big fleets, grand armies are the trimmings. My sort of people win the prizes. After this one's over, we'll not see the same world again, or our kind of Navy.'

Rear Admiral Niven stood up, feeling his age. He might go to an hotel and have breakfast. Or give that damned woman, what-was-her-name, a ring.

He paused by the door. 'Young Seaton. *You* fixed it for him?'

'With our new chief, yes.' Venables smiled. 'The air marshal has the right ideas sometimes.'

'I'd have thought a suite at the Ritz would be more the thing.'

'Would you, sir? Rather like the gladiator before his most testing and usually fatal conflict, you mean? A bounty for services rendered?'

The admiral felt his cheeks flushing. 'No, I damn well didn't!'

'Anyway,' Venables was already flicking through his telephone book. 'Lieutenant Commander Seaton would probably tell you what to do with your offer.' He smiled again. 'Or tell me.'

The petty officer Wren passed the admiral in the doorway and waited by the desk.

Venables said, 'I want you to get me a Dorset number.' He glanced at the clock. They were probably together right now. Lost in each other's arms.

He thought of his admiral's inability to understand how men and women could fight and still stay above the stench of war.

He added, 'If I ever get like him, tell me.'

The Wren left the room. It was said she was the only girl who could stand working for Captain Venables. She could not understand why.

16

Citadel

TWO DECKS down in the old *Cephalus's* hull Seaton sat with Venables' folder on his lap, leaning slightly forward as he read the carefully listed contents.

At his desk the captain sat smoking his pipe, careful not to look at Seaton in case he should break his concentration. The new mission training officer, as well as the ship's first lieutenant were also present.

Around all of them the ship murmured and creaked, and from somewhere in her bowels came the muted buzz of lathes and workshop machinery.

Seaton let his eyes rest at the foot of the page, seeing nothing but her face as he had picked up the telephone in the adjoining room.

He had returned to the warm bed. 'Recall.'

The girl had moved against him, caressing his shoulders whispering secret words into his body. Perhaps she had thought of Trevor then. Those times when a message could bring danger or death.

But she had said, 'I love *you*, David.' She had shaken her head as he had looked at her. 'You know it. Don't try to think otherwise. You do not wish to harm me, that I know. The only hurt you can do me is to leave me forever and not to love me also.'

He had dressed in quick, urgent movements, and all the while she had sat on the edge of the bed, naked and with a sheet over her smooth shoulders. It had been terrible, unbelievably so, and he was defenceless against it.

He had said, 'I have no words, Nina. But I love you so much. If someone were to ask me what my love is, I could not tell him. I only know it is there, has always been there, waiting for you to arrive and accept it.'

She had run to him then, all the carefully rehearsed defences going as the tears had broken through.

There was so much he wanted to know about her, so many things he needed to share. She had cried, 'And you say you have no words, my dear David? You are so very mistaken!'

Seaton lowered the folder and closed it, the small sound making the others turn towards him.

'The rocket site is near Brest.' He watched their faces. They were seeing him differently now. Like a condemned man. 'It is over a U-boat pen which has been there for two years.'

The captain tapped out his pipe. He had not even noticed, let alone resented, that he was hearing this top secret information from a junior reserve officer. It seemed right somehow, and like the moment, strangely moving.

The mission training officer said, 'The Germans have kept it very secret. They've added to the protection with a concrete dome, and the whole area is surrounded by flak and heavy armoured units. The nearer our troops get to the port, the stiffer will be the resistance. The Canadians have already run into unexpected difficulties.' Charteris had the floor, and was enjoying it.

But to the depot ship's captain it meant a lot of other things. Time and durability, fuel and navigation for the various rendezvous points He tried not to think that the latter might not be needed. He said, 'Get on with it, Number One. I want all heads of department here right away. And tell the base engineer officer to come over, too.' He leaned back, his gaze passing over Seaton's composed features. 'Make a signal to the towing submarines. Commanding officers to repair on board immediately, and never mind if they've not had breakfast yet either!'

Seaton heard the door slam, knew the captain was making a joke for his benefit. But he saw her face, could almost hear her voice, close to his ear at moments during the night.

How long had they had? Seven days. A lifetime.

Seaton said, 'I'll tell the crews myself, if I may?' He was looking at the captain, but knew Charteris would answer.

'Well, Captain Venables didn't say anything about that.'

Seaton stood up slowly. Unwinding. Feeling unnaturally light. 'I am to lead them. I want them to trust me.'

'I shall have to get authority.' Charteris sounded angry. 'Captain Venables may want to finish the briefing.'

'Captain Venables is not going on this one!' He faced Charteris calmly. 'We are most likely going to be killed. I'd like to be the one to explain why.'

The captain said sharply, 'Of course, David. I'd do the same in your place.' He walked round the desk and clapped him on the shoulder. 'You will not be killed. Take that as an order from me!' But his eyes did not smile.

Seaton handed over the folder and watched as the captain locked it in his safe.

The orders, so neat and methodical, had already formed themselves into grim reality.

The rocket, which Gjerde and so many others had worked to create, was a monster. When it was launched from its underground lair it would rise to a height of over sixty miles before tearing down on its target at a velocity of over three thousand five hundred miles per hour.

And according to Gjerde's information the rocket was far more accurate than the V-weapons. It had a range of three hundred miles, which meant that while the Germans held on to the site they could hit and destroy any target from Liverpool to London. The whole of south-west England, port, bases, harbours and cities would be wiped out.

The captain asked, 'Anything else I can do?' He crossed to a scuttle and looked down at the pontoons and the submarines alongside. 'I don't have to tell you that we'll be giving you every help we can muster.'

Seaton replied, 'This rocket, sir. It's bigger than my own command. Think of it. A rocket which rises to high trajectory and then drops at such enormous speed there's no defence. They say that if you're still alive you'll be able to hear the sound of the thing falling *after* it's exploded! Can you imagine?' He shook his head. 'So it's up to us apparently.'

The captain tried to see Seaton's little hull groping through the mined and netted waters towards this impossible creation.

Instead he saw a young ex-estate manager, a New Zealand marine biologist, a subbie who had barely experienced anything of the Service he had intended for his career, and lastly the little chief who had come to see him about 'getting spliced'.

Charteris said, 'Well, if you do your best–'

Seaton picked up his cap. 'Christ, you sound like my father.' Then he walked out and made for the upper deck.

The captain looked at Charteris's angry face. 'Not your day, is it?'

'Well, there it is.' Seaton leaned on the table in the operations room, feeling like a showman, with an overhead light trained on the carefully constructed model. The model makers had done well. Had even added little trees made out of *ersatz* sponge.

Operation Citadel. It certainly looked like a strange, nightmare fortress. The huge dome, and tiny ones scattered around it like offspring. In fact, they housed multi-barrelled anti-aircraft guns. The original entrance was deep underneath, although it was said to have additional steel gates which were closed at the moment of firing. He wondered what had happened to all the slave workers who had built the U-boat pen and later the massive additions overhead. Probably ended up mixed with their concrete, as the advancing Russians had discovered in their own country.

Seaton said, 'The rocket has one disadvantage to its users. It has to be delivered to the site in sections and then assembled *inside* the ramp.' He saw Lieutenant Farmer, XE 26's first lieutenant, grasp his fingers together as he added, 'Against that, however, it will do far more damage than anything we've yet envisaged.' He looked round at the faces, men he knew, who were withdrawing into strangers. 'It can, no, it *will* smash everything we have on this side of the Channel unless we can knock it out. The bombers can't hurt it, and unless the army get there in time to destroy it, things look dicey for any hope of victory.'

They were probably thinking of the flying bombs which were still falling across London and the south-east. Intelligence had added further reports about the second V-weapon, but even combined they were nothing when compared with the one near Brest. And even Gjerde had admitted there would be more of them under construction once the invasion was turned into another Dunkirk.

Seaton said, 'There will be the proper briefing tomorrow at eight.' He thought of the captain's joke. There would be little breakfast eaten that day.

Gervaise Allenby stood up languidly. 'May I say something?'

'Shoot.'

'I'm not too keen on this little caper. But if, as the felon said to the hangman, go I must, then I'd rather be led across the great divide by you.' He sat down, and there were several nods and murmurs of approval.

Seaton cleared his throat. There was no point in drama and false heroics. But he could imagine the sort of talk Charteris would have given, or Niven's father.

He thought of all the men who had gone. Had known their efforts would be hopeless, at least for themselves. The lonely ones you never met. Who led the prongs of an attack, or waited at the tail of a retreat. The real heroes.

He walked past the scattered chairs, needing fresh air. Silence.

On deck a stiff wind drained the warmth from the sunlight, and he paused by the guardrail to stare up at Portland Bill until his eyes watered. What was she doing now? Still at the cottage, or had she been picked up and taken back to the underground H.Q.? No, surely they would have spared her that. Seeing the little flags being moved on Ruthven's wall chart, nearer and nearer. Then vanishing, to be placed in a tin with all the others.

Someone leaned on the rail beside him. He knew it was Drake.

Drake said quietly, 'The big one, Skipper.'

'Looks like it. Worried?' He turned slightly to watch Drake's strong profile and faraway eyes. Whatever our flaws and weaknesses, we have come through a lot, he thought.

'I'll be glad when it's over. Put it like that.' He grinned. 'Least, if we have to ditch we know the army will come to *us*, eventually.'

The newly-joined diver in XE 26, Sub-Lieutenant Driscoll. hovered beside them then said, 'Letter for you, Geoff.'

'Thanks.' Drake examined it. It was in Decia Niven's handwriting.

The new sub-lieutenant did not go. It seemed to give him confidence to be near the one who would lead. Who had done it all before, and had got back.

He said, 'Mail's just in. Your diver, Richard Niven, gave it to me.'

Drake stared at him. Drake and Driscoll. Both letters in the same rack. Niven could not have failed to see it, to recognise his wife's writing.

Seaton guessed most of it. It had happened at last, and it was too late to do a damn thing about it.

Drake stared down at the oily water. 'Holy cow!'

Seaton walked away, leaving him to his new anxiety.

Tomorrow there might be a letter from Nina. He hung on to the name, her voice and her accent. *Nina*.

Then he swung on his heel and was back at Drake's side almost before he understood what was happening.

'*Listen to me!*' He saw Drake's eyes widen with surprise. 'I really don't give a damn about your affairs. It's no longer important. What is, and I should have made this point in the ops room, is that we will do a good job, no matter what the cost. And hear me, Geoff, if I see cause to blame you for one fault during the attack I will personally drop you overboard with the side-cargoes!'

Drake tried to grin, to laugh it off, but his mouth stayed frozen.

'I *mean* it.' Seaton walked down the side deck without another glance.

The decision to put Operation Citadel into effect, once confirmed, set the chain of command rapidly in motion.

From the Admiralty, through Combined Special Operations and Flag Officer Submarines to the desk of the admiral in Portland, the message was urgency.

The briefing aboard *Cephalus* as she rose above her small brood like a protective parent was taut and exacting. The U-boat pen which had been converted into the rocket site was just one of the great complex of concrete bunkers which had been built along a one hundred mile coastal strip from Brest to Lorient. For months and years the U-boats had left their French bases to probe deep into the Atlantic and reap a bloody harvest. In 1943 the tide had started to turn, and for once U-boat losses overtook the yards' ability to replace them. New methods were employed by the Allies to protect the precious convoys as they fought their way again and again into the Western Approaches. Better escorts, hunter-killer groups, radar, pocket-sized aircraft carriers, and almost as important, the realisation that at last they were starting to win.

Fewer U-boats returned to the concrete pens, and their crews no longer sang as they marched up to their shore quarters past bitter-eyed French men and women.

With the Allied armies now in Normandy it would be a matter of time only before every U-boat base along the Bay of Biscay would have to be evacuated, with the boats having a hard time to reach safety in Germany.

They were all at the briefing. Venables, Charteris, the depot ship and base technical officers, Operations and Met department, and Seaton was glad to see Captain Clifford Trenoweth slip in quietly just before the briefing got started, his familiar limp making several heads turn.

Venables, clear-eyed and brusque, with no hint that he had barely slept for days, cleared one point after another.

The target was some twenty miles south of Brest. It had never been very useful as a U-boat pen, mainly because of the twisting shallows which led up to it. For its present use it was excellent for the same reasons. There were a few soldiers present, too. Lean, tough-looking officers in camouflaged jerkins and red berets.

The Airbourne were going to make a drop inland to attack a château which was known to be a German infantry H.Q.

A lieutenant colonel and two majors made notes as Venables spoke of the proposed diversion. Seaton thought it sounded more like suicide.

A strike force of fleet destroyers would pass through the blockading squadrons to cover the withdrawal.

Seaton glanced at Niven, who was writing busily on his pad. Perhaps Drake was wrong? Niven gave no sign of anger or dismay as he compiled the notes for his navigation log.

Drake, on the other hand, sat bolt upright, his eyes fixed on the maps and the model, but his mind obviously elsewhere.

The three E.R.A.'s stayed in a tight group of their own. Jenkyn was grim-faced and dwarfed by his two companions. But there was an unusual brightness about Jenkyn, like someone inspired, or controlled by another force.

Seaton watched him, feeling a lump in his throat. Would Jenkyn ever find his dream now? His 'nice little party'.

Seaton looked down at his hands. Nina kept emerging, recalling precious moments.

The first dawn, waking together. Watching her at the mirror, the comb crackling through her hair. Walks in the fields, hand in hand like children one moment, desperately in need of each other the next.

The meeting was almost done. Feet moved uneasily. Thoughts of a good meal, writing letters home, or just going over it all in your mind, showed on most faces. Those who would be going. Others who would try to make it as safe as possible for them.

Venables waited for the operations officer to complete his appraisal of coastal defences, then he stood up and walked to the centre of the little stage, his hands in his reefer pockets, his neat head thrusting forward as he surveyed them.

'All this seems to great to digest. And yet in a matter of weeks we have achieved miracles. Soon the cry will be, forward into Germany, the last turn of the screw.' He spoke very evenly, and his words seemed to have more impact because of it. 'It is not our lot to know if each and every part we played in this conflict was vital, or even necessary. This I can say. If we falter now, the sacrifice of every man, woman and child in *our* world will have been in vain. Be proud of what you are doing, for there is no fault in pride. Be determined, but above all, gentlemen, know that what *you* are about to do is the stuff of victory.'

He stepped down from the platform, and followed by his aides walked through the assembled men looking neither right nor left.

Seaton licked his lips, trying to fix the moment in his mind, as he would a bearing or landmark on a chart. There should have been cheers, or a wave of wild and crazy excitement.

He looked around at the others, those who would go, those who would have to wait behind. There was something more than empty excitement here. A will to go through with it. A strength which he had never seen before.

A hand touched his sleeve and he saw it was Trenoweth.

'Good to see you again, sir. It seems so long.'

Captain Trenoweth grunted. 'That man Venables. Never knew he had it in him, quite a speech, I thought. Blast the man, I was almost cheering m'self just then!' He grimaced. 'Almost.'

Seaton waited for the others to move away. 'I was going to write to you anyway, sir. I've some letters and a few personal things.'

'I see.' Trenoweth was expressionless. 'You've made me very proud. To have asked me.' He looked away, swaying heavily on his good leg. 'But it *shan't* happen. Not now.'

Seaton watched him despairingly. *Help me. You know what it all means. You must have gone through it often enough.*

Trenoweth said heavily, 'They've closed down *Syren.* I've come south to take over some little job. I'll miss the old place, and all we achieved together.'

'Yes.' Seaton clenched his fists, suddenly angry. Why had he been thinking badly of himself? He should have seen something was wrong. Trenoweth's world had gone for good. He had done a fine job, they would say. Then they'd forget him. Another old warrior, used and thrown away.

He said gently, 'I'm selfish, sir, but I'm glad you're here. I was feeling a bit down. You always managed to perk us up when we needed it.'

'Did I?' He sounded miles away. 'Poor old Duffy's no longer with us.' He poked the deck with his stick. 'Went off in his sleep. Still miss the old bugger, bless him. Buried him above the loch.'

Seaton nodded, seeing it. The old captain with his stick, the ungainly dog sniffing along the loch at dusk. Inseparable.

'I'm very sorry. You know that.' Trenoweth's loss seemed to steady him, to pull him together. Perhaps it was the simplicity of it after all the grim technicalities of the briefing.

Trenoweth made a great effort. 'Wish we had time for a gin. But I expect you'll be wanting to get ready, eh?' He smiled sadly. 'I've not forgotten the feeling.'

Seaton held out his hand. 'Thank you again, sir.' He did not know how to tell Trenoweth what he had done for him. Instead, he drew back and saluted.

Trenoweth limped out on to the slippery deck. It must have been drizzling, he thought. Then he peered down at the three small submarines which seemed to be swarming with artificers and mechanics. It had all got beyond him. He felt at a complete loss amidst the bustle and purpose of a front-line base.

He saw Seaton down on the pontoons, speaking with an engineer officer.

A good man. No, better than that. He thought of the time *XE 16* had sailed for Norway. His vigil on the hillside with Second Officer Dennison. Helen.

He turned as Captain Venables hurried along the deck, speaking with one of his assistants. It would be Admiral Venables before long.

Venables paused and studied him thoughtfully, his head on one side.

'I've been speaking with the C-in-C about you. A job you might fancy.'

Trenoweth drew himself up, leaning on his stick as little as possible.

But Venables gave him no time. 'Nothing grand, of course. But I'll need someone to take overall command of the new midget base down here, to get them ready for the Far East. Suit you?'

Trenoweth swallowed hard. Then he said simply, 'Thank you. I'd like it.' He nodded. *'Thanks very much.'* Surprisingly, he found it easy to say.

Venables gave his wry smile. 'We make a good team. They like you, and in me there's always someone to hate.' As he turned to follow his agitated assistant he added, 'Second Officer Dennison will be posted to you for communications.' He smiled again. 'And so forth.' Then he was gone.

Trenoweth gripped the guardrail and exclaimed aloud, 'Bless my soul, Duffy, we're not done for yet!'

The operations officer ran his parallel rulers across the chart and said quietly, 'There is this snag to contend with.'

Seaton leaned forward, his eyes rebelling against the harsh reflected glare from the chart table. The two other commanding officers, Allenby and Winters, studied the 'snag' with him.

The operations officer explained, 'With the best of intentions the R.A.F. sent a strike of low-level bombers across your U-boat pen. This was before anyone had a clue about rockets or anything else. A U-boat was returning from patrol. Usual thing, nobody looking at the sky, each chap thinking about a run ashore after the bloody Atlantic.'

Seaton studied the neat pencilled mark on the chart. How simple he made it sound. *Usual thing.* It was certainly true that more submarines were caught on the hop by aircraft when they were returning to base than outward bound.

Winters said, 'The U-boat's still there on the bottom.'

'Right.' The operations officer sighed. 'The Germans can't be bothered to salvage her at this stage of the game, they're otherwise engaged. But the sub does present a hazard. Watch out for the thing. Check your bearings whenever you can. Memorise each detail so that you recognise a landmark without going backwards and forwards to your charts.'

Allenby straightened up and rubbed his spine. 'One thing, old son. It's not so far as Norway!' He chuckled. 'Last week we were moaning about being out of it. Right now, I think we are well and truly *in* it!'

In the dockyard, dressed in his stained seagoing gear, Niven stood with a telephone to his ear, listening to his father's voice. For anybody else there were no private calls with the whole base at top level security. Niven knew it, and wished his father had not used his authority to telephone him from London.

It was too much like school, or Dartmouth. Seeing him off from holiday or leave.

He was in an emergency signals office, where a telegraphist and two Wrens were watching him with unveiled curiosity. They knew who was calling, and who *he* was, too. More to the point, they would know where he was going.

His father was saying, 'I'm not *worried*, naturally. Just wanted to say that I hope it all goes all right. You know.'

'Yes.' Niven stared at the floor. 'Thanks.'

A pause. 'Is that all you've got to say, for goodness sake?'

No, it's not. Decia's having an affair with Geoffrey Drake. She can't keep her hands off him, and now she's writing to him.

In a tight voice he answered, 'I'm sorry.'

Something in his tone made his father ask, 'Look, Richard, is something wrong? We've had our ups and downs, I know. All families go through this sort–'

Niven heard himself stammer, 'Ours is not a family. It's a bloody, hopeless mess!' He saw one of the Wrens cover her mouth with her hand. He said, 'So long, Dad. Tell Decia he got her letter, will you?' He slammed down the receiver.

The telegraphist watched him walk to the door and gave an admiring gasp.

Niven turned and looked at them, his face pale and strained. 'Sorry about that. Bad show. But you see–'

One of the Wrens hurried from her table and said, 'It's all right, sir. *Really.*' Then she leaned over and kissed him quickly on the cheek. 'That's from all of us, sir. Good luck. Things will sort themselves out.'

A red-faced yeoman of signals banged through another door and halted stock still. 'What's going' on? Something wrong?'

Niven lifted his chin and then gripped the girl's arm. 'Thanks for that.' To the yeoman he said, 'Wrong? Nothing at all. It didn't really matter.'

The door closed behind him, and the Wren who had saved Niven's sanity burst into tears.

The yeoman said desperately, 'Gawd Almighty! The day they let girls into th' Andrew was *the bloody day*!'

Seaton was so involved with last-minute preparations it came almost as a shock to find that the day had gone.

The water around H.M.S. *Cephalus* was hazy with the stench of diesel engines, as the maintenance engineers made their last checks on the midgets and aboard the three submarines which would tow them as near as safety allowed to the target area.

Torches bobbed along the pontoons and the out-thrust arms of the harbour breakwaters. Launches snarled into the darkness, and from outside, somewhere in the Channel, Seaton heard the banshee shriek of a destroyer's siren.

He tried to think clearly, to find any loose strands. He had others to think of this time, while within his own command there was a new and latent menace between Drake and Niven. He had warned Drake, so why not Niven? He was the youngest aboard, and yet, as he had proved, could quickly become the most vital man in the crew. Despair, hatred or just humiliation might kill as easily as a bullet.

A seaman scuttled out of the gloom, his oilskin shining like black glass.

'Sir? Senior Officer wants to see you up at the base, right away.'

'What does he want, for God's sake?' He relented, seeing the man's confusion. Why take it out on him? 'All right. Pass the word for the duty motor boat.'

The seaman relaxed. 'Ready and waiting, sir.' He hesitated. 'Best of luck with the raid, sir. A bit of Harry Roughers, if you ask me!'

Seaton smiled. Good old Jack. A phrase which contained everything involved with the job, and excluded all those not taking part.

Perhaps the senior officer had some last minute request. Anyway, it took his mind off things. As he sat crouched in the bouncing motor boat, the 'skimming dish' as she was nicknamed, he went over his own private preparations. Letters for Nina and his father. One for Captain Trenoweth, giving him the necessary authority to dispose of his effects. It was not a lot, but it might help Nina to find time, to discover another hope of happiness.

Into a car and up the winding road to the base. He caught sight of himself in a long mirror as he hurried through some swing doors. It looked wrong in some way to appear so smart. In fresh battledress and cap, the shoulder straps with his new rank for all to see, he barely recognised himself.

Even that brought it back again. Nina setting off with his old uniform to lay a trail for the Germans to find, and draw them from Bergen. She had spoken of his bravery, but what of her own? How that S.S. butcher would have made her suffer was beyond imagination.

He glanced at all the empty racks outside the wardroom, which such a short time ago had been filled with naval caps. British, American and almost every nation which was occupied by the enemy. Where were their owners now, he wondered?

A porter guided him to somebody's office, where to his surprise he saw Air Marshal Ruthven drinking coffee with the base commander.

The air marshal stood up and shook hands warmly. 'Hello, young man, you look better than the last time I saw you.' He looked meaningly at the commander. 'Must be off soon. Back to my Sussex hideout to keep an eye on things.' As the other officer moved to the door Ruthven added, 'It's putting a lot on your shoulders. More than anyone has a right to ask. If I thought there was any other way . . .' He shrugged. 'But now we know for certain. I've had a report just now that a rocket was launched on a test run from *that site*. It apparently had no explosive war-head, but it landed in the Bristol Channel, that's over two hundred miles from the firing point.' He massaged his forehead wearily. 'It fell amongst a coastal convoy heading out of Cardiff. But for the quick thinking of the officer in charge of the escort, I might not have been told. But as he reported, there was this enormous splash which threw up a column of water bigger than anything he had ever seen, and although it was clear of the convoy, it almost capsized one of the coasters.'

Their eyes met, then Seaton said, 'So they'll be assembling the next one right now, sir, Armed and set for a real target. Probably London.'

Faces flashed through his mind. His father and his friends in the pub. The women of London, as conductors on the buses, on the trains, working at machines in factories, tending the injured.

'It looks like it. After that it will be a bombardment.'

Ruthven walked to the door. 'I have to go. Good luck.' He gestured to the other door. 'She's waiting in there, Five minutes.'

She was standing in the centre of the room, her hands clasped, her blue-green eyes fixed on the door. The next second they were together, holding each other so tightly that nothing outside of them seemed real.

He said quietly, 'I never dreamed I could be so lucky.' He lifted her chin with his hand, remembering everything which had grown between them.

She had taken off her service cap, and as he touched her hair with his fingers she moved her arms up around his neck. The scent of her, the feel of her body against his was something which no uniform could mar. She said, 'I shall be waiting, David. And then we *will* be safe. We will have a life. Together.'

Seaton saw her mouth quiver, but knew she would not break now. Not until after the door was closed. She, more than most, knew the value to him of this last moment. To both of them.

Outside, a horn echoed like a wounded stag.

She said, 'Five minutes. Like our seven days, David. They are shorter than everyone else's.'

'Wait here.' He kissed her slowly and with great feeling. When their mouths drew apart it was like being burned. He stepped back. 'I shall never forget.'

She brushed the hair from her eyes. 'You look beautiful, David. And I'm so proud.'

He closed the door quickly and hurried through the other room without looking back.

His driver was ready. 'All set, sir?'

'Yes.'

He sat in silence, remembering her face as he had closed the door.

He thought too of Ruthven. For someone who was sending them almost certain death, he had done all he could to help.

The car swung in a tight arc and he saw the harbour.

The rest was behind him.

17

Goliath

THE PASSAGE to the target area seemed to demand more of Seaton's nerve than any before. Because of the danger of detection, or the possibility of being attacked by one of the many Allied warships which were covering the invasion forces, the three towing submarines took a roundabout route from Portland.

Down channel, then south towards the Bay of Biscay, with the crews getting as much rest aboard their parent craft as their varied resources of courage and experience would allow.

Each slow mile gave Seaton a growing sense of his responsibility in the operation. It was not just another case of risking his neck, with all the excited aftermath to hide the earlier apprehension and fear. This one really was important, and he found it almost impossible to snatch even a cat-nap.

The commander of the towing submarine did his part of the job with practised efficiency. But this time he gave it something extra, knowing what was expected of Seaton and the three tiny X-craft. At regulated times he went to periscope depth, raised his snorkel to suck air for his diesels, while at the same time he monitored the steady flow of signals from the far off Admiralty.

The commander was about the only man within the submarine's hull to whom Seaton confided his thoughts, even his hopes.

But each radio signal was like a slap in the face. A further sighting shot had been detected from the hidden rocket site, and this time it had fallen on land just to the west of Southampton. It had completely destroyed itself, but had made a crater in a stretch of farmland large enough to hold several tanks. With its massive warhead fitted, the effect of an explosion would be appalling.

The submarine commander had said during one of their discussions, 'It seems to take them about two days to assemble each rocket. They'll probably get quicker at it. But now they've got the practice and know-how to range it on a particular area. It's my guess that the next few days are going to tell.'

Seaton lay behind his bunk curtain and stared at the dripping deckhead.

The army was not going to break into the Brest sector in time, and although the R.A.F. had made another heavy raid on the target area, they had achieved nothing, and had suffered terrible losses from flak and fighters.

A few hours before the time of transferring to *XE 16*, Seaton gathered his crew in the submarine's wardroom. The commander had ensured he would be left undisturbed, and even the off-duty watchkeepers had been made to take their rest elsewhere.

They sat around the small table, as they had before. But it even felt different, with a barrier between him and the others.

When he explained about the enemy's second practice shot he saw the effect of it at once. Perhaps, like himself, they had been hoping for a way out. A miracle.

He said, 'The unloading of the rocket components and their entry through the U-boat pen appears to take place at night. It makes sense. This is going to be a rough one, and with no time for messing about. We'll go in at dawn. If we attack earlier the rocket will not be inside to explode with the side-cargoes. The Airborne are doing a red-herring raid for us, so there's not much else we can hope for. It's us or them.'

Drake placed his hands flat on the table and stared at them. 'Seems a tall order.'

Seaton watched him. 'It is. But just remember. That first test shot went two hundred miles plus. I'm given to understand that it can do another hundred and then some at full blast.'

He looked at their faces. Niven, tight-lipped, hiding his feelings. Jenkyn, his narrow shoulders stooped as if only just aware of what he was facing. Drake, unusually grim, wary.

The curtain moved slightly across the door. 'Ten minutes, sir.'

'Well, I think you know what this may mean.' Seaton patted his pockets. How stiff and unfamiliar his new battledress felt. 'But we must try to get clear after the attack. And help each other all we can.' He imagined Allenby and Winters saying much the same to their own crews.

Jenkyn stretched and yawned. 'They're spendin' enough on this one, sir. So we mustn't let the old taxpayer down, must we?'

Outside, in another world, a tannoy rasped, 'Deck handing party muster by the fore hatch. Anti-aircraft gun crews to the control room on the double.' A slight pause. 'Stand by to surface.'

Niven said, 'I'll be glad to get on with it.' He smiled at Seaton, his gaze excluding the others. 'Don't worry, sir.'

Seaton looked away, *He knows I know*. He's trying to tell me in his own stiff way that he'll not let me down.

They heard the inrush of compressed air, the click of the lower hatch being opened.

Seaton waited, standing away from the table or any support, gauging the deck's motion as the big submarine lurched to the surface. It barely swayed more than a few degrees.

Jenkyn had been watching his face, and said, 'Mill-pond. That's summat.'

Then they were moving, hurrying through the boat towards the fore hatch where the seamen had already hoisted out a rubber dinghy.

A few quick glances from the busy submariners, a thumbs up, a brief grin.

Then with the handling party they were on the casing, gasping in the salt air which seemed too strong after the confines of the boat.

Seaton waited for the others to jump into the dinghy and then turned towards the conning tower's dark outline. He knew the commander would be watching him, but aware all the time of his own responsibility, his nakedness on the surface, trimmed as high as possible to help the dinghy crew.

There was a regular off shore swell, but less than Seaton had expected.

They had been steering due east, following the forty-eighth parallel as if walking a tight-wire. To port lay a deadly procession of rocks and tiny jagged islets, and beyond them, away to the north-east, was the fortified port of Brest.

Seaton clung to the rocking dinghy as it twisted and bobbed down the tow-line towards the surfaced X-craft. He could see her black outline, surrounded by lively cat's-paws as she wallowed beam-on to receive her rightful company.

Twenty miles to the target, and dawn was early. It would be dangerous all right.

He pictured the French coastline as it reached out like a protective shoulder above the Bay of Biscay. *Pointe du Raz.* A difficult stretch of land which had cost the lives of many sailors and had claimed a lot of ships down through the centuries.

Nelson's captains must have hated it as they had worked their weather-beaten ships back and forth on blockade duty. Brest, Belle Île, Ushant, names from history.

Seaton watched the seamen making fast to *XE 16* and poised himself to jump across.

Now they were going to add to that same history. One way or the other.

The lieutenant of the passage crew shouted, 'Nothing to report, David!' He grinned through the darkness. 'Sorry! I mean *sir*!' He stood aside as his companions dived past him, each handing over to Drake and the others with a minimum of delay.

Seaton heard someone call, 'Good luck!' Then the dinghy was clear, scuttling back to the submarine like an ungainly water-beetle.

Seaton slipped the tow and hurried to the hatch. When his boots hit the control room deck it seemed as if the others had never left since the last time.

As he watched them going through their checks he found time to notice what a good job the depot ship had done on XE 16. Fresh paint, a sheen of oil on every working part, she was like new.

He heard the back-echo of the towing submarine flooding her tanks as she dived and steered away to safer waters. The other two X-craft would, or should be on their way by now, heading to the rendezvous for one last contact before the attack.

Drake said, 'Checks complete, Skipper.'

'Very well.'

Seaton tossed his cap on to a newly fitted rack of weapons. *He rarely calls me by name now.* Another barrier.

'Dive, dive, dive. Thirty feet. Eight-five-oh revolutions. Course zero-nine-five.' He watched Jenkyn's hands as he opened the main-vent valves. 'Tell me when you're satisfied with the trim.'

Drake and Jenkyn had become so practised and experienced at working together that Seaton was almost able to ignore what they were doing as they pumped water back and forth, adjusting the boat's trim so that she would answer instantly to rudder and hydroplanes.

Niven was leaning over the chart, his eyes slitted with concentration, doing what Seaton often did. Shutting out the others with his back.

Drake reported, 'Trimmed for diving.'

Seaton ducked his head and moved to the table. He said, 'We will stay at this depth and speed until the first fix.'

Niven seemed fascinated by the large-scale chart of the target. It was a narrow inlet, pointing north into the coast like a crack. There was not much depth, and shallows on either side of the entrance.

Seaton said quietly, 'I'll bet many a U-boat commander cursed the mind which planned *that* for a pen.'

Niven ran one finger along the pencilled course. Eastward to the inlet, then a sharp northerly turn, do the job and out again. His finger traced the outward course more slowly, as if examining the idea of survival.

He said, 'The escape run is almost due south, sir. Straight across the *Baie d'Audienne*.'

Seaton replied, 'Better chance that way.'

He followed Niven's finger. The inward and outward courses made one great right angle, like a cocked hat. The three submarines were on their way to the pick-up area already. Their people would be having breakfast. Powdered eggs and tinned sausages.

He swallowed hard, amazed that he could feel hunger at a time like this.

'And there's the *château* the Airborne boys are going after.'

It was about eight miles inland, and unremarkable except for a fine seventeenth century clock tower, according to Venables' information. It would be remembered for a lot more after the raid, Seaton thought grimly.

Niven said, 'At least we're free of mines. They've laid quite a broad field to the south-east, towards Lorient.'

'With rocks to port and shallow water by submarine standards, there's been no need.'

Seaton closed his mind to the possibility that the chart was wrong about those rocks. That would ruin everything before it started if he drove his command aground.

Niven twisted his head to look at him. 'I wouldn't have missed it for anything.' He watched Seaton's surprise. 'At first I thought it was just bravado, big-headedness on my part. Then I imagined I was trying to cover up something, and that my fight with the German frogman was a fluke, outside my nature.'

'And now?'

'I find it hard to explain. Like doing something better than anyone else for the first time in my life. Not merely *well*, or as my father would say, "could have been worse", but good enough for,' he dropped his eyes, 'for *you*.'

Seaton smiled, 'Thank you. But it's your father you really want to impress, isn't it?'

'Once. Yes, it was. My brother–' He shrugged. 'Well, I expect you guessed.'

'Most of it.'

'The funny thing is that my father never really wanted to be in the Service. My grandfather told me one day, when he'd had a row with him about something. I was just a boy, but I never forgot that. You see, in our family it was expected. The thing to do. There was never any question of choice.' He sighed like an old man. 'Maybe that's what he had against me. I actually *like* the Navy, and nothing, not even his success, can wipe out his original protest at being sent to Dartmouth.'

'I see.' Seaton watched him, understanding his need to talk, to explain. 'And you've been fighting him ever since?'

'I suppose so. Decia, my wife, is a bit like that.' He had

wered his voice, and Seaton guessed it was because of Drake.

Seaton did not know what to say. 'It's difficult in wartime. eparation.' He thought of her words to him. About Trevor. overs, but not in love.

Niven nodded. 'Don't I know it.'

Jenkyn called, 'Can someone give me a spell? I'll wet the tea.'

Niven straightened up. 'I'll take over.'

Across the control room Drake watched him dully, his shoul-ers glittering with droplets of condensation, as if he had been anding in summer rain.

Seaton opened his pocket-book, *XE 16's* codename leaping ut of the page at him. *Goliath*. That was most likely Venables' lea, too, David and Goliath.

He wondered what Nina was doing right at this minute. ying asleep, as he had watched her so often in those precious :ven days. Her body perfect in the moonlight, her soft breath-g the only proof that he was not just dreaming.

The book closed with a snap. He must not think like that. She as almost beyond reach now. Every turn of the screw was king him towards the final separation.

Seaton glanced at the clock, Twenty minutes more and then p to take a look around.

He turned back to the chart, but saw instead her face as she ad watched him leave.

I don't want to die. Especially not now. How many had said r thought like that? Like his father's war, on the firestep of a ench in Flanders. A last hope, and then over the top into the ire, the chattering machine-guns. Oblivion.

Jenkyn's face appeared. 'Char up, gents! Cheaper than ons!'

Seaton swung round, showing himself to the others. He uld not give in yet. He owed it to these men. Now more than er before.

He grinned. 'When it's over we'll have something stronger.'

Jenkyn grimaced. 'You're on. Though it's right bloody now I eds it!'

Seaton licked his lips and shivered. The strain of waiting was aking him ache all over. It even seemed to reawaken the juries he had received from the German boots in Bergen.

255

It was hard to accept that the other two midgets were clo[se]
by, or ought to be by now, manoeuvring into position just sou[th]
of the last headland before the inlet.

He swallowed, tasting Jenkyn's tea. He must have half fill[ed]
the mug with sugar. A thick corned beef sandwich complet[ed]
their breakfast. Or was it a last supper?

'All ready?' He touched the periscope hoist. The cont[rol]
room lights were all extinguished except for essential ones abo[ve]
controls and chart. It would give the man at the periscope [a]
better chance to accustom his eyes without delay.

'Ready, Skipper.'

'Right. Two-five-oh revs. Periscope depth.'

XE 16 tilted very gently towards the surface, her mot[or]
vibrating in response to the reduced speed.

'Nine feet.'

Seaton was already on his knees, his hands controlling t[he]
periscope's slow rise, his body moving with it as it broke t[he]
surface.

The sky was the first thing he noticed. Very clear, with a f[ew]
tiny stars to prove that night was still retaining its grip. But [he]
could see the land, black and solid above the sea's oily shee[n.]
God, but it looked hard and unwelcoming.

He heard Niven say, 'The headland should be about n[ow,]
four-five, sir.'

Seaton eased the periscope round carefully, feeling the h[ull]
sway more noticeably in the undulating swell.

He watched the land reaching away in clinging darkness. B[ut]
it would not be long now. Behind him the newly fitted R/T s[et]
was spitting and murmuring to itself as evidence that it w[as]
switched on. It was like hearing the fish speaking their o[wn]
special language.

Seaton tensed as something moved above a long, unbrok[en]
roller.

'Stand by to dive!' He steadied the handles and murmur[ed]
quietly, 'God Almighty.'

The others knew better than to speak, but he could feel th[eir]
anxiety.

He said, 'It's a man in the water.'

He made himself follow the bobbing head as it idled slow[ly]
towards the periscope. The leather helmet and brightly colour[ed]

ae West told him it was a ditched airman, probably from that
st big raid over the rocket site.

The lens had him perfectly now, and Seaton could see the
ay his arms were spread out on the surface, wide apart. His
ad was thrown back, the mouth open as if in one last appeal, a
ıal curse against those who had sent him here to die.

Seaton wanted to lower the periscope, but could not do so. It
ıuld be cheating, an insult to a man who had died alone. He
w the face right by the periscope, held in the crosswires, the
ıpty eyes ignoring it.

He heard Niven gasp as something scraped against the hull.

Seaton said, 'His boots.' Then he swung the lens away to
ave the sea empty once more.

To Niven he said, 'Take over here. I'm going to see if this
ımn set works.'

As Niven ducked down to control the periscope their eyes
et.

Then Niven said, 'Poor devil. It seems wrong to leave him
ere like that.'

Seaton sat by the small steel cabinet with its twin red lights.
e took the handset off its clip and pressed the button.

Niven would in all probability be dead in a few hours. Yet he
ıuld find pity for one who was beyond aid.

He said, 'Hello, *Dodo*, hello, *Dodo*. This is *Goliath*. Do you
ad me? Over.'

More crackles and clicks, then a voice came through the
eaker, faint at first, but unmistakably Allenby's.

'Hello. *Goliath*, this is *Dodo*. I read you loud and clear.
ver.'

XE 26's codename was *Oyster*, and Winters' response was
earer and louder.

They were all on station. No faults. No breakdowns.

Seaton said, 'This is *Goliath*. Proceed as planned. No
anges. Good luck. Over and out.'

There was no point at this stage in exchanging useless
marks. But knowing that each was nearby made all the differ-
ıce.

And they had gone over it, and over it again, until they could
emorise every known detail. *Known* detail.

Gervaise Allenby would lead in *XE 19*. His would be the

honour, as he had put it. He was experienced and highly skille
But not so much as Seaton. If anyone was going to catch it,
would be the one in the lead. They all knew that, no one mo
than Allenby.

Winters had only done one previous operation in a comma
of his own. He was to enter last, or hold back if the wo
happened and try again later. It had sounded fine when t
operations officer had explained it at the briefing.

'Like waitin' for the N.A.A.F.I. to open,' Jenkyn h
remarked.

Seaton said, 'Lower the stick. Take her down to thirty fee

He scrambled to the table, feeling it tremble slightly as Dra
depressed the hydroplanes. He moved the parallel rulers on
again, checking the bearings, knowing there was no need. B
just in case.

'Alter course, Alec. Steer zero-five-zero.'

'Thirty feet, Skipper.'

'Increase to eight-five-oh revs.' He looked at Niven. 'St
handing out the Sten guns.'

He had a momentary picture of Major Lees and
formidable sergeant, McPeake; they had done their work w
Niven showed no trace of surprise as he took out the Stens a
spare magazines.

Now *Syren* would become the Lodge Hotel again, but sur
some memories would remain? Some remnant of the youth a
eagerness which had passed through its doors.

At least old Duffy was still there, watching over the loch.
pale creeping mist and the bitter winter days.

He said, 'Grenades, too, Make sure they're primed.' He s
Niven look at him questioningly and smiled. 'I *know*. But che
everything again.'

Apart from her powerful side-cargoes, these weapons w
the only teeth *XE 16* possessed.

A fat lot of use they would be, Seaton thought. But it g
Niven something to keep him busy, and a small confidence
those who still believed in it.

He tried not to look at the clock, One hour to go. Then o
the top, and the best of luck.

He thought suddenly of the cottage. Maiden's Nettle s
asleep beyond their window. Her arm across his chest,
mouth touching his skin.

258

The memory was so clear, so deep inside of him that he felt defenceless, the pain of it pricking his eyes like smoke.

Jenkyn kept his gaze on the ticking gyro repeater, holding the boat on course with little effort. There was hardly any motion, and even when they had been at periscope depth it had been as gentle as a loch. Making it easy for them. The last ride to bloody hell. He thought of that creepy sound, thudding and scraping against the hull. Poor sod. Drifting all alone. Somebody, somewhere would be waiting. Hoping. Husband, son, lover? What difference now?

At least we will all be together when it happens. Snug in our tin coffin.

I hope she doesn't take on too badly when the news gets to her. We'll get the Victoria Cross for this little lot. It will be something for her to have. To show Gwen when she's grown up enough to understand why the world once went raving mad.

Drake heard him sigh and shifted his buttocks on the hard seat. Like Jenkyn, he was thinking it was all too smooth. When you had a lot to do, like when they were in Italy, or probing towards Bergen, the time passed swiftly. He picked a shred of corned beef from his teeth. The condemned man ate a hearty breakfast.

He thought of Decia and that letter. Was she scared or repentant? Or just saying it to tempt him to some new mischief?

Just thinking of her lithe, sensuous body, her demands and her submissions, made his mind swim.

He heard a click and turned to see Niven watching him, a Sten gripped in his hands, the muzzle aimed at his stomach.

Niven said softly, 'No magazine.' He turned away. 'This time.'

Drake stared at him. He wanted to explain. To tell him. But how could he? The others were here. The old firm. How the hell would he start?

Niven looked at his watch. Thirty minutes. He felt parched, although he had drunk his tea and plenty of water as well. Parched and sick.

The look on Drake's face. Guilt, astonishment, momentary fear. But Niven had found no enjoyment, only disgust with himself. Not for making Drake think he was going to shoot him, but for knowing he could have done so.

It was all suddenly plain. His blind anger and hatred told him

that. He was still in love with Decia, and nothing which Drake
had done would change it. But it made it all the harder to bear.
Knowing that Drake had been with her when he had not.

His words fell in the quiet control room like stones.

'I'm all right now.' He waited for Drake to face him again.
'But don't imagine I couldn't have done it. Before, when I
thought I knew, I wanted to take you outside and beat hell out of
you.' Nobody spoke or moved as he continued flatly, 'But I knew
you'd win. It's your way. And then I'd have been no better of[f].'

'Look, Richard, let me explain!'

Seaton said quietly, 'In case it's slipped your notice, we're
about to go into action.'

Niven looked at him, his eyes pleading. 'That's why, sir. I
didn't want you to think we were letting you down because of
our own troubles.' He turned to Drake. 'I don't need
explanations. Not any more. I've grown up. Too late, as it
happens, but I have. Do you honestly think she would see
beyond your body? My God, you're the one who needs pity if
you imagine she'd throw her life away on you, *friend*.'

Drake breathed out very slowly. 'I know. That's what was in
the letter. The brush-off. I wanted to tell you.' He shrugged
heavily. 'I don't know what to say.'

Jenkyn did not move his eyes from the compass. 'I think
you've *said* it, chum! The bloody pot-full! Now, for Christ's sake
let's do what we come to do, an' *try* to stay sane!'

Seaton said, 'Well put, Alec.' He looked at the others. It had
cost both of them a great deal, but at least it had cleared the air.
'We started as a team. Let's keep it that way.'

Less than half an hour later *XE 16, Goliath*, reached the
shallows by the inlet and turned her nose towards the north.

In his bunker beneath a Sussex farmhouse, Air Marshal
Ruthven sat with his chin on his hand, watching the activity
beyond the great window behind his desk. There was only one
reading light on in his office, and he could see the girl's reflection
as she poured coffee for both of them.

She was a beautiful girl. Strained to the limit, sometimes near
to tears, but with an inner strength any man would be lucky to
have.

A phone buzzed and he lifted it with his other hand. Below

he ops room counters were being moved or replaced, acts of abotage marked on the wall chart with angry scarlet stars. Railways, bridges, ammunition dumps. It must be driving the nemy wild, making him even more dangerous.

The voice in his ear was Venables'.

Venables sounded alert. Confident. But Ruthven was a good udge of men. He knew Venables would never show weakness, ven at the point of a knife.

'All reported going well, sir. Towing submarines and upporting destroyers are in position Zebra.'

'Good.'

He had a feeling that Rear Admiral Niven was with Venables, ut he said nothing about it. The admiral was probably under he weather. Ruthven had heard he had had a row with his son. A bad start of *Citadel*, but he had seen it coming for a long time. Rear Admiral Niven was a front-man. But without people like Venables backing him, he was empty.

Ruthven saw some girls below his room moving blue ounters across the water towards France. He felt a chill up his pine. The Airborne, the Red Berets were on their way. He heard he girl put a fresh cup of coffee beside him, knew she was vatching the chart. Not seeing the counters, but only the small netal flag with the name *Goliath* painted on it.

He said, 'Thank you, Walter. Keep me informed.'

The reply was quick and dry. 'I expect you'll know before I o, sir.'

Ruthven turned in his chair and looked at her. Neat and trim n her uniform, but so easy to imagine as Seaton must have seen er and held her.

Ruthven had not expected her to ask to be here. He had ffered her leave, or duties elsewhere, but she had insisted. Now, e would not insult her by commiserating or offering false opes. She was above that, as she had proved ten times over vhen she had worked with Trevor.

The girl seated herself on Ruthven's small leather settee, ushing off her shoes and tucking her legs up beside her without ven knowing what she had done.

She did not wish to talk, and she knew that Ruthven would ot demand it of her.

All she needed to do was watch the little flag. And pray.

18

With Daring

THE SOUND of the periscope hissing from its well seemed deafening.

Seaton checked its rise and watched the water becoming clearer, changing to shark-blue before it broke surface. He held his breath, forcing his contracting muscles to relax, loosening his grip on the periscope when before he had been holding it with all his strength.

The entrance to the inlet was less than half a mile wide, and each side was marked with steep rocks, against which the current made a lively necklace of spray. He saw a wide band of wet rock too, which showed how the tide had dropped in the last hour.

He moved the periscope very carefully. It was a grim looking place. Hills beyond the shoreline, a few trees, and some abandoned houses right at the water's edge.

He said, 'It's like a bloody scrapyard.'

It had been his custom to tell the others what he could see. His eyes were all they had, and it helped to keep him calm as well. In the strengthening light he could see some of the chaos left by repeated air-raids. The abandoned houses were roofless, and the place was pitted with craters, strewn with buckled girders and smashed masonry.

On one hillside he also saw evidence of what the raids had cost. Scorched grass and bushes which marked the path of a crashing bomber. Further along the same hill he saw another aircraft lying on its back, the wings torn off and scattered down on the foreshore.

'Let her fall off to starboard, Alec.' He tensed, watching the stern of a half-submerged wreck as *XE 16* crept past it. 'Steady as you go.'

It had probably been a small coaster, commandeered by the Germans for patrol work.

Flotsam and trailing wire grated against the hull, It was like a place of the dead. Nothing moved at the water's edge, not even a dog. But he saw several concrete pill-boxes dotted about the hillsides, and imagined a dozing sentry peering down at the tiny periscope.

Without looking at his watch he knew that the Airborne must have started their attack. Eight miles away, but it could have been a thousand for all the signs of activity here.

'Hello, *Goliath*. This is *Dodo*.' Allenby sounded unusually clipped. 'I am approaching sunken U-boat. There seem to be booms at either end of it. Jerry has used the gaps for tipping his rubbish.'

Niven took the handset. 'This is *Goliath*.' He glanced at Seaton for confirmation before asking. 'Hello, *Dodo*. What do you intend?'

There was a roar of static and then Allenby replied, 'I think the bloody thing's blocking the entrance. I shall have to go over it.'

Seaton glanced swiftly from the periscope to the depth gauge. Allenby would have to surface to do that. Of all the bloody bad luck. The one thing nobody had considered. And it made instant sense. Now, when it was too late. The rocket parts were brought to the waterside by road and then ferried into the pen on barges. It doubled the chances of getting through without being damaged by bombing, it also did away with the risk of attack from the sea. The Germans did not *need* an entrance for vessels of any sort from seaward.

Allenby spoke again, his voice calm and unemotional. 'Just took another peep and have sighted the target. Not surprised they've been unable to smash it.' There was a long pause, and then, 'Getting ready now. Wish me luck. Over and out.'

Seaton crouched, his fingers on the hoist button, counting seconds. *Now.*

He ducked to the periscope as it rose and said, 'Steer a point to port.'

He forgot Jenkyn at his wheel, everything but the sight in his lens. The U-boat pen spanned the end of the inlet like a colossal dam. The towering concrete structure above its original roof linked the hills on either side, and further back, curved and camouflaged like the one on the model was the great protective dome. It was grotesque and sinister, more so because there was no sign of life. But it was all there, with the small jetty close to the pen's entrance from which the rocket parts were unloaded. The barges, Seaton assumed, were moored by the U-boat slipway deep inside the citadel.

Seaton said, 'Tell *Oyster*, I am in sight of target. He'll want to know where we are.'

He concentrated on the scene across either bow. The tangle of broken vehicles and equipment which the Germans had pushed into the water, and which marked the ends of the wrecked submarine better than any buoys.

He depressed the periscope until the slow-moving lens was partly awash. He had seen a movement at last. It was a soldier, hurrying along a path by the ruined houses, his agitation quite obvious, despite the poor light and the distance he was away.

Seaton watched him. Of course, at eight miles the soldier would be able to hear the anti-aircraft guns, even the Airborne troops' mortars. From the submerged X-craft everything was kept silent, lifeless.

A second soldier had emerged from somewhere. He had a rifle across his shoulder, and seemed to be holding a cup in one hand as he watched the other man striding towards him.

They had almost met when it happened. The man with the cup pointed wildly across the inlet, the cup smashing in fragments by his feet. The other soldier swung round, and then froze, as if stricken by some terrible disease.

Seaton knew what had occurred even before he saw it. Slowly at first, then with gathering haste, Allenby's boat began to surface, the black hull glittering like coal in the early light. He must have seen the soldiers, for even as he crossed over the hidden wreck he began to dive again.

Seaton lowered the periscope, the picture of the two startled soldiers still firm in his mind. One or both would run to a telephone. Every line would be busy because of the Airborne attack. It was possible that some of the local troops would have to be sent to help stem the intruders from the sky.

He said, 'Get ready to surface. I'm going over the wreck.' To Niven he added, 'Tell *Oyster* to stand-off. He stands no chance now. Too far astern.'

Seaton raised the periscope again. *Must be quick.* He checked the sloping tangle of rubbish and scrap at either end of the wreck and said sharply, 'Fifty yards. Stand by to surface.'

He swung the periscope to port, vaguely aware that his mind was very clear, empty of everything but the approaching mass of concrete. He saw only one soldier. The man was on his knee, the rifle to his shoulder. Seaton saw a brief flash, then heard Drake curse as a bullet cracked against the hull. The soldier had seen the periscope. Seaton pressed the button. He did not want to go in blind. *'Surface!'*

The hull shuddered and took a violent blow on the keel as it collided with part of the wreck. The grating seemed to go on and on, and the noise was joined by at least two more bullets hitting and ricochetting away from the casing.

'Over!' Seaton wiped his face. 'Periscope depth again. 'Lively!'

There was a hollow boom, which rocked the hull drunkenly from side to side. It did not sound like a depth charge, but it was big enough to worry about.

Seaton pressed the button, his fingers slipping with sweat. There was smoke drifting from the entrance to the pen, and he felt something like despair as another explosion sent a procession of waves surging out into the daylight.

'Hello, *Goliath*! This is *Dodo*. Do you read me? Over.' A pause. *'Do you read me, over?'* He sounded desperate.

Seaton snatched the handset from Niven. 'This is *Goliath*. Over.'

Allenby said, 'Bastards dropped a couple of explosive charges. I'm right inside the place. Suggest you shove off, old son. I don't think we'll be going anywhere.' Seaton heard someone coughing and retching. 'Bloody side-cargoes have been released, but my poor old girl is done for.'

Seaton said urgently, *'Bale out.'*

The R/T was getting faint. 'Can't, old son. Bloody hatches are jammed solid. I expect–' The sound was cut off completely.

Jenkyn muttered, 'Wot a way to go!'

Seaton looked at Drake. 'We're going in. Might be able to do something.'

A glance at the clock. It had been only minutes, and felt like an eternity.

Another quick look through the periscope. It was amazing they had got this far. The entrance to the pen was towering across their approach, and inside he could see a launch idling beside one of the ramps, some faces peering outboard into the water. The explosions had probably been demolition charges which had just happened to be nearby. They were all it needed to turn Allenby's boat into a tomb.

Something moved at the edge of his lens and he said, 'They're going to shut the gates!' He saw a steel framework of criss-crossing girders moving very slowly from one side of the entrance.

It was all quite clear what he must do. He snapped, 'Surface!' Then he was at the hatch, loosening the clips as he shouted, 'Cover me, Richard!'

Like an ungainly porpoise, and as if she were aware of the urgency required, *XE 16* surged noisily to the surface, her snout-like stem cutting through oil and filth and making the moored launch stagger violently, hurling the occupants into the bilges.

Seaton was through the hatch, his mind registering nothing but the coldness of the Sten in his fingers, the damp misery of the air around him.

He heard cries from the launch and saw them running towards the bulwark again, pointing at the surfaced midget and then ducking as he fired a burst directly at them. One man dropped over the side and vanished, the others stayed hidden.

Niven had struggled through the hatch to join him. 'Here, sir, take a grenade!'

Together they dragged out the pins and flung them into the open launch. Then they fell prone to the deck, their eardrums all but splitting as the grenades exploded together. Splinters punched holes through the launch, hissed into the water and scythed across the concrete like hail on a tin roof.

As the smoke rolled away towards the inlet, Seaton heard

someone screaming. A tortured, inhuman sound which stopped suddenly, as if cut off by a soundproof door.

XE 16 had stopped at last, rocking defiantly above her reflection as if trying to decide what to do next.

Niven said breathlessly, 'I can hear artillery!' He laughed, and looked incredibly young. 'Good old Airborne!' He swung round, firing from the hip, as a shadow dodged round a doorway and tried to reach some steel stairs.

The gates across the entrance had stopped moving, and as the running man slipped and then pitched headlong down the stairs, Seaton guessed he had been the one working the mechanism.

Somewhere a long way off he heard a klaxon shrieking insanely. The alarm, but it was too late now.

Seaton shouted, 'Try and call up Allenby again!'

He reached out to seize a trailing wire from the ramp and wound it loosely round a bollard. He heard Niven yelling at Drake through the hatch, his voice hollow inside the control room. Allenby and his crew were right here. Probably feet away. He dare not drop the charges until he was certain nothing could be done to save them.

It was deathly quiet. Seaton crouched on one knee and trained the gun towards the stairs and to another opening by the slipway. He made sure the spare magazines were within reach and tried to remember what the instructor had said about faults and stoppages.

Niven dragged his head from the hatch. 'Got him, sir! They heard the firing and thought the Jerries had caught *us*!'

Seaton said, 'Keep your eyes peeled. We shall have company in a minute. They probably imagine there are more of us.' Then he asked, 'What do you think, Richard? You're the diver.'

Niven said, 'I'd risk being killed. Especially in their case. I'd plant a few grenades under the W & D hatch. That should shift it. They might be safe from the explosion in the control room.' He fired a long burst into the shadows and said, 'Blast! Nothing there!' As he jammed in a fresh magazine and cocked the gun he added, 'Even without escape gear they should be able to get out once the hull is flooded. It's only a few feet deep here. We could help.' He pivoted round. 'God, what's that?'

Machine-guns were chattering beyond the entrance, and they both stared with surprise as Winters' boat probed through the opening, sparks flying from her hull as she was pursued by bullets.

Seaton said, 'And I ordered him to-' He gripped Niven's arm. 'Get down and tell Number One what to do.'

He watched the third X-craft draw abeam and Winters' head and shoulders thrusting through the after hatch, a Sten already aimed and ready.

He saw Seaton and grinned. 'Came to join the party!'

'We're going to get the others out if we can.'

Seaton looked up as boots hammered overhead, echoing and re-echoing along one of the catwalks which obviously led to the rocket launching chamber.

He called, 'Tell your diver to come up. We should be safe enough if we cover the stairs and that opening. You could hold an army from here. They'll not want to use anything heavy under their precious rocket.'

A bullet slammed past Seaton's head and splintered into concrete. A longe-range shot from the outside. He peered astern and saw bobbing figures scurrying along the water's edge. It must be a fine old rumpus at their H.Q., he thought.

Niven appeared again. 'I got through, sir.' His chin lifted defiantly. 'I told Number One, and he said for *me* to do it.'

He knelt down and retrieved his Sten gun. 'Just as well. The set's packed up completely.'

They looked up as more shouts echoed along the roof, and then several shots were fired from out of the darkness. A man, or men, had got into one of the air shafts and had gained advantage from height and shadow.

Winters threw up his Sten and raked the metal shaft from end to end, the holes appearing as if by magic as Niven joined with his gun. They heard a brief cry and the sound of a body slithering down the shaft. Then nothing.

Then the water seemed to light up, and for a terrible second Seaton imagined that one of Allenby's charges had exploded prematurely.

He watched the vivid orange flash fade as quickly as it had appeared, to be replaced instantly by a great bubbling froth of released air.

'They've done it!'

Niven and the diver called Driscoll plunged into the filthy

water without pausing even to kick off their boots.

A burst of tracer ripped across and through one corner of the entrance. Winters, who had been peering into the water, was hurled headlong across his casing, blood spurting from his chest and stomach. His body was smoking and torn open by the tracer, and as he choked and gurgled, his heels drumming on the steel as if to ward off his agony, another burst tore across his boat and threw him into the water. He floated away, the blood trailing behind him.

Seaton cupped his hands. 'Keep down! Your skipper has bought it!' Another few feet and the burst would have done for them both.

He dare not watch Niven and Driscoll for fear of a sudden attack along the slipway. But he heard them floundering and splashing, and then Allenby's unmistakable voice as he managed to gasp, 'My Number One's dead. Martin's in a bad way, too.'

Martin was the diver. A quiet-spoken man. Quiet even when Allenby made fun of his diving ability.

Seaton felt them dragging themselves aboard, their bodies stinking of oil. He heard someone sobbing and knew it was the diver. Quiet as always.

Allenby put a wet hand on his shoulder as he groped for the hatch. 'Thanks, old son. I'll not forget.'

Seaton said, 'Tell them to release the side-cargoes. Pass the word to *Oyster*, too.'

He wiped his forhead with his hand and took a firmer grip on the gun. They thought only one would get in. And we all made it. Trenoweth would be a proud man.

Niven grabbed Driscoll by the wrists and hauled him on to the casing.

Seaton said, 'Well done. Now we're getting out.'

He had felt the hull quiver, more so because she was surfaced, as the two side-cargoes were allowed to fall clear.

Six charges in all. Enough to knock down St. Paul's.

'Someone on the catwalk!' Niven raised his gun and then gasped, *'Jammed!'*

Seaton peered up at the shadows and saw something move. He fired a long blast, seeing the sparks fly, wondering why the hidden man had not fired first.

Something clattered and bounced on the other X-craft, and Niven yelled, 'Grenade!'

The explosion was deafening, and it was only then that Seaton understood what had happened. The grenade had bounced through XE 26's open hatch and had burst inside the control room. With a hissing roar, a tongue of fire mushroomed almost to the roof of the pen, while splinters cracked through the flames and sparks with the sound of a rivet gun.

Driscoll, who had been about to step aboard, was spun round in his tracks, blood spurting down his chest to mingle with the water on his battledress.

Niven looked away, retching helplessly. Driscoll, the one who had taken the letter to Drake, had no face.

As his hearing returned, Seaton heard the crackle of sparks on the other boat's switchboard and knew it was a matter of time before she was gutted by fire and her fuel exploded. Then she would sink and join Allenby's boat beside the charges they had brought so far.

'Clear the casing!' A bullet whimpered between him and Niven. 'Tell Number One we're going out stern first!'

He saw something splash across the casing and knew it was the blood of the man who had dropped the grenade.

The deck trembled, and he saw the immediate surge of bubbles around the screw.

Niven released the mooring wire and paused to pick up his Sten. Then he toppled forward and clutched his stomach. He stared at Seaton, his eyes shining in the light from the inlet.

'Oh, God.' He swayed as the boat gathered sternway. 'I'm hit!'

Seaton kicked the guns and magazines over the side as he ran to his aid and half carried him to the hatch.

Allenby was peering at them, and seized Niven's feet to guide him through.

Seaton jumped down after him, seeing the shadows on the slipway hardening into running shapes, firing as they came, spraying the smoking X-craft and Driscoll's corpse which lay beside the hatch, one arm blazing like a torch.

The control room was crammed with figures. Allenby and his E.R.A., his diver, eyes and hands bandaged, but mercifully free

271

of pain as the morphine swept him into unconsciousness. Niven was lying beside the chart table, his eyes wide as Allenby tore open his clothing and tried to control the bleeding.

Like that other time when he had fought the German frogman.

Seaton watched as his skin appeared in the chart light, saw him grimace as Allenby thrust a great shell dressing over the wound. Not before Seaton had seen it. A gaping hole, blackened around the edges. Tracer.

Niven said between gasps, 'The pain! Oh God, the pain!'

Jenkyn was wrestling with the wheel as metal clanged against the hull.

'You'll be okay! You promised to buy me a pint after this lot, remember?'

'Not . . . this . . . time . . . Alec.' His head lolled. 'Done . . . for.' His voice was fading away as the drug took over. 'Don't . . . want . . . to . . . die.'

Jenkyn tore his eyes from the compass and stared at Seaton. 'Called me Alec! An' I thought–'

He turned back to the compass, but not before Seaton had seen the tears in his eyes.

Seaton said, 'Bring her about!' He gritted his teeth as more bullets clattered over the hull. It only needs one vital spot. 'We're going out on the surface.'

Drake said desperately, 'They'll pick us off! No chance!'

Allenby covered Niven with a blanket and put a lifejacket under his head.

'Wrong, old son. Surfaced you've got more speed. Besides which, there's a strong chance there might be a bright German watching. If he sees us, and knows about the two we've left behind, he'll not want to hang about and wait for the bang!' His voice hardened. 'Bloody obvious, I'd have thought.'

A sharp explosion thudded against the lower hull, and then more heavy splinters.

Allenby said, 'They must have a mortar ranged on us.'

Seaton nodded. 'Start zigzagging, Alec.'

He winced as another deep-throated bang punched up from the bottom of the inlet. If the screw gets a splinter, that's it.

He said, 'Give her all you've got. Maximum revs and to hell with the gauges!'

The diesel was getting louder and vibrating to such an extent that every loose piece of equipment rattled and rolled about in chaos.

Seaton pressed the periscope switch and had just put his eye to the lens when more machine-gun bullets swept across the casing in a deafening bombardment of steel. He felt the periscope jerk violently and saw the picture of the nearest foreshore vanish completely while water spurted across his wrists.

He moved quickly to the immobile search periscope and peered through it, watching the tangle of debris which nobody had known about and which had almost done for the mission completely.

A small scout car was tearing along the cratered roadway, a Spandau firing from the rear seat. It reminded Seaton of the one he had seen in Bergen.

'Come on, *Goliath*!'

He pounded his fist against the cold steel, seeing the water churning back from the blunt bows to show the little submarine's efforts to get clear.

'We're over the wreck!'

He seized hold of the smashed periscope as another explosion rocked the hull, playing with it like a giant's hand.

'Take her down to fifteen feet. Any more and we might hit something.'

He listened to the water surging into the tanks as the diesel cut out and the clutch was broken to allow the electric motor to take over again. It was a wild, unnerving sensation. Hurrying through the inlet, unable to see, even to know what was happening.

More thumps, but they were further away, and Seaton wondered if it was possible for hope to exist after all.

Allenby said, 'My guess is that the Jerries will run for it. If the rocket had been ready to fire they would have done it, with or without a set target. But they weren't quite ready. Remember what they told us? They shut the gates at the moment of firing.' He wiped some more oil from his face and neck. 'They'll know that we've done all right. It'd take a brayer man than me to sit there fiddling with a rocket with all that explosive under his bum!'

His E.R.A., Petty Officer Turbett, exclaimed, 'Martin's

stopped breathin', Skipper.'

Allenby reached over the diver with the bandaged eyes an felt his pulse. Half to himself he said, 'Martin set the grenades t blow the hatch. One went off almost in his face. He wanted me t leave him.'

Seaton tried to imagine it. The hatch blown off, filling th boat with splinters. The water rushing in, forcing up the pre sure. Yet Allenby had taken the precious seconds to wrap crude bandage around his diver's head. He had been prett brave himself.

Drake said thickly, 'What about Richard?'

Allenby was still looking at the dead man. He could ha been asleep.

'Depends. If the rest of the operation works out, we might g him to a surgeon in time.' He yawned, the strain lining his fa like dark scars. 'Even then...'

Drake blinked to clear his vision, trying to hold on to h self-control.

'I wanted him to know about the letter. It was just a stup lapse. She realised that afterwards.'

Seaton watched him. 'It takes two to make a *lapse*, as you p it.' He turned and looked at Niven's face, the skin waxy in th chart light. 'I wish she could have seen him back there. H father, too.'

Allenby cut in, 'What now, David? Are we ditching? Or sha we keep going as long as we can?' He tried to smile. 'You're t boss.'

Seaton stepped over Niven's body and peered at the cha

'We'll keep going. Like the man said, it's all laid on.' H looked at the other E.R.A. 'Can you make tea as well as Ale

The man grinned. 'Better, sir.'

Seaton added, 'And lace it with something.'

He saw their expressions. They knew. When *XE 16* surfac again it might be for the last time. The enemy would be out fo kill, and no holds barred.

One hour after they had careered out of the U-boat pen t combination of charges and explosives thundered through t water like some nightmare monster bellowing in a cave. *XE* had reached open water and had gone as deep as possible avoid the effects of the massive explosion, but she was hurled c course and went into a steep dive, completely out of control.

Sparks danced across the switchboard, and a gauge shattered with the sound of a pistol shot.

The depth gauge wavered at one hundred feet, and with Drake and Jenkyn working like madmen they held her, brought her under command, and kept her so. A few more feet and they would have plunged bow-first into the sea-bed.

Shakily, they returned to a depth of thirty feet, and while Jenkyn checked the motor Seaton sat at the helm, feeling the boat responding, answering his touch.

It was strange, he thought. But he had not actually seen the great rocket. Now, with any sort of luck, nobody would.

When it was time to surface again Seaton said quietly, 'Whatever happens, I'd like to thank all of you.' He looked at the dead man by the watertight door. 'And the others who didn't get this far.'

He looked at Drake. 'Ready, Geoff?'

Drake nodded jerkily. 'As ever, Skipper.'

'Surface!'

He crouched at the search periscope, half-blinded by a shaft of sunlight. Then he said, *'Aircraft!* Six of them!' So they had been caught out after all.

A red flare floated down towards the sea, changing colour as it passed through the sun's eye.

Seaton clung to the deckhead, holding his forehead against the rough metal.

At last he was able to speak without emotion. 'Some of *ours*, bless 'em! Captain Venables kept his part of the deal!'

He swung round. 'Open the hatch!'

The noise of the aircraft was deafening as they swept and circled overhead.

Seaton felt something touch his ankle, and looked down to see Niven staring up at him. For a moment more the elation of escape could wait. He knelt down and gripped Niven's hand, watching as he stared at the open hatch, the circle of blue sky and the flashing shapes of the protective aircraft.

Niven said, 'We did it.' He spoke so quietly that Seaton had to put his ear almost to his face. 'Wouldn't have missed it. Tell Decia, will you? I'd like her to hear about it from you.'

Seaton gripped his fingers more tightly. 'Tell her yourself.'

He glanced at Allenby, saw his quick shake of the head.

Niven murmured, 'I'm cold.' He moved his head to watch as another aircraft thundered above the hull. 'I wish–' His stare became fixed and unmoving.

Seaton gently released his hand and stood up.

Jenkyn leaned on his wheel, resting his forehead on his hands, while Drake stared at the body, unable to accept it had happened after all they had done and come through together.

The other E.R.A. said quietly, 'They'll be expectin' a signal, sir.'

Seaton nodded. Then he unclipped the Aldis from its rack and climbed up until he was waist-high through the hatch.

He looked around his small scarred and chipped command. There was the line of the French coast, a towering black column of smoke rising higher and higher towards the sky.

He saw the aircraft, and another group prowling between him and the land.

Then Seaton turned and shaded his eyes, seeing the darker shapes of surface vessels, destroyers surging out of the horizon towards him.

He was barely able to read the diamond-bright signal lamp. Their faces kept misting over. Winters and his crew, Allenby's Number One, then his diver. And now Richard Niven.

Seaton pressed the trigger and shuttered his number, then the codename, *Goliath*.

As the acknowledgement was flashed back towards him he made one last signal. *Out of the deep we are here*.

It was over. And she would be waiting.

DOUGLAS REEMAN

Author Douglas Reeman creates exciting
novels of courage and daring in modern-day
warfare on the high seas! Read them all.